MISSING MOM

Other Books by Joyce Carol Oates

MISSING MOM

A NOVEL

joyce carol oates

An Imprint of HarperCollinsPublishers

Designed by Claire Vaccaro

ISBN-10: 0-7394-6836-7
ISBN-13: 978-0-7394-6836-4

Printed in the U.S.A.

Scattered throughout the text are references to bread-baking taken from BREADCRAFT *by Charles and Violet Schafer (Yerba Buena Press, San Francisco, 1974).*

In Memory of
Carolina Oates (1916–2003)

part one

last time

Last time you see someone and you don't know it will be the last time. And all that you know now, if only you'd known then. But you didn't know, and now it's too late. And you tell yourself *How could I have known, I could not have known.*

You tell yourself.

This is my story of missing my mother. One day, in a way unique to you, it will be your story, too.

mother's day

May 9, 2004. One of those aloof-seeming spring days: very sunny but not very warm.

Gusts of wind rushing down from Lake Ontario in mean little skirmishes like hit-and-run. A sky hard-looking as blue tile. That wet-grassy smell lifting from the neat rectangular front lawns on Deer Creek Drive.

In patches lilac bushes were blooming up and down the street. Vivid glowing-purple, lavender like swipes of paint.

At 43 Deer Creek, my parents' house, where Mom lived alone now that Dad had died, there were too many vehicles parked in the driveway and at the curb. My brother-in-law's Land Rover, my Aunt Tabitha's old black hearse-sized Caddie, these made sense, but there were others including a low-slung lipstick-red sports car shaped like a missile.

Who did Mom know, who'd drive such a car?

Damned if I wanted to meet him. (Had to be a him.)

My mother was always introducing me to "eligible bachelors." Since I was involved with an ineligible man.

It was like Mom to invite people outside the family for Mother's Day. It was like Mom to invite people who were practically strangers into her house.

I parked the car across the street. I'd begun to whistle. It seemed to tamp down my adrenaline, whistling when I was in danger of becoming over-excited. My father had whistled a lot around the house.

Mother's Day: I was bringing Mom a present so soft, so gossamer-light it seemed to have no weight but lay across my outstretched arms like something sleeping. I'd spent a frustrating half-hour wrapping it in rainbow tin foil, crisscrossing the foil with multi-colored yarns instead of ribbon; I had a vision of the sort of wild/funny/funky look I wanted for the gift, and had to settle for this cross between New Age and Kindergarten. I'd taken a half-day off from work to find an appropriate gift for my mother who presented a riddle to her grown daughters, for she seemed in need of nothing.

Anyway, nothing we could give her.

We'd wanted to take Mom out, of course. My sister Clare and me. Why not, for once, a Mother's Day meal in elegant surroundings, the Mt. Ephraim Inn for instance. No need for Mom to prepare one of her complicated meals, work herself into a state of nerves inviting guests at the last minute like a train hooking on extra cars, careening and swerving along the tracks!

No need. Except of course Mom resisted. Maybe when Dad had been alive, if he'd insisted on taking her out she'd have consented, but now Dad was gone, there was just Clare and me hoping to persuade our mother to behave reasonably.

You know how I love to cook. This is the nicest Mother's Day present you girls can give me, my family visiting and letting me cook for them.

Then, vehemently as if protecting her innocent/ignorant daughters from being swindled *Pay prices like that for* food? *When I can prepare a meal for us for a fraction of the cost, and better?*

There were three ways into Mom's house: front door, side door, through the garage. Most days I used the side door, that opened directly into the kitchen.

The door to which Mom had affixed little bells that tinkled merrily, like a shopkeeper's door, when you pushed it open.

"Ohhh Nikki! What have you done with your *hair*!"

First thing Mom said to me. Before I was through the doorway and into the kitchen. Before she hugged me stepping back with this startled look in her face.

I would remember the way Mom's voice lifted on *hair* like the cry of a bird shot in mid-flight.

Mom had a round childlike face that showed every emotion clear as water. Her skin was flushed as if windburnt, her eyes were wide-open greeny-amber. Since Dad's death she'd become a darting little humming-bird of a woman. Her shock at my appearance was such, I'd have sworn what I heard her say was *What have you done with my hair?*

Innocently I said I thought I'd told her, I was having my hair cut?

"Cut."

Meaning, what an understatement!

I was thirty-one years old. Mom was fifty-six. We'd been having these exchanges for almost three decades. You'd have thought we were both ac-customed to them by now, but we didn't seem to be. I could feel Mom's quickened heartbeat like my own.

This time, the situation was pretty tame. I hadn't run away from home as I'd done as a teenager, or, worse yet, returned home abruptly and un-expectedly from college refusing to explain why. I hadn't announced that I was engaged to a young man my parents scarcely knew, nor even that I'd broken off the engagement. (Twice. Two very different young men.) I hadn't quit my current job in a succession of boring jobs. Hadn't "gone off" with a not-quite-divorced man nor even by myself cross-country in a rattletrap Volkswagen van to backpack in the Grand Tetons, in Idaho. All I'd done was have my hair cut punk-spiky style and darkened to a shade of inky-maroon that, in certain lights, glared iridescent. No strand of hair longer than one inch, shaved at the sides and back of my head. You could say this was a chic-druggie look of another era or you could say that I looked like someone who'd stuck her finger into an electric socket.

Mom smiled bravely. It was Mother's Day after all, there were guests in the other room. Wasn't Gwen Eaton known in Mt. Ephraim, New York, in the Chautauqua Valley seventy miles south of Lake Ontario, as uncomplaining, unself-pitying, good-natured and good-hearted and in-defatigably optimistic?

Hadn't her high school nickname been *Feather?*

"Well, Nikki! You'd be a beauty, no matter if you were bald."

Rising now on her tiptoes to give me a belated hug. Just a little harder than ordinary, to signal how she loved me even more, because I was a trial to her.

Each time Mom gripped me in one of her fierce hugs, it seemed to me she was just slightly smaller, shorter. Since Dad's death her tidy little body that had seemed to have a rubbery resilience was losing definition. My hands encountered fleshy pouches at her waist and upper back, I saw the raddled flesh of her upper arms and chin. Since turning fifty Mom had more or less abandoned shoes with any kind of heel, mostly she wore crepe-soled shoes so flat, small, and round-toed they looked like a child's play shoes. We'd been the same height briefly (five feet three, when I was twelve), now Mom was shorter than me by several inches.

I felt a pang of loss, alarm. I wanted to think there had to be some mistake.

In my party voice I said, "Mom, you're looking good. Happy Mother's Day."

Mom said, embarrassed, "It's a silly day, I know. But you and Clare wanted to take me out, so this is a compromise. Happy Mother's Day to *you.*"

For the occasion, Mom was wearing a lime-green velour top and matching pants, she'd sewed herself. Pink shell earrings she'd made in one of her crafts classes at the mall and a necklace of glass beads I'd found in a secondhand shop. Her graying-blond hair was attractively if mod-estly cut, her skin looked freshened as if she'd applied some sort of cold cream to it, then rubbed the cream vigorously off. Since Dad used to tease her about having been a glamor girl when they'd met, Mom had become self-conscious about any visible sort of makeup and used even lipstick sparingly. In long-ago snapshots of the 1960s when she'd been a teenager, Mom had certainly not seemed glamorous. She'd been a blandly "cute" high school cheerleader with the doll-like features and achingly hopeful smile of thousands—millions?—of other girls immediately recognizable to any non-U.S. citizen as *American, middle-class.*

"Nikki, my *God.* What have you *done.*"

My sister Clare was staring at me, disapproving. There was a thrill to her voice as there'd been when we were girls and her willful younger sister had finally gone too far.

I ran my fingers through my spiky hair that was stiff like splinters with mousse, and laughed. Clare couldn't bully me any longer, we were adults now. "Clare, you're just jealous! Purple hair would look terrific on you except your family wouldn't allow it."

"I should hope *not.*"

In fact, Clare's husband Rob (in the living room, with Mom's other guests) might have liked to see Clare unwind a little. It was her children who would have been mortified.

Clare was a fleshy-ripe woman of thirty-five who looked exactly that age. Maybe she'd had a wild streak herself as a girl but it was so long ago, it scarcely mattered. She was the mother of two children whom she took as a grimly ordained task. She was the wife of a moderately well-to-do Mt. Ephraim business executive (sales manager, Coldwell Electronics) whom she made every effort to revere, at least publicly. Your first impression of Clare was *A good-looking, sexy woman* but when you looked again you saw the fine white crow's-feet of disapproval, disdain etched into her skin. Her face was a perfect moon like Mom's, seemingly boneless, petulant-pretty and inclined toward doughiness. Except where Mom was open-eyed and innocent, Clare was skeptical. She'd have said she expected the worst of people and was rarely surprised.

Clare's hair was that wet-sand color that was my own natural hair color, and Mom's before Mom went gray, styled in one of those small-town-beauty-parlor-wash-and-wear-perms that fit all sizes of female heads like a Wal-Mart stretch wig. The most sensible of hairstyles for a busy housewife/mother who hasn't time to "fuss." When we'd been girls, Clare was always beyond me: smart, popular at school, sexy-but-"good." Now,

Clare was so far beyond me she'd practically disappeared over the horizon. I couldn't imagine her Mrs. Chisholm life except as the reverse of my own. For everything about Clare was predictable and sensible: lilac polyester pants suit with a tunic top to disguise her thickening lower body, good black leather shoes with a neat little heel. Instead of my numerous funky-flashy rings and multiple ear-piercings, that gave my earlobes a look of frantic winking, Clare had her diamond-cluster engagement ring and white gold wedding band on the third finger of her left hand, worn like a badge, and her birthday stone (boring pearl, for June) on her right hand. Her earrings were proper little gold leaf-clusters, her husband had probably given her for Christmas.

Rob Chisholm. Out of nowhere he'd appeared, to save Clare's life where she'd been languishing (in fact, complaining to anyone who'd listen) as a social studies teacher at Jericho Middle School in the next township. I'd imagined my sister glancing at her watch, noting the time, realizing it was getting late, time to get married! All she retained of her teacherly authority was her upright posture to put others, like me, to shame for slouching; and her air of barely concealed impatience for the slower-witted who surrounded her.

No need for Clare and me to hug, we'd seen each other recently enough.

Mom was fumbling to smooth things over, "Well! It will always grow back, Nikki! Remember, when you were in seventh grade, I'd just been elected president of the PTA at your school and I had to chair my first meeting and I was scared to death—I mean, *me!*—whatever were they thinking of, electing *me!*—some of those people knew me as 'Feather' Kovach!—so I hurried out to get my hair styled at that place next to the vacuum cleaner repair, Doreen's it used to be, now it's the Village Salon, and I said to Doreen, looking the woman in the eye, in the mirror, so there couldn't be any misunderstanding, 'Just a little off, please, about an inch,' and wasn't paying attention reading some mystery book, I think it was Mary Higgins Clark, you know how she draws you right in, you keep turning pages though it will all end sort of silly, and next thing I knew I looked up into the mirror and—my hair was gone! I was this pathetic skinned thing like a—what d'you call them, opossum?—iguana?—and I almost burst into tears crying, 'Ohhh! What have you done! This looks like one of those pixie-cuts, *I am thirty-seven years old*,' and Doreen peered at me sort of nearsightedly like she was only just seeing me, and seeing it was so, her customer wasn't any kid, what on earth that woman was thinking I never knew, I mean I wasn't one of her regular customers because I wasn't a regular customer at any salon, but anyone with eyes should have seen, anyone with any sense should have known, I was hardly the age or the type for a pixie-cut! And Doreen says to me, such a profound thought she slowed chewing her gum, 'Ma'am, I'm sorry but I can't make it longer can I? Hair grows back, I promise.' "

We laughed. We always laughed hearing Mom's pixie-cut story.

Waiting for Mom to continue, for there was a coda, what Dad said when he came home and saw her, but Mom was looking distracted, turned away just as a buzzer went off on the stove like an indignant wasp.

Hawaiian Chicken Supreme, a "scrumptious" new recipe Mom had acquired from one of her senior ladies at the YM-YWCA pool where Gwen Eaton was a much-loved volunteer swimming instructor.

Entering the old house.

Taking a deep breath, like a diver. Except even the deepest breath can take you only so far.

After four years of Dad being gone still I had to check the impulse to look for him. For always Mom was the one to greet visitors, Dad would appear belatedly as if surprised by the intrusion though willing to be a good sport about it.

After four years I wasn't grieving for my father. I don't think so. I'd adjusted to his death. (Though it had been a shock at the time: he'd been only fifty-nine.) Only just Mom seemed so bravely alone without him, in this house. Like a dancer whose partner has left her alone on the dance floor while the music is still playing.

"Nik-*ki*. Wow."

This was Rob Chisholm's greeting. In an undertone.

Rob was staring/smiling at my spiky maroon hair. And at my tiny puckered-black-crepe top that fitted my torso tighter than any glove, nipple-tight you could say; and at my bare, luridly pale feet in gold-spangled high-heeled sandals. (Thrift shop purchases!) The glittery rings and ear studs and bold magenta lipstick with which I'd outlined my pouty lips: these captured the man's attention, too.

There was a stiffness between my sister's husband and me, I hoped no one noticed. We never hugged, only just shook hands briskly and briefly. Then Rob dropped my hand. As if my skin burnt his fingers.

Always so much was happening when we were likely to be thrown together at family gatherings, Rob and I were spared having to confront the fact of each other for long.

"Oh, Aunt Nikki—*cool*!"—a breathless little squeal from my thirteen-year-old niece Lilja, grinning at my hair. And there came Foster, my eight-year-old nephew, a fair-skinned husky boy with endearing chipmunk teeth and a way of mumbling *Hi Aunt Nikki* that made me feel the futility of trying to be anyone's aunt.

In the kitchen, Lilja hovered around me. Plied me with her usual questions. Family occasions at Mom's house were beginning to be a strain for Lilja as they'd been for me at her age. I knew it annoyed Clare, how Lilja seemed to admire me: I was as far removed from Clare and the mothers of Lilja's friends as you were likely to encounter in Mt. Ephraim, New York, population 21,000. (Partly because I didn't any longer live in Mt. Ephraim but in Chautauqua Falls, a larger and more prosperous city about thirty miles due west. There, I worked as a reporter and features writer for the *Chautauqua Valley Beacon* and led what, to a thirteen-year-old, and possibly to Clare as well, might have seemed like a glamorous life.)

"Lilja" was a Danish name, chosen by Clare for its musical/mysterious sound. Luckily my niece was turning into the sort of precocious adolescent—very thin, very pretty—who didn't seem to be fazed by an exotic name.

"Aunt Nikki, tell us what it was like, interviewing Waylon Syp?"

Waylon Syp was a local Rochester boy who'd achieved something of a national career as a white-boy rapper in the sulky/sullen mode of Eminem except not so talented as Eminem and, as an interview subject, a dud. His manager had answered most of the questions put to him by local journalists at a press conference in Rochester and I'd written them up, with a professional sort of zest, for a front-page feature in the *Beacon*. I hadn't acknowledged how ordinary, how bland, how dull, how not-very-good-looking Syp was close up, and seeing the expectation in Lilja's face, I wasn't going to now.

I saw that even Clare was interested. Even Mom, who couldn't have known anything about rap music, and would have thought that Eminem was candy.

"Help Grandma and me set the table, sweetie. And I'll tell you."

Aunt Nikki. Weird!

I'd always been ambivalent about being an aunt but I was fond of my sister's children. I guess I was.

Sometimes, I wasn't sure if I liked anyone, much. How I'd have felt about my own mother, if I'd met her as a stranger.

Yet my sister's children had brought Clare and me closer together. Especially when they'd been babies and Clare had been vulnerable and needy for once; not so judgmental about me, in her obsession with judging herself.

Clare liked me less, now. I wasn't sure how I felt about her.

One thing I knew: I didn't want children of my own. I didn't want to be married. Maybe because my parents had been so happily married, my mother was such a wonderful mother, I knew that I could never measure up.

And maybe I don't want happiness. Not that kind.

．　．　．

Eleven guests at Mom's for Mother's Day dinner!

When we'd last spoken on the phone, Mom had promised there would be "only" seven or eight guests. Originally, weeks before, Mom had assured Clare and me that there would be "only family."

Out of the side of my mouth, into Clare's ear as we were smiling brightly being introduced to the latest, last arrival who looked like an aging Cher in tumbledown silver-streaked hair, layers of witchy swishing black taffeta and red fishnet stockings and high heels, "Why does Mom *do such things*," and Clare never slackened her smile sighing in return, "Because she's *Mom*."

This exotic guest, Mom's newest friend from church whom she'd met, it seemed, only last week, spoke heavily accented English and had to repeat her name several times: "Szyszko, Sonja." Mom introduced her as a "prominent" ballerina who'd performed in Budapest, Hungary, and who had had to leave the country for political reasons, now she lived in Mt. Ephraim and was a housekeeper (house cleaner?) and a seamstress and a singer with a "flawless" soprano voice, who'd just joined the choir at the Mt. Ephraim Christian Life Fellowship Church where Mom was also a member of the choir.

"Mrs. Aiten, I am so, so sorry! I am lost, driving in this, this roads with so many tvists and end-dead where you cannot get *out*. I am looking for 'Deer Creek' in all the wrong place."

Sonja Szyszko fluttered like a flag in the wind, mortified as if she were hours late instead of a half-hour. Mom assured her she wasn't late, not at all. And how beautiful she looked, like a "radiant young dancer"! (In fact, Sonja Szyszko was a hefty middle-aged woman with an eerily white-powdered face, penciled-in black eyebrows and eyelashes so stiff with mascara they looked like a daddy longlegs' legs. Her mouth was a shiny lewd crimson and her fluttery hands were so large and big-knuckled, you'd have almost thought she was a man boldly impersonating a woman.)

Why did Mom do such things? I had an urge, not for the first time since Dad's death, when Mom's "hospitality" began to become frantic, to run away.

But there was Clare watching me. *Don't even think of it, Nikki!*

So I didn't. The way I shook Sonja Szyszko's sizable hand, and listened to her chatter about what a "grazious Christian lady" my mother was, you'd have thought there was nowhere else in the world I wanted to be except exactly here.

Mom's other guests were: Aunt Tabitha Spancic, one of my father's older sisters who'd never had much interest in his family, a severe-looking snowy-haired grandma with an ungrandma-like trick of hanging back to avoid helping in the kitchen, before or after a meal; Mom's oldest "girlfriend" from grade school, a shivery hypochondriac named Alyce Proxmore whom Dad had never been able to stand but who had triumphed over him in death for she seemed to be at 43 Deer Creek Drive every time I returned; the exalted Gilbert Wexley—"Mr. Wexley" as Mom insisted upon calling him—a local pseudo-dignitary with an influential position on the Mt. Ephraim City Council that helped fund the annual Mt. Ephraim Arts and Crafts Festival, with which Mom was involved; and "Sonny" Danto, owner of the ugly red sports car, an ebullient middle-aged man of swarthy good looks with an oily pompadour and sideburns in the mode of the older Elvis Presley, whom Mom had invited just the day before when he'd come to the house on a "life-saving emergency mission."

I asked what the emergency was, and Mom said, pressing her hand against the bosom of her lime-green velour top, "Red ants! An invasion! Remember, Nikki, Clare?—how each spring we'd have black ants invading like an army?—those sort of bristly-black things so large if you crushed them under your foot you could feel them snap in two—oh it was *awful*. But red ants are worse, there are more of them and they're so *small*. I thought almost it was red pepper somehow, spilled out onto the kitchen floor and the counter, and in the sink, though I don't even have red pepper, only black pepper—you know how your father shook pepper on

everything, even eggs? But I didn't know that, I mean I was totally un-
prepared, yesterday morning I came into the kitchen and there was
Smoky mewing and swatting his paws at these columns of red things
marching single file right across the floor bold as you please. As if they
were challenging Smoky—and me—'Here we are, ma'am, and here we
belong.' Up out of that furnace vent by the refrigerator, up the table legs
and swarming over the table, and on the counters by the sink and inside
the drawers, I was so *dismayed*. It was hopeless to try to spray, the way your
father would have done, with the black ants it was a kind of spring custom for Dad, I think almost he looked forward to it, with the aerosol
spray, but I hate those spray cans, I'm afraid they will explode, it always
says 'Keep away from heat' and you wonder what that means exactly,
and I'm terrified of poisoning myself, or poor Smoky, and there were so
many more of these red ants than there'd been black, just kept coming
in a swarm, and they *sting*. And so I looked for help in the yellow
pages, and—"

"Sonny Danto," the oily-pompadour man said, gripping my hand with
a dramatic flourish, "—'The Scourge of Bugs.' "

An exterminator! This was a first.

These mismatched individuals had been invited to Gwen Eaton's
house for dinner on Mother's Day, May 9, 2004, for reasons, near as I
could figure, having to do with the fact that they were mothers, like Aunt
Tabitha, whose children lived too far away to visit her, or were not
mothers, like Alyce Proxmire and Sonja Szyszko, and might be feeling
"lonely and left out"; or that they were sons without mothers, like
Mr. Wexley whose mother was no longer living, or "Sonny" Danto whose
mother was in a retirement village in Orlando, Florida, too far away
to visit.

Why Clare and Nikki were invited was no mystery, at least.

Dinner at Mom's was always more complicated than you'd expect. Not
just the "dishes" Mom was preparing were complicated, and demanded
intense spurts of concentration in the kitchen, in the vicinity of the stove
(where at least one burner of four was likely to be malfunctioning); but

there had to be "appetizers," passed about repeatedly in the living room, and these were invariably "special new recipes" that required commentary, praise. On this occasion Mom had prepared celery stalks with curried cream cheese filling, codfish ball pastry-puffs, deviled eggs heavily dusted with paprika, and tiny hot sausage balls. (The sausage balls were an instant hit with the men, Sonny Danto especially.) While the conversation swerved, ebbed, lurched and languished and gamely revived Mom was anxious to keep the platters in continual motion.

The exalted Mr. Wexley, with the air of a host, jarring to me, who had to wonder exactly what his relationship was with Mom, boasted of having brought "prime" New York State champagne for the occasion. With the self-importance of a small-town politician he lurched to his feet and lifted his glass to propose a toast to my embarrassed mother: "Gwendolyn Eaton! On this special occasion: Mother's Day! Beloved citizen, neighbor, friend, and, um—mother! Who, I've been told"—he winked clownishly, sighting Mom along his long beak of a nose—"as a ver-ry pretty cheerleader at Mt. Ephraim High, Class of '66, was known to her adoring classmates as 'Feather.' "

Everyone joined in the toast. Mom blushed. Sonja Szyszko was smiling broadly, perplexed: " 'Feaz-zer'? As a bird, is it? Bird feaz-zer?"

Poor Mom. Her cheeks burnt as if she'd been slapped. It was impossible to judge if she was pleased by the attention, or mortified; if her laughter was genuine, or forced. Within the family Mom was always being teased; Dad had often led the teasing, though gently. It had been Dad's role to be skeptical while Mom's role had been to be naive, credulous, and ever-surprised.

As we lifted our glasses, I saw Mom clutch at her glass as if not knowing what it was. I didn't want to think *She's missing Dad.*

I touched Mom's arm. " 'Feather'? You know, you've never told us why."

But Mom only just smiled at me, unhearing.

Next, Rob Chisholm proposed a toast. His smile was all gums, glistening. He'd been drinking a succession of beers in the living room as well as devouring tiny sausages and his gravelly voice was buoyant as a rising balloon. "To Gwen, the most terrific mother-in-law any man could ask for if he'd have to have any mother-in-law, know what I mean? 'May the wind be always at your back'—*watch* your back'—whatever it is, that Irish toast. Hail, Mother Eaton!"

There was a goofy looseness to Rob Chisholm this evening, I'd rarely seen in my brother-in-law and found intriguing. A kind of river-current swirl about him as if, with a little stumble, he'd be swept away. Clare laughed sharply, undecided whether her husband was being folksy-witty, or making a fool of himself.

Mom said, fumbling at humor, "Oh, dear: 'Mother Eaton.' Is that what people call me behind my back? Like some kind of—nun? Isn't that what a head nun is called, not 'sister' but—"

Aunt Tabitha interrupted, " 'Mother Spancic' is what my childrens' spouses call *me*. What I have requested to be called. I think the generations should be acknowledged. If you are 'mother' you are spared being a sibling or a buddy to be called by your first name, but you are not just any 'mother'—public property like a street vendor, or somebody with a booth in a flea market. No, indeed! You deserve respect, I think. For what you have endured." Prune-faced old Tabitha spoke with such passion, most of the company at the table laughed, miscomprehending.

To prevent the Scourge of the Bugs lifting his glass in a champagne toast I jumped in: "Here's to *moms*. Without *moms*, where'd we all be?"

A few quick swallows of New York State champagne, Nikki was sounding giddy. Party-girl.

There was something so desperate about this Mother's Day gathering at 43 Deer Creek Drive, it was either giddy or tearful.

Everyone drank to my toast except Mom who was still clutching at her wineglass, observing us with a fond, sad smile as if from miles away. And Foster who was in the TV room watching a baseball game, and Lilja who stood elegantly slouched in the doorway observing us with the clinical detachment of an anthropologist.

Thinking she'll never get our age. Ages. Oh, never!

With the benign-bossy air of a teacher bringing a class to its close, whether the close is logical or not, Clare lifted her glass in an aggressive gesture, leaned forward at the hips and said, smiling so hard you'd imagine you heard small bones crunching: "Where'd you be without *moms* I'll tell you: cooking for yourselves, cleaning for yourselves and picking up after yourselves, sorting socks for yourselves, complaining to yourselves, moping and bellyaching and—"

Hearing the edge to her voice, and seeing our startled expressions, Clare broke off with a dazzling smile, "—and being just adorable to yourselves. And nobody to tell you they love you no matter *what*."

Sonny Danto lifted his glass. In a hearty voice he declared, "*I* will drink to that, ma'am! Truer words were never spoken."

Next, Mom was given her Mother's Day presents.

Of course, Mom had told us not to bring her anything. Every year Mom insisted no presents, every year we brought her presents, every year she stammered in embarrassment, as sincerely as if for the first time, "Oh, you shouldn't have. I . . ."

The burning blush was in her cheeks, she was blinking tears from her eyes. Glancing about the room at her guests, pressing a hand against her velour top, she gave the impression of being uncertain where she was.

I prodded Mom, a gentle little nudge on the arm. "C'mon, Mom! Open your presents, we're dying of curiosity."

I meant to be funny. I was the only person who'd given Mom a wrapped present.

Stiff-backed Aunt Tabitha had brought over a pot of pink mums with tinfoil twisted about its clay pot, which, with a grim smile, she'd presented to Mom in the way of one paying the price of admission—"From Walter, my youngest. In Sausalito, California. He won't mind these mums going to you, Gwen."

"Why, Tabitha! Aren't these beautiful! Thank you."

Mom accepted the pot of mums as if she'd never seen anything so exotic. She leaned over to smell the niggardly little bud-blossoms, though knowing that mums have no scent. Tabitha was complaining of her three children: "Now you'd think, wouldn't you, but you'd be wrong!—that they would at least check with one another, to see what flowers to send me. Friday morning the delivery boy from Curtis Flowers comes to the house with a pot of mums wired from Wendy, in Toledo; Saturday morning, a second pot of mums wired from Aaron, in Scranton; Saturday afternoon, a pot of mums wired from Walter, in Sausalito. Can you imagine! Two pots of pink mums, and one pot of lavender. And the same identical size, which I happen to know, because I inquired, is the cheapest size for wired flowers, and the same identical note LOVE TO MOTHER ON MOTHER'S DAY, and the same identical delivery boy, I was mortified."

"Well," Mom said. "Mums are very beautiful anyway, Tabitha. You should—"

Tabitha interrupted sharply, " 'Should'? 'Should' what, Gwen? Be grateful as a craven little puppy-dog that my children have remembered me at all?"

"Well—"

"It isn't as if they were actual children, for heaven's sake. Wendy is forty-four, Aaron is forty-one, and Walter is thirty-eight. And they did more or less the same thing last year, except it was azaleas they wired." Tabitha drained her glass of champagne vehemently.

From Alyce Proxmire's hands came a cellophane-wrapped pecan-cherry kringle, an elaborately rich Danish pastry in the shape of a horse collar. At Mom's gatherings, Alyce always brought pastries from a bakery in town, removed from the baker's box and re-packaged in one of Alyce's baking pans; Alyce had never outgrown a childish love of sweets, but couldn't be troubled to bake. She was a plain-faced knobby woman with a fretful air, always ill, or convalescent, or "coming down" with something; shivering today in a baggy brown woollen dress, with a baggy white cardigan buttoned over it; the nails of her long bony fingers purplish-blue. Clare and I could recall our mother's "oldest girlfriend" regarding us with looks of mild revulsion when we'd been small children urged to call her "Auntie Alyce" which we'd never learned to do convincingly. Alyce had never married of course. Alyce had had a "tragic" romance years ago. Alyce had been urged into early retirement as a public school librarian who'd been unable or unwilling to learn computer skills and who, at the end of her career, had developed a phobia about allowing certain students (germ-laden? destructive?) to check out books, or even to consult them in the library.

Mom was saying, "Oh, Alyce! You shouldn't have!"—leaning over to squeeze her friend's icy hand. "Thanks so much, love. I've made peach melba for dessert, now we'll have kringle, too."

Love! Clare and I exchanged a resentful glance.

Lilja had made a watercolor card—HAPPY MOTHER'S DAY GRANDMA EATON!—that had obviously taken some time, and was embarrassed by our praise. From the rest of the Chisholm family came a comic Mother's Day card, and a $150 gift certificate from Restoration Hardware in the mall. "Oh, Clare! Rob! Thank you!" Each year, practical-minded Clare gave our mother a gift certificate and each year Mom appeared to be pleasantly surprised.

As a girl, already a model of efficiency and frugality for whom sentiment was a secondary matter, Clare had solved the gift problem by buying items with a festive twist in quantity: boxes of gaily colored tissues, mouthwash and toothpaste in unusual flavors, giant boxes of Dad's favorite cereal Wheaties and a full case of Mom's most-used Campbell's soup cream of celery; without irony or a wish to be cruel, Clare had given me such birthday gifts as flea collars for our cats, a bag of scented Kitty Litter, deodorant, a "giant economy" box of Junior Miss Sani-Pads.

"Oh, Nikki! What on earth . . ."

Mom was marveling over the rainbow-wrapped present that weighed so little. With comical fastidiousness she undid the yarn with which I'd tied it, anxious to preserve the wrapping paper to use another time. "So beautiful, Nikki! Isn't this just like you, so—*imaginative.*"

Was it? I wanted to think so.

Inside the paper was a fluffy white ostrich feather boa, I'd found in a Rochester thrift shop. Mom exclaimed with childish delight, pulling the boa out of its wrapping and positioning it on her shoulders. There was something comical and touching about her, like a little girl playing grown-up. "Nikki, just what I was needing. However did you guess?"

Mom leaned over to hug me. She smelled of white talcum.

After Dad's death, which had been abrupt and unexpected, Mom had lapsed into a phase of showering frequently, washing her hands compulsively until the skin began to wear out, brushing her teeth until the gums bled. She'd dusted herself obsessively with the fragrant talcum powder Dad had given her, even the soles of her feet, so that, when Clare and I dropped by the house we'd be startled by ghostly white powder footprints on the floor outside the bathroom.

Eventually, Mom had returned to normal. We thought.

"I found a feather boa once, ostrich feathers, too, white mixed with black, in my grandmother's attic. I asked the old woman if I could have it to play with, I was just a little girl, and d'you know what my grandmother said?—'No you may *not*.' "

Aunt Tabitha delivered this little speech in an amused voice, as if she'd shifted her loyalties to the long-departed grandmother, not the long-departed little girl. You had to guess that Tabitha didn't much approve of my whimsical present to Mom. And Alyce Proxmire shook her head, frowning in wonderment as at the spectacle of a girl classmate making a fool of herself. Of course, my big sister Clare smiled indulgently: "Nikki always buys us things she'd like for herself."

I felt the sting of that remark. Damn Clare, it wasn't true!

Sonja Szyszko was so exclaiming over the "beautiful"—"glamorous"— boa, Mom draped it over her sturdy shoulders. I felt a moment's concern that Mom would impulsively give the boa to her as Mom often did with things that "looked better" on others than on her.

Talk shifted to thrift shops. On this subject, I was the expert. For Mom's guests I showed off a watch I'd found in the same Rochester shop, slightly tarnished but still very beautiful silver with a delicate midnight-blue face that hadn't conventional numerals, but pale, luminous little stars instead. On the back was engraved: *To Elise with love.* High on champagne, in an excitable mood, seeing how the men were watching me, I heard myself prattling on like an airhead TV personality about my "insatiable" love of browsing in secondhand stores. I seemed to be drawn to old things, as if what was new, raw, untested and "not-yet-loved" hadn't any appeal to me; I seemed to need to acquire things that had already belonged to someone else as if I wasn't sure of my own judgment and had to follow where others had been: "Clothes, jewelry, men."

My slender purple-silk legs were crossed, my waxy-white naked left foot (toenails painted magenta, to match fingernails and mouth) was jiggling in the gold-spangled high-heeled sandal. I'd spoken as if whimsically. I had a way of saying what was serious in a bold-innocent fashion to elicit startled laughs.

Except Clare wasn't laughing. Or Mom, still fussing over the ostrich feathers draped across Sonja Szyszko's shoulders, marveling at their beauty.

Another woman's husband! How can you, Nikki.

How can you expect him to marry you, if he doesn't respect you.

Because if that man respected you he would get a divorce and marry you.

Yes he would! I don't care what century this is.

And if he doesn't marry you he doesn't respect you.

Nikki don't you laugh at me! Your father would be upset about this, too.

Honey I'm your mother. I just don't want you to be hurt.

Everyone marveled at Mom's cooking. Of course.

For Mother's Day dinner we had: the much-anticipated Hawaiian Chicken Supreme, a gooey mélange of very tender chicken, chopped green peppers and onions, hefty pineapple slices, soy sauce and white rice and almonds. Also, asparagus spears, corn soufflé, beet salad with chopped mint. Also, Mom's home-baked raisin/yogurt/twelve-grain bread. And for dessert peach melba with ice cream and cherry-pecan kringle. Except for sulky Lilja who ate only asparagus spears and a teaspoon of corn soufflé, and infuriated her mother by asking to be excused after ten minutes, we all ate hungrily. Even Aunt Tabitha who commented stoically that the Hawaiian chicken was "a little too sweet for my taste" and the rice "just a little undercooked"; and prissy Alyce Proxmire with her habit of cutting her food into tiny portions to be eaten with excruciating slowness as if she were expecting to bite down on broken glass.

One of your mother's lame ducks, Dad used to say of Alyce Proxmire with a bemused roll of his eyes.

For a while as a child I'd actually thought there might be "lame" ducks Mom had rescued, somewhere. She was such a soft touch for stray creatures, predominantly women, calling at all hours or dropping by the house ("I'll only stay for a few minutes, Gwen, I promise") so it would be just like Mom to take pity on limping ducks.

So many people at the dining room table, we'd had to add extra leaves. Rob and me struggling to fit the sections together. Our hands brushing. Maybe it's harder to relate to a brother-in-law if you've never had a brother.

At dinner, the table seemed too crowded. You'd have thought it was Thanksgiving or Christmas and that we were all family, talking and laughing loudly. Trying to sound festive. My eyes smarted with tears, though I was laughing. I kept looking for Dad amid all these faces and was baffled to see Rob Chisholm in Dad's place, across the long table from Mom.

More annoying, the exalted Gilbert Wexley was seated to Mom's right, speaking pompously to the table—"The president will be reelected by a landslide in November, the patriotic American people will never be soft on terrorism"—while Mom looked on smiling and anxious. I couldn't bear to think that my mother might care about this man who so reveled in his own self-importance.

Fifty-six was too old to "date." If Mom didn't know this, Clare or I would have to clue her in.

Beside me sat Sonny Danto, as I'd feared. Before dinner I'd tried to switch name cards, placing myself between Mom and Lilja, Mom had caught me and slapped playfully at my hand. *Nikki no!*

One good thing about Danto, he vied with Wexley for dominance at the table. Though he knew virtually no one here, he wasn't shy in the slightest. Talking, gesticulating, eating and drinking with the zest of a swarm of cockroaches. Even his attempt to speak with me was bustling, aggressive: " 'Nicole Eaton'—your name? In the little local paper?"— smiling with his large stained teeth, leaning toward me so that I wasn't spared seeing each hair, each follicle of the Presley pompadour with unnerving intimacy—"my favorite of all the local writers, I always look for your columns."

"Do you."

Mom must have talked me up shamelessly to Sonny Danto, he seemed to have come prepared. In the local library quickly scanning back issues of the *Beacon*.

Danto confided in me, in a lowered voice, he intended to write his memoir someday—"*The Scourge of the Bugs: A No-Holds-Barred Account of a Real-Life Terminator*. Terrific title, eh?" Or maybe, if he could find the right collaborator, it would be one of those "as told to" memoirs.

He'd been inspired by his grandfather in Tonawanda, who'd been the original "Scourge of the Bugs." Except Danto's grandfather's specialty had been termites, his were carpenter ants. "It reveals a lot about a person, which is his specialty. In the field of pest extermination."

I said, "I think my specialty would be moths. Those little fluttery paper-looking things? That are kind of pretty? Though I guess, I'd have to kill them, wouldn't I. I don't think I would like that."

Danto laughed extravagantly. He must have thought that I was flirting with him. Like an infomercial he began to lecture on the subject of moths, drawing the interest of most of the table away from Wexley: "Now your so-called paper moth can infest a household worse than ants! One day you see there's a few of them, next day you see there's a dozen of 'em, suddenly they're all over the house and know why?—it isn't just woollens they eat. No, they lay their eggs in cereal, crackers, pasta, dry pet food, birdseed, even in tea, anything in your cupboard that isn't canned or packaged airtight. People just don't know! Like poor Mrs. Eaton yesterday who despite a pretty clean household was about overrun with red ants and had no clue how to deal with 'em, which is where the Scourge of the Bugs comes in. You don't ever want to underestimate the power of bugs to take over your house, you need professionals to exterminate 'em." I saw Mom force a smile at *pretty clean household* and exchanged a look of sisterly irony with Clare across the table. How could our mother have plucked "Sonny" Danto out of the yellow pages and foisted him upon us, at this table!

And upon me, her supposedly beloved daughter.

She doesn't know me. Doesn't want to know me.

As usual, Mom was oblivious of any discomfort that wasn't obvious. As long as her guests appeared to be enjoying themselves, eating her food and accepting offers of seconds, what else mattered? Gwen Eaton, incurable optimist! It was hopeless to be angry with my mother, she meant so well. She wanted her Nikki to be happy like her Clare and that meant marriage, kids, home. *Family.*

Inspired by Danto whose swaggering self-confidence must have annoyed him, Rob confided to the table how, as a boy, he'd wanted to be a bacteriologist, or maybe an epidemiologist: "Somebody who would do good in the world not just make money."

Aunt Tabitha crinkled her nose as if Rob had said something vaguely obscene. Alyce Proxmire shuddered, staring at him in disbelief. Clare was looking embarrassed as if Rob had suddenly revealed an intimate secret and Sonja Szyszko clapped her ungainly hands together as if she'd misunderstood.

"Why Rob," Mom protested. "You do good, in your line of work. 'Electronics.' 'Sales.' There has to be electronics in our world, doesn't there? There has to be business, and making money, or there wouldn't be other things like science, would there? You couldn't make a living just from tiny things you can see only through a microscope, who'd have invented and manufactured the microscope without business and money?

Bacteria are so little, not like birds or even bugs." Mom spoke gaily, giddily. She was being funny without knowing why, and seemed pleased at the smiling response.

Danto said belligerently, "Bugs have their own bacteria, you better believe it. Like ticks? Lyme disease? It ain't the ticks that cause the disease, it's bacteria."

"Actually, it's a virus," Rob said curtly. "Lyme disease is caused by a virus."

The subject shifted to Lyme disease: everyone knew someone who'd had it. Alyce Proxmire seemed to come alive for the first time that evening, speaking excitedly of how, two summers ago, in this very house, she'd made the near-fatal mistake of holding Gwen's gray cat in her lap and in so doing she must have picked up a tick from the cat's fur because early next morning she was wakened by a terrible throbbing in her scalp, and managed to see in the mirror an angry red swelling of the kind that is a danger sign meaning infection, and Lyme disease, if you aren't treated immediately with antibiotics.

"I might be paralyzed right now! I might be in an iron lung, right this minute! Thanks to Gwen and one of her strays."

Alyce meant to be joking, even as she was seriously chiding Mom, but her voice quavered with dread.

Mom said apologetically: "Oh, Alyce. I feel so bad about that! Right away I examined Smoky, and took him to the vet, and Dr. McKay could not find a single tick on him, honestly. Not even a flea. 'Smoky is one of the cleanest animals in my practice,' he said, truly, Alyce! I've explained to you. Maybe you did pick up a tick at my house, out in the grass, remember we were walking in the lawn, there are always deer crossing the lawns in this neighborhood, and Lyme disease comes from deer ticks. I'm sure the tick didn't come from Smoky."

Alyce murmured petulantly that Gwen always defended the cat, as she always defended her strays. Aunt Tabitha smiled grimly, agreeing: there was no telling how many of Gwen's strays were underfoot, she was sure she'd felt something brush against her ankle beneath the table. In her teacherly way of shutting down a subject Clare intervened: "Mom is a sucker for stray animals but her family keeps a close watch on her, she's down to just one."

Mom said, sighing, "Well. Morning Glory passed away. Now there's just Smoky."

"But there was a time, not long ago," Clare said, "when you had four cats. You know how Dad felt about that."

"Oh, dear. Your dad didn't . . ." Mom smiled, faltering. Before dinner she'd draped the white feather boa playfully over her shoulders but now it was slipping off. ". . . actually didn't like animals. Very much."

"Not animals, Mom. Strays!"

Clare was smiling brightly. I knew I had to help her, she'd blundered leading us to this subject. We would tease Mom to deflect her attention, make her laugh with embarrassed pleasure. Telling of her weakness for strays: the cosmetics saleswoman who'd begun to weep during her sales spiel, confided in Gwen how lonely she was, promptly Gwen invited her for dinner, the woman had a "breakdown" and wound up staying the night, and in the morning, Dad was the one to ask her please to leave. Even worse, there was "Cousin Darlene"—a remote relation of Gwen's from Plattsburgh who arrived unannounced and disheveled with a six-month infant, telling a terrible story of her husband abusing her, and threatening her life, and naturally Gwen made her welcome; and within a few days Darlene was running up long-distance telephone bills, leaving the colicky baby with Mom for much of the day and expecting Mom to cook and clean up after her, until again Dad had to intervene, contacted Darlene's family in Plattsburgh to please come get her. " 'Cousin Darlene'! She'd be here yet, camping out in my old room," Clare said vehemently. "She'd stolen from her own family. She wasn't even married. That baby didn't have any father."

Faintly Mom protested, "Oh, but whose fault was that? A baby doesn't choose . . ."

"And last summer? I dropped by the house here, and there's this Ozark-looking individual, I swear his arms were covered in tattoos, in a muscle T-shirt and what looks like swim trunks out in the yard pretending to mow the grass. Except the mower kept sputtering. I asked Mom who on earth this person was and she tells me Reverend Bewley 'spoke up' for him, he's a parolee from Red Bank of all places."

"Oh but just for some small thing, really," Mom said, blushing, "like forging checks, or . . ."

"Auto theft, Mom! Burglary! Who knows what else he did, he never got caught for! Your precious Reverend Bewley is as naive as you are! And, get this," Clare said in triumph, "his name was 'Lynch.' "

"But Clare, a person can't help what his name is . . ."

" 'Lynch' was his first name! 'Lynch' was certainly a name the man could have changed." Clare's eyes glistened with righteous fury, she had the rapt attention of the table. The mood of the moment was wayward and comical. Mom blushed with a kind of embarrassed pleasure at such chiding. I could see my father's figure hovering in the background as often, when Clare and I were visiting with Mom, having coffee or herbal tea together in the kitchen, or on the patio, I'd become suddenly aware of Dad as he stood in a doorway seemingly wanting neither to join us nor to leave us; content with listening in, getting that gist of what was so entertaining to his three girls as he called us fondly, without wishing to participate. ". . . so I'm with Mom in the kitchen and we aren't hearing the lawn mower, and I go outside to investigate, and there is this 'Lynch' in front of the garage where there was oil spilled on the concrete he must have spilled himself, and what is the man doing?—I couldn't believe my eyes, he was practicing slipping and falling. Falling! This guy, in his late twenties, one of those skinny hard-muscled guys, scrubby little goatee and sunburnt-looking face, sort of positioning his hand on the ground, and lowering himself, preparing to fall hard, turns out Mom had hired him for yard work in some 'Christian Fellowship Out-Reach Program' sponsored by Reverend Bewley, and what's he doing but practicing an 'accident'?—so he could pretend he was hurt, and blackmail Mom? Sue Mom? So I call out 'Excuse me, mister, just what the hell do you think you're doing?'—and that got his attention." Clare spoke vehemently as one giving testimony on Court TV. The color was in her fleshy face from the wine she'd been drinking, and now the rapt attention of the table. "And all this while Mom is trailing behind me wringing her hands—'Oh dear, oh dear! Don't be hard on him, Clare.' Lynch at least has the decency to be embarrassed when I confront him, he's mumbling *Nothin, ma'am, I ain't doin nothin just finishin' up here* and I say, 'That's right, mister. You are doing nothing. You are finished working for my mother, you will leave this property immediately and not ever return or I will call the police and you'll be back in Red Bank where you belong.' "

Amid the laughter of her guests Mom tried feebly to protest. "But he meant well, I think. I mean, at first. I'd talked with him, he wasn't a bad person, really—told me his 'only trusted friend' was his grandma. I know it looked suspicious how he was behaving, I'm sure Clare is right, but how can a parolee support himself, how can he avoid committing more crimes, unless someone gives him a chance . . ."

Clare cried, "A chance to exploit you! A chance to rob *you*!"

"But how could I know, Reverend Bewley said . . ."

"So I called the Reverend. Oh boy did I call the Reverend and give him a piece of my mind. 'No more charity cases! No more phony Christian ex-cons preying on my tender-hearted mother! Gwendolyn Eaton's family takes care of her just fine, thank you.' And the Reverend, too, had at least the decency to apologize." Clare was breathless, triumphant. Each time she told the Lynch story it was becoming more embellished, crueller and funnier. In the earliest version which Clare had told me on the phone, on the very day of the episode, it hadn't seemed so clear that lawn worker had been practicing a fall, only just behaving suspiciously in Clare's eyes, in the vicinity of the garage. (While Dad was alive, the garage had been kept relatively clear, and he'd insisted that the car be parked inside every night. After Dad's death, Mom tended to park the car in the driveway, and the garage was filling up as a kind of storage space.) This new version was such a success in the telling, even prim-faced Tabitha and Alyce Proxmire were reduced to fits of giggling, unable to resist the tale of another's hard luck.

Foster, who'd been watching TV in the other room, ran back to see what was going on with us, and there came languid Lilja, cell phone to her ear: "Mom? What's so funny? Why're you guys laughing so hard?"

It took me a moment to register, Lilja's "Mom" wasn't Mom but Clare.

In Mom's guest bathroom where the predominant smell was sweet potpouri and "floral" soap. Where the hand towels were prissy little linens Mom had embroidered with rosebuds, you'd never dare soil with your actual hands.

Nikki what have you done with my hair seeing my pale startled reflection in the mirror and the fright-wig dyed-maroon hair on my head that looked weirdly small. *What have you done with my Nikki.*

"I'm thirty-one years old! I'm not your Nikki any longer, Mom."

Whose Nikki, then? I'd had a few glasses of wine and wasn't thinking with my usual laser clarity.

Ran cold water, splashed my feverish face. Winked and smiled flirtatiously at myself. " 'My specialty would be moths.' " Pursed my lips in a mock kiss trying not to see that I wasn't so sexy/funky/glamorous close up. Was it seductive or silly, or sad, the way my puckered-tight black top had a tendency to ride up my midriff showing a swath of skin? No wonder Rob Chisholm, Gilbert Wexley, "Sonny" Danto snagged their eyes on me as I'd excused myself from the table.

Lilja on her cell phone. She'd been bored out of her skull by her grandma's Mother's Day dinner.

I'd brought my cell phone too. Arrived at the house by 6 P.M. and it was 8:35 P.M. now and I had refrained from making a single call. (I knew Mom would notice. Seeming so unsuspicious, Gwen Eaton had eyes in the back of her head, and ears, too.) I was feeling empowered not having called my voice mail in Chautauqua Falls which would determine for me had I been expecting a call, or not; was I hoping for a call, or indifferent; was I oblivious of what might, or might not, be waiting for me on my voice mail in my darkened apartment in Chautauqua Falls.

In fact, I couldn't risk it. Hearing the recording click in. *You have no new messages.*

"This has gone better than we expected."

"Well, Nikki! That isn't saying much."

Next morning Clare and I would have to concede, speaking on the phone, that the crazy quilt of Mom's guests had worked, sort of. If we'd taken Mom out to dinner at the stately Mr. Ephraim Inn she'd have fretted over the prices ("Twenty-two dollars for *chicken*! Twenty-eight dollars for *lamb*!"), she'd have been overly friendly with our waitress out of an embarrassment with being waited on ("I'm never waited on at home, am I? I can go to that service station and pour ice water for myself, it's no trouble") and, when the check came, she'd have tried to talk Rob into letting her "help out."

At 9 P.M. Mom's guests were still at the dining room table. Showing no signs of preparing to depart. Wexley and Danto and Rob Chisholm had established an unexpected alliance, criticizing state government officials. In the kitchen Mom was brewing fresh coffee ("real" and decaf). Through the evening she'd been on her feet half the time, into and out of the kitchen in her usual flurried zeal to serve her guests. Mom was a small woman but could be fierce in forbidding anyone to help her: "Now! You're my guests tonight. Even my daughters, you just *sit*." As if Aunt Tabitha and oldest girlfriend Alyce needed to be told.

In the midst of a meal Mom had a way of slipping into the kitchen to surreptitiously rinse a few plates at the sink, place them in the dishwasher and return smiling innocently to the table. *Getting a headstart on cleanup* was for Mom what illicit sex was for other people.

I followed Mom into the kitchen carrying dirtied plates. And there came Clare with more. When Clare scolded, her nostrils flared: "Mom! For goodness sake let Nikki and me take over. Enjoy your guests, *you* invited them."

I laughed. Clare glanced at me, incensed.

"Well, it's so. No one but Gwen Eaton would have invited these people, thrown them together to sink or swim, and hopped up and down from the table all evening abandoning them to one another."

Mom mildly protested, "Clare, I have not. I have not been hopping up and down and abandoning my guests. You're being unfair."

Quickly I intervened: "Clare is being Clare, Mom."

Clare had been doubtful of the evening from the start. Tomorrow was a school day for Lilja and Foster and that meant getting up early and getting the children up etcetera. Worse, Rob seemed to be drinking more than usual. And enjoying himself more than usual.

I smiled to think this wasn't Rob Chisholm at home.

Mom was asking, anxiously, "Don't you think the evening is going well, really?" and Clare and I said, "Oh, Mom: yes. Of course." I complimented Mom on such "lively, original" guests and Clare complimented Mom on "how pretty" the table looked. "But do you think people really like the food, or are they just having seconds to be polite?" Mom asked, all but wringing her hands, and Clare and I laughed at the very question: "Mom, the food is delicious. Of course."

"But the Hawaiian chicken, Tabitha thought was too sweet . . ."

"Tabitha!" Clare laughed. "Didn't you notice, she heaped her plate at least twice?"

"She said the rice was undercooked."

"Because it wasn't gummy," I said. "Aunt Tabitha doesn't know the first thing about serious cooking."

"Well. Maybe."

"Mom, please! You're a terrific cook."

Mom had promised more ice cream for the table, to accompany the remains of the peach melba and the kringle, and it was my task to poke through the crowded freezer in search of another pint. I tried not to be distracted by the numerous snapshots held by tiny magnets to the refrigerator, mostly family pictures. There were layers of these going back to when Clare and I were teenagers. My smiling parents in summer clothes, looking startlingly young and happy. Clare and Rob on their wedding day, also young and happy. Clare with infant Foster in her arms, looking like an athlete who has won a prize. Blond Lilja at age eight, squinting at the camera with a beautiful shy smile. And there was almost-eighteen-year-old Nicole in high school graduation cap and gown, over-exposed white in a dazzle of sunshine: "Nikki" not yet spiky-haired, darkish blond and smiling wistfully at the camera (held by Dad) in the grassy backyard at 43 Deer Creek Drive.

Strange, to see an old photo of yourself. All that was so crucial at that time (senior prom, boyfriend, sex) melted away now like last year's snow.

I'd located the ice cream, raspberry ripple. The carton was covered in a fine frost-film, icy-cold against my fingers.

". . . and Lilja, she scarcely touched her food. Oh Clare, I worry about her . . ."

"Please don't."

"But her wrists are so thin, little sparrow bones . . ."

Between Lilja and her adoring grandma there'd been a special bond, it had seemed. But not recently.

Lilja was a sensitive topic Clare refused to discuss with Mom, in fact with anyone. I avoided this subject as I'd have avoided a live wire. (I'd have taken my niece's side, anyway. Rebelling against her so-efficient mother must have been delicious.) Mom knew better, but couldn't help herself. Clare bustled about the kitchen in a way to make you think she was shoving Mom and me aside though she hadn't so much as touched us. She grabbed the steaming teakettle off the stove, tossed two fresh bags of Almond Sunset herbal tea into the ceramic teapot, poured boiling water carelessly into the pot and slammed back into the dining room.

Mom said, hurt, "Well, I do worry. You read about anorexia, it's on TV all the time. It isn't just Lilja is thin, she's so edgy and, I don't know, not-there when you try to talk to her. This little sweater I want to knit for her, in a light cotton yarn, she hasn't picked out the style yet and her birthday is only two months away . . ." Mom's voice trailed off wistfully.

I could imagine Lilja's polite interest in Grandma's latest knitting project. I didn't want to think how vulnerable Mom was to hurt.

"Well, Mom. Lilja will be fourteen. She isn't a little girl any longer."

"Oh, I know! Girls that age. I see them at the mall, and at the pool, they seem so self-sufficient, somehow. I smile at them and their eyes go right through me. When you were that age, Nikki . . ."

"Was I more immature, Mom, than I am now?"

Mom laughed, perplexed. Knowing this was a joke even if it wasn't wholly logical.

I loved to make Mom laugh. These last four years it seemed the best I could do for her.

All this while Mom had been fussing with the coffee percolator which was made of glass that had become too stained for use with guests, coffee made in it had to be carefully poured into a gleaming silver pot to be carried into the dining room. And the ice cream, which I'd simply have passed around in its carton, naturally had to be scooped into a "nice" bowl to be presented with a silver serving spoon.

Nice. That was the measure of Mom's life.

As if she'd been tracking my thoughts Mom said suddenly, in an anxious undertone, "And you, Nikki? How are *you?*"

"Terrific, Mom. As you can see."

I brushed at my spiky hair tufts with both hands.

Mom was peering at me, smiling uncertainly. Her greeny-amber eyes appeared moist as if, in fact, she was trying very hard to see who stood before her.

"You've been distracted by him, haven't you. All evening."

"Mom, please. Not that tired old subject."

My response was quick, sharp. I would realize later that I'd been waiting for this, for my mother's murmured words of the gentlest reproach, and that quivery look to her face, the rapid blinking of eyelids signaling *Your mother is blinking back tears. She is being brave on your account. She is a good loving mother of a willful self-destructive daughter intent on breaking her heart.*

"Nikki, it isn't tired to *me.*"

"Look, you don't know him. You've met him once, you have no idea how it is between us. So, please. Let's drop it."

" 'Drop it.' What a thing to say. As if I could 'drop' my own daughter."

"Mom, your guests are waiting for you. We'd better go back."

"Oh, what do I care about them! I don't know why I invited them, a kind of madness came over me. 'More people! More people! If I can't be happy myself I can make them happy!'—maybe that's it. But I only care for my family, I care for *you*."

Mom made a clumsy move to touch me, and I drew back. Quick as if a darting little hummingbird had struck at me with its beak, I'd reacted without thinking.

Suddenly we were speaking in low excited voices. My heart was beating with painful clarity, unless it was my mother's heart beating. I could not breathe, she was sucking the oxygen out of the room. I wanted to push her from me, I was frightened of her power. I could not bear to be touched by her, as, in the waiting room at the hospital when we were told of Dad's death, I could not bear to be touched by any of the family for the outermost layer of my skin had been peeled away, I stood raw, exposed. Mom was saying words I had heard in her mouth many times and imagined many times more, I must break up with that man, he has been such an evil influence in my life, even if he divorces his wife think how unhappy he has made her, and me. How can I expect him to marry me if he doesn't respect me and how can he respect me if I don't respect myself. How can I drift as I've been drifting. These years. Drifting downstream. As if I'd been rowing a canoe, and I'd let the paddle go, now the canoe is just drifting downstream, with me in it . . .

"Maybe you haven't drifted enough, Mom. Family isn't all there is."

"Without family, *what is there?*"

Afterward I would think, Mom was asking this question sincerely.

Wanting to know, and how could I tell her. I could not reveal to her I didn't know.

"Mom, you are not me, and I am not you. And thank God for that."

All that I said was true. I had thought such mutinous thoughts many times. Yet now, suddenly I was uttering them aloud in a hurt, childish voice.

It was at this point Clare pushed open the kitchen door.

By 9:40 P.M. the party had broken up. Finally.

Driving back to Chautauqua Falls I thought *I will punish her, I won't call her tomorrow.*

Maybe the next day.

Maybe not.

... then judge me

When we were growing up. When we were harsh in our judgments of others as adolescents are apt to be. " 'Walk a mile in my footsteps, then judge me.' That's what my mother used to say."

Mom wasn't scolding us exactly. She spoke gently, and she was smiling. Clare understood the rebuke but I had such a literal mind I'd try to work out how you could walk in another's footsteps: in snow? in mud? in sand?

Mom rarely spoke of her mother Marta Kovach who'd died when Mom was only eleven. She'd died of some mysterious "eating-away" nerve disease.

Even decades later the subject was too painful for Mom to discuss. It alarmed Clare and me, growing up, to realize that our mother had been a stranger's daughter, she hadn't always been our mom but a little girl of eleven who'd come home from school one day to a shingle-board row house on Spalding Street in downtown Mt. Ephraim to discover that her mother had "passed away" in her sleep and she would not be allowed to see her.

Mom had been in sixth grade at the time and would have to repeat the grade, everything she'd learned had been wiped away.

"It was like a blackboard being wiped down. I just forgot everything."

Mom smiled wistfully. I wondered if it could be true: forgot everything? Her name, how to read and write? I doubted this.

We were alone together in the kitchen. Mom was looking so sad, staring out the window at the bird feeder where a swarm of small birds—chickadees, sparrows, juncos, a flashy red cardinal and his olivish-red mate—were fluttering and darting at the seed. Yet she didn't seem to be seeing them.

I felt an impulse to hug her. But I was fifteen at the time, I wasn't into hugging much.

Anyway, the moment passed.

missing

Two days after the Mother's Day dinner, late afternoon of Tuesday, May 11, the phone rang and since I was finally working, after an all-day procrastination of epic-neurotic proportions, I tuned it out.

A few minutes later it rang again. Somehow, the rings sounded like my sister Clare.

"Nikki! I've been trying to reach you. Have you spoken with Mom today?"

"Not today."

Actually, not the day before, either. Wally Szalla had re-entered my life, the man whom Mom had said was an "evil" influence on me. Wally and I had not been communicating for six days, fifteen hours and forty minutes, and so had catching-up to do.

Not that I'd tell Clare this fact. Or Mom.

Though that morning I'd called Mom, around eleven. Knowing she probably wouldn't be in, weekday mornings were Mom's busy times, at the YM-YWCA pool with her aquatic seniors, church committee meetings, garden club, library/hospital volunteer, lunch with women friends, crafts classes at the mall. Sometimes, just outside digging in her flower beds. Driving to my first interview appointment of the day I'd left a hurried message via cell phone *Sorry I didn't get to call yesterday, Mom. Mother's Day dinner was terrific. Everyone had a wonderful time and the food was wonderful, I finished the corn soufflé for breakfast this morning, absolutely delicious,*

THANKS! Oh and hey, I think I've fallen for the Scourge of the Bugs. You were right, Mom, we're a perfect match! We'll name our firstborn little roach after you: Feather. Bye! Mom would know it was a joke, I hoped. Not adolescent sarcasm.

Since Sunday, I'd come round to seeing the humor of the situation, and was feeling regretful that I hadn't been very sociable after Mom and I had exchanged words in the kitchen. After the other guests left, Clare and I stayed behind to help Mom clean up; this was our usual routine when Mom invited us to dinner. We'd never let Gwen talk us into leaving her to a massive cleanup! But I hadn't talked much; listening to Mom and Clare chatter about the party I'd tuned out; I'd been hurt by what Mom had said about drifting, drifting downstream, for possibly Mom was right, and I'd drifted now out of Wally Szalla's life too, or he'd drifted out of mine, and I loved him, and wanted him to love me, and was feeling sorry for myself as you're apt to feel on Sunday night preceding Monday morning and the hectic beginning of another work week, I'd left the house at 43 Deer Creek Drive as soon as the last rinsed plate was set in the dishwasher. (Mom had invited me to stay the night in my old room she'd converted into a guest room, but I'd declined. Had to escape!)

Had I hugged Mom goodnight, I wasn't sure.

I thought so. Probably. Mom would've hugged *me*.

Clare was saying, "Mrs. Kinsler, Mom's friend from church, called me to ask if I knew where Mom was, they were supposed to meet at the mall for their crafts class this morning at ten-thirty, then have lunch with some other women. But Mom never showed up, which isn't like her, and never called to explain, and hasn't been answering her phone all day."

"Clare, it's only a little after five P.M. What do you mean, 'all day.' "

"I mean, it isn't like Mom to miss a date with a friend, or one of her classes. Even if her car broke down, she'd have called."

Clare was trying to speak calmly. Clare was allowing me to understand that this might be serious, or it might not be serious. But she, Clare, the elder and more responsible of the Eaton sisters, was the one to provide information.

I couldn't think how to reply. My mind felt shredded. I'd been trying not to think of Wally Szalla while struggling to make sense of the mottled quality of the tape I was transcribing, wondering if it was my example that caused Wally too to be drifting, years had passed since he'd begun filing for a divorce from his wife, wondering if it was my fault that the tape was so difficult to decipher or whether it was the fault of the new, compact, Japanese-manufactured recorder, that made me want to cry. I had only until tomorrow morning to type into my computer some sort of coherent and entertaining "human interest" feature under the byline "Nicole Eaton." Now, I saw that the tape cassette was still turning, soundlessly. In my haste to answer the phone I'd punched the volume and not the on/off button.

"Fuck."

"Nikki, *what*?"

"—I mean, I did call Mom around eleven this morning. But she was out, I just left a message."

"And she didn't call back?"

"It wasn't that crucial, Clare. Just thanking her for the party, no need for Mom to call back."

"But Mom always calls back . . ."

"Look, did you drive by the house?"

I'd asked this innocently, should have known better. Clare exploded, "Did I drive by the house! In fact yessss, I drove by our mother's house, Nikki. In the midst of this crazed day, one errand after another, already I've driven Lilja halfway across town to a friend's house, and swung around to pick up Foster from soccer practice, and waited for the plumber who finally came forty minutes late and now I'm due in fifteen minutes to pick Lilja up again and drop her off at home and drive out again to a late-afternoon dentist appointment I've already rescheduled not once but twice, and his office is in that new medical/dental center up North Fork, and you have the gall to ask me from Chautauqua Falls a very convenient thirty miles away did I drive by our mother's house which is across town from my own, yesss in fact I drove by the house

41

but Mom isn't home, or wasn't home around four, her car wasn't in the driveway."

"You didn't check inside . . ."

"No. I didn't 'check inside.' If Mom's car isn't in the driveway, she isn't home."

I supposed this was so. For Mom never parked the car in the garage as Dad had wanted her to. In all weathers it was parked in the driveway becoming ever more rust-stippled, dotted with white bird droppings like accent marks.

Clare spoke of calling Mrs. Higham, Mom's neighbor across the street, asking her to look out the window, see if Mom's car was back, I told her this sounded like a good idea, then Clare immediately objected, in a way that echoed Dad who dreaded neighbors becoming overly involved in the private life of our family as he'd have dreaded bubonic plague, "Oh, but that might embarrass Mom, you know how she prizes her independence, once Gladys Higham knows we're worried about Mom she will tell everyone in the neighborhood, you know how people are, and Mr. Higham is retired with nothing better to do than gossip, it will get back to Mom and she'll be upset with us."

I felt a tinge of alarm. It wasn't like my sister to fuss in this way. I said, "The last time we were worried about Mom, remember?—it turned out she'd been talked into emergency babysitting over at Rhoda's." (Rhoda Schmidt was a cousin of ours with whom we'd never been especially close.) "And before that, around Christmas, someone called us from the hospital, where was Mom for her gift shop shift, and she'd been at a movie matinee with friends, the woman at the hospital had made a mistake about scheduling and Mom was annoyed with us, and I don't blame her. 'I didn't realize I had to report my hourly schedule to my daughters,' Mom said. 'Maybe you should put one of those ankle radar things on me, they put on parolees.' "

We'd laughed, Mom had been funny about it. But she'd been humiliated, for we'd called a number of her friends.

I did feel guilt, sometimes. About having moved away from Mt.

Ephraim. About leading a slapdash kind of life, unmarried, unsettled-down, that life of drift and impulse of which Mom so disapproved. But I'd left home several years before Dad died, and Mom became a widow.

How is it my fault! I wanted to protest.

"Why don't I drive over this evening, Clare. Between six-thirty and seven. If Mom isn't back by then, I mean. You've already done enough running around, have dinner with your family and I'll call you around seven. I'm sure we're exaggerating all this, and Mom is fine. There are only a few places in Mt. Ephraim Mom is likely to be, right?"

"But she gets involved with people. She's such a soft touch. If this is 'Reverend Bewley' exploiting her again . . ."

"Clare, stop worrying. I'll call you after I check the house. In the meantime maybe Mom will call one of us back. Or we'll get through to her."

"Well. If you promise . . ."

"Promise! I just said I would, didn't I?"

"You're not always reliable, Nikki. A call from your editor, and you're off. Or some friend. Or, well—your friend Szalla turns up, you might disappear for days into a time warp."

"Wally has 'turned up,' you'll be pleased to know. We had a time warp yesterday, thank you. And this evening I intend to drive to Mt. Ephraim to check out Mom, as I said."

"Fine! Let me know. 'Bye."

We hurried to hang up, a habit of years. Which one of us could get off the line first.

I was trembling, I wanted to think because of my bossy sister.

I checked the time: 5:08 P.M. I would leave for Mt. Ephraim in about an hour.

I rewound the cassette and returned to transcribing the flawed tape, hunched over my laptop trying to catch crucial sentence fragments and key words, typing in frantic flurries for I had to e-mail the feature to my editor at the *Beacon* no later than 11 P.M. that night. It had to be no more, and not much less, than 1,000 words to fit into the insert supplement *Valley News & Views*. The subject was a ninety-nine-year-old bluegrass and country-and-western performer named Jimmy Friday who'd had several hit singles in the long-ago 1950s and was still locally active, a Chautauqua Valley celebrity of sorts who performed wherever and whenever invited, produced his own CDs and had just published his memoir *Songs My Daddy Taught Me: The Mostly True Tales of Jimmy Friday* with a local press which was the ostensible occasion of the interview. At the time of the taping that morning I'd been basking in the erotic/emotional afterglow of the time warp with Wally Szalla and so in a mood to be utterly charmed by Jimmy Friday, as Jimmy Friday had been charmed by me, marveling at my punk haircut, wondering if it was too late for him, his hair was a beautiful floating-frothy white and he was in fact a handsome elderly man who required only a cane to walk with, he had a wicked sense of humor and a way of presenting himself that was both gallant and frankly sexual. About old age he'd been blisteringly funny. "The most praise we can hope for is *Oh! he isn't completely deaf!—Oh! his wheelchair is so well-oiled!—Oh! his dentures don't clatter*" except hearing these remarks now, or what was coming through of them in the tape, as I was trying to type with increasingly desperate fingers, causing the little spell-check alarm to cheep every few seconds, I didn't think that Jimmy Friday was being funny at all. I swallowed hard and forced myself to continue until the tape stopped abruptly as if broken in the midst of one of my inane questions *Mr. Friday, what advice can you give to—*

There was silence. I was alone in the empty apartment. Five rented rooms on the third, top floor of an elegantly shabby Victorian brownstone in a residential neighborhood of Chautauqua Falls approximately thirty miles from 43 Deer Creek Drive, Mt. Ephraim. Strange how, as I was here, I was also there. Well, I wasn't really here, I was there.

Since speaking with Clare I'd been waiting for the phone to ring but it had not rung. I'd been waiting for Mom to call but Mom had not called. And I was made to realize that, if Clare hadn't called to upset me, if Mom had called in her place, I would have peered at the caller I.D.

screen, seen EATON, JON and probably would not have picked up because I was working: because I didn't want to be interrupted in my work.

And it came to me *Here is what you deserve: never to hear your mother's living voice again.*

I was frightened suddenly. It wasn't 5:30 P.M. but I left for home now.

finding mom

I was so disappointed! Clare had been right, Mom's car wasn't in the driveway.

Though I'd known what to expect. On the drive to Mt. Ephraim I'd punched out Mom's number repeatedly on my cell phone. And always the phone at the other end rang four times, then came the click, and the eerie computer-generated voice *This is 716 737 2695. There is no one home please leave a message at the sound of the beep.*

We'd insisted that Mom have a computer voice installed, after Dad died. Not use her own voice. So no one could guess that an older woman lived by herself at that number.

Not that there was crime in Mt. Ephraim: there wasn't. People left their doors unlocked during the day, car keys in ignitions. There had probably not been a break-in or burglary in any residence in Deer Creek Acres in years. But still.

While Dad was living, Dad's taped voice was what you'd hear when you called my parents' number. So stiff and self-conscious, Dad had re-sembled a computer voice. We'd teased him about Hal in the movie *2001.* Both Dad and Mom had been reluctant to leave messages when they called. In recent years Mom had become more practiced but ini-tially, when voice mail was new for them, they'd hang up quickly as soon as the recording clicked on, like guilty children. I would arrive home to a series of hang-ups on my answering service and think, Oh, Dad.

Mom. When I called back, I knew not to embarrass my parents by alluding to these.

So exasperating! Our parents! Why won't they leave messages!

As soon as I turned onto Deer Creek Drive, a block from the house I could see that the driveway was empty. My heart beat hard in disappointment, dismay.

I was beginning to be worried about Mom but also: I'd wanted to prove Clare wrong, she'd been so adamant that Mom wasn't home. We were adult women in our thirties but every exchange between us was a tug-of-war of wills, and Clare invariably won.

Strange to be returning to the house, so soon after Sunday. It seemed as if I'd just left. Unlike Clare, who lived in Mt. Ephraim, I didn't visit home often. I tried not to feel guilty: Mom tried not to make me feel guilty. But a kind of constriction came over me when I returned, an invisible clamp across my chest. *When will you get married, Nikki. When will you settle down, have children. Without family, what is there?*

Mostly this was unsaid. And yet I heard.

Waning sunlight slanted across the front of the house, which was set back from the road in a grassy lawn pocked with dandelions. There were vividly blooming lilac bushes along the driveway. The air was fragrant with lilac. My mother's house was small but attractive, the most ordinary of suburban houses, I guess you'd say. As a family we'd never lived anywhere else except this single-story redwood-and-stucco "ranch" at 43 Deer Creek Drive. Four bedrooms, a living room and a dining room and a "family" room with sliding glass doors opening onto a rear patio. The subdivision had been built in the late 1950s and each lot was one-and-a-half acres.

Growing up, Clare and I had bicycled everywhere in Deer Creek Estates. We had classmates, friends who lived in the subdivision and we knew half the residents by name. Away at college when I'd been lonely I'd played a game: lying in bed, eyes shut tight I would see myself bicycling along the curving roads of Deer Creek Estates. There was Deer Creek Drive intersecting with Green Glade Drive; there was Cedar Point beyond Oriole, and the cul-de-sac Cedar Point Circle where larger, more expensive ranch houses and handsome white colonials had been built. There was man-made Deer Creek Lake beyond Lakeside Drive, and beyond that a stretch of woods, birches, pines, oaks, and the raised embankment of the Chautauqua & Port Oriskany railroad. Beyond that, Mt. Ephraim. My memory began to wane.

Directly across the road from our house was a near-identical ranch with a plate glass "picture" window mirroring, or mimicking, our own. For as long as I could remember, Mr. and Mrs. Higham lived there. They'd grown old, within my memory.

Mom was friendly with Gladys Higham, who was in her sixties. The women admired each other's lawns and flower beds. Dad had been standoffish with Mr. Higham as he'd been with most neighbors but Mom had always liked Gladys. I was sitting in my car thinking maybe Gladys knew where Mom was, Clare should have called her. And then I thought, with a childish thrill of hope, maybe Mom was at Mrs. Higham's: that was where she was.

I had to resist the impulse to run over to Mrs. Higham's. To avoid entering Mom's empty house.

I'd parked in the driveway as I had hundreds of times. This was the season of my classy-looking 2002 Saab well beyond the range of a *Beacon* reporter's buying power except a friend of Wally Szalla had been the dealer. I left the keys in the ignition thinking I would be right back. I left my cell phone on the passenger's seat thinking I would have no need for it. I would enter the house by way of the kitchen as everyone in the family did. I had a key of course. I'd never not had a key for the house at 43 Deer Creek Drive though I hadn't lived there for almost a decade.

It was 6:05 P.M. The sky was riddled with beautiful bruised clouds above Lake Ontario to the north and in the west the sun was partly obscured amid clouds yet still high above the horizon as if reluctant to set. I thought, again with that childish thrill of hope, It's still day, nowhere near night.

And yet: 6:05 P.M. And now 6:06 P.M. My mother would not have been away from the house for so many hours. If she'd left for the mall at about 10 A.M., rapidly I calculated she'd been gone now for almost eight hours.

Today was an ordinary Tuesday in Gwen Eaton's life, I was certain. She'd planned no ambitious outings, there was nothing in her schedule to account for this absence. If there had been, Clare or I would have known.

Mom would have told us, she told us everything.

Oh, why was my heart beating so hard! As I walked slowly up the driveway, approaching the side door. The concrete stoop upon which Mom had placed the usual pots of geraniums: red, pink, white. At its base she'd put in purple pansies, I could smell the wet pungent earth-smell. I saw that no lights were on in the kitchen. The door was unlocked. When I pushed it open I heard the quick welcoming tinkle of the little sleigh bells overhead.

I wondered if I felt so edgy because it was unnatural to be entering Mom's house in her absence. Now that I no longer lived here, and so much time had passed.

I never "dropped in" as Clare was always doing. My visits were pre-meditated. I would not have wished to make the trip home, to be disappointed by an empty house.

No one to greet me at the door with her breathless little hug: "Why, Nikki! Hi, honey."

I imagined this. I imagined Mom at the door, after all. (The Honda was being serviced at a garage. Mom would pick it up in the morning.) This time, Mom wouldn't be so shocked at my hair. She'd shake her head ruefully, she'd laugh.

I'd be a beauty, Mom insisted. No matter if I were bald.

"Mom? Are you home? It's . . ."

Silly. I heard my silly voice.

There came Smoky, Mom's burly gray cat, to push against my ankles and mew. The cat was behaving strangely, I thought. Smoky was a friendly cat, at least with people he knew, but he was behaving now edgily, anxiously. When I stooped to pet his head he stiffened, ducked, seemed about to run away. "Smoky, it's me. Don't be afraid of me." I stroked his head, I coaxed a hesitant purr from him. I saw that his plastic food bowls were empty and the water bowl nearly depleted.

There were other things wrong in the kitchen but I couldn't seem to see what they were. I saw, but wasn't registering. Somehow, I kept waiting for Mom to appear. I was waiting for her footfall, her voice. "Nikki? Why honey, what a nice surprise . . ." I was remembering a day years ago when I'd come home from school and Mom was supposed to be home but didn't seem to be home and I'd wandered through the house sort of looking for her and finally calling, "Mom? Are you home?" in a whiny voice but really I wasn't thinking much about it, at the age of fourteen you don't think much about anyone except yourself, certainly you don't think about your mom, you don't imagine a life for your mom in any way separate from or independent of your own, and finally happening to glance out a window in my room into the backyard I saw Mom in her garden clothes and straw hat weeding in one of her flower beds, exactly where Mom would be. And immediately I turned away and forgot whatever vague edginess I'd been feeling, not to remember for seventeen years.

Well, here was a wrong thing: one of the kitchen chairs looked as if it had skidded across the floor to collide with the refrigerator. If you knew Gwen you'd know that she would never have dragged the chair there, unless maybe she'd been mopping the linoleum floor, but she would not have left the chair there, as she would not have left soiled dishes untended to for even a short period of time.

I replaced the chair. I think I was acting unconsciously. I would not want Mom to know that the chair was out of place, that I'd seen it out of place and might have worried.

There was a strange smell here, too. My nostrils constricted, I could not identify it.

"Smoky! Poor guy."

I poured dry cat food into a bowl for Smoky, and replenished his water bowl. Though Smoky ate hungrily, he seemed wary of me, cringing when I moved to replace the cat food box in the cupboard, freezing and glaring as if, for a split second, he hadn't known who I was. "Smoky, come on. You know *me*."

Mom talked to Smoky constantly, she'd talked to all our cats and when we'd had parakeets she'd talked to them. It became a joke in the household how Dad would reply absentmindedly, "What, Gwen? What did you ask?"

I kept up a bright one-sided banter with Smoky, for it seemed important to soothe the nervous cat. He needed to be assured that he'd be fed, everything was normal and routine at 43 Deer Creek Drive.

Through the rear kitchen window, framed by ruffled sunflower-print curtains Mom had sewed, I saw the bird feeder which Dad had positioned to be at about eye level; it, too, seemed to be depleted of food. Small birds hovered and fluttered in the evergreens nearby, chirping as if querulously. I could see most of the backyard: Mom wasn't visible.

I was beginning to shiver. That day had been warm, a glaze of sunshine through a mostly overcast sky, now as daylight waned a decided chill rose from the earth. I'd run out of my brownstone apartment in jeans and a sweatshirt, bare-headed. With my hair so very short, the nape of my neck felt exposed.

At the *Beacon* yesterday my co-workers were about evenly divided between those who thought my new look was "cool"—"sexy"—"fantastic, Nikki!"—and those who smiled ambiguously and offered no opinion.

When I passed by his food dish, Smoky cringed and froze in a momentary panic. I went to check the bathroom in the hall: the "guest" bathroom where Mom kept her special floral-scented soaps in a little wicker basket on the back of the toilet. There was a reassuring smell here of potpourri and soap and my face in the spotless mirror did not appear so waxy-pale and drawn as, from inside, it felt.

The dyed-maroon hair looked like a fright wig. Something to be slapped on a head at Hallowe'en. Seeing me, Wally had blinked and smiled and laughed and had to concede: Nikki Eaton was about the most unpredictable female he knew.

Of females he'd been involved with, in any case.

Beyond the guest bathroom was an alcove, a short corridor that led to the basement door and the garage door. I would check these later, I thought.

The basement door was shut. If Mom had been down in the basement, running a load of laundry, ironing, she would have left the door open.

In the dining room I saw with a shock that something was very wrong.

Chairs had been yanked away from the table. The breakfront drawers were open and spilling their contents. On the carpet was the green silverware box, looking as if it had been flung down, spilling forks, knives, spoons in a glittery jumble. I stepped on something that rolled beneath my feet: a broken candle.

It took me a moment to realize: our silver candlestick holders were missing from the dining room table and from a serving table against the wall. Only candles remained, flung down and broken.

We'd been burglarized.

My heart was beating rapidly now. The house had been broken into, ransacked. Through the doorway I saw items in the living room strewn about. I could smell an acrid odor, as of perspiration. A man's odor.

In the family room, the television set lay on its side, on the carpet. Not a very new or a very large set, it must have been dragged from its perch on a low table, then abandoned by the thief as too cumbersome.

The door was open to Clare's old room, now a sewing room. Here also drawers had been yanked out of a bureau and lay on the floor spilling such mundane contents as sewing supplies, napkin rings, woven place mats. My old room, now a spare room with matched floral bedspread, curtains, and chintz-covered easy chair, had been similarly ransacked.

I went into my parents' bedroom at the end of the hall, now I was very frightened. Pulses were beating in my head, in my eyes. I saw bureau drawers pulled out here, overturned on the floor with a look of violence.

Mom's things scattered on the carpet: her inexpensive jewelry, stockings and socks and underwear, sweaters. The glamorous white ostrich feather boa . . .

The closet door was open, Mom's shoes lay on the floor as if they'd been kicked about. Size-four crepe-soled shoes with laces, black ballerina flats, a single patent-leather shoe with a small heel. Clothes had been torn from hangers, flung into a heap on the floor.

Even the bed had been disturbed, the hand-sewn quilt Mom laid over her pink satin bedspread lay partway on the floor.

He'd been looking for money, I thought. But my parents kept no money in the house.

I was stepping on an old purse of my mother's, a bulky leather handbag she hadn't used for years. And there was a glazed straw purse decorated with cherries. And a beaded white silk purse, Mom had last used for the wedding of a cousin of mine. These were yawning open, empty.

In the hall bathroom, the mirrored medicine cabinet door was open. The narrow glass shelves of the cabinet had been cleared as if with an angry swipe of someone's hand, a tube of toothpaste, a toothbrush, a plastic cup, deodorant in a blue plastic container and other toiletries had fallen into the sink and onto the floor.

And vials of prescription pills, spilled onto the floor. He'd been looking for drugs.

I couldn't keep from staring into the toilet bowl. I thought, He has used this toilet. But the water was clear.

All this while, a part of my mind was detached and warning me: get help, run outside, call 911. This part of my mind understood that I was in danger, I should not have remained in the house after I'd realized what the situation was. Yet, I seemed to be reasoning that, though something had happened, and this something might involve my mother, yet until I acknowledged that something had happened that required outside help, it was not altogether established that something had happened to my mother. But once I called for help, it would be established.

I saw a movement in the corner of my eye, I turned and there was nothing. But in a mirror at the end of the hall, a woman's thin, ghostly figure seemed to be floating. My eyes were flooding with tears, I could not see who the woman was.

Smoky had followed me at a wary distance. He was mewing in short anxious bleats as a cat mews when desperate to be let outside.

I returned to the kitchen, Smoky ran ahead of me panicked. Now in the kitchen I saw what I hadn't seemed to see before: the phone cord had been ripped out of the wall, the avocado-green plastic receiver lay on the counter unattached.

All day we'd been calling Mom's number, Clare and me. Our calls had been automatically deflected onto the voice mail service. If we'd heard a protracted busy signal, one of us would have come over earlier.

I went to the basement door and opened it, slowly. A cold damp air lifted to my nostrils. "Mom?"—my voice was childlike, wavering. I might have been thinking, Maybe Mom is hiding in the basement.

A weak fading light from the narrow windows penetrated the dimness. The washer and dryer glimmered like dream-objects but other shapes close by were indistinct. No movement! No sound! Yet I could not force myself to descend the cellar stairs.

The door leading from the kitchen into the garage was ajar, I saw. I seemed not to have noticed this until now.

For a while I stood in the doorway staring into the garage. I told myself *You can see better here, it's safer here.*

I was smelling something strange. I was thinking of the butcher shop on Mohegan Street. Where when I'd been a little girl my mother had brought me "meat shopping" with her. I'd drifted off to stare as if hypnotized at sculpted cuts of raw meat inside the display cases while Mom talked and laughed with the butcher giving her orders in a surprisingly knowledgeable voice.

A smell of blood. I knew.

I thought *Something has died here. An animal.*

My father would have been upset to see how cluttered Mom had allowed the garage to become. Now that he was gone. There wasn't even room for Mom to have fitted her car inside if she'd tried. Everywhere were trash cans, garden tools, bags of wild birdseed and peat moss and fertilizer and wood chips. Lawn furniture including years-old chairs whose plastic slats had long ago rotted and ripped. Here were discarded household furnishings—worn-out chairs, an old portable TV, shadeless lamps and lampless shades. Both my parents had been reluctant to dispose of their handsome matched and monogrammed leather luggage, a wedding present in long-ago 1968 before the advent of wheeled suitcases. You never knew when fashions would change, my father stubbornly believed.

I was staring at a shadowy shape on the concrete floor about fifteen feet away. It appeared to be a small rolled-up strip of carpet, an oddly shaped box or bundle of some kind . . . I switched on the light and saw that it was Mom.

I called out to her. She did not move.

She must have fallen, I thought. Tripped or something, or fainted and fallen. You are not accustomed to seeing a fallen person, almost you can't identify what you are seeing. There appeared to be a dark oily liquid spread beneath Mom and on her lacerated neck and chest and lower body yet I continued to think that she must have fainted and struck her head. I believed that I could see her breathing. Pulses beat so violently in my eyes, I could not be sure what I was seeing. As in a dream I approached her. I seemed to be floating and yet I must have stumbled, I'd struck my leg on the handle of something metallic for there would be a bruise on my shin afterward, I felt nothing at the time. Mom was lying awkwardly on her right side, her right arm outstretched as if reaching for help and her left arm twisted beneath her. Her face was turned upward, her skin was deathly white as I'd never seen it before. Her eyes were partly opened and I believed that they were aware of me.

I was sobbing, pleading: *Mom! Mom! Mom!* I was kneeling beside her. I touched her, tried to move her arm that had stiffened. I tried to lift her. I tried to revive her. But her skin was so strangely cold. I thought, There is something wrong, Mom's skin is so cold and it isn't winter now. When I leaned over her something ruptured and began bleeding in my chest.

Mom's pretty clothes, stained in blood! A blue linen jacket, a floral print blouse that matched a blouse Mom had sewed for me back in high school. Blue cotton knit slacks stained in blood.

I panicked, on my feet and swaying. I could not faint: I could not give in. I fumbled to open the garage door. The switch, where was the switch! My fingers were slippery. It was crucial, my mother needed fresh air, to help her breathe. The sickening stench of blood in this confined space must have caused her to faint, and fall.

The garage door opened so slowly! A rumbling of gears overhead. My bloody fingers would leave their imprint on the switch that operated the door. The bloodstained soles of my shoes, jogging shoes with articulated ridges, would leave their imprint on the concrete floor and on the asphalt drive outside: clearly at first, then diminishing as I ran from the garage. I knew that I had to get help for Mom for I could not revive her and yet it was a terrible thing to leave her alone, and so helpless. I was partway down the drive when I heard my name called in a faint anxious voice *Nikki!*

I understood: I was the only one. I was all that Mom had.

When I returned to the garage I saw that Mom was moving. I saw that Mom was breathing. Through my pulsing eyes, I saw. I ran back to her, and tried to lift her. It seemed to me in my confusion that if Mom could be lifted to her feet and if she could stand, she would be revived, she would be all right. It was a matter of balance, wasn't it? Mom was looking at me now, her glassy eyes fixed upon my face, I saw that she recognized me, always I would believe that she recognized me, yet her head fell back limp, her mouth was open in a way unlike her and there was a terrible raw wound beneath her chin. So much blood, so many hidden wounds. Her skin was clammy as before, her body was oddly stiff and resistant and heavier than I had known it and she had not moved, she had not been breathing, and yet she had called to me, I'd heard her!

This had been a mistake, whatever had happened. My mother had been stabbed many times. Someone had been angry with her to stab her so, and that was not possible. There'd been some mistake, whoever had done this had come to the wrong house. He could not have wanted Gwen Eaton, it had been a mistake.

Tenderly I laid Mom back onto the floor. I pulled a strip of canvas partway beneath her. It would be difficult to explain afterward what I'd done or had intended to do and yet it was logical at the time, and necessary. I would make Mom comfortable, I would position her at rest. She would appear to be sleeping. There is peace in sleeping. There is not horror, pain, ugliness in sleeping. I must have shut her eyes. I must have touched her eyelids, to shut them. Never had I dared touch another person's eyes in such a way, no lover's eyes, never my parents' eyes, yet I must have touched my mother's eyelids, to shut them. I promised her *You will be all right, Mom. I won't go far.*

I stumbled away. Another time I collided with something metallic. Then I was outside. How strange, the air smelled of lilac! I ran doubled over, a sharp pain in my chest where something had broken. I was trying to call for help, trying to scream. The sounds issuing from my mouth were hoarse, choked. But I was able to run across the street to our neighbors' house. This was the Highams' redwood-and-stucco "ranch" built to the same model as our own for there was the large rectangular window facing our window as in a subtly distorted mirror, there was the same grassy front lawn, less pocked with dandelions than our own because Mr. Higham squatted out there, armed with a hand hoe, to dig the gnarly weeds out.

I ran to the side door of the house, that like ours opened into the kitchen. I was brash, reckless as a child. In fact I was a child. I was crying, "Mrs. Higham! Let me use your phone! Something has happened to my mother."

rupture

Something ruptured and began bleeding in my chest when I bent over my mother, when I saw my mother in that way. It will happen to you, in a way special to you. You will not anticipate it, you cannot prepare for it and you cannot escape it. The bleeding will not cease for a long time.

In my case, no one could know. No one would think in pity *Why, that show-offy woman with the spiky purple hair is bleeding inside.*

More likely it was thought *That silly woman! What a sight! Couldn't she have known that her mother might be murdered, isn't she ashamed!*

"murder"

There was a taffy-colored plastic phone receiver in my shaking hand. I managed to dial 911. A woman answered with startling abruptness and I heard my dazed voice: "I—I need to—I need to report a—murder."

The voice responded with an audible gasp: "You need—*what?*"

"A murder. My m-mother. We are at—"

The look in Gladys Higham's face! As if I'd shouted at her, given her a sudden rude shove. As if, Gwen Eaton's friend of more than twenty years, she could not comprehend the words issuing from my mouth.

Gwen? Gwen? Not Gwen . . .

I saw then: my hands were not clean but sticky. I would realize afterward that I'd left faint smears of blood on Mrs. Higham's plastic wall phone that was a twin of Mom's kitchen phone in design, lightness.

Speaking with the 911 dispatcher, I seemed to be having trouble with the simplest words. My tongue had gone numb. There was a ringing in my ears. Pulses in my head beat like electric current. I was distracted by elderly Mrs. Higham clutching at her throat in alarm and disbelief, stumbling to sit down, heavily, in a kitchen chair. Gladys Higham was not a young woman, she was older than Mom by perhaps ten years and much less fit. Her old-woman legs were thick to bursting in brown support hose.

In Mrs. Higham's kitchen that was a mirror of our kitchen across the street there were two cages of fluttery little birds: daubs of greenish-gold beating their wings as they flew about excitedly inside their brass cages, swing to bar, bar to swing, tittering and chirping brightly. You'd have thought that I had blundered into their cages, the little birds were so aroused. The dispatcher was instructing me please to repeat what I'd said, to speak more clearly, more loudly, I had to wonder what this stranger must be thinking, a desperate call to report a murder made in the presence of tittering and chirping birds. I was repeating my name, not Nikki, for Nikki wasn't serious, but Nicole, I was Nicole Eaton calling to report the murder of my mother Gwendolyn Eaton, Mrs. Jonathan Eaton of 43 Deer Creek Drive in the Deer Creek subdivision . . .

Mrs. Higham was ashen-faced, blinking and panting. Her eyes were elderly eyes, lashless and brimming with tears. I hung up the sticky receiver, it slipped from the wall and clattered onto the counter. Parakeets, canaries! What a commotion! I was sorry to have frightened Gladys Higham, I had not meant to upset her. She was calling for her husband Walter, in another part of the house. I was trying to comfort her, I think. I'd barged into her house, into her kitchen to grab at her telephone, to leave smears of my mother's blood on the plastic receiver. I thought, how terrible Mom would feel, upsetting Gladys Higham! Upsetting any neighbor! What was private, spilling over across the street, into a neighbor's house! Mom had made us promise, Clare and me, years ago when she'd had a biopsy for a pit-sized growth in one of her breasts, that if the test came back "positive," if the growth was malignant, we would tell no one.

We'd promised, of course. Clare and me, exchanging a look of complicity. How could such news be a secret, in Mt. Ephraim! Where so many people knew Gwen Eaton.

But we would promise, wouldn't we, Mom begged.

Mom dreaded people talking about her as a cancer patient. Feeling sorry for her or worse yet feeling they should feel sorry for her.

The biopsy came back negative.

A false alarm! No cancer.

Elderly Walter Higham was staring at me now. Gladys was clutching at his arm, repeating what I'd said. The look in Walter Higham's face! Such a tittering of birds!

Now it would begin. Now was the start. Nothing could prevent it. Nothing could shield us from it.

Gwen? Gwen Eaton?

Not Gwen! No.

It isn't possible: Gwen Eaton?

I don't believe it. Can't believe it. No.

My God, no. Not Gwen.

Of all people, not Gwen.

Gwen Eaton! Gone.

Murdered.

I stood in the driveway, shivering. I was aware of the garage, the opened door, at my back. By now the sky was beginning to darken, in the west the sun had become a broken, bleeding red yolk. It was the kind of mottled-luminous twilit sky you might lose yourself staring into, in other circumstances.

I wondered if I should move my car. There would be emergency vehicles, my car might be in the way. I peered through the window and there was my cell phone on the passenger's seat. I retrieved it, and called Clare's number. My fingers were clumsy, I punched out the wrong number and had to begin again. At the same time, I was aware of Mom in the garage, on the concrete floor where she'd fallen.

It was difficult to resist thinking: Mom is going to be all right. I have called an ambulance, Mom will be taken to the hospital and will be all right. A part of my mind was urging me to believe and I was weakening yet I would not give in.

As if she'd been waiting impatiently for my call, Clare answered immediately, like the 911 dispatcher. Clare answered before I was ready to speak with her. I'd hoped for more time. I'd hoped for Clare's voice mail. I was saying, "Clare. I'm at the house. Mom has been hurt." Clare cried,

"Hurt! Oh, God! I knew it. What—" I could not speak, my mouth had gone dry. I saw a Mt. Ephraim Police patrol car turning onto Deer Creek Drive, moving swiftly. And another patrol car, close behind. They braked to a stop in front of our house, at angles to block the street. I was distracted by these maneuvers so deftly executed. Across the street at 44 Deer Creek Drive, Walter Higham was standing in his driveway, staring. I had not remembered Mr. Higham so white-haired, a stoop to his shoulders. Talking with Dad at their mailboxes, which were side by side as if companionable, on solid wooden posts on the Highams' side of the street, Mr. Higham had been my father's height which was at least six feet.

Clare's voice was sharp and fearful in my ear. I tried to explain: Mom was hurt. Mom was badly hurt. I could not utter the word *dead,* and speaking to Clare I could not utter the word *murder.* I did not want to break down! It was my responsibility not to break down now that I'd summoned police.

One of the uniformed officers approached me to ask if I had called 911, if I'd reported a murder. "Do you mean, am I the one who made the call? Yes." I was sounding excited, angry. Yet calmly the officer asked my name. "What does it matter, my name! My mother needs help." Officers had entered the garage. I ran to join them but was prevented from entering. I pushed at arms, restraining hands.

I could see where Mom was lying. Where she'd fallen. Strangers crouching over her.

My cell phone was in my hand. I'd forgotten it. A small voice screamed out of it, ". . . Nikki? For God's sake . . ." It was Clare. I told her that Mom was badly hurt, someone had hurt Mom and she must come immediately. "Mom is *hurt?* How—is Mom *hurt?*" I heard myself stammer that Mom was dead and the cell phone fell from my hand.

The house at 43 Deer Creek Drive, Deer Creek Acres had been transformed. From a short distance, you would believe its occupants were being celebrated.

The street was blocked by police vehicles. Residents of the neighborhood were being rerouted. When they asked what had happened they were politely told to move on.

Vehicles, turned away, moved slowly and haltingly. Some stopped altogether. People were coming out of their houses to stand in the street, staring. Teenagers, younger children. There was a fearful wish to know: what was it? whose house? fire? ambulance? so many police cars—why?

"Somebody has been hurt."

"Hurt—how?"

". . . Mrs. Eaton, in that house."

"Mrs. Eaton? *Gwen?*"

A chill was lifting from the grass. The air smelled damply of lilac. Strangers were asking me questions. The same questions were repeated. Wildly I thought, If Dad was here—! Dad would be the one to speak to the officers.

I was feeling light-headed, dazed. I was not feeling adequate to the situation. It seemed to me a terrible thing, I had told Clare *Mom is dead*. She would hate me now. Between us now there would be the unspeakable *Mom is dead*.

Yet it seemed to me plausible that I'd been mistaken. I wanted to interrupt the police officers to ask: "But is my mother really . . . dead?" The more I considered it, the more I doubted my judgment. Emergency room physicians might see that Mom was still breathing, her heart was still beating, oh why hadn't she been taken to the hospital, why were they leaving her broken and helpless in the garage . . .

In the confusion Clare came running. Clare was frightened as I had never seen her. She saw my face, and stumbled past me without a word, toward the garage. For it was obvious, what had happened to Mom had happened in the garage. "I'm her daughter! I'm Gwen's daughter! Let me see her! *Let me see her!*" Police officers prevented her entering the garage. I heard her sharp raised voice. I heard her scream.

Later, we embraced. Like drowning women clutching helplessly at each other.

My brother-in-law Rob Chisholm was trying to comfort us. My uncle Herman Eaton, Dad's older brother. There was Lucille Kovach, my mother's cousin. There was Fred Eaton. Other relatives, mostly men, I had not seen in a very long time. Gil Rowen, chief of Mt. Ephraim Police, who'd gone to school with "Johnny" Eaton and had known "Feather" Kovach in the old days when they'd all been young, newly married.

Gil Rowen appeared deeply moved. Firmly he clasped my hand in his. He clasped Clare's hand. He introduced us to one of the plainclothed officers, Detective Strabane, who would be heading the investigation into "your mother's murder."

We were meant to shake hands with Detective Strabane. Oh but why! And then I was sitting down. I seemed to be sitting in the grass. Maybe I had fallen. Voices conferred over my head: "daughter"—"found the body." It was suggested that I be taken to Mt. Ephraim Medical Center but I refused angrily.

I saw that the knees of my jeans were stained with something dark. My hands were sticky. Vaguely I recalled, I had wanted to wash my hands. But I'd forgotten, and kept forgetting. There were things I meant to recall but had forgotten even as I told myself I must not forget. I thought *I've had no practice at this! Nothing has prepared me for this.*

Clare was being questioned now. Clare had regained something of her schoolteacher poise. The detective was calling her "Mrs. Chisholm" and she was calling him "Detective." A wave of childish relief came over me, Clare would shield me.

I had been the one to discover Mom. I had been the last person to touch Mom. The last person Mom had seen.

It seemed to me yes, Mom had seen me. Had Mom tried to speak to me? I didn't want to make a mistake, I was in fear of saying the wrong thing.

Had I said the words *Mom is dead!*

And now the word *murder* was being uttered, as a statement of fact.

Murder, dead. Multiple stab wounds. Caucasian female fifty-six years old. Resident of. Wife of. Mother of.

The Pedersens next-door were offering us their house so that Detective Strabane could ask his crucial questions. The Highams offered their house. Clare was sitting beside me in the grass now, to comfort me. Clare was holding me as you'd hold a young child. Suddenly it was dark and everywhere there were lights. Police spotlights, blinding. Clare and I stared at our house, where every window blazed light. It did look like a celebration. Even the grimy basement windows emitted a faint warm glow.

"Poor Dad. He'd be so embarrassed . . ."

"The garage, you mean? All that junk . . ."

"The basement windows. So dirty."

Clare laughed, suddenly. It was the first hint that Clare might not be so composed as I'd thought. "He always took such care of the house, and the lawn. Now people are trampling the lawn. Mom's flower beds. And all those lights on, Dad would rush around switching them off. 'A penny saved is a penny earned.' "

We laughed, shivering. We resisted being re-located to our neighbors' house. Yes, Rob Chisholm was right, it was the sensible thing to do, to go inside, but Clare and I resisted. Detective Strabane squatted beside us, to speak with us. He meant to humor us for we were the daughters of the murdered woman. We were children, Gwen Eaton's children. We had become childish, excitable. Strabane was an earnest man in his late thirties, not young. His features were swarthy and simian and his necktie was twisted. My impulse was to straighten the necktie. As Mom had straightened Dad's neckties, or his shirt collars, with a sweet little apologetic murmur *There! That's better.*

Strabane was saying how sorry he was to disturb us at such a "tragic time"—"a time when you just want to be alone"—but it was crucial to ask us a few questions immediately: about our mother's bank account, her credit cards, car; whom she'd been scheduled to see that day, who might have been scheduled to come to the house; who might have been at the house recently—plumber? carpenter? lawn crew?

It was a surprise to me, in my confused state, to be made to know the simplest thing, obviously taken for granted by everyone else: my mother had been murdered, there was a murderer or murderers to be apprehended.

I knew this, with a part of my mind. I'd known immediately, seeing my mother's body. Yet somehow, I had not absorbed the knowledge.

Mostly, Clare answered the detective's questions. She knew names, even the correct spellings of names. She knew with certainty what I would have guessed: Mom's bank was the Bank of Niagara. She knew that Mom had only a single credit card, a Visa. (Dad had not "believed in" credit cards. If he'd had his way, we would have had none.) In her clear brave voice Clare recited the names of workmen who'd been in the house in the past several months and this litany of names was provided to the detective, who took notes in an old-fashioned spiral notebook. When Clare failed to recall a name, Rob provided it. I was made to realize how much my sister and brother-in-law knew of my mother's life, that I had not known! I was made to realize how irresponsible I had been, and how negligent. Suddenly it was clear, the detective would know, how I was the daughter who had abandoned her widowed mother while Clare was the good daughter who'd remained.

Strabane glanced at me, brooding.

"Ma'am? Ms. Eaton? Anything you can add, any name . . . ?"

My mind was blank. I could not think. I was tamping down my spiky hair, of which I'd become acutely ashamed. Like the Statue of Liberty, I must have looked. And my face dead-white, and my lips caked with an acid-vomit taste.

I didn't remember vomiting. Anxiously I wiped at my mouth, I saw that the front of my shirt was dappled with something whitish, sour-smelling.

Clare said suddenly, "Oh. 'Danto.' He's an exterminator, he came to the house a week or so ago, to exterminate red ants."

I said, "Clare, no! 'Sonny' Danto would never . . ."

"Detective, his name is 'D-a-n-t-o.' 'The Scourge of the Bugs' he calls himself." Clare was becoming fired-up, vindictive. "My mother was a

66

lonely, vulnerable woman, a widow. She was so friendly to everyone, so trusting. I hated it how people took advantage of her!"

But Danto was a joke, wasn't he?—just one of Mom's many eccentric acquaintances, not to be taken seriously.

Strabane was saying, for my benefit, that "all names, any names" of persons who'd been in my mother's house recently were urgently wanted for purposes of the investigation. "Ma'am, if there's weeding-out to do, I will do it."

It was taken for granted that the person or persons who'd murdered our mother had also taken her Visa card and her car, her wallet, various household items we would be asked to identify in the morning. It was taken for granted that our mother had probably walked into a burglary in progress which had resulted in her death. (Dad had had a security system installed, but after his death, since Smoky was always tripping the alarm, Mom had asked Rob to dismantle it.) In my confused state I'd known that Mom's car was missing but I had not seemed to grasp that it had been stolen, and might be the means of finding the murder or murderers.

Rob asked Strabane if whoever had done this would be that stupid, to drive a stolen car, and Strabane said, "Yes, sir. They are all stupid."

I could have told the detective that my mother's car was a metallic-green Honda, a fairly new model, four-door, but Rob Chisholm knew precisely that it was a 2001 Honda Accord for he'd been the one to accompany Gwen to the dealer and help her make the purchase. I could not remember anything of my mother's license plate number but both Clare and Rob recalled the first three digits—*SVI*—and Rob also knew the name of the garage where she took the car to be serviced: the manager could give police more information.

I saw how I was being left behind. How Mom was being left behind.

I saw how the police investigation would move swiftly and professionally, as if I did not exist. I saw how others seemed already to know much more about what had happened to my mother than I knew.

I was frightened by this realization, I think. I could not accept it. In the garishly lighted garage (so cluttered, so embarrassing, what will strangers think of us!) my mother's small lifeless body was being examined and photographed by strangers who had not known Gwen Eaton and for whom she was but a body, a "victim." Her designation was lurid: "murder victim."

Soon, the "murder victim" would be removed from the garage. It was to be transported to the Mt. Ephraim Township morgue. This was a place, you could say it was an institution, to which neither Clare nor I had given the slightest thought, ever. Yet, for many others, it was a known place. It would be a known place, for us.

We would have liked to accompany our mother's body to the morgue but we were not allowed this privilege. Nor could we approach our mother simply to touch her, in farewell.

Our mother had passed beyond us, suddenly. We could not claim her.

Strabane must have finished his questions, temporarily. For Clare was on her cell phone speaking with Lilja. In a shaky but careful voice explaining, "Something has happened to Grandma Eaton but . . . No, honey, your dad and I are all right . . . Yes, we'll be home soon and in the meantime do me a favor honey, don't turn on the TV? Promise?"

As soon as Clare broke off the conversation, Lilja would rush to the TV. Obviously!

Still more vehicles were arriving on our street. Radio voices squawked loudly. Seen from a distance we must have looked like a carnival. I thought *This can't be happening, it was meant for someone else.*

This long day: had it really begun with ninety-nine-year-old Jimmy Friday wisecracking and flirting through his interview with me that morning, inscribing my copy of *Songs My Daddy Taught Me: The Mostly True Tales of Jimmy Friday* in an extravagant old-fashioned handwriting TO BEAUTOUS NICOLE FROM "ONE & ONLY" JIMMY FRIDAY!

I remembered now, I'd thought I would buy a second copy of the elderly musician's memoir and ask him to inscribe it to Gwen Eaton, she'd been one of his admirers from long ago.

A TV crew had arrived but was not allowed past the police blockade.

Hastily Rob called their home again on the cell phone, to ask Lilja please not to turn on the TV.

"Just don't, honey. Daddy is asking you. Promise?"

Now we were being fingerprinted. I was on my feet, I'd been able to wipe my hands clean with a cloth soaked in rubbing alcohol. Detective Strabane was explaining the procedure, why it was necessary, for our fingerprints, Clare's, Rob's, mine, would be everywhere in my mother's house. His hair grew in odd stiff tufts like quills, slanting forward as in a brisk wind. I had a whiff of something like motor oil. "Ma'am? May I . . ." Strabane took my hand in his in a diffident gesture and pressed my fingertips against a black-inked pad, then he pressed them against a sheet of stiff white paper, rolling them carefully onto the paper: each finger separately, then the four fingers together. Tears leaked from my eyes, Strabane made no comment. My fingers were icy, Strabane made no comment. We were almost the same height, but Strabane outweighed me by fifty pounds. He was stocky in the chest and shoulders, with a whistling sort of breath as if his sinus cavities were partly blocked. A fleeting thought came to me of Wally Szalla clasping my cold bare feet between his warm sprawling-big bare feet playfully shuddering *Brrr! Cold toes, cold heart!*

I'd been supposed to meet my lover, the "evil" influence in my life, that evening at eight, at an inn on the Chautauqua River that was one of our places, a discreet distance from Chautauqua Falls where Wally's family lived. I'd forgotten completely and would now forget again for my head was so empty you could hear wind whistling through its cavities, you could see scraps of litter and straw blown about.

"Now, ma'am. The other hand . . ."

Strange to be called *ma'am* for I certainly wasn't the type. I was made to think that my social status had changed, as the daughter of a murdered woman.

"My name is Nikki, officer. 'Nicole.' "

Strabane's forehead was low, and deeply furrowed. One of those individuals who has been frowning—"making faces"—since childhood. He frowned now, repeating the ink-procedure with my left hand that was limp and unresisting. I heard myself say suddenly, "Officer, if you'd known my mother! She didn't deserve . . ."

"Nobody does, Nicole. None of it."

". . . she was not a woman who, who could . . ."

"Ma'am, I know. Please accept my condolences."

"But you don't *know*. None of you, you can't *know*."

Clare pulled me away. Smiling hard, and digging her nails into my shoulders. Whispering in my ear, "Don't you become hysterical, Nikki! Just hold on."

Rob gave Strabane his telephone number but I stammered and stuttered trying to remember mine. The detective waited patiently. At the third or fourth try, I managed to remember. I was blushing deeply now, I was becoming angry.

"You are free to go home now. We'll be contacting you in the morning."

These were practiced words, obviously. Detective Strabane had uttered them many times before.

I was examining the card he'd given me. It seemed so trivial, a business card at such a time. Dad had had a stack of similar little cards after he'd been promoted to senior vice-president of Beechum Paper Products. It seemed like there were hundreds of these cards, winding up in drawers, fallen into the cracks of things and behind cushions.

DETECTIVE ROSS J. STRABANE

MT. EPRHRAIM POLICE DEPARTMENT

TEL: (716)722-4186 EXT. 31

HOME: (716)~~817-9934~~ 722-1874

Strabane was urging us to go home, get a good night's sleep.
A good night's sleep! The bastard.

". . . this way of thinking when I was a young kid, a kind of superstition like in a primitive part of the brain, that a bad day was just for that day, a 'bad luck' day, and the next day had to be different. But when you grow up, you know that bad days can come one after another, there's no connection between them. So, the exhaustion will hit you, what has happened today, that is too much for you to comprehend, you should try to sleep tonight."

It was a touchingly mangled speech. Clare was staring at the detective in astonishment. For a moment no one spoke. Rob thanked Strabane, and said we would all try.

All this while I'd been watching the garage anxiously. I could not see my mother's body any longer. I wasn't sure if it had already been loaded onto an emergency vehicle backed up to the garage entrance.

I said, "I want to go with Mom. I have a right, I think."

It was explained to me, I could not go with Mom. I did not have a right, in fact.

I said, "I'm not leaving her." Then I said, as if there were any logical connection between the two statements, "This house is my home. It is my *home*."

Clare tugged at my arm, annoyed. "You're coming home with us, Nikki. Don't be silly."

"No. I don't think so."

"We need to be together. You can't drive back to Chautauqua Falls in the state you're in."

A wisecrack bristled on my lips *I'm in the same fucking state you're in, Big Sis: New York State.*

"My car. I can't leave my car here."

"Rob can drive your car to our house, Nikki."

"Why are you in a 'state to drive,' Clare, and I'm not?"

"Nikki, the shock was worse for you. You were the one to find Mom . . ."

"Well, I don't want to leave her just yet."

I must have spoken sharply, I'd become an object of attention.

Gil Rowen, who'd known "Johnny" Eaton and "Feather" Kovach forty years before, was advising Clare that "your sister" be taken to the medical center after all: I wasn't looking good, I'd had a "severe shock." I turned on him with a savage grin: "You can speak directly to me, Chief Rowen. I'm not brain-damaged."

I resisted Clare's fingers on my arm. I resisted a herding movement of my brother-in-law, to urge me in the direction of the Chisholms' Land Rover. I wasn't a sick child, to be taken care of by responsible adults! I was filled with rage suddenly. I wanted to scream, bite, tear with my teeth.

At this moment there came a darting movement in the grass in front of the house, a furtive dark shape. Dad had planted two willow trees in the front yard when I'd been a little girl, these had grown to their full height, the graceful branches arcing, falling toward the ground, beginning to quicken with new spring growth. The shape darted from the base of one of these willows to the other, I saw a flash of tawny reflector-eyes. Smoky!

In the commotion my mother's cat had run outside, terrified. I had completely forgotten him until now.

What a nightmare for a cat! The house was blazing with lights, strangers speaking in loud voices. Smoky had lost his only companion in Mom, now he'd lost his place of refuge in which he'd been safe for almost ten years. In a seductive voice I called "Smoky! Kitty-kitty!" and tried to approach him even as he retreated before me, ears laid back. Smoky was a football-shaped cat, burly rather than fat, his fur was not glistening-silky but dull gunmetal-gray, Dad had called him about the least graceful cat he'd ever seen, some strange hybrid between a cat and a small species of pig, but Mom had loved him. And he'd loved Mom, and would never be able to comprehend that she was gone.

Clare called to me, but I ignored her. She and the others were staring at my odd posture as I crept across the lawn, hand extended. They hadn't seen Smoky, they had no idea what I was doing. Rob was calling me, too. I ignored them, pursuing Smoky who was at the corner of the house now, by the lilac hedge, poised to disappear into oblivion. The pretense was that I had something to feed Smoky, something in my hand, but Smoky was too shrewd for me, and frightened of the loud voices of strangers and the activity in the driveway. I turned to shout at these intruders: "Don't talk so loud! Please lower your voices! You're scaring my mother's *cat.*"

Smoky bolted from me around the corner of the house, and disappeared. Hunched almost double as if in pain, in fact my gut was livid with pain as with molten lead, my hand still extended into the shadows, I ran after him.

oblivion

Toward dawn I fell asleep. I think.

There was a promise that, whatever had happened that hurt so badly, it would be rescinded by morning.

Like DELETE on the computer. Click onto DELETE and whatever it is you want to get rid of, becomes *was*.

Except it wasn't the right sleep somehow. Maybe it was someone else's sleep, sloshing onto me by accident. A kind of gritty froth-foam slapping over my face, then withdrawing. I was lying where I'd fallen on a lumpy beach. Pebbles, cold wet sand. Too exhausted to move my head. This kind of gritty-filthy surf washing over me and for a fleeting second or so I would be sleeping and then the surf would withdraw leaving me exposed and my eyes sprang open in terror.

Mom? *Mom?*

It was so, I'd gone home with Clare and her husband.

I hadn't been able to find Smoky. I stumbled and fell in a neighbor's backyard. I wasn't crying but I was very tired. I had to concede, Clare was probably right: I wasn't to be trusted driving a car in the state I was in.

Mental state, Clare meant.

And it wasn't a good idea for me to be alone that night. The police chief who'd known my dad and mom insisted. No! not a good idea, Nicole! Not alone in a rented apartment in a shabby-chic brownstone in Chautauqua Falls where possibly I would be in danger.

"You're coming with us, Nikki. *Now*."

Clare climbed into the high cab of the Land Rover like a general climbing into his military vehicle. Clare grim-jawed and glarey-eyed like one going to war.

Rob followed behind us in the Saab. I was the lone passenger.

"Until whoever did it, the murderer or murderers, the cowardly bastards, is caught. You will be with *us*."

I was not able to think clearly but I did recall the police officer with the swarthy simian face who'd assured us that after a bad day you can expect a good day, anyway a less-bad day. Some kind of superstition but maybe it was so?

On the way home, Clare swung around to stop at Luke Myer's house. Dr. Myer had been our family "primary care" physician for as long as I could remember and he had not yet heard of Gwen Eaton's death and was stunned, shaken, by what Clare had to tell him but recovered enough to provide Clare and me with something to help us sleep that night.

A quick-acting "mild" barbiturate.

Clare made it clear, she did not believe in drugs. But tonight was an emergency situation, especially where I, Nikki, her younger and more emotional sister, was concerned.

"You see, Nikki was the one to discover the—"

Clare felt the need to begin again. "Nikki was the one to find Mom. She's taking it pretty hard as you can imagine."

Clare's eyes flashed like scimitars. Not with tears.

. . .

It would be said in Mt. Ephraim that Nikki, the younger Eaton daughter, had collapsed after discovering her mother's body but this was not true! I had not collapsed at the time. I had not collapsed for hours. Not so that anyone could see.

As soon as I was alone upstairs in the Chisholms' house my head seemed to come unhinged from my neck and fell heavily forward. It had been my intention to shower immediately, to tear off my blood-smeared clothes and wash my hands which bore traces of black ink, but in the bathroom I became frightened, flushing the toilet involved so much noise. I seemed to lack the strength to take a shower, I was shivering badly and unable to remove my clothes. Sweatshirt, jeans. My punk-cut hair I'd been tamping down with both hands like a monkey displaying grief.

I was too exhausted to take the sleeping pill Dr. Myer had given me. I couldn't make the effort to run water into a plastic cup, lift the cup to my mouth. I staggered into the attractively furnished guest room that Clare was providing for me at the end of the second-floor corridor of the house, I'd never slept in my sister's house before and was comforted by a familiar scent of our mother's floral soap and potpourri for this room closely resembled Mom's guest room and in fact a number of Mom's things were here: an oyster shell afghan Mom had knitted, a macramé wall hanging, coral shell knickknacks and clay vases. I fell heavily onto the bed. Onto the oyster shell afghan. When someone knocked hesitantly at the door—"Nikki? Are you hungry?"—I burrowed more deeply into the afghan and did not answer for I could not bear facing my sister's children with the terrible knowledge between us of what had happened to their grandmother, I could not face them just yet.

Nikki! Don't leave me, honey.
　Honey, I need you. Come help me.
　If you'd come earlier . . . Nikki!

. . .

Toward dawn I fell asleep. I think.

And in a dream there was the whispered promise that what had happened that hurt so badly would be rescinded in the night. What had happened that had no name would be rescinded by morning. I had not been a little girl for many years but I was willing to believe as a little girl might believe. For there was Mom wearing the clumsy oven mitts she'd bought at a church bazaar, three sizes too large for her, stooping to pull a bubbling casserole out of the oven and unaware of me watching. And there was Mom feeding her "strays"—three very hungry cats jostling for her attention, in a corner of the kitchen. And there was Mom casting a sidelong look at Clare and me who were acting silly about something *Oh really, you two! Make yourselves useful.*

For why should things be serious, couldn't you turn them into a joke? Better to smile than to frown. Better to laugh than to cry. Deflect a remark that might wound with a quizzical lift of the eyes, an innocent/mischievous twitch of the lips. Dad was the worrier in the Eaton family. Dad was in need of "lightening"—"cheering up"—for Dad took his responsibilities seriously, supporting his family, this damned recession in western New York State that seemed never to be turning around the way politicians were always promising yet taxes remained high, taxes were steadily rising, where was it going to end!

Go give Daddy your valentines. Go on, Daddy is waiting. And give Daddy a kiss, whether he asks for a kiss or not.

Mom was sewing a quilt. Not a full-sized quilt but a baby-sized quilt, for one of my older Eaton cousins was having her first baby. The quilt was "patchwork"—squares of all different colors, designs—pale green, pale lavender, white bunnies, red cardinals, orange giraffes, sunflowers. As the needle in her fingers darted and winked Mom hummed loudly to herself.

I was jealous! I was too old for a baby quilt.

You've had your turn, sweetie. This is for a new baby.

. . .

I didn't wake until after 10 A.M. Sunshine was beating into my face. I smelled of my body and of what had happened in the garage and my brain was aching as if broken glass had gotten inside my skull. I seemed to be wearing the identical blood-stiffened sweat-smelling clothes I'd worn the day before. Sweatshirt, jeans. I'd kicked off my running shoes but hadn't the energy to pull off my dirty socks. My underarms were caked with stale deodorant and my mouth tasted like tar. I'd been sleeping on my face, the entire right side of my face was imprinted with the whorled knit of the afghan like a bizarre tattoo.

The childish thought came to me, Is Mom still dead? Maybe something happened while I've been gone, to change that?

case closed!

There is a romance of mystery, but when my mother Gwen Eaton was murdered there was no romance, and there was very little mystery. For within four hours of her reported death her murderer had been tentatively identified by Mt. Ephraim Police and within twenty hours he'd been positively identified. Within forty-eight hours, he'd been arrested and charged with murder, kidnapping, robbery, burglary, theft, criminal trespass, and credit card violation.

None of this was like TV or the movies. Believe me. It was not suspenseful or what you'd call exciting. It was revealed to us, Gwen Eaton's family, those whom newspaper obituaries call "survivors," as a rapid-fire recitation of facts so bluntly presented, we were like Little League batters at the plate as adult hardball pitches slam by at one hundred miles an hour. Maybe we'd assimilate these facts at a later time, but only later.

And maybe not ever.

Mom had been murdered at approximately 11 A.M. of the morning of May 11. Approximately forty-five minutes earlier, at the Mt. Ephraim Tiger Mart service station on Route 33 north of town, evidently on her way to the Northland Mall, Gwen was seen giving a ride to an individual who approached her on foot as she was waiting for her car to be serviced. By chance this individual, a Caucasian male twenty-nine years old with a history of methamphetamine abuse, was known to the proprietor of the Tiger Mart who, after news of Gwen's death was broadcast on local TV that evening, would call police to report what he'd witnessed.

Once the hitchhiker was in Gwen's car, he forced her to drive back into Mt. Ephraim and to 43 Deer Creek Drive where he would ransack the house looking for cash, credit cards, pawnable items, and he would stab her with a weapon similar to a Swiss Army knife some thirty-three times, including six separate stabbings in the throat. He then fled in Gwen's car, with some of Gwen's jewelry and household items. At approximately 11:45 A.M., a man attempted to use Gwendolyn Eaton's Visa card at the Wal-Mart on Route 33 south of Mt. Ephraim, but fled when a cashier called a store manager to examine the card with a woman's name on it. (This transaction was captured on Wal-Mart videotape.) Forty minutes later, the same individual succeeded in using the card, forging Gwendolyn Eaton's signature, at J & J Men's Discount Clothiers a few miles farther south on Route 33 where his purchases were: a $23.98 cotton shirt, a pair of $29.99 chino trousers, a pair of $34.99 running shoes, and a pair of $2.98 socks. At approximately 12:45 P.M., this same individual approached a gas station attendant at Hal's Mobil Service at the intersection of Routes 33 and 39, asking for the key to the men's room, where it was believed he changed his soiled clothes. (He was wearing a canvas jacket, not visibly stained, over a bloodstained T-shirt and jeans. He laughingly attributed the way he looked to an "accident with a chain saw" he'd had while trimming trees that morning.) The attendant became suspicious and noted the license plate number of the 2001 silver-green Honda this individual was driving, which he'd report to police that evening after the 10 P.M. local TV news.

A bundle of bloodied men's clothing—T-shirt, jeans, socks—would be discovered next morning in a Dumpster behind a McDonald's twelve miles west on Route 39: so carelessly jammed into a J & J Men's Discount Clothiers plastic bag, it was spilling out and immediately caught the attention of the trash pickup workers who reported it to police.

At approximately 7 P.M. of May 11, in a Radio Shack near the

Dunkirk, New York, exit of Interstate 90, the murderer attempted to purchase a $376.99 CD/video player but again fled when the salesman questioned the Visa card with a woman's name on it; this time, the murderer left the card behind.

By 10:25 P.M. of May 11, a tentative I.D. of the murderer of Gwen Eaton had been made by New York State police. Fingerprints found in Gwen's house would substantiate the I.D. The murderer had a prison record: he'd served five years of a seven-to-ten-year sentence at Red Bank Men's Facility for drug-related felonies, check forgery, and burglary. He was tracked to his grandmother's residence in Erie, Pennsylvania, about twenty-five miles beyond the state line, where the stolen 2001 Honda registered in the name of Gwendolyn Eaton was found in a barn and where he was taken into custody without offering resistance.

Amid numerous items in the car, officers found Gwen Eaton's emptied wallet. Beneath the driver's seat, a bloodstained Swiss Army knife.

"See, most criminals are stupid like I told you. Especially meth-heads looking for quick cash."

It was Detective Strabane who told us these things. Though he frowned and squinched up his monkey-face, swiped at his nose and shifted his shoulders inside his dun-colored sport coat (not only unbuttoned but missing one of its plastic buttons) you could see that the plain-clothed officer had all he could do to suppress his excitement and elation. Oh, he felt good about this professional police work! *He* had been at the prow of it, you could be sure.

We stared at him, stunned into silence. Clare, Rob, me.

Finally Clare said, " 'Ward Lynch.' That was his name. I'd gotten it backward. I met the man myself, once. At Mom's. I'd thought he was a joke. One of Mom's lame ducks, to tease about. Oh, Jesus."

In the Chisholms' living room ("cathedral-style" ceiling, hardwood floors) Clare and I were seated on a sofa, Rob was a few feet away in a chair. And there was Detective Strabane leaning forward, earnest and eager, elbows on his knees, in another chair. My niece and nephew had been banished upstairs, what the "policeman" had to say wasn't for their ears.

Clare had begun to cry, bitterly. Yet not hiding her face as you'd expect, just sitting rigid and furious, fists clenched at her sides. I knew that I was expected to cry with my sister, to hug her tight, but my arms were like lead, my legs were like lead, I hadn't the strength to turn to her, couldn't move an inch. She might have been on the far side of the room.

evil

Reading The Diary of Anne Frank *when I was fourteen.*
"Mom, you just can't face it that some people are evil."
And Mom said quickly, "Oh I know that, honey. Some people are evil. I know."
But speaking without conviction like someone agreeing the earth is round though
in her heart she knows otherwise.

part two

crazy

"Well. People have to eat, you know."

These were Mom's brave, bright words, after Dad's funeral. At the crowded buffet brunch in Aunt Tabitha's old stone house on Church Street. Where so many people were turning up—"company people" from Beechum Paper Products, unknown to most of us in the family—it was a good thing that Tabitha had prevailed over Gwen, hosting the funeral brunch in her house and not in the smaller house at 43 Deer Creek Drive. So many people, and all so hungry.

It was one of those January days: cold, blustery, bracing. A glitter of fresh-fallen snow and the ground frozen solid so there was no procession of hearse and cars to the cemetery.

The widow, exhausted and feebly smiling. Fifty-two years old and looking younger except for the hurt bruised look around her eyes. *How brave she is! Poor Gwen.*

Mom had insisted upon providing some of the food for Tabitha's table including the home-baked bread for which she was known.

Saying fiercely, "My husband loved my bread. He would want it served. He would be so *pleased*."

Practical-minded Tabitha had wanted the meal catered, wasn't that the sensible solution? She'd been so shocked by her younger brother's death (of a coronary thrombosis, aged fifty-nine!) she hadn't any energy even to think about food, and poor Gwen, what a shock it had been for

Gwen who'd actually been present when her husband died, collapsing in his own home in the TV room in his favorite old leather chair watching a rerun of his favorite TV program *Law & Order* (even new *Law & Order* shows were reruns, Dad conceded, but the formula was so soothing, somehow), how could Gwen be expected to prepare food at such a time?

But Mom insisted. Mom might have been exhausted, practically staggering on her feet, an untimely bladder infection kept her hurrying away to the bathroom every half-hour, and she was crying and swiping at her eyes, still in a fury of energy Mom managed to bake six loaves of Dad's favorite bread—buttermilk/hazelnut/cranberry with a thick nutty crust—on the eve of his funeral.

"Oh, I couldn't sleep anyway! I need something useful to do."

Rising at dawn to prepare another of Dad's favorite dishes, Waldorf salad (a gigantic quantity requiring three large salad bowls to be toted to Aunt Tabitha's) with fresh-chopped pecans, to be served on iceberg lettuce leaves.

Gwen had never succeeded in training Jon to prefer any other lettuce over iceberg: "That's just how his taste was formed, back in the 1950s." Gwen spoke with a rueful little smile, fingers pressed to her bosom, sighing.

Why, they're crazy. People are plain crazy. A man dies, falls over dead, struck down like a beast felled by a sledgehammer blow on the way to the slaughterhouse and people stand around talking about—what are people talking about?

"Well. People have to eat, you know."

Sounds like Mom, doesn't it? In fact, it was Clare.

After Mom's funeral. At the buffet brunch in Clare's house.

Have to eat. Have to eat. Have to eat. Why?

· · ·

Mom's funeral! As Clare said, "I can't believe this."

So many mourners crowded into the Mt. Ephraim Christian Life Fellowship Church they had to stand in aisles and in the vestibule, filled the choir loft at the rear, and were herded into the basement to listen over the sound system. (Where I wished I'd been instead of trapped in the first row of relatives between my quivery sister and Aunt Tabitha weepy and blowing her nose through an entire small box of scented blue Kleenex as Reverend "Bob" Bewley spoke of "our dearest friend Gwen Eaton, the most Christian lady of this community and the most beloved" and several times paused to blow his nose also, in the way of a bull elephant clearing his trunk.) Our Eaton relatives who'd tended to take Gwen for granted as just a housewife/mother who'd married right out of high school were stunned to see that Mom had so many friends but Clare and I knew better: most of the "mourners" crowding into the church scarcely knew Mom at all. They'd read of her violent death in the newspapers, they'd watched the extensive coverage on TV. Even Mom's obituary was featured on the front page of the *Chautauqua Valley Beacon*.

Well, some of these people knew Gwen from high school, or from her church and volunteer work, some could even claim to be related (the Kovachs were a large sprawling tribe of mostly disconnected individuals, as Mom described them, rattling about like loose buttons in a drawer), but they hadn't any personal ties with her, really.

I wanted to think this! I didn't want to share Mom with so many others.

The evening before, Clare and I had been instructed to arrive at Klutch Brothers Funeral Home (est. 1931) for what was called a private viewing. By this time, four days after Mom's death, we were getting used to the idea that Mom was *dead*, we were about ready for Mom to be *buried*.

At least, we thought so.

At least, we wanted to think so.

That weird, stepping-on-eggs way people speak of the dead! Like

"Gwen's body"—"Gwen's funeral." As if the dead were somehow still present more or less as they'd always been except now there was this new, disembodied entity that was the spirit of Gwen with the capacity to possess a body, a funeral. Where Mom used to be exactly what you'd see when you saw her, now what you saw was "her" body. *But where was Gwen?* The worst was some dimwit calling from the Mt. Ephraim Township medical examiner's office with the cryptic message: "Your mother's cadaver is ready to be released."

Politely I said, "Thanks! I'll tell her."

Startled silence at the other end of the line. Then we both hung up.

How Mom would have giggled at *Your mother's cadaver.*

Like that old wisecrack *Your father's moustache.*

Clare drove us in the Land Rover to Klutch Brothers. I tried to make her laugh telling her about the medical examiner's office. I tried to make her laugh mispronouncing "Klutch" as "Klutz." But Clare ignored me, frowning. She was taking medication to settle her nerves and help her sleep but I preferred my raw, ready-to-snap nerves and miserable nights. I was vain enough to believe that I could "do" my mother's death the way I did most of my life.

Capably, that is. Not quite fucking up.

There would be no public viewing of Gwen Eaton, we'd been advised this wasn't a good idea considering how she'd been injured. (Oh, how had Mom been injured? We didn't want to think.) In fact, Mom had not had a public viewing for Dad, either: he'd made her promise never to display him like a wax dummy and so she had not.

"Mrs. Chisholm! Ms. Eaton. Come."

The elder and more blustery of the Klutch brothers greeted us at the door. Took our hands, half-bowed. We had thought that we'd be asked to sign more papers, but Klutch led us directly to the viewing room for our "private time" with our mother.

We were told to take as long as we wished, there were no other viewings scheduled in the room that evening.

The viewing room was long as a bowling alley. Mom's coffin was at the farther end amid a bank of ghastly white lilies. (I hadn't thought the lilies were real, but they were. Pollen came off on my nose when I stooped to smell them.) Heavy burgundy-colored drapes covering windows and walls were stirred by gusts of air-conditioning like those spooky wall hangings in the House of Usher.

I knew: a primitive part of the human brain needs to see the dead individual close up to comprehend that the individual is truly dead and not just off somewhere traveling. So this viewing-ritual was necessary for Clare and me, maybe. Except Clare began sneezing and I began shivering convulsively.

I groped for Clare's hand. She tried to ward me off, then gave in. Clare's hand surprised me, dry and at least body-temperature. My own hands had been icy-cold for days.

Gripping each other's hand, awkward as a three-legged race, we approached Mom's coffin. It made sense to say *Mom's coffin* since we could see Mom inside it, just her head and shoulders. Like a part-convertible canoe. Shiny as plastic, and so large! Massive. Mom would laugh, did we think she was an Egyptian mummy?

Mom had weighed only 108 pounds. Her murderer weighed 180.

All that was visible was Mom's head, not her neck or shoulders. Her head had been carefully positioned on a white satin cushion. Her face had been virtually remodeled with some kind of flesh-colored putty. It was still a round face but appeared flattened somehow. There must have been bruises in the skin for vague purplish blotches showed through the putty layers like old water stains. Yet this was a wax-doll face attractively powdered, rouged, lipsticked in a warm rose-pink to suggest innocence, purity. There was the barest suggestion of mascara on the lashes of the shut eyes. The hair that had been graying now appeared lightened, almost silvery, fashioned in a way to evoke an era before Gwen Eaton had even been born: was it crimped? marcelled? Dad would have teased Mom for being a glamour girl and Mom would have been stricken with embarrassment.

You were meant to think *Why, she's only sleeping.* So peaceful!

Except this wasn't sleep, and it wasn't peaceful. More like a coma.

Clare sneezed violently, and blew her nose. I hated to give up her hand.

I watched to see if Mom was breathing. I thought it might be a matter of looking closely, patiently.

Clare appeared to be whispering to herself. I didn't want to peer at her, was she saying *Oh, God? Oh, God?*

It's rare to see just a head poking out of a shiny wooden box. And the eyes of the head closed, so you can't make eye contact. It took time for me to grasp that Mom's neck was hidden beneath a kind of silky pink ruffle to her chin: someone had skillfully arranged it to disguise what the media persisted in calling multiple throat wounds. I felt such regret, I hadn't thought to bring over the glamorous white ostrich feather boa along with the more ordinary clothes we'd provided for Mom to be buried in.

"Clare. I can't."

"Can't—what?"

"Can't do it."

"Do *what?* Stop shivering, you're driving me crazy."

"Do this. You know."

"I don't know!"

". . . Mom."

"Well, you are. You are 'doing' it, just like me."

Clare blew her nose, crumpled the soaked tissue in her fist and shoved it into a pocket of her nubby black trouser suit with the fluted tunic top, that fit loose as a skirt over her hips. She glared at me and gave me a poke in the arm. My shivering began to subside.

"You know that Mom would expect us to behave like adults, at least. You know Mom believed in rituals."

"Mom didn't! Mom laughed at things like this."

"Mom pretended to laugh. But really she took it all seriously, and you know it."

"Mom never pushed us, Clare. Beyond what we could do."

"She tried! You've never wanted to accept it, Nikki, you couldn't live up to Mom's hopes for you."

Did I hear this correctly? I let it pass.

"Clare, Mom looks so lonely there! I wish they'd made her smile."

"The bastards. They're supposed to."

"And the way that ruffle-thing sort of bunches up over her ear, Clare. It makes her look frivolous."

"Nikki, don't touch it! There's some purpose to it."

"Mom would wonder why we're whispering like idiots."

"Mom would wonder why we gave her to strangers, to fix up like a voodoo doll."

Clare went to stand on the other side of the coffin so that we could look down on Mom between us, head positioned on the white satin cushion. I wanted to think that a kind of low-wattage heat was being generated, lifting to Clare and me from Mom.

A long time passed. I had time to think *This is crazy* and to think *This is beautiful*.

Clare was staring at Mom so hard, I thought she must be memorizing her. My eyes kept filling with moisture so that I had difficulty seeing clearly as they did often in normal life: when I was looking at Wally Szalla, for instance. And Wally's face would fade in, fade out of my vision without his knowing.

Finally Clare touched Mom's cheek. Then I touched Mom's cheek.

Clare stooped over to kiss Mom's forehead. Then I stooped over to kiss Mom's forehead. It was cool and smooth as ivory. It wasn't any colder than my own lips. I was happy suddenly! I thought *Mom will always love me, this will be all right*.

Clare said, with that little thrill to her voice she'd had as a girl sometimes, as if making a secret vow, "We'll see he is punished, Mom. With his fucking life."

I wasn't sure I'd heard this, either.

Why, people are plain crazy. You knew.

. . .

After Mom's funeral service, Mom's burial.

There was a conspicuously smaller gathering of mourners in the cemetery. Still, more than we'd have expected. And many strangers.

In the early 1900s the Eatons and their in-laws had begun to take over a corner of Mt. Ephraim Cemetery. This wasn't the Catholic cemetery in downtown Mt. Ephraim where my Kovach grandparents were buried but a larger, more attractive cemetery on the outskirts of town with a view of sloping meadows, pine woods, and the Chautauqua River. It was a mile and a half drive from the Mt. Ephraim Christian Life Fellowship Church so you had time to ponder where you were headed.

One day when I was in middle school, Dad came home whistling and looking pleased with himself: "Bet you can't guess what I did today, girls!"

We were all Dad's girls: Mom, Clare, Nikki. When Dad was in the right mood.

His news was, he'd bought a family plot, a "real bargain," in Mt. Ephraim Cemetery. Not just for him and Mom but for Clare and me, too. "If you want to join us. If you don't have other, fancier plans."

Clare and I snorted with laughter. Our dad was so weird sometimes.

Eighteen years later Dad's bargain grave was lush-grassy-green and looked all settled in. You had to suppose that the man was pleased with himself. We'd chosen his headstone after much deliberation: a large dignified dark-granite marker engraved

Jonathan Allan Eaton

February 16, 1941

January 8, 2000

Beloved Husband and Father

There was no matching headstone for Gwendolyn Eaton, yet. That would come later. Mom's grave was, well—a fresh-dug hole, with steep vertical sides. It was discreetly covered with a shroud of synthetic turf but I'd peeked.

Reverend Bewley led us in another prayer. This time, for the repose of Gwendolyn Eaton's soul. In a sudden brisk breeze, "Bob" Bewley's carefully wetted, slicked-down hair lifted from the curve of his scalp to reveal it was an ingenious comb-over.

Clare hadn't been crazy about the idea, but she'd given in to a request from Mom's Senior Swim Club friends that they be allowed to release doves in the cemetery. The ceremony ended with several elderly women trying to coax three doves out of a wire cage, which took some time. Finally, two emerged from the cage flapping their wings agitatedly into the foliage overhead; the third held back, wary and confused, until at last I lost patience, grabbed the cage and tilted it sharply so the dove had no choice but to tumble out onto the ground, and flap its wings in a panic to escape. "Go! Fly! Get as far away as you can!"

It must've been me, that shrill voice.

I will punish her, I won't call her.
I don't need her love! Not me.

After Mom's burial, Mom's funeral luncheon.

Where, once again, Mom's home-baked breads were served.

"Isn't this just like Gwen!"

"She would take such pleasure, if she knew."

For it happened that, when Gwen's relatives, neighbors, friends checked their freezers, it was discovered that they'd stored away bread Mom had given them. Clare had a full loaf of raisin/yogurt/twelve grain. Aunt Tabitha had buttermilk/cinnamon/pumpkin seed—"Maybe just a little stale." Alyce Proxmire had small portions of several loaves including High-Fibre Sugarless/Saltless Carrot/Wheat Germ that Mom baked especially for her. And there were scattered others with Oatmeal Muffins, Almond Squash Pound Cake, Date-Nut Brownies, Grandma's Molasses Brioche, even gaily frosted Christmas cookies of Gwen Eaton's, they were eager to bring to the funeral luncheon to be served with the catered food Clare had ordered.

Oh, it would be a festive occasion! I hid upstairs.

A tentative knock at the door and there was my niece Lilja blinking at me. "Aunt Nikki, I don't want to be downstairs, either. But Grandma would want us to, you know."

Downstairs, I hid in the guest bathroom. Fantasizing a romantic/lurid interlude with a lover. Or, a cigarette. Marijuana, crack cocaine. Anything to wipe my mind out!

There came a sharp accusing knock on the door. My sister's knuckles against wood, recognizable anywhere.

"Nikki. Get your ass out here. People are asking about you, don't you dare embarrass Mom, and me, *unlock this door*."

This was shocking. This was serious. Clare hadn't spoken to me in such a way since high school. I had no choice but to unlock the door, immediately.

For the occasion Clare was what we'd call "revved-up." It must have been the medication Dr. Myer had prescribed, her eyes were unnaturally glistening and her speech rapid, percussive. Having so many guests in her house was a natural high, putting color in her cheeks like rouge. As an "executive wife" Clare was expected to "entertain" her husband's numerous colleagues and clients, which obligations she fulfilled in the way of a teacher executing a lesson plan. My practical-minded sister had virtually stopped having family gatherings except a catchall open house on Christmas Day.

As Mom had naively observed, you'd almost think that Clare didn't much like her family, wouldn't you?

"C'mon, Nikki. You're on."

Clare was the one who was *on*. Stylish in her nubby black trouser suit that fitted her snugly, almost sensuously you might say, at her generous hips and stomach. Her face was a startling glowing-creamy cosmetic mask that obscured, at least at a respectful distance, the sharp vertical lines between her eyebrows. Her eyebrows flared provocatively and her lipstick was Revlon Fire Engine Red, she'd been wearing since high school. Beside Clare, I was looking like a disco casualty. Not-new but still serviceable black "silk" (i.e., silk-seeming) trousers with flaring cuffs, a three-quarter-sleeved smoke-colored see-through designer shirt designed (of course) to be worn over naked breasts but, in this case, worn over a tight black T-shirt top with no pretensions other than sexy. Nikki's signature smear of purple lipstick but no makeup otherwise. I'd tamped down my hair so that it lay almost flat on my head, a punk chicken with wetted feathers.

On my bare luridly white feet, smoke-colored leather-and-Plexiglas platform shoes with a hint of glitter.

Clare's swift assessing gaze took me in, wetted-head to shoes, pitilessly. However I looked, I was *on*.

"Oh, Clare. I just don't think . . ."

"Then don't! Don't think. Like me."

After a funeral service, after a cemetery trip on a bright windy chilly spring morning, mourners are naturally hungry. Food is their reward, and they deserve it. Still I was stunned by the quantity of food on Clare's beautifully decorated dining room table. Mom's baked things were a small part of it, really. The caterer had set out lavish platters of smoked salmon, cold sliced meats, deviled eggs, stuffed mushrooms; there was creamed chicken to be served over biscuits; there were rice, pasta, vegetable salads. There was even a huge bowl of Waldorf salad, prepared from Gwen's recipe. And there were desserts. Many.

Always set out more desserts than you think your guests can eat, Mom used to say. So that they leave a few behind, and can feel good about their diets.

I'd never seen Clare's house so crowded. Dining room, living room, glassed-in family room, vestibule. The showy cathedral ceiling seemed appropriate, as in a hotel lobby. "Oh, Nikki! *Oh.*" There came Alyce Proxmire lurching in my direction to embrace me in an unexpected hug, her rail-thin arms surprisingly strong, her breath hot and anxious in my face, so stricken with grief at losing her oldest friend she'd been suffering from insomnia, migraine, irritable bowel, and her white blood cells had "plummeted" leaving her vulnerable to infections. There came Aunt Tabitha in a black rayon dress with a drooping bosom, watery-eyed, sniffing loudly, suddenly looking old, befuddled: "Poor Gwen! Of all people! Hadn't I told her and told her! Oh, hadn't I told her! Not to become so *involved*, not with people outside the family, oh I *told her*! You and Clare know! And she wouldn't listen! Oh, she listened, she pretended to listen, you know Gwen, you know that sly way of hers, that little smile of hers, if a cat could smile it would smile in that way—'Yes yes I agree! but I intend to do just what I want to do.' That's what a cat would say, and that's what Gwen was *think*ing! Oh, Jon's sweet little wife, he married so young, Gwen never grew up, somehow. Oh, what a tragedy! Oh, Nikki, all our lives are in danger! Oh, I wish I hadn't been so critical of your mother, Gwen did the best she could, oh that dear woman did the very best she could which is more than most people can say for themselves. Oh, and Gwen was so—*good.*"

There was the exalted Gilbert Wexley frowning and somber as he piled food onto his plate, speaking in a high-pitched voice of his plan for Gwen's memorial service: "I know just the place for it. Not that church, the new Arts Council building. I will organize it! I have the staff! We at the Arts Council are so very grateful to Gwen for all she's done for us, the bake sale, the crafts festival, fund-raising, her committee work, what a dear friend, what a lovely woman, there should be a plaque in Gwen's honor, *I will direct my staff to look into it.*"

There was "Sonny" Danto in a dark suede sport coat, sharp-creased black trousers, a necktie that appeared to be made of black leather, vigorously shaking hands with Rob Chisholm as if they were old friends, offering him condolences in a rush of words: "Mrs. Eaton was the grandest lady, the nicest and most wonderful lady, you are so lucky to have a mother-in-law like Mrs. Eaton not like some, I can tell you, oh man can I tell you," shaking his head and grinning as if, in fact, he couldn't have told Rob, or anyway Rob would not have believed him. And there was Sonya Szyszko waiting her turn with my brother-in-law, in swishing black velvet with a plunging V-neckline, crimson-mouthed, wiping at her elaborately made-up eyes and blinking nearsightedly as if grief were a performance, she'd prepared for its public display and was eager to begin. There were Eaton relatives I hadn't seen since Dad's funeral, and there were Kovach relatives I'd have sworn I hadn't seen before in my life. There was Aunt Maude, there was Uncle Fred, there were my cousins Jill, Barbara, Tom. There were middle-aged men speaking wistfully of "Feather" even as they heaped their plates with food. There were my high school girlfriends Sylvie, Janet, Annette, Noreen and there were my high school boyfriends Vic, Marty, Steve, Sonny, and Davy Petko you'd think would not dare to show up, that bastard. And there was my ex-fiancé Dick Gurski who grabbed me and held me so tight, I felt the hot throbbing length of him as if it was high school again: "Nikki, Christ. What a shitty thing. Your mom was *tops*." Another of my ex-fiancés Lannie Bishop came to embrace me, his wife closely behind him regarding us with anxious eyes. "Nikki, darling. I couldn't believe when I heard the news. Gwen wanted us to go through with it, why'd you back out?" I laughed nervously pushing away from Lannie: "We were too young, for heaven's sake. We were just crazy in love and it would never have lasted." Lannie squeezed my arm so hard it hurt: "It would have! We'd have had kids, for Christ's sake. We'd hang in there like everybody else."

There came Sylvie LaPorte frantic to hug me, and pull me along the hallway into the guest bathroom where she offered me a swallow, in fact more than one swallow, from the pint bottle of Johnnie Walker Red Label she'd produced out of her handbag. I'd heard that Sylvie had a drinking problem since her divorce, in fact she'd been a drinker in high school. Sylvie hugged me hard, planted a wet, hot kiss near my mouth saying she'd freaked when she heard the news on TV, I would never get over losing my mom who was the nicest, kindest, most generous person she'd ever met, not that that was saying so much considering certain members of her family and guys in Mt. Ephraim but Gwen Eaton had been a saint, I would never get over the loss of her: "When I heard, Nikki, I just started screaming. I mean, I started breaking things. This meth-head murderer, he's got to be given the death sentence. I'll jam in the needle myself."

The look in Sylvie's tear-brimming eyes, I could believe her.

After Sylvie, I blundered into the Scourge of the Bugs with a plate of food, chewing deviled egg and staring at me with melting eyes: "Nicole! Please accept my heartfelt condolences for your loss. Your mother was a grand, gracious lady. May I call you? This week?" And there came Sonja Szyszko in chill rustling black taffeta and jasmine perfume, to grip me against her foamy bosom: "Your poor momma! How could such a terrible thing happen! In Mt. Ephraim where everybody is so friendly! Mrs. Aiten was my dear friend, I will never have another friend like Mrs. Aiten again." Sonja was so shaken, I ended up having to comfort her.

Overhearing a two-hundred-pound cousin of my mother's, Lucille Kovach, a woman with a flushed moon face and an appetite for pastries, speaking vehemently to another wide-beamed Kovach relation: "I loved Gwen. We were girls together on Spalding Street, she had a hard life. All this bullshit of the Reverend's, like Gwen was some kind of angel, *she was not.*"

In the front hall, Rob was trying to calm Clare who stood at the door barring the way to an astonished-looking Reverend Bewley and his wife: "Reverend, we don't want you in this house. You brought that murderer into my mother's life. *You* are responsible for my mother's death." As Bewley opened his mouth to protest, Clare spoke in a shriller voice: "You! Call yourself a Christian! You are *Judas.*"

I pushed through a knot of guests in the hall, escaped into the kitchen where the caterer's assistants were busily working. A young woman asked if she could help me and I said thanks, no. My hands were trembling as I poured wine from an opened bottle into a glass, and swallowed thirstily.

Tart white wine, stinging my mouth in a way I liked. (Clare hadn't wanted to serve alcohol at the funeral luncheon, only just sparkling water, sodas, coffee and decaf. Certain of the Kovach relatives, we knew from past experience, weren't to be trusted with an open bar.) I had time to admire my sister's custom-designed "country kitchen" that was twice the size of Mom's and bore the approximate relationship to my kitchen in Chautauqua Falls that a football field bears to a Ping-Pong table: state-of-the-art appliances, gleaming Mexican tiles and copper pans hanging from hooks, that looked as if they'd never been used. Here and there amid the glossy color-coordinated surfaces were poignant remnants of Mom: a glazed pot with a lid marked COOKIES, a russet-red plaster-of-Paris rooster, terry-cloth dish towels. Beyond the kitchen door was the dining room, and an alarming tide of voices. So loud, so *alive*. I couldn't help but wait to hear Gwen Eaton's voice among them. It terrified me to realize I would not hear that voice again.

"Ma'am? Would you like—?"

"I'm *family*. I'm the sister of Mrs. Chisholm, who hired you."

I poured a second glass of wine, left the bottle on the counter and went outside, onto the flagstone patio. Impressive: a built-in barbecue, hefty redwood lawn furniture, Martha Stewart–style waterproof cushions in a bright floral pattern. Unlike our mother, Clare hadn't time or patience for gardening, even small flower beds. Her lawn was solid, sodded grass without a dandelion in sight and like most of the professionally landscaped lawns in Fox Hunt Acres, its showplace center was a swimming pool.

More people! More people! If I can't be happy myself I can make them happy.

I'd been thinking a lot, about these words. What Mom had said to me in her kitchen, after the Mother's Day dinner.

Since seeing Mom in the canoe-coffin, I was having difficulty recalling her as she'd been in life. Kept seeing her in that ridiculous thing, only her head exposed. The putty-face that wasn't exactly Gwen Eaton's face, the marcelled silvery hair that wasn't exactly Gwen Eaton's hair. Rouge, glossy shell-pink lipstick, ruffled scarf hiding her throat.

" 'Your mother's cadaver.' "

I laughed. My face seemed to crack, I could feel fissures in my cheeks. Through the kitchen window, the caterer's assistants were probably watching me. Maybe some of Clare's guests were watching me, too. I decided not to care. I swallowed down the last of the wine, left the glass on a table, and walked away.

I would leave my things upstairs in Clare's guest room. On the bedside table was my broken wristwatch, the delicate little watch inscribed *To Elise*, somehow in the night stumbling to the bathroom I'd stepped on it where it had fallen to the floor, don't ask how. I would leave without saying goodbye to family, friends. I would leave and neglect to call Clare for several times to apologize or even to explain, I would fail to return Clare's numerous messages on my answering machine. I saw that my car, the sturdy Saab that Wally Szalla had helped me acquire, was hopelessly blocked in the Chisholms' driveway but this didn't deter me for I could walk: I could walk into Mt. Ephraim, and call a taxi. Not thinking *I could call Wally, of course there is Wally* even as I saw, a half-block away on Mockingbird Drive, a car idling at the curb, spewing exhaust like a smoker: a chunky Buick the color of tarnished brass, I'd recognized at once. The owner of that car had been criticized for being a man who hurt others, who was selfish, careless, "evil." Yet this man had had the sensitivity not to attend my mother's funeral, and not to show up at my sister's house.

Clare would accuse me on the phone of having gotten drunk in her kitchen but that wasn't so, I was excited and anxious but not at all drunk in my glittery black platform shoes fleeing out the Chisholms' crowded driveway and into the street. I was breathless, muttering to myself. A gust of wind like a prank dislodged my wetted-down punk-purple hair. The tarnished-brass car had leapt into motion, pulling up beside me now as the smiling driver leaned out his window. In a blur of tears I saw that the side of the Buick was lightly splattered with mud like the finest lace.

"Darling Nikki! Climb in."

and the boy said, "*Her* upset, what about *me* upset? Always it's *her*, or it's *you*, fuck what about *me* for a change?" and the man said, "Your mother is under the impression you'll be back with her tonight, she's sure that you promised her," and the boy said, disgusted, "*I* promised her?—fuck I did not. *You* promised her. The only way to get out of the fucking house is to promise Mom some pathetic fucking thing nobody has any intention of doing—*jeez.*" Tears glistened in the boy's stricken eyes. He had the preening public style of an MTV rock star. In his Snoop Dogg T-shirt trampling the heat-wilted lawn as his father followed after him, trying to reason with him. Here was my interview subject, a prominent Chautauqua Falls resident, something of a public figure, losing a quarrel with his teenaged son. His thinning gray-brown hair was disheveled, his white shirt was rumpled and stained with perspiration across his broad back like folded wings.

I would have slipped away and escaped but my car was parked at the curb, on the far side of the disputing father and son.

The outburst resembled TV except, unlike TV, it wasn't scripted. It was a true family quarrel limping and lumbering and careening on like a train wreck in slow motion. It reminded me of quarrels I'd had, not with my parents, no one in my family, but men whom I had misunderstood or who'd misunderstood me, the fury of wounded pride, the need to wound another. When Szalla tried to touch his son's arm in a restraining gesture, the boy threw off his hand as you'd throw off a cobra: "This sucks, Dad! This totally sucks! All this summer has sucked, Mom acting crazy on account of you, and you living in this dump, but tonight is different, I'm going to Rochester with the guys, I'm not giving up that ticket." The resemblance between the boy and his father was striking: what was sharply chiseled in the young, brattish, good-looking face was thickened and creased and apologetic in the middle-aged face. Both son and father were of the same height, about five feet ten, but the boy was trim and lean as a weasel and the man was at least thirty pounds overweight, his bulk concentrated in his midriff. Like an aging athlete, he was panting and left behind, outmaneuvered by his opponent who suddenly changed directions wasted twenty minutes driving to the far side of town, made a fool of myself breathless and beaming like a girl TV anchor ringing the doorbell of an impressive old-style red-brick colonial on prestigious Ashburn Avenue, being nervously informed by a Guatemalan maid that "Mr. Zal-la" was no longer "resident" at that address even as I distinctly heard, in the background, a woman on the brink of hysteria crying, "Tell her to go away, Nina! Whoever it is, go away! *We don't know where he is.*" Several frantic calls on my cell phone later, I was directed across town to Riverview Luxury Apartments, 8A: a ground-floor apartment with a door that opened directly onto a front stoop. This stoop was so littered with old newspapers and flyers, I would have thought no one was home except as I uneasily approached the door I could hear voices inside.

All this was disheartening! The name *Szalla* was close to our Chautauqua Valley equivalent to *Rockefeller* in the larger world. But Riverview Luxury Apartments wasn't and Wally Szalla, that overweight dad trotting pathetically in the wake of his adolescent son, had the glamour of a well-worn old shoe.

Szalla! And I'd been hearing he had the reputation of being a "womanizer."

Troy came charging back out the door, carrying a black backpack into which he was stuffing a cell phone. He'd jammed a rakish Buffalo Bills cap on his head and his expression was fierce and triumphant. Behind him, Wally Szalla followed in the self-punishing way of a large aging dog trailing a smaller, faster, younger dog. As Troy jogged down the street without a backward glance Szalla paused at the curb cupping his hands to his mouth: "All right! But you call me, Troy! God damn, you use that cell phone at eleven P.M. and call me and if I call you you'd better answer or I'll have you picked up by state troopers! You hear?" By this time, Troy was out of earshot.

I'd had plenty of time to study Wally Szalla by now, and wasn't much impressed. A deflated-looking middle-aged man, staring after his vanished son. Not just he reminded me of an old shoe, he was wearing old shoes: the kind my father had called "moccasins." Dad had owned a favorite pair of these shoes, meant to resemble deer hide, something Native Americans might have "tanned" and "sewn" in frontier days, now machine-made with floppy little tassels: slipper-shoes so worn, so splayed, Dad had shuffled around the house in them like an elderly invalid, exasperating the rest of us. Mom had tried to dispose of the moccasins but somehow Dad managed to retrieve them from the trash saying in a wounded voice: "Gwen, these shoes *fit*."

Well, Szalla was wearing moccasins. And summer trousers that might have been stylish in another season but were badly worn now, and soiled across the buttocks. His limp damp incongruously formal long-sleeved shirt had pulled out of his trousers at the back, looking like a pajama top. I was embarrassed to see Szalla panting so badly, wiping his eyes on his shirtsleeve.

Vaguely I was headed for my car. A mud-colored Datsun compact so nondescript I kept forgetting what it looked like, in parking lots. Szalla saw me, and quickly tucked in his shirttails. With unconscious vanity he tried to suck in his stomach. "Excuse me: you must be Nikki from the *Beacon?*"

I said yes but we could re-schedule the interview, if he wanted. I could see that this wasn't an ideal time for him.

"No, no! I mean, yes. I can't think of a more ideal time. Please don't leave."

The way Wally Szalla was headed toward me, across a patch of grass near the curb, you'd think the desperate man meant to block my escape.

Quickly I said, "Mr. Szalla, I think I'd better call your secretary, to reschedule. I know what adolescents can be like, pure hell."

"You do? I mean, *you* do? You're too young to have a sixteen-year-old."

"Not have one, Mr. Szalla: I used to be one. Made my parents anxious over me, it doesn't seem that long ago."

Szalla laughed eagerly. "Rock concerts? Ten thousand screaming fans? 'Heavy metal'? 'Ecstasy'?"

" 'X' is after my time, Mr. Szalla. If that's what you mean by 'Ecstasy.' "

"Not what I mean by ecstasy. No ma'am."

Szalla stood close beside me, considering. He was looking less distraught, eyeing the very short very tight white cord skirt and lacy red top that fitted my torso snug as a sausage casing. I felt the powerful swerve of his interest. My heart was beating just a little quickly. And I felt sympathy for the man: I knew the wish not to be left alone as evening came on.

Thinking, in my naïveté, that Wally Szalla would have to spend any evening of his life alone if that wasn't his wish.

Still I felt obliged to say, "Mr. Szalla, it doesn't seem appropriate. A reporter could take advantage of you, asking pushy questions. You've had an upset just now."

" 'Mr. Szalla' is my eighty-two-year-old father, Nikki. Please call me 'Wally.' "

"Well. 'Wally.' "

I felt my face burn pleasantly. "Wally" was such a comfortable old-shoe kind of name.

Apologizing profusely for his rudeness in ignoring me and for his son's rudeness, Wally Szalla escorted me into his apartment. I was conscious of his fingers lightly on my elbow. Szalla was saying of his son Troy that his rudeness wasn't intentional, it was purely unconscious: "That age, most of life is unconscious. Other people, especially older people, don't register."

I wasn't sure how true this was. But I saw that a father would want to believe that his son had no conscious wish to defy or wound him.

"May I get you something, Nikki? Coffee, or a soda, or—?"

Szalla was wanting to say "something stronger" but decided against it. I declined his offer, setting up my Japanese-manufactured tape recorder near an electrical outlet, on a low, glass-topped table in Szalla's surprisingly small living room. To find a space for the recorder, we had to push aside layers of clutter—newspapers, magazines, an empty pizza carton, scattered CDs (heavy metal rock, white rapper) that must have belonged to Troy. I could see Szalla hovering over me preparing to ask if I needed help with the machine which, as I paused and fumbled my two-inch polished fingernails and muttered to myself, it appeared that I did. But Szalla decided against interfering, he meant to keep a respectful distance.

I was grateful for this. A father who knows not to crowd his children. Daddy had crowded Clare and me, sometimes. Not that he showed his impatience but you could feel it, a quivery heat and exasperation lifting from his skin.

Szalla rubbed his hands vigorously. "You don't mind if I have a drink, do you, Nikki? Having your heart chewed up by a bratty kid makes a man thirsty."

In the kitchen Szalla got himself a cold beer from the refrigerator and, for me, a can of Diet Coke.

Saccharine, caffeine, and chemicals! Exactly what I craved at this hour of the day when my blood sugar was dipping and it was too early for a serious drink.

The "luxury" apartment was chilled with air-conditioning but the air smelled of beer and stale pizza and something more intimate: unwashed laundry, sweaty socks. Through the kitchen doorway I could see the kind of casual mess you'd expect of a father and son who've been camping out together for a few days.

Despite the name "Riverview," there was no view of the Chautauqua River from Wally Szalla's windows: his apartment faced the street. Venetian blinds on the living room windows were partly drawn, each at a different height. Furnishings looked as if they came with the apartment: stylish but charmless leather sofas in neutral colors, chromed-edged chairs and tables, rugs like wild boar skins strewn casually about. An upscale bachelor's pad you might see in a *Playboy* photo feature except this one had been invaded by a teenager and bore signs of incipient shabbiness, like Riverview Apartments itself, that had opened only a few years before but was beginning to look tacky on the outside. Monthly rentals here were several times what I paid for my funky third-floor brownstone apartment in a less prestigious part of Chautauqua Falls but I didn't have much envy for the residents.

"And are you a 'career' journalist, Nikki?"

"What is a 'career' journalist?"

"A very serious, very dedicated journalist. An ambitious young woman on her way out of Chautauqua Falls, using the *Beacon* as a springboard."

Szalla had to be teasing. The *Chautauqua Valley Beacon* was as springy as cooked spaghetti.

We laughed together. Szalla sat across from me, sprawled in one of the leather chairs. Where his wrinkled shirt was unbuttoned at the throat, a spidery mass of graying hairs sprang out. There were matching hairs on the backs of his big knuckles. His large splayed feet were bare in the worn old moccasins, as white as the insides of my thighs.

Awkwardly I began: "Please tell me about your background, Mr. Szalla? You were born in—"

Szalla lifted a forefinger as if in warning. " 'Wally.' "

"Oh, yes. 'W-Wally.' "

I fumbled my notebook, staring at the questions I'd diligently prepared. Pages of questions! The palms of my hands were moist, I couldn't believe that I was nervous. Wally Szalla was the least discomforting of men, nothing like the pushy arrogant guys I was always meeting, or who were always meeting me. Guys with names like Dale, Brock, Kevin, Kyle. Guys with names nothing like Wally.

"Born in Chautauqua Falls, W-Wally, in—"

"Haven't you done your homework, Nikki? I bet you have."

"Well, but—"

"You're checking, are you? To see if what I tell you tallies with what you already know?"

"Mr. Szalla, no! I just—only—"

Szalla was laughing at me, but in a kindly way. The only person who ever laughed at me like this, as if my fumbling and blunders were precious to her, was Mom.

I was feeling mildly high, as if it wasn't Diet Coke I was drinking in Wally Szalla's bachelor pad but something much stronger.

As Szalla settled in to being interviewed, sipping at his bottle of Sierra Lite, he became professional, serious. He spoke slowly and lucidly into the tape recorder. He was reminding me of my most admired university professors, who'd spoken not in breathy snatches of words like the majority of people but in carefully thought-out and articulate paragraphs. Szalla said, "I've been misquoted, Nikki, many times in the past. Forgive me if I overcompensate now."

I was embarrassed to realize that I'd underestimated Szalla. No one should be judged by the figure he cuts with an adolescent child.

Of course it was so, I'd tracked down a few facts about Wally Szalla. I knew that, though he looked years older, he was only forty-three. (Only! Forty-three, to me, seemed ancient. About as old as twenty-eight would seem to Szalla's son.) Wally Szalla hadn't been an outstanding student at Chautauqua Falls High but he'd been president of the class of 1976 and a popular football player; and beneath his smiling yearbook photo was the quotation *I contradict myself? Very well, I contradict myself.* After graduating he'd lived in Washington, D.C., for a year, working as an intern for his uncle Joseph Szalla, a Democratic U.S. congressman from our district; he'd taken courses at George Washington University, transferred to the State University of New York at Buffalo, and graduated in 1981 with a degree in business administration and communication arts. In 1982, he'd married his college sweetheart, a TriDelt who'd been Homecoming Queen. The couple had three children of whom the youngest, Troy, was born in 1985. The Szallas of Chautauqua Falls were well-to-do businessmen and civic leaders, mostly aligned with the Democratic party: Szalla's father Otto had served as mayor of the city for two terms, one of Szalla's cousins was a state senator, and Szalla himself now served on the County Board of Supervisors, an elected position. In interviews Szalla spoke of himself as an "investor in my home territory"—"an investor in hometown dreams"—and so he had a history of quirky projects: refurbishing the old, baroque Cameo Theater in downtown Chautauqua Falls, remaking an immense bankrupt bowling alley out on Route 33 into an indoor ice rink, introducing a summer jazz festival in Riverside Park, campaigning to bring a film festival to the Chautauqua Valley region. (The Cameo Theater had since been remodeled into a CineMax with eight screens. The ice rink was closed. The jazz festival was "tentatively successful." The film festival organizers had decided they preferred the more scenic Adirondack Mountains.)

Two years before, Szalla had purchased a local radio station, WCHF AM-FM, with the intention of "revamping" it. When I'd been in high school, WCHF AM had been the station to tune in to for pop-rock and country-and-western, nonstop except for the interruption of noisy ads, like most AM stations. I'd stopped listening to it years ago, like everyone I knew. Then suddenly Wally Szalla had stepped in to save the station from shutting down, and to rejuvenate it with NPR programming, local news several times a day, and, amid the ubiquitous rock music, interludes of classical jazz, "opera highlights," American popular music. There was a morning call-in program that dealt with women's issues called "No Holds Barred," hosted by a female personality who'd obviously learned a few tips from Oprah Winfrey; there was even, several nights a week from 10 P.M. to midnight, Wally Szalla's own D.J. program, "Night Train." Mostly Szalla played jazz CDs, tapes, and old 78s from his private collection, chatting in the way of a mellow old friend who takes for granted that you have time for him and if you don't, if you switch him off, that's cool, too. When I happened to be home at that hour, alone—which I tried not to be—I'd gotten into the habit of switching on "Night Train" to hear the D.J.'s rambling voice, cozy and intimate as a voice in my ear. Yet, to tell the truth, I hadn't even been aware of the D.J.'s name, I listened to the program so haphazardly. Only when my editor at the *Beacon* pushed this assignment onto me, to interview Szalla, did I realize that I knew the sound of the man's radio voice.

I knew the kind of jazz Szalla favored, to my untrained and impatient ear so unemphatic and repetitive it was about as exciting as listening to crickets. I did like brassy-bright Dixieland I could bop around to, to make my body think I might be dancing in a club, effervescent and sexy as hell and whoever I was dancing with didn't actually need to *exist*.

Szalla was a skilled interview subject. If he didn't care to answer an awkward question ("Mr. Szalla, it's said that WCHF AM-FM is 'struggling to survive'—is that so?") he simply answered another question in its place, smiling and upbeat: "Serious radio programming in the United States is a constant challenge to maintain, it isn't just TV we compete with but . . ." (Of course, I wasn't the kind of aggressive reporter who persisted in unwanted questions. The reader-friendly *Beacon* was hardly the *New York Times*.) When I asked Szalla the only pointedly political question of the interview, a question one of my fellow reporters had told me to ask him, about the possible "conflict of interest" in his serving on the County Board of Supervisors when a number of his relatives and associates were involved in developing land in the Chautauqua Valley, Szalla frowned thoughtfully, drained the remainder of his Sierra Lite, and said, fixing his warmly brown, kindly eyes on my face: "As I've said, Nikki, I see myself as an investor in 'home dreams.' In the Valley, where I was born. Where my great-grandparents settled, in 1899. The role of local business to plow back money into the local economy, hire locally and demonstrate faith in the future of this beautiful region that has suffered economically in recent years like much of upstate New York." Szalla spoke with a sincere sort of hesitancy as if these words were utterly new to him. I felt the thrill of his old-fashioned idealism. And I liked it that, as if he couldn't help himself, my interview subject (only my third, since joining the *Beacon* staff) was staring at my lacy red top with the 1930s shoulder pads, my very short very tight white cord skirt that had ridden up to mid-thigh, and my long slender legs that a second-to-last lover had described as skinny.

To conclude the interview, which had already gone beyond the spare forty minutes Szalla's protective secretary had granted the *Beacon*, I asked Szalla to describe his personality, and he responded with boyish enthusiasm, as if this was the very question he'd been awaiting. "As a boy, I was fascinated by machines. The way voices came out of the radio, and voices and images out of the TV, and all there was inside was wires, mostly! I loved to dismantle household things like vacuum cleaners, clocks, radios,

phonographs, even a TV, once: sometimes I could put the things back together and nobody knew what I'd been up to, but sometimes not. See, a
machine is a puzzle. Most people, normal people I'd suppose you might
say, just look at it from the outside, as its function. But to someone like
me, the machine is also a riddle: how does it work? why does it work?
who put it together in this way, and is this the most efficient way? Is there
something 'hidden' about it? Machines people take for granted are constantly being re-imagined, re-styled. Look at computers, that were once
massive. Any machine that's being manufactured, you can be sure that it's
already being re-styled in someone's imagination. As a little boy I could
spend hours poking around in my mother's appliances, I remember once
I dismantled most of the refrigerator when she was out, it was just the
most thrilling thing I'd done yet in my life."

"How old were you?"

"Maybe four."

"Four! That doesn't seem possible."

"Trouble is, I couldn't put the damned thing back together again. I
guess looking back at it, I might've been slightly autistic, or afflicted
with this Asperger's syndrome, I think it's called, where a kid, almost always a boy, becomes fixated on something, it could be baseball scores, it
could be counting how many airplanes fly overhead, it could be taking
machines apart and seeing their insides . . . I grew out of it, eventually. I
really don't have any talent for engineering or mechanics. So now I'm a
radio man, you could say that I'm inside the radio myself—one of those
mysterious voices. I tape most of my shows so I can listen to myself 'over
the radio.' And sometimes I perspire from just thinking as if my brain is
all cogs and wheels, a kind of crazy machine except it's also a flesh-and-
blood brain . . ." Szalla broke off, embarrassed. He'd been thinking aloud
as if he had forgotten the tape cassette, and me; as if he'd forgotten his
surroundings altogether.

I heard myself say, with a bright smile, "Well! It must be wonderful,
Mr. Szalla, to pursue your dream as an adult." Even as I spoke these in-
nocuous words they sounded phony and trite, insincere and tossed-

together as my conspicuous clothes which Clare was in the habit of calling (to my face as well as behind my back) "Nikki's costumes." Except
Wally Szalla smiled happily and reached over, as if impulsively, to squeeze
my hand. "Nikki, yes! That is what my life is about: pursuing my dreams
in the hope that they will be others' dreams, too."

His fingers closing over mine were warm. And strong.

The interview ended. I was shaky from the strain but I was very happy.
As I prepared to leave his apartment Wally Szalla hovered beside me smiling awkwardly and tamping down his unruly hair and finally he cleared
his throat to ask if I was free that evening for dinner?

"No," I said. "I'm not free. But after I make a brief call on my cell
phone, I will be."

Hours later we were still together. Still talking, or anyway Wally Szalla
was still talking. He was gripping my hand on the tabletop between us
and telling me that our meeting had been the strangest of his life.

I asked him why.

He said, staring at me, "Nikki, I think you know."

2.

Ridiculous! Wally Szalla wasn't my type.

Not a man at whom, in the street, I'd have glanced at twice.

Too old! Overweight, and losing his hair. No more glamour than
Dad's scruffy old moccasins.

Another woman's husband. And a father of three.

"Clare, I am not 'seeing' a married man, who told you such a thing! I
happened to interview Wally Szalla who's the new owner of WCHF AM-
FM, that's all. We've become friends, you know I have lots of friends and
this one happens to be separated from his wife and we've discovered that
we have some interests in common. That's all."

Clare spoke. At some length. I listened, until my face began to burn as if my sister had slapped me and my hand gripping the receiver began to shake. Even then, I was exceedingly polite. In the sweetest and most cordial voice you could imagine I said: "Wally Szalla is a remarkable man but there is nothing between us except friendship and in any case Wally is separated, there is nothing remotely 'wrong' in seeing him. You can tell Mom, too, in case she's wondering."

Nikki? Can I see you tonight? I know it's late and we didn't plan for tonight but I didn't go with Isabel and the children to visit my in-laws at Lake Placid after all and on the way back from the station I began to feel very lonely for you, Nikki, and I'm wondering if you are feeling lonely, too?

He brought flowers—"Corny, but can't help it." He brought CDs, blues classics by Nina Simone, Billie Holiday, Bessie Smith. He brought aromatic New Age candles for me to light. He brought champagne. He brought delicious pre-roasted chickens from The Food Shoppe and he brought a clutch of those miniature books called "inspirational": *Joy of Everyday Life, 101 Reasons to Love, The Zen Path of Enlightenment: Poems of Solitude and Wisdom.* Gravely he read aloud to me, holding a miniature book close to his face, like a character actor in a sweet, corny Hollywood film of the 1950s: William Bendix, Ernest Borgnine. " 'The song of the yellow oriole/echoes in the forest./Warm sun, gentle breeze,/willows green along the shore./The ox has no place to turn in the brambles.' "

"The *ox?*"

Wally frowned. "It's a Zen concept, I think. Searching for the 'ox' is a spiritual quest. Or the ox is the physical body, to be overcome."

"But why an *ox?*"

"Nikki, don't be so literal. It doesn't have to be an ox, I suppose, it could be, well—a bear, a deer. An elephant."

"Why'd we be hunting one of those? It seems so cumbersome, somehow."

There was something of Troy in my voice. It seemed to come naturally, teasing Wally Szalla when the man was trying to be serious.

Wally said, exasperated, "Make it an oriole, then! The point is, Nikki, the philosophy of Zen Buddhism is *now*."

"Now what, Wally?"

"Now *what*?"

Wally laughed, as if baffled, and ran a hand through his hair, and allowed his eyes to glide up onto me as if he'd been holding back his warm, brown, liquidy gaze.

By this time, exactly seventeen days since the interview, the two of us had some "history" between us, you could say. We had come pretty quickly to that point in a relationship between two people who essentially don't know each other very well when they are beginning to think that they like each other a lot and are mildly dazed by this revelation as you'd be dazed to take your temperature and discover that you were running a fever of 102°F and yet you'd been feeling normal, or better than normal. It's that stage when the two of you are still play-acting, a little.

Wally was saying, in the serious voice of the interview, "What Zen Buddhism means, as I understand it, is that 'now' is the realization of how precious life is. The ordinary things of life. Not that an ox is ordinary for us, but maybe for them. These poems are from long ago, I think. And it isn't an ox, as I said, it's, well—all things we don't notice, we're in too much of a hurry."

I laughed, and stretched. I was feeling frankly sexy. "*I'm* not in any hurry, Mr. Szalla. I'm mellow, like a Siamese cat in a negligee."

Wally sputtered with laughter. He never knew what I might come out with and I felt to myself like a leggy girl skater out there on the ice, free to improvise with every eye on her.

"You're laughing at me, yes? You think I'm too old for this."

"For what? Zen Buddhism?"

"For *this*. You know."

"Tell me: what do I 'know'?"

Wally laughed. His face was pleasantly flushed. Maybe he was thinking that, in Nikki Eaton, he had his kids again, the brash playfulness of adolescents when they adore you and wish you well and not the other, that hurts like hell. In the romantic-subdued lighting of my funky apartment, one of Wally's Nina Simone CDs playing in the background, I had to concede that Wally Szalla didn't look so middle-aged after all. In fact, with each sip of wine I was finding him more attractive, more my age and more my type.

It wasn't just Zen poems he'd brought me this evening. We'd shared a greasy roast chicken from The Food Shoppe, heated up in my lopsided oven, and German potato salad devoured out of the plastic container, and a loaf of Russian rye bread, and most of a bottle of Italian red wine that tasted as if it cost a little more than the "luxury" twelve-dollar wine with which I was more acquainted.

Wally said ruefully, "*This*. Me falling in love with you, and you a little bitty skinny girl scarcely troubling to hide your scorn."

"Oh."

"Oh, *what*? Surely you aren't surprised? Surely this isn't exactly 'breaking news'?"

I was taken aback a little, I hadn't expected this. My fingers made complicated by two-inch bright-polished nails I had to be overly conscious of, not wanting to crack the damned things, or chip off the polish I'd applied only that evening, these fingers fumbled for my wineglass on the carpet beside my bare twitchy toes. Again I murmured, "Oh!" as I nearly overturned the glass.

Falling in love. Men didn't say such things, usually. Or anyway not to me. Nor did I say such things to men. Usually. *Falling in love* was words from a blues song of the 1940s lamenting the fact, funky-funny but not to be taken seriously like lacy red tops with boxy shoulder pads, high-heeled sandals with leather straps that looped and tied around the ankles, disco hair. *Falling in love*: the punch line to a joke.

"If you want me to leave now, Nikki, I understand."

Wally made a move as if about to lurch to his feet. (He'd half-sat, half-collapsed into a sling chair. It was more a trap than a chair and not intended for a tall, stocky male.) By an alarmed gesture I allowed him to know no! I didn't want him to leave.

"What you've said has surprised me, that's all." I smiled, eager to make a joke of it. " 'Little-bitty-skinny.' That's a compliment, I guess?"

"And beautiful, Nikki. Mostly beautiful."

"Oh."

When I'd heard Wally's footsteps on the stairs outside my apartment, earlier that night, I'd quickly removed my phone receiver from its hook. I'd turned off my cell phone and my computer. I'd lowered the lights for a suitably "romantic" atmosphere. (The first thing you saw, stepping into my low-ceilinged apartment, were elegant old lamps, both table and pedestal, with rose-tinted shades or gauzy rose-tinted fabrics wrapped about their shades. The second thing you saw might be satiny wall-hangings, or antique-looking mirrors framed in brass or ivory. Deep-cushioned plush velvet settees, chairs draped with afghans (knitted by Mom in rainbow colors), and attractive carpets from the remnant store covering the ruined hardwood floor. The lipstick-red plastic table I used for a desk, my computer and printer, shelves of books, were in my bedroom, facing a window with southern exposure. This back-bedroom area was my "real" self, the other the "feminine." Most visitors never got beyond the "feminine.") Knowing that Wally Szalla was imminent, I'd felt my heart beat and plunge about like a bird trapped inside my rib cage. I'd smiled at my reflection in a mirror: "Nikki! Lookin' good." Now I was feeling confused and wishing almost that I was alone, to think these things through. The presence of an *actual man*, only a few feet away, staring at me, was disconcerting.

True, Wally Szalla and I had become "lovers"—we'd "had sex"—the kind of sex you'd call "promising"—still it was unexpected to hear Wally speak to me as if, suddenly, he wasn't play-acting but sincere. In a halting voice he confided in me that his separation from his wife Isabel was "painful" for him; it had been Isabel's idea, not his; though he'd come to think, since she'd asked him to move out of their house in May, three months before, that probably it was a good idea for them both. They had married too young, begun having babies too young. They'd been drifting apart for the past decade and needed to reassess their future: "If we have one."

Wally supposed that Isabel was right: he had a deeply flawed character. He was immature, irresponsible. He threw his money away on "harebrained hobbies"—"playthings"—like WCHF AM-FM; he neglected his serious business affairs, the myriad stocks and investments in Szalla family holdings that generated their real income. Wally was a "soft touch" who did favors for people who didn't deserve them, he lent money too readily without charging interest. His very friendliness in public annoyed Isabel: the way he shook hands, vigorously and with a big smile, like a politician. Wally believed that he and Isabel loved each other but were no longer *in love*. Wally could live with that, he had his work, he had a complicated and rewarding life outside the marriage, but Isabel's pride was hurt and (maybe) her vanity so she seemed always angry at him for something neither of them could help.

"Call it change, time. 'Fate.' "

Wally fell silent. He wiped his eyes on his shirtsleeve. Instinctively I reached over to squeeze his hand. He gripped my hand in his, tightly.

"And what about you, Nikki? You've told me so little about yourself."

What about Nikki! I sat very still, my mind struck blank.

Men rarely asked me about myself. As if my*self* apart from the sexy-flirty female gazing at them with adoring listener's eyes had not much existence. I was an ideal interviewer, asking questions of others. Frankly, I liked it that way. Nikki Eaton didn't greatly interest me. She never had, as the younger and less personable of the Eaton sisters. I'd always accepted it that my parents loved Clare better than they loved me, or anyway recognized that Clare was so much more accomplished than I was, even when we were girls. It seemed so self-evident to me, I wasn't even jealous. So now, Wally Szalla looking at me in that way of his, expecting me to confide in him as honestly as he'd confided in me, I could not speak. I could not confess that often I lay awake in the night wondering when I would be in love again, when I would have sex again, when I would have a "meaningful" relationship again, and sometimes I was tormented by these thoughts when I was in fact lying beside a warm slumbering male body.

Finally I told Wally that what he'd said about himself was true of me, in a way. Being "separated." Since high school I'd been involved with boys and men, I'd been engaged and almost-engaged and *in love* and *out of love* more times than I could count and right now you could say that I was *separated*: "From my past. Permanently."

"From your entire past? Or just—men?"

"My past."

"But you have a very supportive family, Nikki, don't you?"

"I *do*?"

"Well, your mother. People who know Gwen Eaton have told me so."

" 'People who know Gwen Eaton'—? Wally, who are these people?"

Wally shrugged evasively. Of course, he had friends in Mt. Ephraim. He had friends, acquaintances, associates and "contacts" everywhere in the Chautauqua Valley, and beyond. He was a Szalla, and the Szallas knew everyone. Of course.

I was made to feel like a small child who'd told a fib. Not an outright lie but something tiny and trivial, to make me blush.

"Well. My mother is special, I suppose. She's a terrific mom. One of those 1950s housewife-mothers who lives for her family, exclusively, hasn't much life of her own, but she's happy that way, or mostly. Now Dad has died and Clare and I are grown, Mom lives for the community, I guess. Her church, her friends. 'Other people.' She makes such a fuss over my work for the *Beacon*, you'd think that I was a best-selling novelist. She doesn't know me, really. She never has. And what she knows, she doesn't approve of. When Dad was alive I think she defended me against his disapproval but now that Dad is gone, and Mom is getting older, she's becoming more concerned about what she calls my 'future.' If she learns about you—"

Wally frowned. " 'Learns about me'—what?"

"Well. That I'm seeing you. And you're married."

Married. The word tasted sour in my mouth. I hated to be the one to utter it, as if in accusation.

I wasn't being altogether honest with Wally. (Are we ever honest with men with whom we're "involved"?) By this time I had reason to surmise, from reproachful remarks of Clare's, that Mom knew about Wally Szalla and me. Or knew something.

"I won't be married forever, Nikki. I'm fairly certain, Isabel and I are moving in that direction."

I wondered what this meant. What Wally meant it to mean, telling me. Still he was speaking in that somber, thoughtful voice, not at all affable, or playful. The corners of his mouth were downturned, ponderous. His eyes glistened. I had to suppose that divorce wasn't his idea, either.

"It's just—I've been hurt, Nikki. My wife has hurt me with the things she has said, and my children . . . You met Troy, I mean you had a fleeting glimpse of Troy in action. His older sister Katy is even angrier. And Andrew, our oldest, who's been flunking out at Colgate since he enrolled . . . They've made me feel as if everything I do is wrong, ridiculous somehow and pathetic. Mostly, I don't feel that I'm real. Some people think the world isn't real, other people aren't real, but me, I wake up in the morning thinking, Is this *me*? and the guy I see in the mirror sure isn't. If I could shave wearing a blindfold, I would. I'm afraid if I sneeze suddenly, I might disappear."

"Oh, sweetie. The size of you, you aren't likely to disappear."

I laughed, Wally was being funny now. We were getting back on safer ground. I went to Wally, as he struggled to hoist himself up out of the sling chair, and we kissed. It wasn't our first kiss but it felt like a first kiss, eager and awkward and wetter than you'd wish, like spaniels kissing. I slid my arms around Wally's warm, solid torso and I pressed the side of my face against the front of his white cotton shirt, the top of my head snug against the bottom of Wally's fleshy chin. I heard his heart beat slow, strong, certain, not rapid-fire like my own.

"My ox."

"Hmmm?"

"*My* ox."

By this time, well past midnight, the aromatic candles had mostly burnt down.

How quickly your life can change: a day, an hour.
And all the hours flowing from that, weeks and months. Years.

Not until January 2002 did I dare to introduce Wally to Mom.

Of course, by then Mom "knew." Whatever Clare had been telling her, or ominously hinting. *Why of course we haven't seen much of Nikki lately, you know Nikki: doing her own thing.* There was a network of female informants eager to tell Gwen any news of her wayward daughter living in Chautauqua Falls, but especially scandalous news. *Gwen! You know I hate gossip, I hate to be the bearer of upsetting news but I think you should know, I mean in your place as Nikki's mother I would certainly want to know, that Nikki is involved with this married man over in Chautauqua Falls, he has three children, he's separated from his wife, he's one of the Szallas, he's twice Nikki's age or anyway much older, his car is always parked outside her apartment and it's there in the morning . . . Gwen? Did I upset you? Are you still there, Gwen?*

So I imagined. Probably, the reality was worse.

On a clear, very cold, chalky-smelling winter day Wally and I drove to Mt. Ephraim, to take Mom out for an early dinner at the historic old inn on the river and afterward to a spirited Bach chorale at the Mt. Ephraim Arts Center, performed by students from the Rochester Music Conservatory. I'd planned this evening for weeks: initially in my head, as a fantasy of bringing together the two people who meant the most to me in all the world; then, with Wally; and then with Mom. Gwen had been reluctant to meet my "current man friend" but at last she'd given in, and as soon as they met and shook hands and Wally was his usual kindly, cordial, smiling self, I could feel Mom's distrust of him melt away.

Seeing how Mom looked up at Wally Szalla, blinking and smiling, as if she'd been expecting someone very different, I realized that Wally was probably reminding her of my uncle Fred Eaton, one of Dad's younger brothers whom we didn't often see and who had, like Wally, a boyish-battered face and a stocky build. *Trust me!* Uncle Fred's warm brown eyes seemed always to be urging.

"Mrs. Eaton, I've heard so much about you from your daughter, who adores you. It's an honor to meet you at last!"

Mom laughed, blushing. "Well. I'm not exactly the Queen of England, Wally. Please call me 'Gwen.' "

" 'Gwen.' 'Gwendolyn.' A rare beautiful name."

I'm not sure if it was a coincidence, but Mom had begun listening to WCHF AM-FM recently. Her favorite programs were "No Holds Barred" and "Afternoon Pop Classics." ("Night Train" came on too late for her. Most evenings, Mom made it a point to read for at least an hour before turning on TV to her favorite cable channel, Animal Planet. She was in bed by nine-thirty.) Wally was cheered by Mom's enthusiasm for "No Holds Barred" and suggested that Mom come visit the radio station sometime, he'd introduce her to the call-in show hostess whose name was Gloria Silberman. "Gloria would love to meet you, Gwen. She could interview you on the show."

Mom said, startled, "Interview *me*? Oh, dear. I don't think so."

"But why not? Gloria interviews all sorts of women, not just 'career' women."

Mom shook her head, laughing.

"On the radio? Live? I'd be tongue-tied. I couldn't think of a thing to say."

"You won't know until you try, Gwen, will you? There's always a first time. I'd never tried my hand at being a D.J. until 'Night Train' and as soon as the sound engineer signaled me I was *on the air* I just started talking. You'd be a natural, Gwen. I'll call you one of these days. When the weather isn't so unpredictable. You and Nikki could both appear on 'No Holds Barred,' Gloria would love it."

For much of our dinner in the elegantly spacious candlelit dining room of the Mt. Ephraim Inn, Wally drew Gwen out in a way I had never witnessed. At family gatherings, no one had much bothered with Gwen Eaton, Jon's wife; but then, no one had much bothered with any of the wives. Conversation was limited to a very few, predictable topics: weather, food, family/neighbor/household problems. But here was Mom talking with Wally Szalla about radio and TV programs they'd liked when they were young, and almost you'd have thought that Gwen Eaton and Wally Szalla were of the same generation. Wally had the uncanny ability to so empathize with others, he seemed to mirror them. He and Mom talked animatedly of Frank Sinatra, Perry Como, Rosemary Clooney, "Young" Elvis. Mom spoke of having seen a production of *West Side Story* in Rochester in 1964, when she was sixteen: "That song 'I Feel Pretty' is still in my head! I hear myself singing it sometimes, even now." Wally asked Mom if she and her husband had enjoyed dancing and Mom said, "Oh, I loved to dance! In high school, I mean. I'd just dance with other girls, mostly. Jon was older, you know—seven years older than me. He was always so serious. His attitude was, 'Jumping around like a lunatic isn't my idea of a good time, Gwen.' But really it was because he didn't want to try anything he couldn't already do well, in any public way."

"Is that it, Mom? That was the reason?"

"The reason why your father didn't try many things," Mom said, sighing. Wally had insisted upon pouring a little white wine into her glass, and she'd been sipping at it; something she'd never have done if Clare and I had brought her here. "You see, he didn't want people 'looking' at him. He didn't want people 'laughing' at him. All the Eaton men are like that. Jon needed to be perfect, so he didn't have to be anxious. Trying new things, being vulnerable to making mistakes, made him very anxious. He needed things to be perfect around him, too. At Beechum, and at home. That was why he was such a reliable employee at Beechum, and, at home, why he kept up home repairs almost before they were needed." Mom laughed, almost giddily. "My friends complained how their husbands were so slow to get things fixed but not Dad! If the furnace was just 'acting funny,' he'd call in the repairman. If there was a single drip from a ceiling, he'd call in the roofer. And remember how upset Dad was every spring at the dandelions in our neighbors' lawns? Because the fluffy little seeds would blow over onto our lawn, there was no way to keep them out."

Wally said quickly, "Well, that kind of personality is needed in the world. Otherwise we'd have chaos."

We were talking so animatedly, with such outbursts of laughter, diners at other tables glanced in our direction, smiling. Mistaking us for a family?

Wally would say afterward, he hadn't expected my mother to be so young. And vivacious. I thought it was something of an exaggeration, "vivacious," but it was so, Mom's skin was glowing, she'd put on lipstick for the occasion, she was wearing a pale green dress of some crinkly-velvety material that brought out the color of her eyes and around her neck was a necklace of small jade stones, I'd found in a thrift shop and given her for one or another birthday. For the occasion, I was wearing a velour top Mom had sewed for me, dark lavender in a tunic style, that fitted me rather loosely; of the items Mom had made me over the years, the tunic tops were the most glamorous. My ears were studded with piercings, my fingers flashed with inexpensive glittery rings. There was a fever in my usually pale-sallow skin. *You can always tell when Nikki's in love* girlfriends of mine were given to say and maybe this was so.

Without my wishing it, talk had turned to my "journalism" at the *Beacon*. Of course, Mom saved every article and interview that appeared under my byline in the paper, and friends and neighbors supplied her with extra clippings, for "Nikki Eaton" was about as famous as anyone was likely to get in Mom's social circle. Both Mom and Wally were lavish in their praise of my writing which made me want to hide my face in my napkin. "Oh, please!" Mom must have scrutinized my interview with Wally Szalla, which had appeared months ago, for she had questions to ask about it, and one of them was whether the interview had been when we'd met?

"Yes, Mom. That was exactly when we met."

I reached over, and stroked the back of Wally's hand. The gesture was affectionate and possessive and not so spontaneous as it appeared but I wanted my mother to see *I am serious about this man, this man is special.*

For Wally had filed divorce papers, finally. His lawyer and his wife's lawyer were "negotiating."

There'd been a difficult time, at Christmas. Wally had felt obliged to spend much of the holiday with his children whom he'd been, as Isabel charged, neglecting. And so we'd had some painful discussions. And I'd been emotional, which wasn't like me. Or wasn't the way I wished to be. But now in the New Year 2002 things were much improved. Much!

I was telling my mother about a suggestion I'd made half-seriously to my editor at the *Beacon*, that I travel to Europe in the summer and write a column for the paper, "Mt. Ephraim Abroad." It would be comical in tone but serious, too, with travel tips and suggestions. "My editor is enthusiastic, he thinks travel agents will want to advertise in the paper. But he can offer only a 'limited budget' and I know what that means."

Wally said, "I'll stake you, Nikki. It sounds like a terrific idea to me."

Mom was smiling at me, uneasily. Any talk of "travel"—"going away from home"—made her uneasy. Impulsively I said, "I'll take you with me, Mom. We can travel together. We never have, just the two of us. You always did want to see Paris, and Rome, and Daddy was never very enthusiastic."

Mom shook her head, frowning. No, no!

"Mom, why not?"

"Since what happened at the World Trade Center, I'd be afraid to fly. And I'd be anxious about you flying, too."

"We'll go by boat, then. A romantic crossing of about five days."

It was pure impulse. I was becoming carried away, having had a glass or two of wine in the company of the two people who meant more to me than anyone else in the world, who couldn't help but smile at me indulgently as if Nikki were the bright brash child to be adored, encouraged, and yet sensibly restrained.

"Well, Nikki. Maybe."

"Mom, I'm not going to let you get away with pretending to be *old*. Because you are not *old*. You are what's called middle-aged, which is practically the average American age now. Young!"

I'd taken Mom's hand, which was small-boned, and surprisingly cool. The more I thought about taking Mom on a trip, the more excited I became. After Dad's death, Clare and I had vague plans to "take Mom somewhere" but these plans had never materialized, for Clare was always busy; and Mom, in her timid/stubborn Kovach/Eaton small-town way, hadn't encouraged us. But now, the prospect of taking my mother to Paris, Rome, maybe Spain, the two of us traveling together, had seized my imagination; and maybe, just maybe, for of course this was a vital part of my fantasy, Wally Szalla would be traveling with us, too. Wally would certainly be traveling with us. By summer, which was more than five months away, Wally would be divorced. Wally would be "free." In fact, the trip might be a honeymoon. On "Night Train" Wally would joke about his honeymoon with his mother-in-law. He'd be sweet and charming and funny and bring tears to listeners' eyes.

Tears flooded my eyes now. Surreptitiously I wiped them with my linen napkin, leaving a mascara smear.

Seeing that Mom was becoming uneasy, Wally shifted the subject to vacations closer to home. Mom told him of our Star Lake cottage in the Adirondacks, where the Eatons had gone for years. How lovely it had been, and how peaceful—"Except when the girls got to be teenagers, and lost interest. They hated to be separated from their friends so it all came to an end."

"Oh, Mom!" I laughed. "Ancient history."

"Well, your father and I weren't about to go alone. And Key West, where we'd been on our honeymoon, this beautiful old 'historic' inn called the Windward, we were always planning to go back, but never did. Jon promised for our thirtieth anniversary, but we never quite made it."

Mom spoke with a wistful smile. How like the elder Eatons: *never quite made it.*

"Did you enjoy the roast chicken, Gwen?"

"Oh, yes! Thank you, Wally. It was delicious."

Though she'd managed to eat only about one-third of it. As usual, Mom had ordered the least expensive entree on the menu. I was relieved that she hadn't launched into her familiar refrain of how overpriced restaurant food was, the Mt. Ephraim Inn especially, when chicken was a Bargain Buy at Pennysaver this week, sixty-nine cents a pound . . . I was relieved that Mom hadn't engaged our waitress in conversation, establishing that she and the waitress's mother had gone to school together, or the waitress's elderly grandfather was one of Gwen's swimmers in the Senior Swim Club at the Y . . . At the end of the meal Gwen glanced around for the waitress, her purse in her lap, wallet in her hand; I knew that she was going to insist upon paying for her "share" of the dinner, but Wally, dear suave Wally, had anticipated all this without my having to tell him.

"Gwen, I've already settled the bill. Shall we leave for the concert?"

The look on Mom's face! So surprised by Wally Szalla's maneuver, which no Kovach/Eaton from Mt. Ephraim could have imagined, she hadn't a chance even to protest.

That night, after the Bach concert, after taking Mom home and driving back to Chautauqua Falls, Wally stayed the night with me as he'd been doing lately on weekends. And in the morning, while Wally was shaving, I called Mom trembling with excitement.

"Well! What did you think of him, Mom? Isn't he *nice*?"

My voice was lowered, surreptitious. There was a pause before Mom replied.

"Nikki, no. I don't think that your friend Wally Szalla is 'nice.' "

Mom spoke so quietly, I almost didn't hear her. I'd been smiling in expectation of a very different response and now my face froze.

"You—don't? Oh."

Mom was saying that Wally Szalla seemed "nice." Of course. About the "nicest" man she'd ever met, except for Dad.

"But he isn't, Nikki. Obviously."

"He isn't?"

"Nikki, the man is an adulterer. A hypocrite. A manipulator. He has made my lovely sweet daughter into a—an 'other woman.' I was awake all last night thinking this, and how wrong it was for you to ask me to meet him, and for me to accept. Oh, I feel just terrible! I couldn't say one honest word to either of you, I just—'made conversation.' I am so ashamed of my*self*. But, Nikki"—Mom's voice lifted alarmingly, as if she were about to miss a step on the stairs— "I intend to send you a check made out to that man, to pay for my share of our dinner bill."

I was so stunned, the receiver slipped from my fingers.

Nikki, your mother is a lovely woman!

Except she seems a bit lonely.

Why don't we see more of her, Nikki? Take her out again, sometime soon?

I liked her so much, I hope she liked me.

Yet there was the night, months later. Wally said, "Nikki, I need to move back with Isabel for a while, there's been a crisis," and I felt a sensation like a knife going in, through my ribs—not a sharp knife but something crude and dull. And I thought *Sure. That's the way this was always going.* And I thought *Mom knew.*

There was more but I'd stopped listening. The word *Isabel* was repeated in the man's guilty faltering voice but I wasn't listening. *Hospital, overdose, needed at home* and again *crisis* and when he came to hold me I stood still and stiff and calm in his arms, and I didn't cry, and I tried not to sound sarcastic when I said, "Why doesn't this surprise me, Wally?" but I think I did.

Sound sarcastic, I mean.

3.

"Darling Nikki! Climb in."

He drove me back to Chautauqua Falls. He rescued me from my sister's house. He would arrange, he said, for someone to pick up my car and drive it back to me in the morning.

When news of Gwen Eaton's death was first released, Wally had called me immediately to leave a message on my machine—*Nikki. I'm here. Let me know when you want me*—and I had not responded. All thoughts except of my mother had been pushed out of my mind.

He knew not to talk. He knew to touch, to hold, to hold tight. At the brownstone he knew to half-carry me up the stairs when I stumbled and in my third-floor apartment that was chilly and airless on this mild May day as if its tenant had been absent for months instead of less than a week he knew to lie with me on my bed and hold me in his arms and let me cry. For I was falling, breaking into pieces. I had thought that this grief had happened already and that I had overcome it as I had urged the frightened white dove out of its cage to fly away out of the cemetery for I would be strong from now on as Clare was strong, and after Dad died, as suddenly and unexpectedly as Mom was to die, Mom had been strong, Mom had not been weak and self-pitying. But I was made to realize now that grief would come in waves and there would be wave after wave, there was not a single massive wave to be overcome or even endured, I'd been mistaken for I had had to flee my sister's house in my weakness, and in my weakness I was pleading, "Don't leave me again, Wally. I need you so. Don't go away, Wally, ever again." And Wally said, "Nikki, I won't. I won't leave you, I love you." In the crook of his arm, against his fleshy rib cage. My face pressed against his chest, feeling the coarse wiry hairs through his shirt-front. The warmth of the man's body, and the comfort of his body, the strong hard beating heart.

4.

"We'll work things out, Nikki. This time, I promise."

"smoky is waiting"

Your mother's big gray cat is with us, Nikki. Safe and sound. Any time you want to come get him, Smoky is waiting.

Of the many calls on my answering machine this was the most welcome: *Smoky is waiting.*

The call was from Frannie Haber, a neighbor on Indian Village Road. Frannie and my mother had been friendly for years and were approximately the same age though Frannie had let herself go—"let herself go" was an expression I'd hear repeatedly in my young suburban life, it had connotations of a frazzled female running mad in the street, tearing at hair and clothes and screaming obscenities though in fact it meant nothing nearly so exciting, only just young-but-fattish women, not-so-young-and-fattish women, who took time only to smear lipstick on their mouths, push back their perm-damaged hair and forget it. The Habers' daughter Ruthie was a classmate of mine and my off-and-on friend since grade school. Half the time Ruthie and I couldn't stand each other and half the time we were close as sisters. Or almost.

When I spent time at Ruthie's, she warned me about her mother— "My mom will ask you questions like she's our age, so chill her out. She's fun, sure. She can be. But you can't trust her, that's what I learned. I bet you can't trust your mom, either."

I wanted to say *Mind your own mom.* Instead I laughed.

"You'd have to be a real dope, Ruthie, to trust anybody with your secrets. Including your so-called girlfriends."

Now I was thirty-one years old. I hadn't seen Ruthie in years. I hadn't seen Frannie Haber in more years. I'd lost my mother. I was desperate to retrieve my mother's cat. Fumbling the phone, close to breaking down, I called Frannie Haber back and told her I'd be over to pick Smoky up the next evening. Thank God, Frannie had called me and not Clare. I could imagine Clare crying, "Who wants that cat! Take that damned cat back to the shelter!" and slamming the receiver down.

It was tricky to return so quickly to Deer Creek Acres. I plotted my route in the way of a military strategist hoping to avoid snipers and land mines. If I entered the subdivision by Lilac Way, I could take Pinewood Drive to Indian Village, and avoid Deer Creek Drive entirely. I wore over-sized dark glasses that left red marks on my nose, I wore the sporty green canvas hat with WCHF AM-FM in white letters, the station gave away for promotional reasons. This hat I pulled down on my forehead, to shield my tear-corroded face. In a frantic mood I decided to wear black nylon slacks that fitted my buttocks to advantage, at least I'd been so assured by one or another male acquaintance, and I wore a fuchsia satin shirt with COWGIRL stitched in black above the left breast. I wore plastic-looking sandals. I seemed to have left off my glittery jewelry. I began, then gave up on, "makeup." (What is it we make up when we apply makeup? Do we "make" up something that isn't there, or do we "make up" for something that is, we couldn't bear otherwise? I wished I had Mom to ask, she'd have taken the silly question seriously.)

My silly-Nikki questions. Who would take them seriously, now.

Anyway: I threw together a costume. The dark glasses and the hat were most helpful. My face was a loss, forget the face. Puke-pale and swollen as with a mouthful of infected teeth. I plunged out of the house into some kind of mocking sunshine hoping people would not stare at me in the street *Oh God there's the Eaton girl, the one whose mother was murdered.*

. . .

"Why, Nikki! Sweetie."

As soon as I stepped inside the Habers' house and was greeted by
Frannie Haber in a crush of a hug, as Ike Haber, rubbing his jaws in sympathetic misery, looked on, there came Smoky mewing anxiously and
nudging against my ankles, and when I picked him up, he kicked a bit
but began purring loudly, you might say frantically, his glaring cat-eyes
fixed on my face. "Smoky! Where were you, I was so worried about
you . . ." Suddenly I was happy. As Frannie and Ike looked on, I was becoming very happy. I might have laughed aloud, as a child laughs out of
sheer happiness.

Thinking I would bring Smoky back home. I would hurry to show
Mom. *See? He was never lost, what did I tell you.*

For we'd had lost-cat scares, over the years. A few.

They hadn't always turned out happily, though. Not like this.

Smoky was kicking more energetically now. I had to be embarrassed,
he was behaving as if he didn't know who the hell I was.

Frannie was saying apologetically, "Oh, he wouldn't eat! You can feel
his ribs, almost! He was hiding in our garage behind the lawn furniture,
at first we thought it was, oh, a wounded rabbit, or raccoon, except we
heard mewing, we had no idea whose cat he was, where he'd come from,
I left food and water for him in an open place but he wouldn't touch it,
even when no one was around. But then—"

Ike Haber interrupted, "—my idea, to put out tuna."

"—real tuna, like for humans—"

"—and boy oh boy did he eat that, gobbled it down—"

"Oh but, Ike," Frannie felt obliged to correct her husband, "he threw
most of it up, he'd gobbled so fast. Though, later—"

"—when he came inside the house, finally—"

"—just ran in, when I opened the door—"

"—like somebody had called him he trusted—"

"—he did eat some cat food, dry food out of a box—and this 'Tender

Vittles' kibble, he liked. And he drank so much water, the poor thing was *so thirsty*—"

"—he knows nobody is going to hurt him here, but still—"

"—the least little noise he runs and hides—"

"—we weren't sure whose cat it was, except—"

"*I* knew it was Smoky! I knew, and Smoky knew me, I swear the poor thing ran to our house because he knew he'd be safe here—didn't you, sweetie?"

Frannie was stroking Smoky's tomcat head, for a panicky moment I thought the cat would erupt out of my arms hissing and clawing but thank God he did not.

The Habers looked on, sorry for me. An adult woman behaving as I was behaving pressing my face against Smoky's fur. And it wasn't soft fine fur, it was coarse, slightly matted fur. And Smoky wasn't behaving like a loving-rescued cat, he was behaving like an almost-crazed cat. He was purring loudly, like a noisy air conditioner. He was kneading his claws in my hair, and in my satin cowgirl shirt where he was doing damage, yet I managed to carry him out of the Habers' kitchen even as, with seeming sincerity, Frannie Haber was inviting me to stay for supper, sniffing and wiping at her eyes, and poor Ike Haber was blinking and staring (at my snug-fitting black nylon slacks, how could any reasonably normal man fail to stare) and swallowing hard wracking his brains for something sensible to say to me that wouldn't provoke his wife into outright bawling, still less me. All Ike could come up with was, with ghastly enthusiasm, "Be sure to come back and visit again, Nikki, real soon!"

to nikki with love

"We will. We'll—start soon."

"Next Monday."

"Next Monday! Yes."

We were adamant, Clare and me.

We were breathless as girls plotting a risky adventure in a way that, as sisters growing up in the house at 43 Deer Creek, we had not been for we'd never been allies. My older sister would have disdained any adventure undertaken with only just *me*.

"Rob says he wants to help. He thinks we'll be overwhelmed, exhausted. But I don't want him, Nikki, do you?"

Clare spoke so fiercely, I was grateful to be spared telling her in no uncertain terms *We don't want an outsider touching our parents' things.*

"No, Clare. I wouldn't feel right with Rob, either."

"Of course he's right, we need to clear the house and clean it and put it on the market before it's midsummer, and people don't look at houses. Every realtor I've spoken to has said this. But Rob doesn't think we're capable right now, he thinks I'm still upset. 'Not yourself, Clare.' " Clare laughed harshly, enjoining me to ponder how ridiculous this was.

I laughed, it was ridiculous. That Clare Eaton could ever be anyone except herself!

Clare fumbled in her purse for a cigarette. She had not smoked since she'd been pregnant with Lilja and she often boasted of this fact yet some-how, since what had happened to Mom, she'd begun smoking again.

What happened to Mom was how we alluded to it.

Sometimes, we had only to say *it*.

Or, uttering the word *Since*—in a certain tone of voice and breaking off with a wincing expression, no need to utter a syllable more.

"—yesterday I think it was, or maybe it was Thursday, after taking Lilja to her dance class, driving on Lincoln Avenue downtown, I saw Mom's car?—the way sometimes I did, you know?—and Mom and I would honk at each other and wave as we passed. And, well, I saw this car, exactly like Mom's except it wasn't." Clare paused, not knowing where to go with this. She'd been recounting the story with a bemused frown to signal that it was a story on herself meant to illustrate a radical and puzzling alteration in her normally faultless behavior. "—And next thing I knew, I had a cigarette in my hand. I didn't even realize I'd bought a pack!"

Clare laughed. She was wearing glasses so dark I could almost not see her slitted eyes.

I wasn't sure how to react. Frankly, I didn't believe it, not the part about discovering a cigarette in her hand.

Vaguely I murmured what sounded like "Me, too."

"*You?* Since when did you stop smoking?"

Clare's voice was sharp. I had to wonder if we were quarreling.

It was a Saturday in late May. Clare and I were sitting in Clare's car parked in front of 43 Deer Creek Drive. We were not parked in the drive-way but at the curb, and Clare had not yet turned off the motor. It was shocking to see the grass so grown and ragged and weedy and the drive-way littered with newspapers and flyers. Neither of us wished to sigh aloud *If Dad could see this—!*

Clare had forgiven me, to a degree. For my "rude"—"immature"—"typical Nikki behavior"—on the day of our mother's funeral. For days had passed. Each day passed slow as a train of lumbering rattling boxcars but once it was past, the day seemed to have gone swiftly and there was regret in its wake. "Something I forgot to do . . ."

Clare picked a piece of tobacco off her tongue, peering at me through her dramatic dark glasses.

"Nikki, what?"

"What?"

"You said something."

"No. That was you."

"Just now? That was *you*."

We were annoyed with each other. Almost, we didn't need a reason.

The modest redwood-and-stucco ranch house at 43 Deer Creek Drive was our joint inheritance. Our mother had willed her estate to both of us equally. I hadn't wanted to tell Clare what I'd felt, that Mom really should have left three-quarters of the estate to her and her family, and one-quarter to me, for fear that Clare might have quipped, "Well, you could correct that, Nikki, couldn't you?"

I'd driven to Mt. Ephraim thinking that Clare and I were to begin our task of sorting, clearing, cleaning the house today. Our parents' property was no longer designated as a crime scene, the shiny yellow MT. EPHRAIM POLICE DEPT. tape had been removed and the redwood-and-stucco house was again available to us. Arrangements had been discreetly made through the police chief Gil Rowen who'd known "Feather" and "Johnny" in the old days for a private contractor from Rochester to clean those parts of the house and garage that had been despoiled, that Clare and I would be spared these sights.

Soon there would come to be the pretense between Clare and me, that I had not "seen" anything that Clare had not seen. I had not blundered into the house, and into the garage. I had not been the one to see our mother where she'd been struck down.

As Rob had offered to help Clare and me with the house, so too Wally Szalla had offered to help. "It may be rougher than you think, Nikki. And it always takes much longer."

I'd thanked Wally but declined his offer. He had no idea how my mother had disapproved of him. How upset she'd have been to know that, after her death, Wally Szalla might enter her house and "go through her things."

I'd prepared myself for today but it seemed we were going to begin on Monday. Clare was one to change your mind for you without your consent and then to chide you for it. "Monday, you'll be prepared, Nikki? Promise."

"Well. Monday after work."

"How long after work?"

"Maybe six? I'll try to get here by six."

"Six! That's impossible for me."

"But—"

"Nikki, I have a family. *I* have responsibilities."

Clare turned the key in the ignition and her car leapt forward. She was very annoyed with me as if I'd misled her. I tried to make amends: "Wednesday afternoon, I can come early. I can be here by one o'clock. Is that better?"

"Wednesday is Foster's soccer game. And Lilja has something after school called 'Hi-Lo.' You know that Wednesdays are horrendous for me, Nikki!" Ashes from Clare's cigarette scattered onto my clothing, into my hair. I flinched seeing that Clare was driving much too fast for these narrow suburban streets.

I said, "Maybe Thursday? I can ask for the entire day off."

"Please do! And don't forget to let me know."

Clare spoke reproachfully as if forgetting to inform her of my days off from the *Beacon* was a familiar failing of mine.

We were both trembling. I'd been gripping my cell phone in my moist hand, though it was switched off and Wally Szalla could not have called me if he'd wished.

Clare said, exhaling smoke through both nostrils, "Yes-sss. Next Thursday might work out. We'll get to the house early and if we don't become distracted we should be able to finish it all in one day. And between now and then we'll have time to"—Clare braked at an intersection, nearly having run a stop sign and collided with another car—"prepare ourselves."

By the time we returned to Clare's house, Clare was in a good mood. We were both feeling we'd narrowly escaped some danger. I understood that Clare had forgiven me for my most recent bad behavior when she instructed me to reach inside her handbag and see what she'd brought me.

It was the beautiful little tarnished-silver watch I'd left behind at her house, broken. The watch with the midnight-blue face. Clare hadn't only returned it to me, she'd had it repaired at the jeweler's.

I was touched. I hadn't expected this. Clare was always so busy and breezy, and this meant she'd taken time for me. I thanked her for her thoughtfulness and asked how much I owed her?

"Don't be silly, Nikki. All you owe me, you'd never be able to repay."

It was a joke of course. Between sisters.

The delicate hands on the midnight-blue face read 4:17 P.M. I held the watch to my ear, I heard the minute ticking.

Turning it over I read the finely-engraved inscription *To Elise with love*. For a fraction of a second I felt a childish pang of disappointment as if I'd expected to see *To Nikki with love*.

"remanded for trial"

Yes. I attended the preliminary hearing in the Chautauqua County Courthouse on June 1, 2004, where the murderer of Gwendolyn Eaton, an individual named Ward Lynch, twenty-nine years old, of no fixed address but with family ties to Erie, Pennsylvania, was officially remanded for trial— "To be determined at a later date."

It was at this hearing that I saw my mother's murderer for the first time. I swallowed hard, I stared. I felt a terrible weakness in the pit of my stomach. Beside me Clare was rocking in her seat and making a low whimpering noise like a dog in pain and though we'd been instructed not to stare at the man, not to risk making eye contact with him, we stared, we blinked and stared and could not look away for the first several minutes of the hearing.

"Oh! He's so ordinary."

This was me, whispering in Clare's ear.

"So—nothing. *Oh.*"

I was groping for Clare's hand. My frantic fingers closed about hers that were icy-cold, in a tight grip.

Ward Lynch was brought into the courtroom walking in stiff baby steps because his legs were shackled at the ankles. His arms were shackled at the wrists. He was a tall bony-faced man with pitted skin, ropy-greasy dark hair straggling between his shoulder blades, haggard eyes. The corners of his thin-lipped mouth were downturned into a smirk. He had a bumpy receding forehead and a narrow receding chin and his chest looked caved-in. *Wasted* was the druggie word. *Strung out, burnt out, meth-head.* The kind of guy who isn't young any longer but isn't grown up, either. Drives a motorcycle when he has the money for it, works at a gas station or with a lawn crew. You'd see him having a smoke outside the 7-Eleven. You'd see him hanging out at the mall, eyeing girls half his age. Hiking along the interstate in the rain. You'd see his sulky face in a WANTED BY F.B.I. notice in the post office.

You wouldn't want to see that face confronting you on a deserted stretch of city sidewalk. As you climb out of your car in a darkened parking lot, or in your own garage.

Much was made of the fact that Ward Lynch had served three and a half years of a five-year sentence at Red Bank State Prison Facility for Men, on a charge of auto theft, burglary, and check-forging. That he'd been paroled for "good behavior." That he'd lived in halfway houses, in homeless shelters in Buffalo and Rochester, he'd been enrolled in the Christian Fellowship Out-Reach Program and it was in this program that he'd initially met Gwendolyn Eaton.

"Oh. I hate him. Oh, Nikki."

Clare was squeezing my fingers so hard, I expected to hear a sudden crack.

Ward Lynch was a murderer and yet: he'd been gotten up in a bright orange clown suit. A child might laugh at him, missing the expression in his face. In a public place, he'd have been the center of attention. In this courtroom that was predominantly men and every man wore a suit, dress shirt, necktie, Lynch was wearing an oversized orange jumpsuit like TV footage. Like the Oklahoma bomber Timothy McVeigh. On both the front and back of Lynch's uniform was CHAUTAUQUA COUNTY MENS DE-TENTION in black letters.

What wasn't ordinary about Lynch was what he'd done. The use he'd made of his hands.

You would expect to see monster-hands. Oversized brutal hands. But these were ordinary hands, though with bony knuckles. I saw discolorations on the backs of both hands like deep bruises.

Lynch's face was flushed. He'd been made to look foolish in public. Shuffling to a seat at the front of the courtroom, every eye on him. He'd lurched, and sat clumsily. His mouth that looked like a rubber band pulled thin quivered.

Beside Lynch, a harried-looking man in his forties, Lynch's public-defender attorney, murmured into his ear as Lynch stared into space. The prosecutor who was trying the case had told us that Lynch's attorney had been reluctant to accept him as a client, but had had no choice. Very likely, the attorney would advise Lynch to plead guilty in exchange for a sentence of life in prison without parole, sparing Lynch the likelihood of a death sentence, and sparing us all a trial.

Clare had objected to this, initially. She'd been tearful, vehement: Mom's murderer deserved to be executed.

After she'd had time to think it over, after Rob and I had reasoned with her, Clare agreed. Let him plead guilty, let the state put him away for the rest of his life.

I hoped this would happen. I didn't believe in capital punishment.

I didn't want to hate Ward Lynch. It was hard for me to hate, the way Clare hated. I didn't want to hate anyone. Our mother had taught us to see the "good" in people and while I doubted that there was much "good" in Ward Lynch, I knew that Mom would not have hated him, her very murderer.

Probably, knowing Mom, she'd have figured out a way to "forgive" him.

Beside me, Clare leaned around to stare at Ward Lynch. I'd stopped looking at him, I'd seen enough. I held Clare's left hand while Rob, seated on her other side, held her right hand. She was quivering, trembling. In Clare, hatred was a force like a geyser. I could feel it building up, aching to discharge. Of the two of us, I had always been the "emotional" one but that was only on the surface.

People had told Clare to avoid the hearing, her presence wasn't necessary. Of course, she'd had to attend. I'd been told that, as soon as my testimony was over, I might leave. But I would not.

The hearing began twenty minutes late, and passed in a buzzing blur. There was nothing exciting or dramatic about it. A calm recitation of facts. As the "witness" who had found Gwendolyn Eaton's body, I was required to testify under oath. I had told my pathetic story a dozen times to various official parties and each time my words had been taped and yet, here I was testifying again. Yes: I'd entered my mother's house at 43 Deer Creek Drive on the early evening of May 11, 2004. Yes I'd entered the house through the kitchen door, that was unlocked. Yes I'd seen signs of "intrusion and upset" inside the house. Yes I'd entered the garage and yes, I saw—on the cement floor of the garage, I saw—

I began coughing. I could not stop coughing. Tears leaked from my eyes though I wasn't crying. Out of the buzzing blur someone, a man, a man whose name I had forgotten, handed me a glass of water. I was called *Ms. Eaton*. I was told to *take my time*, to *speak clearly*. I saw that everyone in the courtroom was observing me, listening to me. The judge, an older man seated at a slightly raised desk to my right, wearing an ordinary dark suit and not judicial robes, appeared to be listening sympathetically. I continued my testimony, gripping my hands in my lap. I'd memorized these words as a tightrope walker might memorize each inch of the high wire she must cross, and cross again, and again re-cross without daring to glance down. I'd been coached by the prosecutor and was looking toward him as I spoke, I did not want to glance at Clare, or at Rob, or at anyone in the courtroom whose face was familiar to me; above all, I did not want to glance over at the defendant sitting slump-shouldered in his bright orange jumpsuit who was staring at me.

"Thank you, Ms. Eaton. You may step down."

In that instant, as I was released from my ordeal, I lifted my eyes to glance in Ward Lynch's direction, and for a fraction of an instant before I looked away our eyes locked.

I stumbled back to my seat, to Clare. I had seen in Ward Lynch's eyes nothing but glassy belligerent emptiness.

The prosecution attorneys had warned me not to look at Lynch, and Wally had warned me. *Look at the attorney who is questioning you, look at the judge. But not the defendant. Don't make eye contact!*

Now I was frightened, my heart was beating hard. Until this moment I had not thought *If he could, he would hurt me. He is a murderer, he would hurt me, too.*

"Nikki! I love you."

Clare gripped my hand tight to pull me close beside her. Clare slid her arm around my shoulders to comfort me, for I seemed to be crying after all. I was shaking, I was so frightened. Why had I glanced at Ward Lynch, when I'd been warned not to! Somewhere at the rear of the courtroom my lover Wally Szalla was seated, he'd insisted upon coming to the hearing for he was concerned for me, why hadn't I looked for him!

I was shaking, I was so frightened. How naive it seemed to me now, how childish, to think of "forgiving" Ward Lynch—as if the man wanted to be forgiven, and by me.

As if I had the power to make him repent. As if anyone had the power.

I was made to realize: if I'd returned home while Lynch was still in the house, if I'd walked into the house or the garage, having seen my mother's car in the driveway and calling *Mom? It's me, Nikki* as I'd done a thousand times, Lynch would have killed me, too.

Of course. This was so obvious.

I must have known, and yet I had not wished to comprehend. I had wanted to think that, now the murderer had been arrested, and would stand trial, it was in my power to "forgive" him. At any rate, not to press for his execution.

Of the witnesses for the prosecution who followed me, the plain-clothed Mt. Ephraim detective Ross Strabane gave the most detailed testimony. Strabane had spoken with me on the phone several times about the upcoming hearing, but I had not seen him in weeks. I had forgotten what he looked like. His skin was olive-dark, swarthy. His eyes were earnest. He was edgy in the courtroom, aware of the judge's frowning scrutiny: he had a maddening habit of squinching up his face in the way of an edgy teenager, and he cleared his throat compulsively. His clothes! Earnest, off-the-rack. A stone-colored suit with oddly wide lapels, white nylon shirt and braided necktie in smudged-aqua. (Braided neckties? Where did men find these? Somehow, Dad owned several, and persisted in wearing them often. His brothers Herman and Fred favored braided ties, too.) Strabane was sitting square in the witness seat as he spoke, leaning slightly forward out of nervousness. Or maybe he was excited. I was touched to see that he wore mismatched socks: both were dark but one was just perceptibly striped and the other not.

Reaches in a drawer, he's in a hurry, distracted. Puts on his socks not noticing they're a mismatch.

Or, seeing they are, he's got more important things on his mind and what the hell.

Strabane was describing the "events" of May 11, 2004: the actions of the defendant Ward W. Lynch from approximately 10 A.M. onward. In his nasal accent describing Lynch's behavior after he had "abducted" Gwendolyn Eaton who'd given him a ride in her car, until police arrested the defendant in Erie, Pennsylvania, on May 13, at the home of his maternal grandmother Mrs. Ethel Makepeace.

I found it difficult to listen to the detective's testimony. I found it difficult to continue to watch him. I thought *I don't have to hear this!* I felt a strong impulse to lower my head, my forehead against my knees, I was very tired suddenly, frightened. It was the sensation I'd sometimes had as a girl, at the end of a diving board. *I don't have to do this, I can turn back. I don't have to be here.*

. . . the discovery of Gwendolyn Eaton's 2001 Honda, and her Visa credit card, emptied wallet in a barn on the Makepeace property. The discovery of the "murder weapon": a Swiss Army knife bearing traces of Gwendolyn Eaton's blood, as identified by DNA testing, and covered in Ward Lynch's fingerprints.

The buzzing in the courtroom grew louder. I was gripping Clare's hand that was cold and sweaty as my own. My eyes had begun to hurt. I was frightened of what the detective would say, I was frightened of his knowledge. I could not bear listening to him. Yet I understood, *He is a good man. He is helping us.* I was having trouble concentrating for I yearned to be somewhere else. I was smiling, I was already somewhere else. Mom would comfort me, if I could find her. But Smoky would comfort me, too. I knew where to find Smoky. He was waiting to rub against my ankles when I returned to the apartment. He would purr loudly. If a cat can purr anxiously, Smoky would purr anxiously. He would purr aggressively. He would purr seductively. He would purr percussively. He would purr like a jealous lover. A mildly deranged lover. Oh, I smiled to think how I would discover in my bedspread, a quilted spread of squares, triangles, and pineapple figures that Mom had sewn for me, the warm imprint of Smoky's burly body, and a scattering of silvery cat hairs.

". . . may step down, Detective. Thank you."

Was it over? Strabane's testimony? I opened my eyes, disoriented. Strabane was looking grim, yet elated. He'd spoken well, he'd been forceful and persuasive. He'd presented "facts" as a narrative of what-had-happened. He was a professional, the rest of us were amateurs.

Especially Clare and me. "Daughters of."

Amateurs in grief.

Afterward I would remember: Detective Ross Strabane passing close by us. He was feeling good about himself, was he! A homely man made impressive, on the witness stand. Except his stone-colored suit fit him oddly in the legs, the trousers slightly too short. And the smudged-aqua braided tie, a fashion blunder. His dark-lashed eyes slid onto mine. His mouth wished to twitch in a smile.

I am your friend, trust me!

I looked quickly away.

. . .

In all, the hearing lasted three hours, forty minutes.

Like squeezing out your blood drop by drop. Those three hours, forty minutes.

"Prosecution" witnesses. Called to the witness stand, sworn to "tell the truth, the whole truth, and nothing but the truth so help you God." Uniformed police officers, plainclothed officers, forensics specialists, the proprietor of Tiger Mart on Route 33, garage attendants, store cashiers, a county sanitation worker who'd discovered, in a Dumpster behind Hal's Mobile Service at the intersection of Routes 33 and 39, a plastic bag crammed with bloodied men's clothing to be identified as belonging to Ward Lynch. During some of this testimony, Lynch squirmed and shifted in his chair like a restless teenager. He scratched at his caved-in chest, he shivered. But during some of the testimony, his face was slack as unbaked bread dough. His narrow jaw drooped, his mouth twisted suddenly into a yawn he didn't trouble to hide with his hand.

Seeing that yawn, Clare whispered in my ear, "Oh! He's *bored*! I want that man *dead*."

At the time of his arrest, Ward Lynch had "voluntarily confessed" to Mt. Ephraim police officers but later, after acquiring a lawyer, he'd "recanted" his confession. Now, Lynch's lawyer (who was looking grim and defiant, like the coach of a badly losing team) announced that his client would not be testifying. There was but one witness for the defense, Lynch's grandmother Mrs. Ethel Makepeace, a stocky woman in her midsixties with ragged-looking tea-colored hair and a belligerent manner with even her grandson's lawyer. On the witness stand Mrs. Makepeace declared shrilly that her grandson Ward had not only been staying with her for "all of May" in her home in Erie, Pennsylvania, but on that day, May 11, he'd been "always never" out of her sight for twenty-four hours. Lynch's lawyer asked quizzically, " 'Always never,' Mrs. Makepeace? Do you mean, 'almost never'?"

Ethel Makepeace sneered at him. Her hair had an explosive look that contrasted with her creased, tired-looking face. "You know what I mean, mister, don't you be putting words in my mouth, any of you. My grandson Ward did not plunder and kill any lady up here in what's-it-called, I am here to swear on a stack of Bibles he *did not.*"

The judge ruled that charges against Ward W. Lynch were not to be dismissed and that the defendant was remanded for trial, the date for which would be set on another day.

The hearing ended. Ward Lynch in his glaring-orange jumpsuit was led away by guards, hobbling in shackles. Mrs. Makepeace had to be restrained by bailiffs, shouting: "What? What is going on? Where are you taking my grandson? I told you, Ward is *innocent.*"

Suddenly, I wanted to be with Mom.

I wanted to run away from everyone, to be with Mom.

We staggered out of the Chautauqua County Courthouse and into the startling sunshine of a day in early summer.

So exhausted! And this had been only the "preliminary" hearing.

On the pavement in front of the mournful limestone courthouse Clare and I were surrounded by well-wishers. Some of these were relatives who'd crowded into the small courtroom to show their support, others appeared to be strangers. But by this time I knew to pretend that I recognized faces, for probably I'd met these people at Mom's funeral or Clare's luncheon. I was learning that public grief is a social responsibility, you can't hide your face like a child or turn away crying *For God's sake leave me alone, I am so tired!*

We were being told that it wasn't likely that there would be a trial, since evidence was overwhelming against Lynch. Possibly his lawyer could try a plea of not guilty by reason of temporary insanity caused by methamphetamines but that wasn't likely either, Lynch's lawyer was a sensible person who'd never let the case come to trial.

"But maybe there should be a trial," Clare said, "and let jurors decide. If our mother's murderer should be executed."

Weakly I said, "Oh, Clare. No. I don't think I could endure a trial. I was only up there a few minutes and I'm wiped out and I don't even want to think about it, ever again. *No*."

"Nikki, you will do what you have to do. For Mom."

We were headed for the parking lot at the rear of the building. We'd come in separate cars but I knew that Clare wanted me to remain with her and Rob for a while, before they drove back to Mt. Ephraim. I wondered if Clare had noticed Wally Szalla amid the crowd and if she was expecting me to introduce her to him. ("Your friend" Clare alluded to Wally, sometimes in a wicked mood, "Your married friend.") And I knew that Wally, gregarious Wally Szalla who wanted everybody to love him, was eager to be introduced to my sister and brother-in-law.

Wally was never to know how my mother had disliked him. He'd have been heartbroken since he'd liked Gwen so much and had been devastated by her death.

Lately, Wally had been spending several nights a week with me in my brownstone apartment. Sharing me, as he said, with Smoky-the-cat. (Wally was mildly allergic to cat dander, we'd discovered. So Smoky was welcome in my bed only on those nights when Wally wasn't there.) Our days were spent apart for Wally was enormously busy with the radio station and other responsibilities, he traveled frequently to Rochester, Buffalo, Albany and New York City. Since the so-called crisis of several months ago his wife Isabel had decided, yes she wanted a divorce, but on her terms, and these would be mean-spirited and acrimonious terms, but at least negotiations were moving forward now, finally. More and more often Wally and I were seen together if mostly in romantically dim-lighted inns and restaurants in the Chautauqua Valley and weekends out of town. "I'm your 'other woman,'" I teased Wally. "The one you can't bring home."

Wally had said, "I've been expelled from that 'home.' It's time for me to make another."

I hadn't wanted Wally to come to the courthouse that day. Not because I was ashamed of our relationship but because I was concerned that, if I broke down on the witness stand, Wally would want to come forward to comfort me. Wally was an emotionally extravagant and impulsive man who sometimes behaved in ways not in his own best interests.

Well, I hadn't broken down. A coughing spell, but I'd managed to continue. *Nikki you were wonderful! You spoke so bravely* I could hear Mom insisting.

Outside in the bright sunshine my eyes were aching. Clare had slipped on her oversized dark glasses that were both stylish and a little sinister, white plastic frames and near-black lenses. We were in the parking lot now, Rob was jingling his car keys and asking if I'd like to have a drink with them, we all needed to unwind didn't we!

In the corner of my eye I saw Wally Szalla on the sidewalk, hesitating. Waiting for me to acknowledge him.

Oh but I loved Wally Szalla! And yet.

Clare nudged me in the ribs: "Nikki. Your friend."

In this way, without my needing to make a decision, the matter of introducing Wally Szalla to the Chisholms was decided.

"the house where the lady was murdered"

So disappointed! Clare's car wasn't in the driveway, or anywhere in sight.

It was ten days later. Ten days after the hearing. Thursday morning, 8:38 A.M. I'd driven from Chautauqua Falls to Mt. Ephraim to meet Clare at Mom's house, to begin our task of sorting through her things, house-cleaning, preparing the house to be sold.

Strange how calmly we spoke of these matters. Clare had a way of saying *Putting the house on the market* as if the house we'd grown up in was only just *the house* and not something more.

On the market was a neutral matter-of-fact term. It was one of Rob Chisholm's terms, brisk and businesslike.

Arriving at 43 Deer Creek Drive and seeing that Clare wasn't here yet, I tried not to be upset. Not to be angry. Parked my car in front of the house. (Not in the driveway. Nowhere near the garage. Though I understood that the garage had been "thoroughly cleaned.") The redwood-and-stucco ranch house with its flat graveled roof was looking forlorn and vacant. Someone had drawn blinds shut over the plate-glass "picture" window, like a large clumsy bandage.

The house where the lady was murdered. So neighborhood children would speak of it, staring as they bicycled quickly past.

Thank God, Rob had arranged for a lawn service crew to mow the raggedy grass around the house and to clear away the worst of the weeds

springing up in Mom's flower beds. I knew that neighbors had been picking up newspapers and flyers from the driveway, which was kind of them,
but still litter was accumulating.

It's as if, in a neighborhood where there is an empty house, litter just
naturally accumulates around it: blown into shrubs like confetti, wrap-
pers and Styrofoam cups and advertising flyers in the stubby grass.

It wasn't Thursday June 3 as Clare and I had originally planned but
Thursday June 10. We'd had to postpone our meeting at the house because after the court hearing we'd both been sick for several days ("flu"
was the catchall word, "a touch of the flu" as Mom would call it) but we'd
had a definite plan for this morning.

Clare had even insisted on arriving before me, to open up and "air out"
the house, that had been empty now for almost a month. "No problem for
me, Nikki! I can't sleep past dawn anyway." There was the unspoken acknowledgment that stepping into our old house might be harder for me
than for Clare.

Except: where was Clare?

She'd suggested that I arrive at about 8:30 A.M. We would work
through the day. Naively we believed that the task of "sorting through"
our parents' possessions might be accomplished in a day.

Mom had never gotten around to seriously sorting through Dad's
things, we knew. It hadn't been a task either Clare or I had much wanted
to help her with.

I waited for a few minutes, listening to WCHF FM on the car radio,
some National Public Radio news, and a startling interlude of "Opera
Highlights" (Maria Callas as Tosca), but Clare didn't show up and so I
called her on my cell phone.

Five rings. No answer. I wanted to cry, this was so frustrating. My
brother-in-law's genial recorded voice clicked on *Hello! No one can come to
the phone right now but if you wish to leave a message . . .*

"Clare? Are you there? Please pick up, Clare. This is Nikki."

As if Clare needed to be reminded who I was!

I tried to speak calmly. Since what had happened to Mom, my

behavior with others was divided, not equally, between Calm Nikki and Gone-to-Pieces Nikki. I was having some luck keeping the Gone-to-Pieces Nikki private, now that Wally Szalla was more reliably in my life.

"Clare, I'm at the house. I guess I should start without you. I hope nothing is wrong over there. Give me a call, will you? You have my cell number."

Actually it felt good to be angry at my sister. There is nothing like a wave of indignant anger toward a bossy older sister to dissipate panic.

I stuffed my cell phone into my pocket, got out and crossed the lawn. Vaguely I was headed for the front door. *Not the kitchen door! Mom's tinkly little sleigh bells overhead.* But maybe I should wait for Clare, before I went inside. I'd brought plastic garbage bags, for trash. Clare was bringing more bags, plus boxes and cartons. We assumed that Mom had a store of garbage bags (in the garage) as well as boxes and cartons in the attic. And Mom had plenty of cleaning supplies in the house, as well as a new light-weight vacuum cleaner to replace the bulky old vacuum she'd been thumping and thudding around the house with for years.

Go inside. Use the front door. Hurry!

What was I afraid of, the house was certainly empty. The front stoop was littered with yellowed old flyers, newspapers. Though Gwen Eaton's mail delivery had been discontinued, the mailbox beside the front door was stuffed with junk mail.

I began to toss things into a garbage bag, with a kind of fury. My heart was beating so strangely it felt like choked laughter.

It was 9 A.M., and then it was 9:20 A.M., and no Clare.

For today's adventure in Mt. Ephraim, I was wearing comfortable old clothes. Not Funky-Chic Nikki but Grab-Bag Nikki. Sleeveless black T-shirt, khaki shorts, WCHF AM-FM hat pulled down over my now-flattened punk hair. I had to suppose that neighbors were aware of me, those who were home. Deer Creek Acres was that kind of place, you might describe as vigilant/concerned or plain nosey depending on your mood.

As an older teenager, I couldn't wait to escape. But since what had happened to Mom, people in this neighborhood had been so warmly supportive, so genuinely grieving for Mom, I'd had to re-think my old feelings.

Clare was less certain. She was beginning to think that Mt. Ephraim was making almost too much of Gwen Eaton, so many people claiming they'd been her best friends. Clare had thought maybe we should go through Mom's things at night, with the blinds drawn, in the hope that no one would see and come to bother us.

I told Clare no thanks! That sounded like a terrible idea.

Clare said she hadn't been serious. Of course.

As Clare had said she hadn't been serious, a flippant remark she'd made about Wally Szalla, after meeting him the other day in Chautauqua Falls.

So that's Wally Szalla! He doesn't look the type.

I was drifting about the yard picking up fallen tree branches. My legs felt weak and I was beginning to sweat. More and more I seemed to be feeling someone watching me.

The Highams were home across the street, no doubt. And there was Mrs. Pedersen next-door, her station wagon in the driveway.

Young mothers pushing children in strollers, in the street. Dogs trotting beside them. Nikki Eaton had been gone from Deer Creek too long for any of these young women to know me, but possibly they'd known Gwen Eaton.

The house where the lady was murdered. They would not utter such scary words to their children yet somehow their children would know.

Schoolbuses had arrived and departed in the subdivision. There wasn't much local traffic, delivery vans and repairmen. Each time a vehicle appeared on Deer Creek Drive I glanced up expecting to see Clare's car, and each time I was disappointed.

Back of the house, the lawn crew had cut the grass in crooked careless swaths. Debris from a recent storm lay scattered everywhere and Mom's flower beds were choked with weeds. Her purple and and yellow irises, her beautiful roses. We'd teased Mom about fussing more over her flowers than she did over us. (Though it wasn't true.) Mom said, "You're not stuck in one place like flowers. If you get thirsty or crowded with weeds, you can do something about it."

I tried not to think how shocked Mom would be, if she could see how things were deteriorating.

Dad, too. He'd been the one to really fuss over the house, more obsessively than Mom.

In my room at the back of the house, sometimes I'd hear my father whistling as he prepared to mow the grass. (We'd never had a professional lawn crew. Most people did their own lawns in Deer Creek Acres.) Once, when I was about twelve, I squatted by my window and whistled through the screen like an echo, and Dad whistled back, assuming at first (as he said afterward) that it was a bird.

A bird! We'd teased Dad over that for years.

Poor Mom never could whistle. She'd try, pursing her lips as we instructed her, but all that came out was a feeble hissing sound. But Mom hummed and sang to herself, outdoors as well as indoors.

How they'd cared for this modest property, Gwen and Jonathan Eaton! And now it would be sold. Placed *on the market*, in the hope that strangers might buy it.

The house where the lady was murdered. In a town as small as Mt. Ephraim, it might be difficult to find these strangers.

Our backyard was defined by a four-foot redwood fence that had come to look permanently waterlogged. Probably it was rotting, and would have to be replaced. Mom had grown morning glories, climber roses, clematis and sweet peas in profusion on this fence. I was tugging at a willow branch that had fallen into the climber roses when I heard someone behind me.

"N-Nikki?"

I turned, startled. It was Gladys Higham.

"Oh, I'm sorry! I didn't mean to creep up on you, Nikki."

My heart beat hard and sullen *Go away! Leave me alone!* but of course

I forced myself to greet Gladys with a smile. I had to be polite, I was Gwen Eaton's daughter.

Gladys was wearing a shapeless floral print dress, cotton socks and crepe-soled shoes of the kind Mom had worn. Her heavy legs were waxy-white. Except for her tight-permed bluish hair that fitted her head like a cap, she was looking slack-bodied, blowsy. Older than I'd ever seen her looking. She approached me hesitantly as if uncertain of her welcome.

"Oh, Nikki! I saw the car out front, I—I thought it must be one of you—you, or Clare."

Gladys hugged me, and I tried to hug her back. I held my breath against the faint chemical smell of her hair.

"Nikki, dear, you're *thin*. You are taking care of yourself, I hope?"

There was no avoiding conversation with Mrs. Higham. To deflect questions about me, I asked how she and her husband were, and Gladys told me. I asked after her children, and grandchildren, and Gladys told me. I was certainly sincere. Mom would have been pleased with me. I hoped that Gladys didn't notice how impatiently my toes were twitching inside my sandals.

Now I was more disgusted with Clare than ever. Where the hell was she!

"—Walter was saying just the other day, 'I suppose the next step is, the Eaton house will be sold. And no telling who will move in.'"

Gladys spoke anxiously. Her large pillowy sliding-down bosom heaved with a sigh.

"Well, yes. Neither Clare nor I would ever live here, it's only practical to sell the house."

"It is practical, yes! But so sad."

Damned if I was going to apologize. My smile persevered.

"Your mother and father lived in that house for at least thirty years. I remember them when they were so *young*! Walter was saying, 'It isn't a good real estate market right now.' Something about interest rates?"

Gladys spoke slowly, doggedly. Behind her bifocal glasses, her eyes brimmed with moisture. I dreaded this stout elderly woman bursting into tears, and making me cry, too; I dreaded her hugging me again, or even touching my arm. As in a nightmare I was forced to recall how desperately I'd run to her, into her kitchen. How I'd interrupted this innocent woman's life. Those chittering canaries, parakeets. I'd upset them, too.

There was an intimate bond between Gladys Higham and me, I could not bear to acknowledge.

"Gwen just loved this house! All her growing things. She was just the happiest woman, you know, Nikki. I loved to hear her sing. She loved people, and she loved life."

I murmured yes, that was so. But now—

"—except Japanese beetles, Gwen did not love. Oh, those nasty things, eating our rosebushes." Gladys laughed, sadly. " 'Why did God make Japanese beetles, Gladys, do you know?' she'd ask, and I said, 'Same reason He made rattlesnakes.' Walter, he'd say, 'Same reason He made Bill and Hillary: to test us.' " Gladys laughed, shaking her head. "It breaks my heart, to see her irises in that state. And her American beauties, in that bed there. When my daughter Liddie had her trouble, you know, two surgeries in six months plus Dwight Junior falling off that railroad trestle and breaking both legs, it was Gwen who always asked after her. *That* was Gwen."

"Gladys, I know. But now, if you don't mind . . ."

"The funeral was lovely! So many flowers. And the music. And that minister spoke so wonderfully, I don't agree with people who say he talks too much. I know, Clare doesn't like him. I can understand that." Gladys spoke quickly, as if making amends. The flesh of her upper arms was so white, and so terribly raddled, I had to look away. "And Clare's luncheon, so lovely. What brave girls you are, you and Clare! Walter was saying, he'd never seen such a large party in a private house. So many people we didn't know. Your sister's house is quite something, isn't it? The rooms are extra-big, and even the furniture. And that swimming pool in the back! Walter was saying, he wouldn't want to pay taxes in that neighbor-

hood. But I gather Rob Chisholm has a good job at what's-it-called—
Coldwater Electric? Gwen used to say. *I never was one for swimming, like
Gwen.* People said she was the most wonderful—patient—instructor at
the Y. Her seniors adored her! After your father passed away, you know,
Gwen was at the pool every morning. She told me, 'In the water you feel
so free.' "

Politely I murmured yes. I'd gone back to picking up storm debris and
shoving it into a garbage bag.

Glady's chatter was a sincere form of grief. I supposed.

Mom hadn't approved of Dad brusquely cutting off neighbors who
tried to engage him in inane chatter. She'd scolded Clare and me for being obviously restless, in the presence of prattling elders. There is just no
excuse for being rude to anyone, Mom believed. Because you never know.

Never know what? I'd asked.

What might come out, to surprise you.

"—never told the police, or anyone. Not even Walter. I wanted to,
Nikki, but—"

I looked around to see Gladys all but wringing her hands. Suddenly I
understood that my mother's friend had something to tell me.

"—just couldn't. Because I wasn't sure. The police questioned me and
made me so nervous, Walter was listening and Walter is always correct-
ing me because I get things wrong, but he gets things wrong, too!—
goodness, even my grandchildren do. But when you're my age, that's
when people notice. Over and over in my mind I tried to remember what
I'd seen. I do remember Gwen backing out of the driveway that morning,
I know it was before 10 A.M because I'd just gone out to hoe in the peony
bed. And Gwen stopped the car and called out, 'Gladys, why don't you
come with me? It's my crafts class, out at the mall. A bunch of us have
lunch afterward.' And I just wasn't dressed, you know. I mean, it wasn't
the right time for me, right then. Now he's retired Walter is at home
mostly all day, he'd want to come with me. And he'd complain afterward—'So many women yakking.' I'd told Gwen I wanted to take a crafts
class at the mall, I'd been telling her for a long time and she'd always

invite me, but it was never the right time, I guess. And that day, Gwen was probably just being polite. But if I'd gone with her!" Gladys paused, wiping at her eyes. Her face was flushed as if with exertion. "What happened would not have happened, would it? He would not—that man— wouldn't have come over to Gwen's car—if there'd been two of us."

I stared at Gladys, astonished. Had she been blaming herself? For such a thing? As if any of this could be her fault.

"—and later, when Gwen came home, I mean, when I saw her car—"

"You saw Gwen come home? With—*him*?"

This was something none of us had heard before. No one in the neighborhood had told police they'd noticed Gwen drive back to the house, to her death.

No one seemed to know whether Lynch had forced my mother to drive back here, or whether he'd overpowered her somehow, had her captive in the car and drove back himself. Or possibly, naive as she was, Mom had voluntarily driven her murderer back to the house, for some "sensible" reason: having hired him to do lawn work, or handyman work as she'd hired him the previous summer. When Lynch had impulsively confessed to Mt. Ephraim police, he hadn't provided such details.

"Nikki, that's what I don't know. It's all a blur to me. I think I saw Gwen's car pull into the driveway, like she'd come home early from the mall. Like maybe there wasn't a class, or she'd forgotten something. The strange thing was, she didn't park where she usually does in the driveway but halfway inside the garage which I noticed because—why'd anyone do that? Unless it was raining and you wanted to go inside the house through the garage door. But it wasn't raining. And really I wasn't exactly seeing any of this, at the time. I wasn't paying that kind of attention. Gwen was always driving that car! She was always going somewhere, and coming back from somewhere. Since your father passed away . . . She was kind of lonely, I think. But of course, Gwen loved to be busy. So many activities! Church committees, and her swim class for seniors, and the arts council, and hospital volunteer, and there's some friend who'd get her to sub for her at the public library, Gwen was always willing to help out.

And of course her crafts classes, and Garden Club, and seeing friends for lunch or if they were sick, Gwen was so faithful to her friends, even the most awful people, nobody else could stand. Well, I don't get out the way I'd like. Gwen was always after me. Except there's Walter, he's jealous of my women friends, he's even jealous of our children having more to say to me than to him, but what would they say to him, he's always complaining! Well, Gwen had her own special way of seeing things. They said she'd had a hard life in her own family, her mother dying young like she did, and the Kovachs not having much money, but I never knew that from her. Sure she missed your father, they'd been sweethearts since high school. Except maybe Jon was older. Oh, Gwen never complained of being lonely! 'Jon and I had thirty years together,' she'd say, 'I would be so selfish, to want more.' She meant it, too. Gwen meant these things she'd say. She had so many friends who loved her. Of course, some of them, I won't name any names, they took advantage of her good nature, and Clare was onto one or two of them, I remember. And Gwen had her church. And she could visit Clare, anytime. Or almost anytime. She said she had a 'standing invitation' for Friday evening dinners, at the Chisholms'. She could see her grandchildren, living right here in Mt. Ephraim. *My* grandchildren, I get to see twice a year if I'm lucky. And Gwen was so proud of you, Nikki, writing for the *Beacon*. Wednesdays when the paper came in the mail, she'd be so excited looking to see if—"

"You didn't see him, Gladys? You didn't see anyone in the car?"

"I—I don't think so. I don't see that well, dear. If I did see something, I might not have known what it was. Shapes are just blurs, sometimes. It's like my grandchildren 'surfing' the TV channels, I can't see to keep up. But if I'd looked harder!—if I'd seen a man driving your mother's car, a strange man, I would—I might—I don't know what I would have done but I—I might have done something. I might have called Gwen—I might have gone over, to check. I might have called 911." Gladys paused, pressing both hands against her bosom. She was breathing heavily. "I've never called 911 in my life! Not once. Until you came to use my phone, I'd never even known anyone who had. So maybe, I would not have called

911. I'd have been afraid, I think. Walter, too. 'Don't get involved' is what he's always saying. Like, you're a witness to a traffic accident, if you give your name to anyone you can be called as a witness, you have to show up in court, or they can arrest you! So Walter would not have called, or wanted me to call. And if I'd seen a man, I might have thought it was some repairman. Like that exterminator man who'd come by, Gwen had had what she called an 'ant invasion.' Well, he showed up in his van, with cartoon bugs painted all over it. 'Scourge of the Bugs'—some catchy name like that. All over this neighborhood every weekday there's TV repairmen, plumbers, roofers, furnace men. You wouldn't give a second glance to any of them. Your poor father had the worst luck, Gwen said, with furnace men: either they didn't come when they said they would, or they didn't come at all, or, if they did, they'd repair the furnace wrong, and make things worse. So, if I'd seen a man over here, I might not have taken any special note. And later, Gwen's car was gone. I'd gone inside by then, and when I came out, the driveway was empty. And the garage door was down. And if I'd thought about it, which I doubt that I did, I'd have thought that Gwen had just gone back out again, which was not so unusual. Now the garage door down, that was unusual, but I didn't think anything of it, I guess. My mind was on other things, you see. We have health problems, I won't go into. Walter's blood pressure, for one. Just that," Gladys said, her stout soft body beginning to quake, "—I might have done something, and I know it. I might have saved Gwen, somehow. Oh, I know this, Nikki! I will always know it, in my heart."

Gladys began to cry. I held her, and comforted her, and managed not to cry. Not just then.

"sorting through"

Next morning, Clare was at the house when I arrived.

It was 8:20 A.M. The front door had been opened wide, as if to welcome me. Radio music was playing inside, loud. Cardboard boxes and cartons had been stacked just inside the vestibule. There was an air of bustle and excitement as my sister swept at me, hugging me in a rib-bruising embrace even as, in virtually the same gesture, she pushed me away, laughing: "Sweetie, you look like a *ghost*. For heaven's sake, this place isn't *haunted*."

It wasn't like my sister to be so effusive greeting me. The quick little hug was in mimicry of our mother's hug but neither of us seemed to know how to perform it, without Mom.

Clare was looking herself. Nothing like a ghost. Her fleshy moon-face had been made up to appear poreless and of no age unless you peered closely, which of course you would not. Her mouth was a moist red wound. Her eyes glared like reflectors. For our day of scruffy work sorting through Mom's things she was wearing a crisply ironed white cotton shirt tucked into belted trousers. The trousers were herringbone, with a sharp crease. All that was missing was a perky little Ann Taylor matching jacket.

"Well, come *on*. I've been wondering when you'd get here."

Clare grabbed my hand, unexpectedly, and pulled me toward the back of the house. This was Mommy-Clare, as she'd been with her children when they were younger. I had a vague jangled impression that furniture in the living room had been pulled out from the walls and slightly rearranged. The bulky carpet had been partly rolled up, exposing bare floorboards. In the TV room it looked as if cushions had been removed from the leather sofa and Dad's well-worn recliner chair and then carelessly replaced. In the center of the dusty TV screen was a glaring yellow Post-it.

"I've been tagging things. I've been clearing out closets. As soon as I arrived, I threw open every door and window to freshen the air. In Mom's and Dad's bedroom—well, you can see! I've been laying out things for us to decide what to do with: what one of us might want to keep, what we can sell to a thrift shop, and what to give to Good Will Charities for their resale store."

Clare spoke energetically, hands on her hips. I was disturbed to see our mother's clothes in a heap on the bed. Mom's familiar "outfits," some of which she'd sewed herself. And underfoot, wire hangers Clare must have dropped without noticing.

"What's this, Clare?"

It was a creased photo of Dad as a young man in his early thirties. I almost wouldn't have recognized him: his hair was thick and dark and grew in startling sideburns on his cheeks. His smile was faint, as if about to be sucked back into his cheeks. His eyes were quizzical, bemused. *Who are you, what do you want of me?* he seemed to be asking.

On the back, MARCH 1972 had been noted in pencil.

"I found it beneath Mom's pillow, Nikki. I wonder how long she'd kept it there."

Beneath Mom's pillow! Oh.

I turned my attention to the clothes heaped on the bed. I was blinking tears from my eyes. Our parents had never seemed to be sentimental about wedding anniversaries, or about each other, at least not in our presence. Dad would not have wished it.

A refrain of Dad's when we were growing up was *Now don't make too much of things!*

I said, "Why Good Will, Clare? Shouldn't Mom's things be donated to her church?"

"No."

" 'No'? Just—'no'?"

Clare was being stubborn, I knew that bulldog set to her face.

"But you know she'd want that, Clare. She was always giving the Christian Fellowship things."

"I don't care what Mom might want. She was deceived by those people, you know how credulous she was. I will have nothing to do with that charlatan 'reverend' of that charlatan 'church.' Kindly do not mention that man's name, or the name of that church, in my presence ever again."

It would only have provoked my furious sister to point out that I hadn't spoken Reverend Bewley's name or the name of the Mt. Ephraim Christian Life Fellowship Church.

"He's lucky that I haven't sued him. If it wasn't for you and Rob, I would."

Clare had me drag more cardboard boxes into our parents' bedroom. Underfoot were plastic garbage bags looking hungry to be filled as boa constrictors. Smaller boxes, some of them containing Mom's jewelry, were on the bureau; this was an "heirloom" bureau, solid carved mahogany that had once belonged to our father's parents.

Briskly Clare said, "We'll divide the jewelry. Mom had only a few good things, most of it was costume jewelry, and 'crafts.' She didn't itemize anything in her will. You have your favorite pieces, and I have mine, and they're not likely to be identical."

"Lilja will want something of her grandma's, too."

"Oh, Lilja! Of course. I can pick out something for her, I suppose."

Everywhere were Clare's Post-its. On the bureau mirror, a yellow Post-it. Another on the headboard of the bed. On the shade of a not-new bedside lamp, a green Post-it. "Red means good enough for one of us to keep, yellow means 'sell!' and green means 'donate-to-charity.' I'd appreciate it if you didn't switch the Post-its around, Nikki, any more than you have to."

Mom had been one to use Post-its in her attempt to organize the chaos of domestic life, but Clare, even as a child, had soon surpassed her. By the age of eleven, my sister had become obsessive about keeping lists—tasks, homework, favorite friends, clothes-to-be-worn-in-rotation-at-school—which she kept posted on the walls in her room.

Some of the Post-its Clare was handing me now looked as if they'd been pre-used, and replaced in the pads. Several had even been written on and the words neatly crossed out.

Meaning that Clare was so frugal, she saved old Post-its. Dad, who'd saved "lightly used" tissues and paper napkins, would have been pleased.

"Be sure to tag everything, Nikki. Don't just toss things into a box. I know, there's so much! You have to just narrow your eyes, like looking through a rifle scope, and proceed! I have about fifteen boxes here, I'll get more if we need them. Rob says, 'Remember, you can't save everything.' He's right, we don't have room. And you don't have room. Beautiful old things like this mahogany bureau—we have to be merciless, and sell them. In Mom's will she left us everything fifty-fifty but really, Nikki, you can take as much as you want of these 'personal belongings.' We'll sell the car, assuming you don't need it, now you seem to be driving a decent car and not that rust-bucket Datsun, and we'll split the money, whatever it is. Rob says he'll make arrangements with the Honda dealer. I thought this morning we'd start with easy things, lighter things like clothes, bed linens, Mom's arts-and-crafts, and later we'll get to the furniture and appliances. Mostly everything will go, I think. Not that Dad's and Mom's things aren't attractive, in their way, but, well—they wouldn't fit in my house."

I heard a faint prideful emphasis to *my house*. Often I'd noticed this curiosity in my sister's speech: *my house, my children, my life*. As if Rob Chisholm wasn't really involved, essentially.

So too Wally said of his marriage: he'd become the man-who-pays-the-bills. All-purpose smiling Daddy.

"Nikki, come help! Don't just stand there."

Clare spoke briskly, shoving boxes out of the way, carrying another armload of clothes out of a closet to let fall onto the bed. I'd been turning in my hand a tortoiseshell hand mirror Mom had kept on the bureau, so old its glass had become spotted, that had once belonged to Grandma Kovach who'd died before I was born. Now I turned to stare at Mom's lime-green velour top, slipping off a hanger on the bed. It was the one she'd worn on Mother's Day: the last time I had seen her alive.

And there, the stylish linen suit Mom had bought to wear to my cousin Judy's wedding a few years ago. There was a straw hat to go with it, festooned with ivory-colored flowers.

On the floor, about to be tangled in Clare's feet, a poppy-colored silk scarf I'd given Mom as a birthday present, back in high school.

Clare said, scolding, "Put that leprous mirror in the trash, Nikki. There are more shoes in the closet and here's the 'old shoes' box. Don't bother tagging the worst of these, just dump them. Oh, so much dust! Mom would be mortified. I never realized how she'd been keeping so much, and Dad was just as bad. I'm terrified of the attic, what we'll find there. It's like an archeological dig. Can you believe, Dad's horrible old scuff-moccasins were still in his closet? It would be funny if it wasn't so pathetic. And those pointy-toed high heels of Mom's, that must date back to the 1970s. Sweetie, no. Don't put this stuff in the green-tag box, I'd be ashamed to take it to Good Will. Just put it in the garbage bag, for trash."

"*All* of it? These shoes—"

A pair of "pumps." Medium heel, black patent leather just slightly cracked. Except the pumps were size four, and except I never wore patent leather, they'd have been perfect for me.

Clare laughed as if she'd only just thought of something.

"A close call, Nikki! When I pulled into the driveway about an hour ago there was Miriam Pedersen putting out the trash, and gaping at me. I hope I wasn't rude but I practically ran into the house pretending I didn't see her. The last thing we need this morning is nosey neighbors barging in to ask 'Can I help?' "

I hadn't told Clare about Gladys Higham. I would shield her from the knowledge that our mother might not have died, if Gladys had been a little nosier.

After Gladys Higham, I'd gone home the day before.

I'd walked the sobbing woman across the street to her house and driven back to Chautauqua Falls, exhausted.

Gladys of course it isn't your fault, don't think any more of it Gladys please! You know what Mom would say.

Of the messages on my answering machine Clare's had been the longest and most agitated. I listened to it several times, fascinated.

"—crisis week for Lilja. I can't sleep past dawn anyway. These bright sunny mornings my brain just clicks *on*. June is a crazed month, anyone with children will tell you. I get up at dawn, I make my lists for the day. I had every intention of getting over to the house, believe me. I make breakfast for my family not that anyone eats at the same time and not the same breakfast certainly. A crisis for Lilja is a crisis for her mother believe me. All very trivial you're thinking but if you're thirteen nothing is trivial so please don't ask me! I promise, I'll be at the house tomorrow. I'll get there early and get things started. I hope you're not angry with me, Nikki, because I can't take that right now. I'd have called you on your cell phone but you neglected to give me the number. Look, I'm sorry! We'll make up for lost time tomorrow. Rob says, the sooner we get the house on the market the better, what with mortgage interest rates—"

I hadn't seen Clare since the court hearing. Most of our telephone calls were messages now. I couldn't determine, listening to this disjointed message, if Clare was somehow angry at me, or just sounded that way.

Lately I'd been having the thought: without Mom and Dad, what were Clare and I to each other, really?

You couldn't say we were friends. If we'd have been cousins, neither of us would have been the other's favorite cousin. If we'd been in the same class at school . . .

I was still bristling at the flippant way in which Clare had referred to Wally Szalla as a "type." When I'd asked her what she meant, she'd only just laughed evasively.

I was a little vain about Wally, I guess. His prominent family, his reputation as a well-to-do civic leader in Chautauqua Falls. Other men I'd gone out with, whom Clare had met, had been more my age and more my "type" but Wally Szalla was special.

This was obvious! A few minutes in Wally's company, you were utterly charmed. It infuriated me, Clare was reluctant to acknowledge the fact.

When we're married, you won't need to see us. Maybe I won't invite you and Rob to the wedding, you'll be spared the embarrassment of declining.

"Nikki, wake *up*. You look like a *zombie*."

Clare laughed, exasperated. Nudging me in the small of the back as she'd done when we were girls, to rouse me.

It was nearly noon. We'd been working for hours. My eyes burned and my hands were covered in grime and my knees ached like hell, from squatting so much. I'd been falling into an open-eyed trance as Clare puffed, panted, grunted, shoved, and charged about with her Post-its, sticking them on helpless stationary objects. I halfway expected to see a green Post-it on my forehead: "donate to charity."

I resented the way Clare was consigning most of our parents' clothing to "sell" or "donate" or "trash"—the way, if I seemed to be hesitating, she snatched an item from my hands and dealt with it herself—yet I knew, of course I knew, that Clare was right. In our history together, Clare was always right.

It was only logical. We had to clear out the house. To whom could we give, for example, Dad's old sport coats, his "dress" shirts, his black-watch-plaid flannel pajamas? To whom, Dad's many socks? (All neatly paired by Mom, of course.) No relative, including Rob Chisholm, would have cared for Jonathan Eaton's navy blue suit with the wide lapels or his spiffy royal blue bathrobe with the gold-tassel belt, nor would anyone have coveted the handsome "hunter green" mohair sweater Mom had knitted for him, now riddled with moth holes. (In fact, Dad had rarely worn this sweater. A massive project for Mom, who'd knitted it in secret for his birthday. But Dad had a chronic "itchy skin," he preferred cheap Orlon or cotton-knit sweaters, better yet no sweaters at all. When Aunt Tabitha chided Mom for going to so much trouble, for such a fussy man, Mom had protested, "But people can change. If they try.") There were well-worn belts of Dad's, with jagged holes. There were dozens of neckties on racks: wide, narrow, dark, "cheery," silky and woollen and "braided." We'd given Dad many neckties over the years and each necktie had represented some sort of hope or gesture but most had been consigned to the nether regions of his closet for he'd worn only a few of them, which resembled one another. (I'd have selected some of the ties I'd given to Dad, to pass on to Wally, except I dreaded a catty remark of Clare's.) I did keep out for myself Dad's silver cuff links, initialed JWE, and two nice tie clips, since Clare didn't want them.

"Isn't it strange, Nikki! Mom kept all this. You have to wonder why."

I didn't have to wonder why.

Hard as it was for me to dispose of Dad's clothes, it was much harder to dispose of Mom's. Especially those she'd sewed or knitted herself. There were "outfits" here dating back to when I'd been in middle school, at least. Each had been an occasion, and each had seemed very special at the time. If Clare wasn't vigilant, I retrieved items from boxes to re-examine. If I stuck red Post-its on something Clare protested: "Nikki! That isn't your taste at all. Lavender? 'Pretty pink pastel'? You with your pierced ears and punk hair, you've got to be kidding." Or, meanly: "Sweetie, you can't seriously think that could ever fit you. Mom was a petite size two, practically a midget beside you."

I resented Clare's tone. Midget!

Clare was just jealous, those hips of hers. The last time she'd fitted into a petite size two, she'd been eleven years old.

"All right, Clare. Not dresses, and not skirts. But shirts are different. Mom and I were almost the same size except in the bust. And sweaters. Especially a cardigan, like this. Isn't it beautiful? And it has a belt. The one Mom knitted for me in this style, its belt has been lost for years. Look at the fine stitching, something I could never do."

Clare laughed as if I'd said something witty.

"Nikki, I wouldn't think so. Knitting and crocheting are hardly your talent."

I resented Clare's superior tone. "Are they yours?"

"Well, I was knitting for a while. In middle school. Mom tried to teach me, but it didn't turn out. I was supposed to be knitting a sweater and it kept getting bigger and baggier, it would've fit Aunt Tabitha if I'd finished it. Such a pretty shade of purple, though."

I protested, "Clare, that was my sweater. I knitted that baggy thing. Remember, you all teased me about it? Mom tried to help me but finally we gave up. I was so *frustrated*."

"Nikki, that wasn't you. Don't be ridiculous, you'd never have had the patience to knit a sweater."

"Actually, Clare, you never had the patience. I liked to help Mom out around the house, for years. Mom taught me to knit but she never taught *you*."

"That's just wrong. She *did*."

"Maybe for a day. Maybe for an hour. Then you lost patience, you'd get angry when you couldn't do something perfectly."

"That was never an issue for you, Nikki: doing something perfectly."

We were laughing, but the air between us had grown tense. How smug Clare was, how complacent and mistaken! I happened to know that she was wrong about the sweater. I was the one who'd labored at knitting the purple-baggy-sweater-for-Aunt-Tabitha, for weeks when I'd been in sixth grade. Clearly I remembered choosing the yarn, with Mom, at a little store called the Sewing Box: a beautiful heather-purple shade. Except somehow I'd tugged at the needles, and stretched the yarn, and finally I'd thrown away what I'd knitted in disgust.

Clare said quietly, stubbornly, "Mom told me not to be discouraged, we could try again. But I gave up, I guess. I was in eighth grade and getting involved in school politics."

School politics! She'd run for class secretary and had won by a handful of votes.

"Clare, it wasn't you. Really, it was me."

"Mom would remember."

"Absolutely, yes. Mom would remember."

The impulse was to call for Mom, since we were here in Mom's house. In fact, in Mom's bedroom. Why?

We were remembering how, when we were girls, in this very house, our quarrels over the most trivial subjects escalated in quick rising steps until suddenly we would begin shouting at each other and Clare might slap at me, and I might kick at Clare, and Mom would rush at us to intervene.

Mom would plead: "Girls! Don't disturb your father, he's trying to relax."

Or, plaintively: "Girls! It breaks my heart to hear you like this."

And one of us would cry, "I hate her!" and the other would cry, "I hate HER!"

We were quiet now, remembering.

We were breathing quickly, not daring to look at each other.

I was planning how, when Wally and I chose a date for our wedding, I would not even tell Clare. She would learn from other sources. *That* would embarrass her.

To my surprise Clare said, as if this were the subject we'd been discussing all along, "Fine, Nikki. Keep anything you want of Mom's. You always were one to encourage her to sew you things, knit you things, she'd spend days and weeks on things you had no intention of wearing. Poor Mom was always asking me, 'Clare, why doesn't Nikki wear that velvet dress, why doesn't Nikki wear that blouse,' so why not hoard her things now, now it's too late? But don't bog us both down, please. This sentimental bullshit of yours. I can't believe how much time has passed and we're still with the damned clothes and we have the rest of the house ahead, we'll be doing this for *days*."

I was shocked at Clare's outburst. For a moment, I couldn't speak.

"—for *weeks*! We'll be stuck in here, together, in this house where I can't *breathe*."

I'd been noticing, Clare was short of breath. Her face that had been so artfully made up when I'd arrived was now flushed with an oily sheen and most of her lipstick had been gnawed away.

"Clare, Jesus! Why are you so hostile?"

"This is a strain, Nikki. I keep waiting for some nosey neighbor to knock at the door, you can be sure everyone is aware of us. 'The Eaton sisters, the ones whose mother was murdered in her home.' I keep looking up expecting Mom to be in the doorway, or Dad, or—what was the name of Mom's gray cat?"

"S-Smoky?"

Even more shocking, that Clare seemed to have forgotten Smoky's name. I'd been wondering why she hadn't asked me about him, how he was adjusting to life with me in Chautauqua Falls?

"I keep expecting something! Some awful unspeakable thing! I'm not the one who's been bristling with hostility, Nikki: that's you. The way you're dressed, that ridiculous hat on your head, hasn't anyone ever told you it's rude to wear a hat indoors, especially a hat advertising some tax shelter of some married-man friend of yours, the way you pull the rim down to hide your eyes so I can't see you when I'm talking to you, that's plain *rude*. And I live with a thirteen-year-old so I am accustomed, let me tell you, to *rude*. Since you've arrived our progress has been one step forward and two steps backward and I believe it's deliberate. I could do this so much more efficiently without you, Nikki!"

I'd been squatting on the floor, awkwardly. Now I managed to straighten my legs, wincing with pain. I saw that Clare was glaring at me with hot acid eyes. I said, stammering, "Because you don't care about Mom, or Dad. All you care about is putting the house 'on the market.' "

"That is not true! Except that I have a family, Nikki, I have responsibilities you could never fathom. My life is other people!—not *me*. I wasn't the one to break away from Mt. Ephraim and lead a selfish life—I didn't practically abandon our mother when she became a widow—I've never slept with a man married to another woman—I've never broken our mother's heart humiliating her in front of relatives and friends: that's you, Nikki. Don't look so wounded, you must know this. That's why you've been so hostile to me, I know you're angry from yesterday, when I couldn't get over here. As if that was my fault! As if I can control my life! Lilja blackmails me with her hysterics and Rob practically runs out of the house to escape us and poor Foster keeps asking about his grandma, children at school are tormenting him, he's begun wetting his bed after years and half the people I see when I go out, including women I'd believed were my friends, turn away or duck into stores to avoid me because they feel so sorry for me. It's a nightmare, Nikki, you seem to have been spared, not living here. As usual, you're spared! It's just me, I am so sick and tired of being *me*."

I fumbled to touch her. This sudden reversal of roles made me shy and ungainly. "Clare, I'm so sorry, I—"

Clare pushed at me, glaring. "Nikki, you are not *sorry*! All you are is *Nikki*."

Clare ran from the room, clumsily. I heard her in the bathroom next door, running water loudly. Then I heard her in the living room, shoving furniture around. Then she was on the telephone, speaking sharply.

I had thought she might leave, and I would have the house to myself. I took advantage of her absence from the bedroom to retrieve several articles of clothing from the boxes. The lime-green velour top, I tried on in front of a mirror. (Tight in the shoulders and a little short at the waist, otherwise fine.) A white silk blouse with a lacy bow, I knew Wally Szalla would admire. (My lover had a weakness for old-fashioned ladylike girls, I'd discovered. He much preferred white underwear on me, whether silk or cotton, to anything more spectacular.) And there was the poppy-colored scarf, and there was the tortoiseshell hand mirror cloudy with age, that had once belonged to my mother's mother. Also, several of my father's neckties I had given him years ago, looking as if they'd never been worn. I would make a present of them to Wally Szalla.

"*Nik*-ki! Come look."

In a voice that sounded almost gleeful Clare called me from our father's study at the end of the hall. I'd been hearing her laughing in there, a sign that her good spirits had returned and she'd forgiven me, or anyway wasn't angry at me any longer.

Immediately, as when we'd been girls, my animosity toward my sister dissolved.

Since Clare's outburst we'd been working in separate rooms, much more productively. We were aware of each other without needing to see each other or to speak. I'd sorted through most of Mom's and Dad's personal items and had moved on to impersonal things like bedding, towels, shower curtains. I was becoming as proficient with the Post-its slips as my sister.

The only temptation was to return to things in boxes destined for "sell" or "donate."

"You'll never believe this, Nikki. Goodness!"

Clare was kneeling on the carpet in front of Dad's old desk. She'd kicked off her shoes. Her white cotton shirt was no longer so crisply ironed but she'd replenished her lipstick and powdered her face. It was like Clare to abruptly switch moods and expect you to switch moods with her.

Weird to be walking into Dad's "home office"! This room we'd been forbidden to enter as girls except at Dad's invitation. (Which was rare.) Since Dad's death, Mom had kept the room more or less unchanged. We joked together, Clare and me, that she was maintaining it as a shrine.

Dad's desk, filing cabinets, bookshelves. His collection of mostly American history books, known as "Jon's library."

It was unsettling, to so freely enter this room, as an adult. To see how ordinary its dimensions were. Its furnishings. Dad's desk had seemed massive and very special to me as a girl, but it was just a standard office desk, aluminum and wood veneer with a simulated stain, smooth and practical as Formica. Somehow, seeing Dad at this desk had seemed so impressive: always I'd wondered what he was doing, what were the documents he frowned over. But now, I could see that the desk was no larger than the table I used as a makeshift desk in my apartment, purchased for fifteen dollars in a secondhand store and painted lipstick red.

On top of Dad's desk was his old electric typewriter, affixed with a green Post-it. Dad had a computer at Beechum Paper Products of course but he'd refused to have a home computer in the belief that the so-called electronics revolution was all about product obsolescence: getting silly people to spend money. If Dad had lived into our era of universal cell phones he'd have been outraged.

"Nikki, come *on*. Nobody's going to scold us."

Clare had pulled out the desk drawers as far as they could go without falling out. She'd been sorting through Dad's meticulously kept records dating back to the early 1980s: New York State and Internal Revenue documents, insurance policies, volumes of cancelled checks and receipts (for purchases as low as $2.98). Mom had said of Dad that he kept everything out of a fear of losing something and I think she meant this approvingly.

Not like me, I'd thought. Who kept almost nothing, out of a fear of losing it.

"The weirdest thing, Nikki: Dad's calendar collection! This stack, I found in the bottom drawer here. They go back to 1981."

These were uniformly large, somewhat bulky calendars with generic landscape and wildlife photographs. What was most striking about the calendars, which Clare had spread out on the carpet, was the maze of emphatic X's, in black ink. Each day of each month of each year had been methodically crossed out, not missing a single square including the very last day of December of each year. The last x'd-out date was December 31, 1999, eight days before Dad's death.

Clare said, "Can you guess what these mean? These numbers?"

You could see, past the black *X*'s, abbreviations and cryptic codes. Not every date contained these, but each date contained, at the bottom, a miniature numeral. In January 1999, the numerals were 188, 186, 187½, 190, 189, 189, 189½, 191, etc. In the earliest calendar, in the month of January 1981, the numerals were 171, 173, 170½, 171½, 173, 173, 173, 174½, etc.

I crouched over the calendars to study the numerals. So carefully recorded in Dad's hand! Day after day, week after week, month after month, year after year. I didn't want to think what this was.

(Dad's weight?)

"I think it must be Dad's weight, Nikki. Imagine, Dad weighed himself every day and kept a record. We never knew, did we? It must have been a secret, he was always teasing us about watching our weight, at least he teased *me*. I'm sure that Mom didn't know. You can see, looking through the calendars, how Dad had slowly gained weight, he'd never been what you'd call heavy but he'd gone from 171 in 1981 to 196 by the time he, well"—Clare paused, suddenly swallowing, as if the enormity of what she was saying in her archly bemused voice suddenly struck her—"died."

Died. That forlorn word. We'd been unable to utter it for a long time, regarding our father.

We weren't yet able to utter it, regarding Mom.

Clare continued to chatter nervously. She wasn't going to tell Rob about the calendars, she said. Or any relatives. She didn't think that I should, either.

I told her no. I would keep Dad's secret of course.

Awkwardly I squatted above the calendars spread out on the carpet, paging through them with a kind of fascinated dread. So many days, hundreds of days, bluntly x'd out in black ink! I sensed with what satisfaction Dad had crossed out the days of his life not seeming to know how finite they were, how rapidly he was using them up.

"Maybe we should just throw them away, Nikki? In this trash bag I've started."

"Well. I guess."

Clare hadn't been able to open the windows in Dad's study more than a few inches, the air smelled of mildew and something faintly chemical. The police forensics investigators had been in this room as they'd been everywhere in the house, but there hadn't been any evidence, we'd been told, that the "perpetrator" had taken anything from this room. Evidently Dad's old electric typewriter, covered with a dusty plastic cover, hadn't tempted him.

A crystal meth-head, the detective had called Ward Lynch.

Desperate for cash, to feed his addiction. Might've chosen anyone, but Gwen Eaton came along.

Gwen Eaton, who saw the "good" in everyone. Who seemed to believe that we're here on earth to "be nice" to people in need.

"Nikki, stay with me. Let's finish up here."

There was a small quaver in Clare's voice. I understood: suddenly my sister didn't want to be alone any more than I did.

After Dad's calendars, it didn't seem so strange or anyway surprising that he'd saved what appeared to be hundreds of paper clips of varying sizes, many of them badly rusted; that he'd saved dozens of loose U.S. postage stamps, many so old they dated to an era beyond memory (when first-class postage was twenty cents?); that, rattling loose in his desk drawers, were countless ballpoint pens advertising local businesses, and all of the pens dried out. There were rubber bands, thumbtacks. Erasers. Telephone directories for 1996, 1997, and 1998 as well as 1999. The antiquated stapler Dad had had for all of our lifetimes and allowed us to use with his supervision, plus a nearly empty box of staples. In the same drawer, several rulers and a badly torn measuring tape from Hamrick's Office Supplies and a cache of Scotch tape dispensers, empty of tape.

Clare held the dispensers in her hand, frowning.

"Nikki, why would Dad save these, once the tape was used up?"

I didn't want to look at Clare, for fear we'd break into hysterical laughter.

. . .

As if we'd been brought to the threshold of a door long locked against us and at last the door has been opened but—what is inside?

We'd planned to drive to the Blue Star Diner for lunch, it was less than a mile away and no-fuss. But somehow, we never got there.

Mid-afternoon, when we were both becoming light-headed from hunger, Clare had the sudden idea of making a meal out of what we could find in the kitchen. "Nikki, Mom would want this! Her leftovers especially."

When I hesitated Clare said, sharply, "You know how Mom fretted, if good food went to waste."

This meant freezer leftovers. I had to wonder how prudent an idea this was, preparing Mom's food in Mom's kitchen without Mom. Only a few steps from the (shut, locked) door to the garage.

"Nikki. Wake up, give me a hand."

Must have been standing there, blank-faced, staring at the (shut, locked) door to the garage.

Clare chattered brightly as I set about tidying the kitchen. When things have been displaced in a familiar setting, it takes a while for the eye to discover them. Strangers had searched our cupboard shelves, drawers. Glassware, china, canned goods, boxes of rice, pasta, tabouleh had been examined and replaced haphazardly. Even Mom's many spice jars, and her herbal teas in rainbow-colored packages. The counters she'd always kept spotless were smudged with some sort of chemical grime, it took a while for me to scrub off with cleanser and a sponge. The once-spotless sink was badly stained as if something dark oily, viscous had been dumped into it.

Even our snapshots on the refrigerator, held in place by little magnets, had been dislodged. I picked up an old photo of myself, smiling happily in some long-ago summer-beach setting, that had fallen to the floor, examined it critically and without thinking tore it into pieces.

"Nikki, what are you doing? What did you *do*?"

Clare slapped at me, disgusted.

"Mom loved that picture of you. What would Mom *say*."

By the time Clare set out for us, in steaming bowls, what appeared to be the remains of Mom's Hawaiian chicken spooned over, not white rice, but buckwheat pasta, we were both giddy with hunger. Other leftovers Clare had discovered in the freezer were the remains of a tuna fish casserole, a half-dozen spicy cocktail sausages, and a half-loaf of buttermilk-pecan bread. I'd discovered a chunk of cheddar cheese in the refrigerator, just perceptibly moldy, we could eat with the bread and a box of All-Grain Melba Toast.

Clare said, "This chicken of Mom's! Maybe it's a little sweet but it is delicious. I was furious at old Auntie Tabitha saying what she did, to upset Mom."

"That's just her way. You know Tabitha."

"So what if it's her 'way'! She'd upset Mom so many times, those seemingly innocent little remarks of hers. Old auntie was plain jealous, her younger brother Jonathan preferred Mom to *her*."

"Tabitha is taking it hard, though. What happened to Mom."

Clare snorted in derision. "But of course. Tabitha and Alyce Proxmire, it's been devastating for *them*."

I laughed. Between Clare and me there had long been the conviction—exasperating, annoying—but somehow comical, as in a TV series—that certain of Mom's relatives and friends exploited her good nature. These were tales told and retold, passed back and forth between us like Ping-Pong balls. I saw now that, though Mom was gone, Clare and I would not relinquish these familiar, comforting old tales of blame, reproach, moral indignation.

"Mom is just too, well—'Christian.' I mean," Clare said, eating, "—*was*."

Now that we were seated across from each other in the breakfast nook I could see the strain in Clare's face. Beneath the smooth cosmetic mask there were bruise-like shadows beneath her eyes and puckers at the corners of her mouth. I knew from Rob that the symptoms Clare had had after the hearing—her "touch of the flu"—had been very like my own.

After my testimony in the courtroom, Clare had avoided looking at me. Glancing sidelong in my direction with a kind of dread as if knowing there might be more I could reveal, of what I'd seen in the garage.

Almost, I could hear her pleading *Nikki don't tell me!*

Then again, at other times *Nikki I must know.*

I never thought of it, now. By "it" I'd come to mean the entire experience, not just the sighting of my mother's body.

I never thought of it and would not think of it except at such times when I was compelled to think of it: giving testimony as a witness. But we'd been assured there would be no trial, Lynch's public defender attorney and the district attorney's assistant were negotiating an agreement to spare us.

"Nikki, aren't you eating? Don't be *silly.*"

"I am, Clare. Stop staring at me."

"Well. You're too thin, you need to eat. It's fine to be fashionably thin, but that anorexic look is *out.*"

Tell Lilja, I thought. Tell your daughter.

Clare glanced up at me. In her schoolteacher mode my sister could read my thoughts as easily as one might observe goldfish swimming in a bowl.

"Lilja is over her 'crisis,' I think. Once school is out and the pressure of her damned 'peers' lets up she's going to be fine."

I was hungry and tried to eat but each time I lifted my fork to my mouth, it began to tremble. The Hawaiian chicken really was too sweet for my taste, and didn't go very well with the overcooked clotted-together buckwheat pasta. The cocktail sausages were no temptation on a near-empty stomach, nor the lumpy tuna casserole that had heated unevenly in the microwave. As if Mom would have served such leftovers!

I busied myself scraping the greenish mold off the cheddar cheese, and ate bits of cheese with crumbly pieces of the buttermilk-pecan bread.

Years ago, Mom had tried to interest me in bread-baking. I'd complained that it took so long and Mom had said that's the point of bread-baking, it takes so long.

"Temperamentally, we weren't each other's type."

"Who? What are you talking about?"

I hadn't meant to speak aloud. It must have been the aftermath of the flu, my brain wasn't functioning normally.

I said, "I wonder if this will be the last of it? Mom's bread."

"No. I'm sure I have some at home, still. Wrapped in aluminum foil in my freezer."

We fell silent. There was so much to say, it made us tired to not-say it.

Outside, children were frolicking in the Pedersens' backyard wading pool. I smiled to think how Dad would be annoyed, complaining of noisy neighbors. Lucky for him, he'd died before the Pedersens acquired the pool.

What I dreaded most wasn't noise but the prospect of someone suddenly banging on the door.

The house was too quiet. Essentially, it was an empty house. You entered a room holding your breath. You were tempted to think that someone might be hiding. Waiting.

That wasn't how Ward Lynch had appeared to my mother. I knew. He'd come up to her quite openly, in a public place. He would not have suddenly appeared in Deer Creek Acres, to knock on the door. He would not have thought of the possibility.

Oh, I'd meant to dismantle the tinkly little sleigh bells above the kitchen door. I thought, if I heard them, I would scream.

Clare was talking as my thoughts drifted. It was hard not to think that, at any moment, one of Mom's friends would turn into the driveway, rap at the kitchen door: "Gwe-en? You home?"

Maude, or Madge. Lucille Kovach, or Gerry Eaton. Alyce Proxmire, Ellie O'Connell, the Barkham sisters. A continuous stream of chattering women five days a week. (Weekends, when Jon Eaten was home, Mom's girlfriends kept their distance.)

More people! More people! If I can't be happy myself . . .

Of course, I hadn't told Clare what Mom said. I never would.

"Do you suppose they *know*?"

Clare was peering past me, into the backyard. She seemed to be looking at Mom's bird feeder. Though it had been empty of seed for weeks,
still there were birds all around the house. That day we'd been hearing
their liquidy cries and calls that meant mating, nesting.

Mom had said that June was the happiest time in the year for her:
when all the birds are singing.

"Who? Know *what*?"

"The birds Mom was feeding. They must know that something is different about this house."

"Well. In summer birds can feed themselves, can't they? You only
need to feed them in cold months, I think."

"Mom put out seed all year round, I'm sure she did. And crusts of
bread."

I didn't want to blunder into an argument with Clare. Not after her
eruption that morning.

"One thing they've noticed, maybe: Smoky is gone."

Clare seemed not to hear. She'd finished her Hawaiian chicken but not
the soggy buckwheat pasta. She'd given up on the congealing tuna casserole and pushed it from her as if she couldn't bear to look at it.

It was maddening, that Clare wouldn't ask about Smoky. I'd been annoyed as hell for weeks. As if Mom's cat had ceased to exist because Nikki
had taken him home with her, and not Clare.

I'd put a kettle on the stove to boil, for tea. When I poured tea into
mugs for us, Clare sniffed suspiciously at hers and wrinkled her nose.

"Nikki, what is this? It tastes like acid."

"This is Mom's Red Zinger."

"I'd have preferred peppermint."

"Peppermint! That tastes like mouthwash."

"Not if you don't make it too strong. This 'zinger,' you've made way
too strong."

"If you'd wanted peppermint, Clare, why didn't you tell me? You must have seen what I was doing at the stove."

"Nikki, I didn't *see*. I wasn't watching your every movement, I was preparing lunch for us. I had to do practically everything myself, you scarcely lifted a finger. You were going to open a can of soup, and you never did."

My face burned. I'd forgotten. We were close to quarreling now.

Clare persisted, "I don't really like herbal tea, I'd have preferred real tea, or coffee."

"Well, you can make it for yourself, can't you? And then we'd better get back to work, if you have to leave early."

"I don't have to leave 'early,' Nikki. I told you when I had to get back home: by six. And I'm not supposed to have caffeine for the time being, with my medication. It's 'contra-indicated.' You know that."

Did I know? I couldn't remember. Clare was glaring at me as if I'd deeply wounded her.

"I can make you peppermint. The water is still hot."

"I didn't say I wanted peppermint. Only that I'd have preferred it to this 'zinger.' That's all I said."

I laughed. I think it was a laughing sound that issued from my mouth.

Clare said suddenly, "It's strange to be here, isn't it. In their house, without them around."

"That's why we're here, Clare. Because they aren't around."

"But it doesn't seem natural. Does it?"

"If you want to sell this house, I guess it's natural. It's what 'heirs' do."

" 'If I want to sell this house'—? Don't you?"

I shrugged. What was there to say. What I dreaded most was a knock on the door. A man's heavy footstep behind us.

"Neither of us is going to live here."

"Right."

Clare rubbed at her eyes. She'd pushed away her cup of Red Zinger tea as if its mere sight offended her. "Wasn't it a surprise, Nikki, Mom's will! All those bequests."

The bequests ($5,000 to the Mt. Ephraim Christian Life Fellowship Church, $3,000 to the Mt. Ephraim Arts Council, $1,500 to the County Humane Society Animal Shelter, etc.) had not surprised me so much as the money Mom had left to Clare and me: $18,000 each. Mom had been so frugal, since Dad's death. It was sad to think of her pinching pennies, saving money for an "estate" to be divided between "my beloved daughters Clare and Nicole."

I said, "I wish they'd spent the money on themselves. While Dad was alive. They'd been talking of going back to Key West for years, where they'd gone on their honeymoon."

"Oh, Nikki! You know Dad. He'd never get around to going."

"We could have encouraged them more. Dad wasn't always so predictable."

"He was! More predictable than we knew, weighing himself every day and . . . Oh, God." Clare laughed harshly, and began coughing. When I made a move to touch her she shoved at me reflexively, unthinkingly as you might shove at a small child or an animal annoying you. In the same instant she lurched to her feet, pushing out of the breakfast nook.

"I guess—I don't feel well. Excuse me—"

Clare hurried to the bathroom in the hall. Quickly I began clearing away our plates, running water at the sink to muffle the sound of Clare being sick to her stomach.

This was the "guest" bathroom kept in perpetual readiness for visitors. As girls we'd been allowed to use this bathroom with the understanding that we would not soil the dainty embroidered linen towels or the fragrant pink soap sculpted into ingenious flower shapes. We might use the toilet, but we must wash our hands elsewhere. Above all, we must not somehow "speckle" the sink or the spotless mirror above the sink.

Dad had avoided the guest bathroom entirely. He'd joked it was the easiest way to stay on Mom's good side.

Strangers had examined that bathroom, I knew. Very likely, strangers had even used the toilet.

Possibly, he had used it, too. The man I had not yet accustomed myself to identifying as my mother's murderer.

By the time Clare reappeared, deathly pale, sullen and repentant, I'd tidied up the kitchen and cleared away all evidence of our meal of leftovers. The last of the Hawaiian chicken, buckwheat pasta, tuna casserole and spicy cocktail sausages scraped into the garbage disposal, and gone.

The remains of the bread, I wrapped in aluminum foil and returned to the freezer.

We didn't resume our sorting that afternoon, Clare wasn't feeling up to it. Nor did she think she could drive home by herself, so I drove her.

In the Saab, Clare began crying. I had never heard my sister cry so helplessly. She was saying she couldn't make it without Mom. She was saying she didn't love anyone anymore. It was too much effort, she wasn't strong enough.

"People make me angry! They seem so silly. I seem so silly to myself. Lilja screams at me, 'I wish I was dead!' and this terrible thought came to me, Why do people keep going, really? What is the point? Lilja won't talk about Mom, not a word. Rob says give her time. I think she's more embarrassed than grief-stricken, and I hate her. I hate my own daughter! And that man. At the hearing, I wanted to scream at him, 'Why? Why our mother? Why us?' Except I knew there was no answer. There is no answer. I don't love Rob. I love Foster, but I don't love his father. I made a mistake marrying Rob. I made a mistake quitting my job. I wanted to go back to school, I wanted to get a master's degree. I wanted to study in New York City. I wanted to travel. Mom was so fond of Rob, and Dad liked him, too. Especially Mom was anxious for me to 'settle down'—'be happy.' And I wanted to make Mom happy, of course! But it was a mistake. I don't love him. I don't even know if he loves me. We're like these people who met at a party and got to talking and wound up trapped in an elevator together, stuck between floors. We try to be civil, we try not to panic or scream at each other, but we're running out of oxygen. Oh, Nikki." In this way my second day at 43 Deer Creek Drive ended early.

love me?

I was thirty-one years old and shouldn't have had to beg.

"Smoky! Come cuddle."

This lonely June night, I'd begun drinking early.

Oh, not serious drinking: just wine.

A glass. Just a glass!

(What harm, a single glass? Let's be serious.)

This lonely June night when I'd made a sensible decision not to be exhausted/depressed/anxious. Two glasses of the terrific Chianti Wally'd brought the other evening, I could hardly recall why I'd imagined I should be exhausted/depressed/anxious.

"Smoky? You'd better love me, buddy. All we have is each other."

(This wasn't exactly true. At least on my part. For after all I had my current married-man-friend who adored me.)

(He said.)

(Well, he did! Said, and said, and said.)

Except here I was being blackmailed by my mother's orphan cat. Emotional blackmail it was. Though Smoky had no one but me, somehow Smoky didn't trust me. Each time I unlocked the door to my apartment and stepped inside, Smoky seemed not to know who I might be, or who might be accompanying me.

As Wally was allergic to Smoky, so Smoky was allergic to Wally.

If I managed to entice Smoky into my lap, to settle down, allow me to pet him, lapse into a quivery drowse and even purr deep in his throat, as soon as he heard Wally's footsteps on the stairs, more recently just the sound of a car door being slammed outside, Smoky would panic and leap from me, digging his claws through the fabric of my clothes into the soft flesh of my thighs.

"Smoky, oh! That *hurts*."

The tiny scratches rarely bled. Maybe just a little.

Still, I longed to hold Smoky in my lap tonight. Longed to stroke his bristly fur, that wasn't so soft and lustrous as it had been in the days of Mom, but still it was fur, and Smoky was a warm creature with a potential to love me.

It was early evening when I decided to have a single small glass of Chianti. Eventually, it become later.

Time for WCHF FM's "Night Train" at 10 P.M. Wally Szalla's radio voice until midnight.

That afternoon when I'd returned from Mt. Ephraim, having taken my weeping sister home first, there'd been two messages from Wally on my answering machine. (There were other messages, too. I wasn't paying too much attention to these.) The first, recorded at 1:48 P.M., was a promise to "Nikki darling" he'd be over immediately after the radio broadcast, which was airing live that evening. The second, recorded at 4:20 P.M., was a harried and evasive message saying he "hoped" he'd be there "as soon as I can get away."

It had been our plan, Wally would be staying with me tonight.

(I think. I'd thought.)

Vaguely I knew there were "new complications" with Wally's family. Not only his "emotionally unstable wife Isabel" but his "very demanding" daughter (whose name I seemed to be blocking though by now, I should have known it as well as I knew my own). And, of course, there was Troy.

I wanted to protest *I'm a daughter, too. Love me!*

Smoky poked his tomcat-face out from beneath my bed. I'd been drifting through the apartment, seductively rattling a package of seafood cat-kibble, pausing now in the doorway of my bedroom. "C'mon, buddy. Midnight snack, then we'll cuddle."

Begging a cat for affection. This poor animal kept prisoner in my apartment.

Smoky's wedge-shaped head had not lost weight, like the rest of his body. If a cat can have jowls, Smoky had jowls. Though I spoke cajolingly, shamelessly to him, still he regarded me with suspicion as if Wally Szalla was somehow crouched behind me ready to spring.

"Nobody here but me, Smoky. And you know me."

Smoky resented it, he wasn't allowed outdoors. At Mom's house he'd been allowed absolute freedom but there was too much traffic in my neighborhood and anyway I knew he would run away, if I let him outdoors, and I'd never see him again.

Smoky is safe with me, Mom. I promise.

I shook a small amount of kibble into Smoky's green plastic bowl in a corner of the kitchen, watching as the gray cat ate in the quick-darting way of a traumatized creature. I would make Smoky love me, I vowed. I would win him over, as Mom had done when she'd brought the scrawny skittish six-month-old cat home from the animal shelter.

Any cat that qualifies as a lame duck, Dad said dryly, your mother will locate. And bring home with her.

". . . and now, here at WCHF FM in the heart of the historic Chautauqua Valley, as the hour moves past eleven P.M. 'Night Train' is going to take us on a sentimental journey to the Sweet Basil Jazz Club in New York City, 1953 . . ."

I had to keep the radio volume low. Smoky glanced up nervously hearing the D.J.'s familiar voice: low throaty sexy as an alto saxophone.

This was Wally's radio voice, not exactly his own voice. But you could recognize it. Smoky's ears pricked, his stubby tail switched restlessly.

"He isn't here, I said. Not yet."

Since I'd become involved with Wally Szalla, I listened to WCHF FM obsessively. In my car, and in the apartment. Every waking hour, and more. "Night Train" (10 P.M. to midnight, five evenings a week) was naturally my favorite program. If I couldn't be with Wally, next best thing was listening to him.

Sipping a third glass of wine, listening to Dave Brubeck. To console me for my loneliness. To prepare me for Wally's arrival.

Wally would ask how the "sorting-through" had gone. I would tell him, *fine*!

No, I wouldn't tell my lover about my sister's breakdown that day. I hadn't told him about Gladys Higham the day before. (I hadn't told Clare, either.) When a man shares with a woman his marital/domestic problems, the kind of problems that seem never to be solved but only to morph into yet more complicated problems, like hair snarls proliferating, sympathy flows in one direction only. By instinct a woman knows it's naive to expect the flow to reverse.

And maybe I didn't want sympathy, really. From Wally Szalla or anyone.

Much of the programming on WCHF AM-FM was taped. But Wally preferred to do "Night Train" live. He liked the edgy excitement of live radio, the thrill of receiving calls while on the air. There was something boyish and appealing about his D.J. personality you'd mistake for a lonely middle-aged guy with no one to love him, no one waiting for him when he left the studio.

Clare had called Wally a "type." As if Clare knew the first thing about him!

". . . a special request has just come in for 'N.E.' . . . who I hope is listening somewhere out there in the Chautauqua Valley on this mellow June night . . . 'N.E.': this is from 'someone who adores you . . . who hopes you will be patient with him' . . . the incomparable Duke Ellington in a 1943 recording of 'Mood Indigo' followed by 'Pretty Woman' followed by 'Just Squeeze Me.' Mmmm!"

I laughed aloud. Smoky, who'd settled at last in my lap, almost asleep, glanced up irritably.

. . .

Soaking in hot fragrant sudsy water preparing for our lovemaking.

If Wally left the radio station as soon as "Night Train" went off the air, he'd be here by 12:30 A.M. I had a luxuriant hour to anticipate his arrival.

I'd decided that I would save Dad's neckties for another time, to give to Wally. Or maybe I should give the ties to him singly. I had brought them home from the house, neatly laid out on a closet shelf. Clare needn't know. What I took from our parents' house was none of Clare's business.

Yes Clare: sex is terrific between Wally Szalla and me. You can imagine!

No Clare: because I sleep with Wally and have been sleeping with Wally for more months than I care to tabulate on the fingers of both hands it does not mean that the man does not respect me. It does not mean that the man will never marry me.

Don't you judge us, Clare: you don't know Wally Szalla. You don't even know me.

When I woke, the bathwater was tepid. It was already past midnight. Hurriedly I stumbled from the ungainly old bathtub and toweled myself dry. The stippled-red claw marks on my thighs smarted. I was surprised to see such clusters of scratches. Some were old, and nearly healed; others were fresh. When Wally had first noticed a few days ago, he'd reacted with alarm: "My God, Nikki, did I somehow do this?" and I'd laughed at him, and kissed his mouth. Telling him that yes in a way he had, but not directly.

"bearer of bad news"

There'd been a time. Such a sweet time. When Mom and I left secret messages for each other around the house.

I LUV U in cake frosting. I LUV U 2! in toothpaste.

Naughty Nikki daring to squirt Dad's shaving cream onto a mirror knowing that Mom would find it first, not Dad. MRS H IS TAKING US TO THE MALL BE BACK BY 6. U-KNOW-WHO.

Valentines bought at flea markets. Old used scenic-sights postcards scribbled over in strangers' handwriting. Tiny plastic bunnies, ducklings, Cracker Jack whistles attached to pieces of cardboard: 4 U from ME. Beads spelling out CRAZZE 4 U. A photo clipped from a magazine of a herd of white-tailed deer including fawns gazing pensively at the camera—DEER NIKKI COME PLAY!!! A Chinese fortune inside one of Mom's herbal tea packets, ingeniously inserted: LOOK FOR THE SLIVER LINING. Homemade cards for birthdays, Easter, Halloween, Ground Hog's Day. More valentines. Mom's flower beds were great places to leave messages for her since only Mom would find them there, part-covered by loose dirt or leaves. Also Mom's sewing machine, kitchen cupboards, bureau drawers. Mom left messages for me on and beneath my pillow, in my textbooks (where I'd discover them in school), inside my socks (I'd discover when I put my socks on). NIKKI PLEASE PICK UP YOUR ROOM PLEASE PLEASE U-KNOW-WHO. And clever Nikki responded PICK UP MY ROOM & TAKE WHERE? PLEASE INFORM! U-KNOW-WHO.

There were messages spelled out in jelly beans—and lima beans—on the kitchen table KISSKISS! There were messages coiled about the collars of Miranda and Suzie-Q., our cats of the time. Some of the messages were practical exchanges of information but most were plain silly. Most, I've long forgotten.

Like most of what Mom and I talked about, all those years.

For such a long dreamy time it seemed, I'd been a little girl. And then, a girl. Eleven, twelve years old. When I was in middle school, Mom had been in her thirties. She'd looked young as a girl herself, running around in jeans, shorts, T-shirts and sneakers, her hair tied back in a ponytail or frizzed in a windblown halo about her head.

Before the days when Gwen Eaton helped senior citizens navigate the pool at the Y, she'd taken us swimming at Wolf's Head Lake summer afternoons. (Dad hadn't cared for swimming, and especially not for the child-centered boisterousness of Wolf's Head Lake.) While other mothers sunbathed, or sat gossiping beneath beach umbrellas, Mom had taught Clare and me to swim, dive. In the murky lake water Gwen Eaton had swum quick and lithe as a fish.

Yes you can do it! Mom would cry.

Oh yes you can.

Mostly, that turned out to be true. I think.

I was jealous of Mom. Dad complained of "open house" on Saturdays when neighbors and women friends dropped by to see Gwen, but he hadn't any idea how busy weekdays could be. A rap on the kitchen screen door, and before anyone invites her inside, there's a woman poking her head in calling: "Gwe-en? You home?"

I'd have said, "No! Nobody's home!" or, more inspired, "Yes! We're home but we've got Rocky Mountain speckled fever. You know, that's so contagious."

But Mom never hid away. Even if she wasn't feeling well, or in one of her rare "blue moods" (Mom attributed merely to "cramps"—"migraine"—"a touch of the flu.") Always she'd hurry out to greet whoever it was who'd barged in, smiling and gracious and ready with Gwen Eaton's perky signature remark: "Why! You're looking *good*."

That summer, when I was twelve years old. Idly pedaling my bicycle along Deer Creek Drive into the cul-de-sac Deer Creek Circle, and back. Lazy figure-eights in the midsummer sun. So bored! Maybe I'd pedal over to see if Ruthie Haber was home . . . Just then I happened to see an unfamiliar vehicle pull up to park in front of our house. It was larger than a car, possibly a minivan. Yet it didn't look like a delivery or service vehicle. From a half-block away I saw a man (maybe in a uniform? maybe not) get out of the vehicle and check the address, walk to the front door and ring the bell. Anyone who knew us would have gone to the side door, this was a sign the man was a stranger or anyway no one accustomed to visiting our house. I knew that Mom was inside, and I knew that Mom was alone. I wasn't really interested but I waited long enough to see if Mom would answer the door, and she did; then I bicycled over to Ruthie's house a few blocks away, but Ruthie wasn't home, only just Ruthie's mom who liked me, and was looking lonely, so I was stuck with Mrs. Haber until a sudden panic came over me, this weird conviction passing through my head swift as lightning *He has come for her. It was all a mistake, that Mom married Dad and had Clare and me. We will never see Mom again because we did not deserve her.* That summer I'd been reading science fiction novels by Philip K. Dick that were both bizarre and matter-of-fact, about alternate universes, time dimensions in which for instance your twin who'd died when you were born is alive but you are dead; time dimensions that were like gloves pulled inside-out. You know that there is an "inside" to things normally only seen from the "outside" but you never think about it. And if you do, it can be scary.

I got away from Mrs. Haber, and bicycled back home, and saw that the vehicle was gone from the curb, and my heart was beating hard by this point, and I'd broken out into a cold sweat. I let my bike fall in the driveway and ran into the house, through the screen door and into the kitchen (no tinkling bells on the door yet), and there was blue-eyed long-haired snowy-white Miranda blinking at me in alarm, from her perch atop the refrigerator. "Mom? *Mom?*" I seemed to know *Mom is gone, this is my fault for leaving her* even as I knew it could not be so, my mother would never leave us, of course Mom would never leave us because she loved us, because she was Mom; and I heard a loud buzzing sort of hum that meant Mom, Mom on the steps from the basement, she'd been ironing in the basement and was only just now coming upstairs carrying an armload of ironed shirts, and seeing me so frazzled and sweaty she asked what on earth was wrong, and I told her nothing, nothing was wrong, except who'd been that man who had rung the doorbell about fifteen minutes ago, a man who'd driven up in a minivan?—and Mom blinked and smiled at me as if perplexed, seeming not to know what I was talking about. Her face was round and innocent as a full moon. Her eyes were greeny-amber, and her hair looked windblown, in her brushed-back-behind-the-ears style.

"A man, Nikki? What man?"

"Wasn't there a man, just now? He rang the doorbell . . ."

With warm fingers Mom brushed my sticky hair out of my forehead, and laughed at me. Now she remembered: "The electric meter man, you must mean. He's come, and gone."

I felt so silly: the electric meter man!

Of course, that's all it was. That's all it could have been. *The electric meter man. Come to 43 Deer Creek Drive to check the meter, and gone.*

A man's voice, abrupt and jarring.

"Ma'am? Hello? Is anyone inside?"

Through slats in the dusty venetian blind I saw him outside, on the front stoop, only a few yards from where I was crouched in a mounting panic. This had to be a stranger. A neighbor would have called me by name, having seen my car at the curb. A relative would have walked inside uninvited calling *Hey Nikki? You here?*

There was something familiar about the man: stocky-shouldered, with a crown of thick hair erect as a porcupine's quills. I couldn't see his face, except to know that he had an olive-dark skin, and he was wearing dark glasses. On this warm muggy day in late June he was wearing a sport coat that fitted his shoulders tightly but hung loose at the small of his back, of some vague dull color like eroded stone. His manner was both aggressive and nervous. He frowned and gnawed at his lower lip like a man arguing with himself, and losing the argument.

I cringed as he rang the doorbell again. A churchy chime-sound, meant to be musical. "Ma'am? Mt. Ephraim Police. May I speak with you?"

Police! I knew now why he looked familiar.

He'd known that someone was in the house, and seemed to know it was a woman. He must have seen my car parked on the street, knew whose house this was. But I had a right to park there, didn't I? I had a right to enter this house I'd inherited, didn't I? The police officer's own car, a stolid squarish unmarked sedan with tinted windows, was parked in the driveway. The venetian blind slipped from my fingers, making more noise than I'd wished for. I stepped back from the window hoping the officer hadn't heard.

An impulse came over me to hide. Barricade myself in the bathroom. Run up into the attic, or down into the basement. This man had no right to enter the house, had he? If I refused to acknowledge him wouldn't he have to go away?

It was mid-afternoon of a day that seemed to have begun a very long time ago. Yesterday, maybe. I'd returned to Mom's house to continue sorting through her things. Since Clare was otherwise occupied, I'd come alone. For hours I'd been working in the basement and didn't smell exactly fresh. My hair that was partly grown out, at the roots threaded with gray, needed shampooing but instead I'd covered it with a red-polka-dot scarf retrieved from the Good Will box in Mom's bedroom, tied at the nape of my neck. When I'd thrown on clothes that morning the polka-dot scarf had looked funky and stylish in a down-low gypsy way but after hours in the basement it had become bedraggled like the rest of me. Without Clare around to sneer at me, what did it matter what I looked like? Nor was I scheduled to see Wally Szalla that night. My grimy tank top was slipping off one shoulder, my denim miniskirt was creased across my belly and buttocks. Somewhere I'd misplaced my shoes and was barefoot, my feet were filthy. I hadn't dared to glance in a mirror for hours out of a fear of seeing exactly how I looked, no lipstick and oozing an oily sweat on my forehead and nose. This was the true Nikki, nothing like the show-offy glamour Nikki most people knew. The sensible thing would be to hide, and not just because I was frightened of a solitary male visitor when I hadn't expected anyone to intrude upon me because no one should have known that I was here.

I hadn't told Clare that I'd be at the house today. The previous week I'd called her several times, left urgent messages asking how she was, asking her please to call me, I was worried about her. But Clare, being Clare, supremely self-absorbed and indifferent to my concern, hadn't called back. Finally I called Ron Chisholm at Coldwell Electronics, managed to get past a protective female assistant with a plea that this was a "family issue," and there came my brother-in-law on the line to assure me, in a voice somewhere between evasive and apologetic, that Clare had certainly meant to call me, but had been "caught up in the kids' schedules" all this week.

So that was it. I'd been worried about Clare's health, and it was Mommy-Clare she'd retreated to, thumbing her nose at me.

Careful not to sound ironic I said, "Oh. It's the 'crazed time,' I guess?" and Ron said, "Is it! So much is happening at the kids' schools, Lilja has events every day, and weekends, nothing like when we were kids." I surmised that Clare hadn't told her husband about her emotional collapse, the terrible things she'd revealed about her marriage, and she wouldn't have wanted me to speak of her behind her back, even in sympathy. Instead, I asked if Clare had any plans to return to our mother's house soon, or should I proceed alone? I'd asked the *Beacon* for a few days off. I didn't mind working at the house alone. Ron said, relieved, "Nikki, if you can do it alone, I would be so grateful. As much or as little, anything you feel up to. The sooner we can place the house with a realtor, the better. And Clare hasn't seemed to be herself lately . . ."

I resisted the impulse to say, Oh. Is that the worst news, my sister not "herself"?

On the front stoop, the plainclothed detective wasn't about to go away. He'd heard the venetian blind clatter. He'd probably seen me. He was rapping on the door sharply. A curious thrill ran through me. *This man doesn't give up. I can't shake him off easily.*

I'd felt that way about Wally Szalla, two years before. The way he'd pursued me. At the time, it always feels like fate.

As the detective lifted his fist to knock again, I opened the door. "Yes? What do you want?" The man's eyes widened at the sight of me, in a kind of startled pity. Maybe I was part-naked, or my face was smeared with grime, I was too tired to care. Damned if I would invite him inside.

He was showing me his shiny police badge, like something on TV. Identifying himself, Detective Ross Strabane, hoped I remembered him, wanted just a few minutes of my time. Awkwardly, he extended his hand. As if I would want to shake his hand! Every memory associated with this man was hateful to me.

I stepped back into the vestibule. My knees were trembling. *Ma'am* he was calling me. *Ms. Eaton. Nicole?* I saw his lips move, he was speaking to me. I made no attempt to decipher his words. There was a roaring in my ears through which I heard only hissing syllables.

Go away! Go away I hate you.

Mom nudged me. Of course, I knew better.

"Come inside, I guess. This way."

Blindly I walked before Strabane, into the living room. I could feel his laser eyes on me: my sweat-stained tank top, the ridiculous miniskirt puckered at the crack in my buttocks, my long thin too-pale legs and filthy feet. At least, the furniture in this room had been rearranged, by me, more or less as it had been in my parents' time. Almost, except for the partly rolled-up carpet, and a flurry of dust-mice stirred by our feet, you might mistake this for a normal living room in a Deer Creek Acres ranch house.

Belatedly I saw that Clare's Post-its were still prominent: red, yellow, green on selected items of furniture.

"Anywhere. Please sit."

I sank into an easy chair, not very gracefully. Strabane adjusted an up-ended cushion, and sat on a sofa facing me. There was a coffee table between us, heaped with family photo albums, Mom's scrapbooks and envelopes crammed with snaphots dating back to the 1960s.

"My sister and I are clearing out the house. It will have to be sold, no one lives here now." I laughed, wiping at my face. "My mom never threw away a thing. There's a little portfolio there, a dozen snapshots from thirty years back, 'Fluffy's Last Days.' An orange tiger cat, I'd never known."

This information seemed to come from a long distance. My voice was reedy and nasal and wavering. Strabane was trying to smile, as if to put me at ease. "Your mother lived in this house a long time, Ms. Eaton?"

"With my dad, twenty-seven years. Herself, longer."

But Strabane already knew that, probably. I had the uneasy idea that he knew things about me, my family, and what had happened to my mother on the final day of her life, that I would never know.

He was peering at me, frowning as he removed his dark glasses and shoved them into a coat pocket. Asking how I was, how my sister was, how we were "getting along." My answers were monosyllables, mumbled. My memory of Ross Strabane was returning painfully. It was like sensation returning, where you'd had Novocain. The man was familiar to me as a blood relative I'd known long ago, someone I'd known for too long, who'd brought me cruel, crude news. I'd been exhausted by him and I had not wanted to see him again for between us there was a terrible knowledge, I could not forgive him for this knowledge. There seemed a kind of further insult, Strabane's jaws were covered in a bristly dark stubble, the start of a beard! It wasn't a good idea, the beard.

Strabane's hair was now trimmed razor-short at the sides and back to erupt in a cascade of quills across the crown of his head. And his eyes! I resented those eyes.

I wiped my face on the front of my tank top, where it left a smear of greasy damp. Beneath this garment, my breasts were naked and loose and tender, as if they'd been roughly squeezed. I was remembering now, at the hearing in the courthouse when I'd given my testimony, Strabane had watched me fixedly. I'd tried not to look at him. I'd tried not to look at Wally Szalla at the back of the room. Or at Clare, my brother-in-law, any of my relatives. Especially I had tried not to look at the man in the orange jumpsuit, "in custody" and charged with my mother's murder. I'd tried to focus on the prosecuting attorney who was formally questioning me, leading me across a tightrope above an abyss . . . Seeing Strabane, I was back in the courtroom. A rivulet of sweat slithered down the side of my face.

Strabane cleared his throat, uneasily. Trying to smile, but not very convincingly. "I'm afraid I have some bad news, Nicole. There is probably a call on your answering machine, at home. The prosecutor's office . . ."

"Last night, I stayed here. I didn't go home. I haven't checked my calls for a while, officer."

I spoke quickly, to defer what Strabane had to tell me.

It occurred to me: everyone tries this. With homicide detectives, you bet. "I'd left plenty of food and water for my cat, before I came here. I mean, I do that automatically. Whether I stay away somewhere overnight, or not." I paused, my heart was beating rapidly as if this were a flirtation suddenly: but who was this man? and where were we, that looked familiar as a much-dreamt dream, the kind you can't remember? "I became so tired, yesterday. I didn't mean to sleep so long. I lay down on my old bed, my bed-I'd-had-as-a-girl, Mom kept my room as a guest room, about the most frequent guest in that room was *me*. When I woke it was so late, it only seemed practical to stay overnight. But I'll be back in Chautauqua Falls tonight, I think. I'll pick up my calls then. Actually, I can pick them up from my cell phone but—"

Strabane was hunched forward awkwardly, elbows on his knees. His scruffy appearance contrasted strangely with his eyes that were unexpectedly clear: as if you could see deeply into those eyes, so dark as to appear black, into another place in which things made sense and were all right and you should not worry.

Strabane was saying there would be a trial, after all. It looked pretty definite now.

A trial! For a moment, I didn't know what trial he could be refering to.

"—his lawyer's been trying to tell him, explain to him, the guy is plain stupid, he can avoid the death penalty if he pleads guilty and accepts a sentence of life in prison without parole, but, no!—he wants to plead 'not guilty' and have a trial. So, there you are. Like I say, most criminals are missing part of their brain. Especially a meth-head like Lynch who hadn't much brain to begin with."

Strabane spoke vehemently. The dream shimmering around us careened in and out of focus. I'd been hearing words but couldn't seem to process them. My mouth twitched in a smile, as if I'd been nudged.

(By Mom? Wasn't it time to smile? When your visitor seems discomforted, if he has brought you bad news and is very sorry and you owe it to him, to assure him *he has not*?)

Numbly I said, "I see. A trial."

"Asshole's firing his lawyer! That shows you how stupid he is."

Strabane's nostrils flared in indignation. The lapels of his ill-fitting sport coat bunched up as he leaned forward, fists on his knees. Vaguely I wondered: is he carrying a gun? In our house, on this ordinary weekday afternoon? This house, the Eatons' house, in which nothing much had ever happened, in all our memories?

"It's rotten for you and your sister, everybody in your family, this dragging on. You're really nice people, decent people not like any kind a guy like Lynch deserved to mingle with for five minutes. The thing is, the defense always tries to stall, that's to their advantage. They figure, witnesses might move away, or die, or change their minds, or forget. They figure, time is on their side. 'Cause the defendant won't be going anywhere. In a capital case, the idea is there's so much at stake, a 'man's life,' everything has to be done by the book 'cause there will be an appeal if he's found guilty which in this case, for sure Lynch will be." Strabane paused, incensed. He was clenching and unclenching his fists like a man yearning to fight. "Worst thing, Lynch was a suspect in a case ten years back, 'home invasion and sexual assault' in Niagara Falls, except there wasn't evidence enough to charge him, the Falls PD had to let the bastard go, and that time, too, a woman was hurt, so bad she couldn't remember a thing that'd happened, a woman sixty years old! Now an informant, Lynch's own cousin down in Erie, tipped off police about Lynch involved in that. So there's that, Nicole, that if Lynch had been charged, and put away for a long time like he deserved, he wouldn't have been out to hurt—well, anybody else."

Through a ringing in my ears I wasn't hearing this. So much information, so quickly! Like Mom's albums crammed with snapshots, clippings, mementos of long-forgotten occasions: each item was precious as each moment in our lives is precious but there was too much, you felt the terror of falling.

"Could be a year, maybe."

"Year . . . ?"

"Before the trial."

"I . . . I see."

What was this insipid *I see* I kept repeating! This was no way of speaking natural to Nikki Eaton.

"The D.A.'s office should be keeping you better informed, Nicole. It's lucky I can intervene. I have taken a special interest in this case, see. 'Gwendolyn Eaton': I think of that lady a lot. I think that your mom was a wonderful decent special person and him, that piece of garbage, hurting her like he did, that upsets me pretty bad. I should be used to it by now. In theory, I am. I mean, I am a professional, don't get me wrong! We don't have a lot of violent crime in Mt. Ephraim, though. This is more what you'd get in Rochester or Buffalo. I never went into police work for any kind of glamour. You know, like on TV. It's more like *Cops*, on TV. That kind of routine. Mostly you follow procedure, it's familiar. I'm a detective for any kind of case needing to be investigated, not just homicide. We have like one homicide in five years! What I hate is being the bearer of bad news. I wish I could be the bearer of good news for once! To people like you, Nicole, and your sister. When I signed up for the police academy, after the army, this was in '85, I'd been influenced by a thing that happened in my uncle's family. Not to go into details, but there was a violent crime. This was over in Lackawanna. And there was a death, of somebody who deserved better. And this detective, in the Lackawanna PD, was instrumental in helping us through it. I mean, his spiritual person, not just his police work. He was a professional but it went beyond that. Helping people through a bad time. You never know when you will need that kind of help. Thank God if there is somebody who can give it. I vowed I would be of that type. I mean, I would try. It doesn't always work out, people don't always want you. And things get screwed up. It's nobody's fault, the way the courts are. 'Criminal justice system'—it's a lottery. I'm kind of clumsy, I guess. I can see I'm embarrassing you. Hell, I'm embarrassing myself. I need to leave you alone, I guess. You will want to call your sister probably. You will want to commiserate. But the trial will be all right. There's no bail for Lynch, he'll stay where he is. After the trial, he'll be shipped to Attica. 'Death Row.' I vow that. Whatever I can do, I will. We've got the evidence, it's airtight. You don't argue with DNA. You don't argue with so many witnesses. We will get justice for your mom, Nicole. I vow!"

Strabane's face had darkened with blood. His eyes shone with a startling lustre. I stared at him, astonished at this outburst. In his left eyelid a tiny nerve twitched.

"Hey. I'm sorry, Nicole—Ms. Eaton. Got carried away."

Strabane stood, embarrassed. He looked like a man who has stepped into an empty elevator shaft and is still falling.

Shakily, I got to my feet. For a fleeting moment I felt that Strabane might grip my hand, to help me up. If he thought that I was feeling weak or light-headed.

If he'd touched me, his hand would have closed tight over mine.

I knew this. The sensation was so powerful, afterward I would feel that it had happened.

Strabane asked me if I had any questions. He wasn't eager to leave but clearly it was time. I wanted him gone yet as I walked him to the door I heard myself ask, as if casually: "Why are evil people 'stupid,' Mr. Strabane? Why do you think so?"

Strabane blinked at this. As if I'd reached out and poked him.

I knew, I should have called him Detective.

He said, sucking at his lower lip, "Well. 'Cause they don't know how they hurt other people? They're missing a part of their brain that would let them know."

"You're sure of this."

"Ma'am, I'm not sure of anything, much. But this has been my experience, I think."

"You don't believe in 'evil,' then."

"Like 'good and evil'? Like, God?" Strabane laughed uneasily, running a hand through his bristly-porcupine hair. I wondered, if I came to know this man better, would I dare tease him about this hair; or would I find it weirdly attractive. I wondered if there were women who found Ross Strabane weirdly attractive.

He was saying, "Hey, I don't know! I'm not—what's it—'theological.' That's a total different line of thinking from mine. I see what's to be done, and I do it. I see connections between things, to relate how they make sense. If I look back, it's to look forward. To see where to go next. My thought about guys like Lynch is, like Hitler, or some terrorist blowing up innocent people, if they could feel it, the way you or I would feel it, the actual hurt they do to other people, they wouldn't do it. They would not commit their crimes. That, I believe."

It was an amazing speech, from Strabane. I had no wish to argue with him. In a way, I wanted to believe that he was right.

On his way out, Strabane fumbled to hand me his card.

"Call any time, Ms. Eaton. Day or night. If you need me, or—just to talk."

Just to talk! I would pretend I hadn't heard this.

As the detective walked away I saw a glaring red Post-it stuck to the back of his wrinkled sport coat.

DETECTIVE ROSS J. STRABANE

MT. EPRHRAIM POLICE DEPARTMENT

TEL: (716)722-4186 EXT. 31

HOME: (716)~~817-9934~~ 817-6649

Cell (716) 999-6871

Strabane must have forgotten he'd already given me his card. I had no idea what I'd done with it. Vaguely I recalled crossed-out numbers on the previous card and wondered if these were identical, or new. Like Wally Szalla, Ross Strabane had the harried look of a man between addresses. Unlike Wally Szalla, Ross Strabane hadn't the look of a man for whom women are waiting to love in the night.

I held the card between my fingers debating what to do with it.

"As if I'd ever call *you*."

In the end I tossed it into the kitchen drawer with Mom's accumulation of business cards, expired cat food coupons, ragged old grocery lists. I knew she'd have wished this.

blaming mom

why Mom? why Mom? why did you Mom? tell us why Mom? why you are not to blame Mom? because you are to blame! you are! YOU ARE TO BLAME! no one but you Mom! you, you are to blame! you brought him here! you brought him into your life! you brought him into our lives! you trusted him! you trusted everyone! you caused this! how can we forgive you! why Mom? why Mom? weren't we enough for you Mom? you are to blame for what happened! what happened to you! what happened to us! you are to blame! you are to blame! you! you! no one else! Mom, why? Mom, why? why? why Mom? why Mom? WHY MOM? WHY MOM? WHY?

part three

broken pieces

This was the season, people said, that Nikki Eaton broke into pieces. To me, it felt like the season I put myself together, stronger than I'd been.

The first thing Smoky did in his old house was to flop down on the kitchen floor in a patch of sunshine and roll over excitedly, showing his splotched-white tummy. His big-jowled face flashed from side to side and his tawny eyes glowed in unspeakable cat-ecstasy.

The second thing, Smoky scrambled to his feet and investigated the corner of the kitchen beside the refrigerator, where his food bowls had always been set out, on neatly folded sheets of newspaper. These were missing, but I would soon replace them.

The third thing Smoky did was to explore the house, cautiously. Peering into each room with his tawny-quizzical eyes, tail and ears pricked up, looking for someone who wasn't there.

maybe?

Mornings waking in my old bed. In my old room. That Mom had transformed into a guest room. (Actually, I'd been the most frequent guest in this room.) Opening my eyes to see not the patchwork of rock star posters (the guys at crotch-level) and disintegrating cork bulletin board (tacked-up snapshots, clippings from the school paper bearing the byline Nikki Eaton, mementos of trips, dried wildflowers) and whirlwind of clothes, papers, books through which paths would have to be cleared from time to time, but, as in a dream in which years have passed within a few seconds, an "adult" room! Allowing me to know *My God I must be an adult.*

Though it never seemed very convincing.

Smoky slept with me. Smoky was lonely at night and not so bossy as during the day. Leaping up onto the bed with his grunt of a meow, settling at the foot of the bed on my feet, or, better yet, snuggling close beside my left side, or, with a grunting purr, onto my chest.

"Just don't smother me, Smoky. Promise?"

A twenty-pound cat on your chest, oh my.

When a twenty-pound cat decides to wash himself, licking every swath of fur with his deft rough tongue, rubbing behind his ears with his chunky paws, and this can go on for ten long minutes, oh my.

But how happy I was, sleeping. The "grief counsellor" to whom I'd gone for a single session spoke of depression taking many forms and one of those forms exhaustion and a wish to sleepsleepsleep which seemed to me a very good idea except: "How?"

That was before I'd moved back to 43 Deer Creek Drive. That was before I'd moved back into my old room. That was before I'd called the district attorney's office to inquire (I was calm, I was polite, Mom would have been proud of me) if my mother Gwendolyn Eaton had been, in addition to being murdered, "sexually assaulted," and was informed that the medical examiner's report had not noted "sexual assault." And I was suddenly happy, hearing this.

Happy when waking in my old bed, I mean. Happy, as Smoky lapsed into a wheezing sort of purr on my chest.

For when you wake up in your old girlhood bed there is a sweet bubble of no-time when you might be fourteen, or eight, or better yet four. In that luxury of thinking *Nothing has happened yet. And maybe it won't.*

squatter

"Nikki! What have you *done!*"

One weekday morning in July I was on the back terrace working with my laptop, trying to write a piece for the *Beacon* on a local sculptress that was already days overdue, when I heard my sister screaming before I saw her.

"Nikki how could you! I let you out of my sight for a few days and you've moved the furniture back, the Post-its are gone, you've even bought new plants! *New plants!*"

Clare had entered the house without warning. I'd had no idea she was coming. I'd called her a dozen times and left messages but she hadn't answered. Now suddenly she'd turned up, screaming at me through the screened terrace door.

For so long, Clare had avoided the house, and me. It was like her now to show up, indignant.

It was like her to make me feel guilty. Damned if I would feel guilty.

"Look, we'd let Mom's plants die. No one watered them for weeks, all I've done is replace them."

" 'Replace them'! Are you crazy! You can't live here!"

I was barefoot. I was dressed you might say casually. I hadn't expected any visitors. I went to join Clare inside the house, where she was storming through the rooms.

"Nikki, you've been unpacking boxes? These things we sorted through,

I sorted through, I spent hours tagging, that need to be cleared out of the house? You've been *unpacking*? All that we did last month, to get the house ready to be sold, you've *undone*? I hate you."

I tried to calm Clare by touching her shoulder, and she threw my hand off in disgust. I hadn't seen her in several weeks and was shocked at how puffy her eyes were, how middle-aged she'd become. There was a soft knob of flesh beneath her chin and her permed hair was looking limp in the muggy July air. I had to concede I hadn't told Clare what I'd been doing; my feeling was, she'd abandoned the house and me, it was none of her business now.

Nor had I told her about Strabane's visit. My call to the district attorney's office.

I was saying hotly, "That isn't true, Clare. I haven't moved all the furniture back and I haven't unpacked all the boxes. I brought some things over to Mom's church, for their charity store in the basement. I've gotten rid of lots of things including most of Dad's clothes and those old cane-bottomed chairs. If you'd looked more carefully instead of screaming at me—"

Now Clare was truly incensed. I stepped back, anticipating a slap in the face.

"Mom's church? That church? That charlatan church, and that charlatan 'reverend'? I told you, Nikki, we were taking Mom's things to Good Will! *I told you!*"

"Well, you weren't here, Clare. You—"

"We need to sell this house, Nikki. You know that, why are you behaving this way? This is an empty house, no one lives in this house, *we must sell it*."

"*I* live here, and so does Smoky."

Now it was as if I'd tossed a lighted match into a hornet's hive.

"You *live here*? You've *moved in here*?"

"Not exactly. Not all my things. It's just temporary, through the summer. Until—"

"No! You have no right! This house belongs to both of us, Nikki!

You're squatting here! You're a squatter, you're crazy, and you're going to drive me crazy!"

Clare ran outside onto the front lawn. I had to realize how upset my sister was, running outside where any of our neighbors could see us, and hear us quarreling. The color was up in her face, she'd become an incensed schoolteacher challenged by a classroom of rowdy students. When she dropped her car keys in the grass we both stooped to retrieve them, and when I handed the keys to her Clare snatched them from my fingers and shoved me away with the flat of her hand.

"Go away! Get out of here! Go back to Chautauqua Falls! You have your own life, Nikki, *save it*."

messages

The phone began to ring frequently. You'd have thought that Gwen Eaton was still living here. Sometimes I answered, and sometimes I did not. Messages accumulated.

Mt. Ephraim was such a small town, everyone knew everyone else and quickly it had become known that Nikki Eaton had moved back into her family house. Relatives called, a few friends called, Wally Szalla called and so did my brother-in-law Rob Chisholm.

Wally Szalla. Of course I wanted to see Wally: I was in love with Wally.

Telling myself *He is the man I hope to marry. He is the man I intend to marry.*

A few hours after Clare's visit, Rob Chisholm called.

I didn't speak with Rob, but I listened to his message several times before erasing it.

"Nikki? If you're there, will you pick up?" Pause. A sound of harsh breathing. "Well. Clare is very upset. We thought you were going to clear out the house . . . I mean, I'm upset, too. We'd thought it had all been decided—selling the house. But now Clare is saying that you've moved back in?—you've brought back your mother's cat?" Pause. *Cat* had been uttered with faint incredulity. The breathing sound was louder, against the phone mouthpiece. An edge was creeping into my brother-in-law's voice, I had a glimpse of how Rob Chisholm spoke to subordinates at

Coldwell Electronics, Inc. and it was nothing like the affable flirty tone with which he usually spoke to his sexy/hip sister-in-law Nikki when his wife wasn't within earshot. "Clare is upset so possibly she's exaggerating. Will you call me, Nikki? To clear this up? Definitely, we need to talk."

I replied to Rob's message when I knew no one would pick up the phone at the Chisholms'. Carefully I explained that I had not *moved into* the house, I was only just *staying at* the house temporarily. Beyond that, my life was my own business.

the tryst

"But, Nikki: are you living here now?"

Wally Szalla was smiling uncertainly. Walking through the rooms of the house at 43 Deer Creek Drive in the cautious and oddly formal way of a man testing his weight on thin ice, waiting to hear it crack.

I laughed. I kissed my lover's lips.

Too late, Wally laughed, and reached for me as if to kiss me. But the playful moment had passed.

"Wally, I told you *no*. Of course I'm not living here. It's just that Smoky was feeling confined in my apartment, and so was I. And the house here is empty. And there's so much work to be done here, sorting through my parents' things, getting the house ready to be sold, it seemed such wasted effort, driving from Chautauqua Falls to Mt. Ephraim and back so often. And it's summer, and I can work out on the terrace. And my editor at the *Beacon* is agreeable to my coming in to the office only once or twice a week, since we do everything by e-mail and fax anyway." I saw how gravely Wally was nodding. As often I'd seen him nod while speaking on the phone to his wife or one or another of his children. Here was a rational man trying to understand another's irrationality. A reasonable man trying to resign himself to another's unreasonable will. "And I can come to see you, Wally, any time you want me. I'll be driving to Chautauqua Falls often. It doesn't always have to be you driving to Mt. Ephraim to see *me*."

When Wally kissed me, it was with an urgency I hadn't felt in him for a long time. Now I wasn't living ten minutes from his bachelor's quarters at Riverview Luxury Apartments or twenty minutes from WCHF AM-FM. Now Wally couldn't take me entirely for granted, waiting for him lonely and lovelorn after "Night Train."

It was a warm July evening. I was showing Wally through the house, which he'd never seen before. I took care to speak of the house as the "family" house—not "Mom's house"—though Wally knew that Clare and I were co-owners now. So long as Mom had been alive, Wally Szalla had never been invited here. I had to wonder if Wally had wondered why.

Before us, retreating, Smoky skulked away. His tawny eyes glared and his claws clicked on the hardwood floors. As usual Wally tried to befriend the indignant cat, despite his allergy, and as usual Smoky snubbed him. "Smoky is just shy, Wally. It will take him a while to adjust to a new person in his life."

Wally said, "I've noticed that. Well!"

Overweight and inclined to perspire, Wally was dabbing at his face with a damp tissue. The house had air-conditioning but I hadn't gotten around to turning it on that day, though the temperature had been in the eighties. Like Mom, I hated air-conditioning. It had been Dad and Clare who'd insisted on it, in this house.

Gamely Wally was wracking his brains for something to say about the Eatons' utterly ordinary suburban-development ranch house. It was "homey"—"comfortable"—"a great architectural idea, one single floor." No one in the Szalla family, you had to surmise, had ever lived in a ranch house in a place like Deer Creek Acres, even those Szallas relatively down on their luck. Wally was especially praising of Mom's macramé wall hangings, clay flower pots, ceramic vases, needlepoint cushions and quilts I pointed out to him in nearly every room. Her waxed gardenia artificial flowers, Wally thought "so lifelike you can almost smell them."

These things of Mom's were beautiful, really. It made me happy that Wally Szalla should acknowledge them, if only fleetingly. If only to me.

And to me, in such a way, only because I was his lover. Because I'd brought him to my house in Mt. Ephraim, locally known as *the house where the lady was murdered.*

(I wasn't exaggerating this. I wasn't inventing it. I had actually heard these exact words, in a child's wondering voice, borne by the breeze from Deer Creek Drive as a young mother pushed a stroller past the house, accompanied by an older child. The young mother had responded with *Shhhhh!*)

Whenever Wally spoke of my mother to me, his eyes misted over. His voice softened. It was a variant of Wally Szalla's radio voice, the tone he took when speaking of the "late, great" jazz musicians he particularly revered, but it was a sincere tone, and it never failed to move me. Wally's sympathy seemed to spur me to react with a smile, even to laugh, to assure him that I was fine, and didn't require being treated like a convalescent. (Generally, this was how people treated me. Unless they managed to avoid me entirely.)

"Your father was interested in American history, I guess?"

Wally was enthusiastically examining the books (now dusted, and neatly arranged) on the shelves in Dad's study. Clare had wanted to box these and get rid of them at a secondhand bookstore but I'd resisted. Vaguely I planned to read some of these books, sometime; also, someday, Lilja or Foster might want them for a school project. These were titles from the History Book Club to which Dad had belonged for twenty-five years, and some of them were bound in russet-red "special edition leather" with gilt-stamped letters, that looked impressive on the shelves. With boyish eagerness Wally read aloud, "—*A Soldier at Gettysburg—I Fought with Geronimo—Fifty Years on the Old Frontier—The Great Adventure: The Lewis and Clark Expedition—Custer's Luck—Wigwam and Warpath.* It looks like your father was an amateur historian, Nikki."

"Well, yes. Sometimes he said so."

"I wish I'd met him, Nikki! The Lewis and Clark expedition has always been something I've been interested in. I mean, as a kid I'd wanted to hike into the Yellowstone, and float down the Missouri in a dugout canoe. Your dad and I would have had a lot to talk about."

Wally was leafing through one of the simulated-leather volumes, examining antiquated maps and photographs. I couldn't tell him that Jonathan Eaton would have been profoundly disgusted with me, simply for being involved with him: a married man, and an adulterer! If Dad were living, Wally Szalla couldn't have stepped onto this property.

It was true, Dad had wanted to be a historian. So he'd often said. As an undergraduate at the State University at Binghamton, he'd had to make a practical decision to major in business administration, as most of the Eatons did, and not so academic a subject as history; and he'd always regretted it, he said. Over the years, as Dad told and retold the story, it began to acquire a mythic dimension in which Mom played a role: "A man has to have a decent income to support his wife and family. I never shirked my responsibilities." There was an air of reproach to Dad's voice as if Mom had forced the decision on him but, if you figured out the times and dates, you could see that Jonathan Eaton must have majored in business long before he'd even met Gwen Kovach, who was years younger than he was.

When in doubt, blame Mom. I guess it was easiest.

Most evenings, Dad watched TV after supper. Sometimes he'd have one of his history books on his lap, to read during commercial breaks when he'd turn the set on mute. By 9 P.M., Dad would be nodding over both the TV and the book though he claimed never to fall asleep for his eyes were "always open." We knew not to tease him even when he snored. We knew not to ask him too closely about what he was reading. Among the relatives, Jon Eaton was an authority on all things historical and political and his word was never challenged. "That man is a walking talking encyclopedia!"—my female relatives were gushing in their admiration.

Yet when the distinguished Civil War historian James McPherson came to speak at the University of Rochester, while I was enrolled there as an undergraduate, I invited Dad to McPherson's lecture and to a symposium afterward, but Dad turned me down impatiently. He hadn't "time to waste," he said. Unlike people who "frittered away their time" on college campuses, he had to "earn a living."

Now Wally was imagining that he and my father might have bonded over a common interest. I didn't have the heart to contradict him.

"All right if I borrow this, Nikki?"

It was one of the massive fake-leather books, I had a strong feeling my father had never read. The gilt-edged pages looked pristine. *The Way Westward: American Pioneer Adventures.* I told Wally of course he could borrow it, in fact he could keep it: "Dad would be so pleased."

The protocol of staying-overnight-with-a-lover.

Should you bring toiletries? A change of clothes?

Since we'd become lovers three summers ago (so long! yet our relationship was so undefined, the time felt much shorter), Wally kept a number of his things in my apartment in Chautauqua Falls. At first just toiletries—toothbrush, razor, deodorant. (The deodorant was Male Maximum Strength.) Then, articles of clothing—boxer shorts, T-shirts, socks. Selected shirts, trousers. (Not pajamas: Wally slept naked.) With his tucked-in smile meant to signal shyness, though Wally was anything but shy, he'd say, "Nikki, is there room in your closet for—?" When other men had made such suggestions in the past I'd become edgy and guarded but with Wally my response was immediate: "Move right in, Wally. There's plenty of room."

Because there was so little room in my three-room apartment, this had to be a joke. Yes?

Wally laughed, uneasily. "Darling Nikki, I wish I could."

I knew to keep my tone light. Maybe I'd become *an other woman* but I didn't intend to play that role.

The Szallas' divorce proceedings were stalled, Wally told me. Isabel had fired her lawyer and hired a new "very aggressive" lawyer from Rochester and Wally's own lawyer, a friend, was "seriously outclassed." I listened to as much as Wally cared to tell me but didn't ask questions. I knew that Wally was miserable enough.

But now, I seemed to be spending most of my time in Mt. Ephraim, and not in Chautauqua Falls. Somehow this had happened, overnight. I hadn't discussed this change in my life with Wally, or with anyone. And suddenly Wally seemed uncertain of me. When he called me on my cell phone his first question was: "Nikki, where are you?" His second question was: "When am I going to see you?"

Wally wasn't a possessive or proprietary man. You could never imagine him jealous. But now, when I wasn't so accessible to him, he was eager to see me. I had to recall that, before Mom's death, there'd been stretches of time—days, even weeks—when Wally and I hadn't seen each other often, or even spoken on the phone; I'd waited for him to call, annoyed and anxious, and had to hide my vast relief when finally he did call: "Nikki, this has been a crazy time, I've been missing you like hell. Please, can I see you tonight?"

My pride melted like ice cubes dumped in the sink.

Yes! Oh yes.

Wally spent nights with me in my apartment, when he could. Sometimes twice a week, sometimes several times a week. If he was traveling on business, I might not see him for a week. If there were "complications" with his family, I might not see him for a week. It was rare that I stayed overnight in his apartment. The pseudo-"luxury" quarters weren't very comfortable. I dreaded one or another of his children showing up without warning. Like much younger children they left clothes and possessions scattered through the rooms. In the wake of Troy, pizza crusts, beer cans, smelly socks and soiled sodden-wet bath towels on the bathroom floor, it fell to me, as a concerned female visitor, to hang them up to dry. If I was foolish enough to hang around long enough, I ended up doing massive laundries.

Of course, Wally had a cleaning service. But the husky Russian-born girls came only once a week, by which time the apartment was a pigsty.

Wally sighed. "I love my kids, and they know it. 'Doormat Dad' is the

T-shirt for me." You'd have to know Wally to understand that this wasn't a complaint but a boast.

One day, in June, I'd happened to see Wally in the company of two of his children, in the showy Chautauqua Valley Shopping Mall. Stepped out of a store and saw, to my shock, my lover Wally Szalla walking with his son Troy, now nineteen years old but no less sulky, and a young woman who had to be Troy's twenty-two-year-old sister Katy, who appeared also to be sulking. Here was a middle-aged man speaking earnestly to his grown children, half-pleading it seemed, smiling in the tender-wounded way in which Wally sometimes smiled at me. It was evident that the three were related by blood, you could see the family resemblance. Yet, for all his charm, Wally couldn't seem to charm these two, who sauntered beside him as if indifferent to him.

I hadn't seen Troy in nearly three years. He'd grown, he was taller and thicker in the torso, his face coarser. His straggly hair had been shaved. He wore a grungy Hard Rock Café T-shirt and grungy shorts, running shoes without socks. Katy, whom I'd never seen before, more resembled her father, husky and soft-bodied, but with prissy cornrowed hair that flapped about her head and shoulders like skinny snakes, and a petulant mouth. Out of this mouth I heard a drawling rejoinder, "Oh for God's sake Dad-*dy*. Get *real*."

I decided to pass by Wally Szalla with an airy "H'lo, Wally!" and a wave of my hand. Friendly-breezy smile, and gone.

In that instant seeing Wally's startled guilty eyes. And Troy's arrogant male gaze sliding down my rear, my legs, to my feet and up again.

Afterward, I worried that Troy might have recognized me. That sexy-girl reporter from the *Beacon* with the punk-style hair, who'd interviewed his father one August afternoon three summers ago. But when I asked Wally, he only laughed.

"Nikki, don't worry! A kid Troy's age doesn't remember anyone or anything."

. . .

Don't worry you will never meet Troy. You will never meet Katy.

Or the older son, Andrew. You will never enter my personal life, only my sexual life.

"Nikki. God, I've missed you . . ."

Wally framed my face in his hands and kissed me. I tried to kiss him back. I tried to lift my arms, to slide them about his neck in the usual way but my arms felt heavy.

Gently Wally pulled me down onto the bed. We were in my old room—my "girlhood" room as Wally called it. Since I'd left home it was supposed to be a guest room but still the furnishings—maple wood, American colonial style—and the once-chic Georgia O'Keeffe flower posters on the walls were unmistakably mine. I'd been sleeping in this bed, better than I'd been sleeping in Chautauqua Falls, and I'd been missing Wally here, and wanting him here, and I wanted him now, except I dreaded hearing loud footsteps in the hall outside the room and my father's furious voice *Nik-ki! Is someone in that room with you?*

While I'd lived at home, until the age of eighteen, the only visitors allowed in my room had been females. The issue of boys "visiting" me at any time had been, as Dad made clear, non-negotiable.

Long after I'd ceased to be a virgin. Long after Dad knew I was "having sex" (as he phrased it, in the way you might enunciate the name of a repulsive disease).

Now, as Wally kissed me, his mouth seemed unfamiliar, not a mouth I'd kissed before. His warm breath, fleshy warm hands that were eager yet hesitant. I had an impulse to push him from me, to break into laughter. I had an impulse to bury my face in his neck, to press into his arms, and cry.

Poor, sweet Wally! He meant no harm, ever. He loved me, and he loved his family. I'd missed him here in Deer Creek Acres, in my girlhood bed. We had not made love for, how long? A week? I'd been vague about setting a date for him to spend the night, and Wally had had to rearrange his schedule to tape "Night Train" instead of airing the program live. He'd have preferred one of our romantic Chautauqua River inns for tonight. ("Air-conditioning is the best aphrodisiac.") But I'd wanted him here. I'd had romantic plans of making dinner for us, dining by candle-light on the terrace. But somehow, I'd put off buying the food. Somehow, I'd run out of time. The previous day I'd experimented with bread-baking, one of the allegedly easy recipes Mom had tried to teach me, for so-called Miracle Bread (soy flour, wheat germ, skim milk) but the bread hadn't risen, a disappointing dead weight in the baking pan heavy as rock. This home-baked bread, I'd meant to impress my lover with. I smiled to think of it, and then I was laughing.

"Nikki. We're all right."

Wally was gripping my shoulders. His face was creased in concern. (Maybe I wasn't laughing?)

"You've been under a strain, darling. You're not comfortable with me here. Look, I understand."

I protested, "But I am, Wally! I want you here, I've even changed the sheets on my bed. I vacuumed until the dirt-bag burst and I had to give up, I didn't have a replacement. I even tried to bake bread for you yesterday—'Miracle Bread.' But it wasn't." Now I did press my burning face against Wally's neck, overcome by a spasm of giggling. "A miracle, I mean."

"I thought I smelled home-baked bread . . ."

"More like home-baked lead."

Wally stroked the back of my head, my tense shoulders. In his arms he gently rocked me. "I didn't think this was a very good idea, Nikki. For you to move into your mother's house in this way, and for you to invite me here tonight. On the phone, you've been sounding—well, too 'up-beat.' And I've heard about the trial. I mean, that there will be a trial. God damn!"

I drew back to look at Wally. My face felt stung, as if he'd slapped me. "But—who told you?"

Wally shrugged. Silly of me to ask. Wasn't he Wally Szalla, one of a network of individuals, primarily men, whose business it was to *know*.

Szalla. In the Chautauqua Valley, the very name vibrated with significance. I had to wonder if, in my wish to become Mrs. Wally Szalla, there
wasn't a childish wish to acquire some part of that significance.

But I loved Wally, too. This kindly/sexy man. So elusive, even when
he was with me. Like the gravelly-voiced host of "Night Train" sounding
so lonely, you wanted to cradle him in your arms.

Except, since I'd opened the front door to Wally, there'd been strain
between us. A charged feeling as in the air before an electrical storm. I'd
been wanting to think that the sensation was sexual, purely erotic: we
hadn't laid hands on each other in so long.

But now it seemed, this sensation might be springing from the house
itself.

"Wally, I want you here! I'm not thinking about the trial, or—
anything. I'm thinking about you. I want you to spend the night, I've
been missing you. I . . ." Wanting to say *I love you*. But the words stuck
in my throat.

"Nikki, are you sure? Tonight?"

"Yes!"

We tried again. Outside the screened window, nocturnal insects were
singing in a quivering web of sound. Frantic coupling, mating. From
somewhere in Deer Creek Acres, the beat/beat/beat of rock music hump-
ing through backyards. I shut my eyes thinking *Upbeat: I'll give you up-
beat, mister.* Thinking *Kiss! must kiss!* even as the curiosity of *kiss* struck
me for the first time: what a weird custom. Was *kiss* natural, or acquired?
A ritual? I must've learned *kiss* from TV and movies. *Deep kiss* I'd certainly never witnessed in Deer Creek Acres.

Wally was perspiring, a burlier man than I'd recalled. Hugging him,
I was reminded of one of the last times I'd hugged Mom: the startling
slackness of her formerly trim body, small pads of flesh at her waist, and
in her upper back. But Mom had been a petite woman, compared to
Wally Szalla who was twice her size.

Wally was fumbling to pull off my shirt. (Why hadn't I shaved under
my arms, when I'd showered earlier that day? And my legs were so care-

lessly shaved, the swirling pattern of tiny brown bristles looked like some avant-garde Braille.) My fingers worked to unbutton Wally's shirt. (Why did Wally Szalla insist upon wearing long-sleeved white cotton dress shirts in the muggy summer of upstate New York? Why did the man never wear comfortable sports clothes, like shorts? And what is the protocol of removing a man's shirt for him, are you expected to unbutton the ridiculous little cuff-buttons, too? A riddle!) As we were kissing I had a flash of how, years ago, not in this room but down the hall in the TV room, thinking that my Mom and Dad were equally involved in a front-yard conversation with neighbors, my high school boyfriend Dick Gurski and I were stealthily making out while ostensibly watching a PBS documentary on the Civil War, and just as Dick shoved his clumsy hand beneath my shirt to clamp onto my cotton-bra-breast, and shoved his clumsy tongue into my mouth, there came a rush of footsteps in the hall and my father's indignant uplifted voice in the doorway: *Ex-cuse me? Am I interrupting something here?*

Again I laughed. I was shivering, and laughing.

Wally said, hurt, "Nikki. Really, you don't want me here."

"But I . . ."

"Not here. Not now."

With as much dignity as he could summon, flush-faced and breathing through his mouth like a winded dog, Wally heaved himself up out of our tangled embrace, that must have looked, from the doorway, like a cubist sculpture of misaligned heads and limbs. Wally shoved his arms into the shirtsleeves he'd just worked his way out of, and began to button the shirt, but crookedly, so that, wiping tears from my face, I had to stop his fingers, and make the correction. We hadn't gotten around to pulling off Wally's trousers, only just his hemp belt, that had fallen to the floor to tangle about his feet like a mischievous snake.

So funny! Mortification and regret would come later for me, that night.

As with my boyfriend Dick Gurski, with whom I'd broken up soon after that terrible scene, mortification and regret had been immediate, and laughter much later.

"Wally! I'm sorry."

I wondered if it was too late to suggest going out to dinner, after all? One of our romantic inns on the Chautauqua River? The mood Wally was in, scowling and panting, I guessed maybe not.

I followed Wally into the hall, clutching at his arm. He was too gentlemanly to throw off my hand as I knew he'd have liked to. Ahead of us was a frantic scuttling, a furry gray shape fleeing into the shadows. I heard my lover mutter under his breath, exasperated: "Damn cat I could wring its neck."

In this way our lovers' tryst in the house at 43 Deer Creek Drive ended much earlier than we'd expected: not yet 10 P.M.

He would call me in the morning, Wally said.

He'd brought two bottles of our favorite Chianti, and when he left, I asked him please to take the second, unopened bottle with him, not to leave it with me that night.

I'd caught up with him at the curb, where he'd parked the chunky tarnished-brass Buick. Why a man with Wally Szalla's money drove such a car was a riddle, you'd think.

Unless Wally Szalla didn't have all that much money? There were hints.

Now we were out of the house, and now it had been decided, no man would be sleeping in my "girlhood bed" that night, we were slightly calmer. Wally was saying how his day had been long, complicated and exhausting, and I was saying how since I'd be driving to Chautauqua Falls early next week, to drop by the *Beacon* office, I could see Wally then?

"Sounds good, Nikki. Yes."

We kissed. We were sleepy, strangely exhausted. As after a strenuous lovemaking.

The subdivision of Deer Creek Acres had no streetlights. On moonless nights like tonight it was alarmingly dark. Lawns that by day were vivid neatly tended patches of green resembled tar pits by night. The only lights were from houses, and some of these were set back from the road, obscured by trees and overgrown bushes. Few vehicles passed. When Wally switched on his headlights swaths of light sprang out onto the shadowy pavement.

The house where the lady was murdered was also the house where Gwen Eaton had lived, and her family had lived with her, and their memories of the house were happy ones, and did not deserve to be obliterated. The house was my house now and I would not shun it, as I would not shun my mother. I wanted to explain these things to Wally Szalla because he was my lover but more than this, I wanted Wally Szalla to know, without my needing to explain.

As I wanted him to know that I loved him, without my needing to explain.

A final time we kissed, through the car window. Our mouths tasted of wine. I stood in the road watching Wally drive away. Winking red lights disappearing from Deer Creek Acres. I'd lifted my arm to wave, not that Wally could have seen. Now I would be lonely, oh God.

I felt a nudge against my ankles, there was Smoky pushing his furry head against me. Petulantly he mewed *Come back inside! What are you doing out here! You have me don't you!*

Aug 5, 2004
Dear Ms. Nicole Eaton,

I have been thinking about our conversation and
want to tell you how sorry I am that I would
seem to you the "bearer of bad news." I know
this is my work and it is expected of me, a
homicide detective as I am, but it does not
make my work easier to bring bad news to those
who have had too much bad news already and who
do not deserve more.

Here I will enclose my card if you have lost
the other. Remember you can call me any time
day or night at these numbers. (The "home"
number has been changed. The cell phone is the
same.)

Yours sincerely

Det. Ross Strabane

Det. Ross Strabane, Mt. Ephraim Police

August 13, 2004
Dear Ms. Nicole Eaton,

On the card I sent to you last week, I
forgot to include my home address. This
is a permanent address now: 3817 North
Fork Road, Mt. Ephraim

Tel. number & cell unchanged.

I understand (I think) why you have moved
back into your old house. It is something
I might also do, I mean in such
circumstances.

There is a patrol in Dear Creek Acres
now, you have probably noticed. But still
you should keep all doors and windows
locked esp. at night but it is advised
during the day also, even in that
neighborhood. Also, keep your cell phone
close by, and in the car when you are
driving. There is not likely to be
anything to happen but you "never know."

Remember that I am your friend, you can
call day or night. I want to stress that
this is "professional" only. Some cases
are special to detectives and this is, to

me. I wish that I could help you and
your family in some way beyond just the
promise that "justice will be done"
sometime soon.

Sincerely,

Det. Ross Strabane

Det. Ross Strabane, Mt. Ephraim Police

emergency!

Fell and hit my head on the pavement. Fell off the bike's pedals and somehow my legs got tangled in the pedals. Oh it happened so fast before I had time to draw my breath to scream. Somehow, my right leg was trapped in the spinning pedal, somehow I was dragged along the pavement for several desperate yards before toppling in a soft broken heap, not just my forehead was bleeding but my right knee through a tear in my jeans and the skin from that knee hanging in shreds, and I was too shocked at first to scream and the breath knocked out of me and it was several seconds before I was able to call *Mom! Mom! Mom! Mom!*

Could have been killed. Could have cracked your skull open. Could have fallen beneath the wheels of a car. Could have died right there on Deer Creek Drive in front of your house that afternoon in August 1984, aged eleven.

If Mom hadn't been home. If Mom hadn't heard me. If Mom hadn't been around the side of the house gardening. If Mom hadn't come running. If Mom hadn't had the car that day, to drive me to the emergency room.

Oh it happened so fast: I'd been showing off.

No one was watching but I'd been showing off.

Riding my bike in the showy reckless way the boys rode theirs. Not sitting on the bicycle seat but standing on the pedals to make the pedals turn with more strength, to propel the bicycle faster. You stand on the pedals rising and falling with the swift turn of the pedals and it's an excited feeling; a thrill in the pit of the belly because you know it's dangerous, you know you can fall, you know you can hurt yourself, rushing down the hill from Deer Creek Circle to Pine Ridge Road so fast the wind makes your eyes tear. And suddenly—

Somehow my foot slipped. Between the pedal and the bicycle frame my foot slipped, and my ankle was caught, I was dragged along the pavement as the heavy bicycle came crashing down onto me slamming my head against something hard. And I drew breath to scream in pain and shock and there came Mom to crouch over me her face drained of blood looking like a porcelain face finely cracked that might shatter into pieces except Mom's hand pressed against my bleeding forehead was cool and calm and her voice quavered yet was calm *Nikki you'll be all right honey, Nikki don't be afraid we'll take care of you* Mom would murmur such words to me to comfort me as I sobbed in terror as blood poured from a three-inch gash in my forehead *Nikki it's just a little cut honey, it hurts but it isn't serious honey, we'll take care of you, don't be afraid honey* wrapping my bleeding head in her sweater, tugging to extricate me from the twisted bicycle, and then half-lifting me in her arms, trying to set me on my feet but I was too weak and frightened to walk so Mom managed to lift me to carry me to the car, hoist me into her arms though I was nearly her size and Mom weighed hardly more than one hundred pounds and we were in the car, I was sprawled in the passenger's seat slipping out of consciousness as Mom drove us to the hospital, two miles to Mt. Ephraim General, to the emergency room driving as fast as she could, braking at corners, skidding and accelerating and at the hospital sounding her horn loud and frantic and screaming for help as the car rocked to a stop in front of the automatic sliding-glass doors and as attendants rushed out to us shouting *Help! help us! my daughter is bleeding from a head wound* and I was lifted by strangers and borne away half-conscious uncertain where I was, what was happening to me, carried into a brightly lighted place and made to lie flat on a table and the blood-soaked material of my torn jeans scissored away to expose the shredded flesh at my knee and there was blood in my eyes, there was blood on my lips, blood soaking my cotton pullover, you would think that blood is warm but this blood was cold, the dampness was cold, I was shivering so hard my teeth chattered as my wounds were cleansed and stitched as if at a distance, I could hear voices at a distance, I could see the faces of strangers at a distance leaning over me and time must have passed, I must have fallen asleep because I was being wakened, called *Nikki* by strangers *Nikki wake up your mother is here to take you home* and there was Mom smiling though looking exhausted and her clothes were stained with something dark, Mom and one of the young nurses helping me to hobble out to the car, marveling what a good, brave girl I was, four stitches in my forehead and seven in my knee and a tetanus shot and a painkiller pill and my head swathed with white gauze and adhesive like the head of a mummy and in the car driving home Mom kept glancing at me, touching my hair, my hand, groping to squeeze my hand in her fingers that were strangely cold *You're safe now Nikki, God has spared us this time.*

teasing mom

Twenty years later I would remember: how Mom had lifted me in her arms. How Mom had carried me to the car, and driven the car to the hospital. How Mom had remained calm. How she'd managed to calm me. How at the entrance to the emergency room she'd leaned on the horn, she'd shouted for help, she'd been fierce in a way I had never seen her. And how, as soon as we returned home, as soon as it was determined that I hadn't been seriously hurt, Mom became, well—Mom again.

At the time, I hadn't realized. Only now. Twenty years later.

As the story of how Nikki fell from her bike and how Mom took her to the hospital was told, told and retold, in the way of family anecdotes, it would develop that Nikki had been "showing off" out in the street and in the hospital while waiting for her to be "stitched up" Mom and the emergency room receptionist had discovered they'd been neighbors back on Spalding Street as girls, the receptionist had been a year ahead of Gwen in junior high, in ninth grade she'd run away to Buffalo with an older boy and eventually she'd gotten married (though not to that boy, to someone else) and had children and gotten divorced and returned to Mt. Ephraim with her children and had been working at Mt. Ephraim General for years and living a few blocks from the hospital and on, and on. As Mom recounted the utterly ordinary life of her old girlfriend Elise Czekaj, Mom's face took on a curious childlike glow of enthusiasm; until Dad would interrupt with a wink, to say, "Well! Poor Nikki was worried her mother had forgotten her, being stitched up like a mummy while Gwen was gabbing away with an old female friend. I'd say Nikki was lucky her mother didn't drive home without her, having totally forgotten her."

And Mom would blush, and laugh. Shake her head in protest: *No!*

Eventually, as the tale was told and retold, Nikki too would join in. At the point at which I was being "stitched up" (somehow, this expression makes people smile) I might interrupt, in the way of a sly tease, to say, "And when I came out of the emergency room, all bandaged up, there was Mom talking with this dyed-beehive-haired fat woman at the receptionist's desk, and Mom squinted around at me like, almost, she didn't want to be interrupted, she'd gotten so involved with 'Elise,' catching up on thirty years of gossip, so I said, 'Mom? You didn't forget me, did you?' and Mom said, embarrassed-like, 'Nikki, *no*. But, goodness, what have you done to your *head*?' "

This was silly. This was preposterous. But everyone would laugh. And Mom would blush, and flail her hands, and laugh in protest: "Nikki, what a thing to say! It wasn't like that at all, and you know it."

We knew, we must have known. I knew, and Clare knew, and Dad knew. And our Eaton relatives knew. Except we laughed. And Mom laughed. And blushed with pleasure, being teased.

If they tease me, if they laugh at me they love me. For I am only just Gwen, to be teased.

rose of remembrance

They were the happiest couple.

They were the most blessed couple.

They wanted to share their news with me: I would be the first in all the world to know.

They brought a blooming yellow rose tree—"Rose of Remembrance"—in a clay pot, in honor of my mother who'd introduced them to each other in this very house.

"Exactly twelve weeks ago, it was. 'Mother's Day.' "

"It was meant to be, Sonny and me. Mrs. Aiten knew. Oh, your mother, in her heart she was so *wise*."

Sonja Szyszko and Sonny Danto. A couple!

Holding hands, their faces suffused with joy. Sonja's face was powdery-white, Sonny's face was oily-dark. Both were smiling so radiantly I involuntarily took a step back from the doorway.

My first impulse was to quickly shut the door. Run away and hide. Not just I wasn't expecting visitors but I didn't want visitors. Not just I wasn't answering my phone but I'd unplugged it.

Nikki be gracious! You know what to do.

Instead of telling these terrible people to go away inviting them inside. Out back, on the terrace.

"Oh thank you, Nicole! Just for a few minutes! We know, you are so private here. Everyone says."

I let this pass. Briskly I led them through the house to the sliding glass terrace door. I'd been working outside, trying to work, on my laptop. A feature for the *Beacon* on a Christian punk rock band that performed locally.

Sonja and Sonny! This was something of a shock. If I'd been shockable. Still my face must have expressed wonderment as the couple excitedly told me of their plans to be married in November. At Thanksgiving because they wished to give thanks. They would be married in the Mt. Ephraim Christian Life Fellowship Church and I was the "first in all the world" to be invited.

"Married! Oh."

"Your mother brought us together, Nicole. We owe this to *her*."

Sonny was setting the yellow rose tree down on the terrace, with a tender gesture. All the buds were open, well into bloom. The tree was a miniature, no taller than Sonny's belt buckle. For a moment I could not comprehend what it meant, why these exuberant people had invaded the terrace. My heart pounded quickly.

The visit would pass in a blur. Several times I thanked Sonja and Sonny for the rose tree. Several times I congratulated them on their engagement. Sonja was displaying her ring, which glittered with a fierce proud fire like her lavishly made-up eyes. Sonny spoke of the "serendity" that my mother had brought them together as if knowing how they were meant for each other.

". . . if it is a girl, we are thinking 'Gwendolyn.' Such a lovely name, it is not so common is it? But then, if a boy . . ." Sonja giggled. Her eyes widened like the eyes of one riding a roller coaster, plummeting suddenly downhill. Sonja's awkward manner of speech made it difficult to know whether she and her beaming fiancé were already expecting a baby or hoping someday to expect a baby.

Quickly I congratulated them. I told them my mother would have been so happy for them if only she'd known.

Next door at the Pedersens' children were squealing and shouting in the above-ground swimming pool. Through the summer I'd been relieved that my father wasn't here to be upset about noisy neighbors.

There was that advantage, to being dead.

". . . 'All you need in life for happiness is a family you love, and a garden, and maybe a cat or two,' " Sonny was saying, reverently quoting Mom, as Sonja exclaimed, "—oh but darling, Mrs. Aiten was joking, I think, 'a cat or two,' she said such things to tease, knowing I am not one for cats, I am *aller-gic* to them, and I do not trust them for they are sneaky animals I believe—but I did not tell Mrs. Aiten this, she would be hurt. She was so kind! She said to me, one Sunday after church, 'You have had a hard life, Sonja, I see in your eyes, but your eyes are beautiful and you have faith, I can see the faith shining in your eyes, you know that every day is a new day, only have faith.' " Sonja's eyes were dramatically enlarged by mascara and iridescent blue eye shadow, her mouth was lush and crimson as one of Mom's peonies, even as she spoke in a tumult of heavily accented words I saw how adoring Sonny's gaze was on her, how inspired Mom had been in bringing these two together, for surely that was what she'd intended. (And I'd imagined that Sonny Danto the Scourge of the Bugs had been invited to Mom's dinner for *me*.)

In the weeks following Mom's funeral, Sonny had left several phone messages for me. He'd asked if he could see me, if he could "drop by." He'd offered a free bug inspection and if his services were required he'd have given me a 20 percent discount. I hadn't gotten around to answering his calls and eventually they'd ceased.

I had to suppose that Sonny and Sonja fell in love shortly afterward.

". . . your mother said, that day I came here to spray for the red ants, 'It's so sad to think, God has created all these creatures and some of them are 'enemies' of one another. And all of these are beautiful to one another as to God, you have to imagine.' I laughed at such a thought, I mean I am not comfortable thinking such thoughts when it's my job to rid households of bugs, but later I was thinking, your mother was right. In her special way of thinking, she was right. She took us to look at her garden, she said, 'Suppose we were blind like these flowers? Like those seashells that are so beautiful to the human eye, but blind to one another? But we are not blind, we can see that tree, that flower. And that makes me happy for it is the secret of life.' " Sonny spoke excitedly. His hairline was receding, but his oily-dark hair lifted dramatically above his tanned dome of a forehead. Mom's wisdom shone in his eyes even if he couldn't express it very clearly. His fiancée was nodding vehemently, leaning forward so that the neck of her dress fell open to expose the milky white tops of breasts tightly clasped in a lacy black satin brassiere. Sonja exuded a rich perfumy air, baubles and bracelets jingled as she spoke. Earnestly she said, "Until Mrs. Aiten was my friend, I was not happy here. I was so lonely here. This place, it is a place of closed doors, to one like myself. Even at the church, I was not made to feel so wanted. And now, because of Mrs. Aiten, I am so happy. I am a new woman. But it is a heavy cloud in my heart, what was suffered by your mother. Such a good, kind woman! Such a Christian woman! And what justice can there be"—Sonja shook her head gravely, her glossy dyed-black hair shifting and shimmering in a lavish spill over her shoulders—"when it is the 'lated'—is that how you say?—'too late'—'belated'—justice of man and not of God. In my country you cannot trust to it, the justice, it is a cruel joke to trust, in this country too, I think, but maybe not so much for there is more hope here, there is more faith, you are a younger country here, you can forget much. Maybe I am not so clear in my speech, saying such things to you, but you know, this man, this terrible man, who did this things to Mrs. Aiten, must be punished. Oh, I will pray for this! That there will be justice." Sonja spoke passionately, her voluptuous bosom shuddered.

"Oh. Thank you."

I was stunned. I'd never dreamt that Sonja Szyszko could speak in such a way. I had underestimated the woman, and probably I had underestimated Sonny Danto, too.

In my smugness. My blindness. My wish to mock.

Sure, I could mock them now. Sonja's fleshy breasts, hips, belly swathed in a crinkling kind of midnight-blue material you'd identify as a shower curtain except it had bat-wing sleeves and a V-neck opening for a head. Sonny who wore a biceps-fitting sports shirt open at the neck to show a fistful of grizzled hairs and the glint of a tiny cross on a gold chain.

Clare! You won't believe who dropped by the house. Who's engaged to be married in November in your favorite church.

"I—I'm very happy for you. Sonja, Sonny. Congratulations."

I went away to bring back a wedding present for Sonja: the white ostrich feather boa I'd given Mom for Mother's Day. It would go perfectly with her hair, her coloring, her overripe showgirl style. Sonja gave a little cry, and hugged me.

Perfumy Sonja, lavish in crinkly midnight blue, gleaming pale-pudgy feet in spike-heeled cork sandals with spangles. And those big pillowy breasts! And Sonny with his slick greasy hair smelling like motor oil. They were the real thing, I'd been a campy imitation.

I walked with the happy couple to the low-slung sexy red sports car parked so conspicuously in front of the house. Nothing like this on Deer Creek Drive. At the car Sonja hugged me again while Sonny looked on misty-eyed. "Of course I will come to your wedding. I promise."

I waved as they drove away. Sonja trailed the fluffy feather boa out the window, in a festive gesture of farewell.

Next day I examined the Rose of Remembrance in its clay pot. I tried to see the little tree with my mother's gardener's eye. She would have noted it was late in the summer to be buying roses. She'd have hoped that Sonny and Sonja had bought the tree from a reputable nursery and at a discount. That her friends hadn't paid full price for a rose tree past its bloom.

avoiding . . . (I)

It was true, as Clare had said: people avoided us.

Not that I blamed them. I guess. Plenty of times in my life I'd avoided people I knew, friends of the family and even relatives who'd lost a "loved one."

In our case, it had to be worse. What do you say to someone whose mother has been murdered?

(Every time there was a new development in the case, however small, local papers would erupt in front-page headlines and photos of Gwen Eaton and Ward Lynch. So often you saw these two faces linked, you'd have thought they were smiling mother and down-looking sullen skimpy-bearded son.)

Some of the people who avoided Clare and me had known our parents for years. They'd visited our house, they'd come to Mom's funeral and even Clare's lunch. Some were old friends and classmates of ours. Some were Eaton relatives!

Most often it happened at the mall, where it's easy to avoid people by ducking into stores, hurrying to escalators. A few times it happened at the Mt. Ephraim Public Library where Mom had been a frequent patron. At the Bank of Niagara where we all had accounts and at Wal-Mart, Home Depot, Eckert's, Pet World, The Whiz, ShopRite, even the Whole Earth Co-Op. Often it happened in parking lots where I'd notice a figure in the corner of my eye hesitating as if he/she had sighted me and was debating whether to acknowledge me, call out hello or discreetly turn away.

Most of the time out of pride I pretended not to notice. But sometimes I'd glance up smiling and wave energetically calling out, "Hey! Hi! I thought that was you."

No escape from such a greeting.

Reporting to Clare *Guess who I saw at the mall today. Who tried to pretend she hadn't seen me. Your best friend from high school Lynda Diebenbeck . . .*

Some of these messages were meant to annoy. I was pissed at Clare for not taking time to call me back. Nor did my sister "do" e-mail.

Actually, I preferred leaving messages. This way my bossy sister couldn't interrupt or contradict me. Or laugh at me. If she erased my messages without listening to them I couldn't know and be hurt.

Clare, you'd never guess who ducked behind the flour bins at the Co-Op this afternoon trying to avoid me: our dear cousin Jill. At check-out she tried to look innocent and surprised when I came up to her and said, Hi! Haven't seen you and your family all summer . . .

Jill Eaton had been a favorite cousin of ours. She'd married a well-to-do local man and had frequently invited the Chisholms, and me, to their larger parties. But not recently.

Jill had always adored her Aunt Gwen. At the grave site after Mom's funeral we'd hugged each other and wept. But how long ago that seemed, now. In Jill's flat gaze and thin forced smile I'd seen the futility of such shared memories.

Of course, I didn't tell Clare that Sylvie LaPorte had pretended not to see me, too. Sylvie LaPorte my wild high school girlfriend! She'd been devastated by Mom's death, for weeks she'd left tearful phone messages for me, sent sympathy cards and miniature inspirational books with such titles as *North of Grief, South of Joy* and *Chocolate Pudding for the Soul*. And there was my ex-fiancé Lannie Bishop, I'd been thinking still had a crush on me, clumsily ducking into an elevator in a multi-level parking garage.

And other Mt. Ephraim men, both single and married, who'd have previously gone out of their way to greet me with a wetly friendly kiss and the suggestion that maybe we could meet for drinks sometime? or dinner? Unless I still had that boyfriend.

Nor would I tell Clare about the most hurtful encounter.

Seeing my niece Lilja with two other girls at the North Hills Mall, skinny-beautiful with long shining hair, tiny halter tops and low-cut jeans baring their midriffs, and waving to Lilja, who seemed not to see me, at least not until I called out her name and approached her. And seeing then the reluctance in Lilja's face as she greeted me, endured a hug from me, mumbled replies to my cheery Aunt Nikki questions. I'd heard from Clare that Lilja was deeply mortified by the publicity surrounding my mother's death and the upcoming trial and I'd vaguely realized that I hadn't seen her or heard from her in some time, but until now I hadn't understood how my niece was estranged from me, too. Clare had told her about my moving back into Mom's house which must have shocked Lilja, for what "weird"—"freaky"—behavior this was, from the perspective of a fourteen-year-old. Not that Lilja was rude, in fact she behaved with a kind of adult graciousness though clearly the last thing she'd wanted was to be publicly accosted and made to introduce her girlfriends to me.

It was then I realized that I wasn't Lilja's cool/chic Aunt Nikki any longer. I'd crossed over to her parents' generation. My dyed-purple punk hair had nearly grown out, I was dishwater blond laced with gray at the roots. I wasn't wearing my funky thrift shop clothes. If I'd smeared lipstick on my mouth that morning, it was probably eaten off by now.

I knew to compliment Lilja on her lavishly pierced earlobes, though. And not to keep her a moment longer. "Well, Lilja! Say hello to your family for me, will you? And come over to see me, before school starts? You know where I'm living this summer, I guess."

Backing off with her friends, Lilja flashed a smile of sheer relief. "Oh sure, Aunt Nikki! I know."

"sharing your grief"

"Ms. Eaton. 'Nikki.' "

Fixing his nickel-colored eyes somberly on me. Arranging the lower part of his face in a small sympathetic smile.

". . . terrible shock you've had. You and your family. Of course you are still in mourning. You are still in shock."

A pause. I fumbled to drink ice water from a crystal goblet and the ice cubes tumbled prankishly causing water to splash onto my face in a way that necessitated a hurried mopping of my face as the nickel-eyes brooded upon me and a waiter hovered in the background.

"I can only imagine. I can only attempt to imagine. Your grief."

Actually it was discomfort I was feeling: a dread of glancing down to see that the front of my shirt had been splattered.

"You could write about it, Nikki. For our readers."

Oh! I was staring somewhere neutral: to my right, through a leaded-glass window, at the Chautauqua River below. Swift-flowing, breaking in a sequence of small frothy rapids.

The editor-in-chief of the *Chautauqua Valley Beacon*, Nathaniel Waldeman, Jr., rarely met with staff writers. More rarely did Mr. Waldeman take them to lunch at the historic Fayetteville Inn.

"You see, 'Nikki,' Dale Wilmer and I were discussing the possibility that you might write about your experience for our readers."

"Nikki" sounded in Mr. Waldeman's mouth like the cute, quirky

248

name of a dog. A Pomeranian, a toy poodle. Dale Wilmer was the features editor of the *Beacon*. My editor.

"Catharsis of grief"—"sharing your grief"—"healing process." As in cartoon word-balloons issued from a man's mouth. The nickel eyes misted over. There was the understanding that, sure this was a cheesy request, or would have been a cheesy request from anyone other than Nathaniel Waldeman, Jr., owner and publisher, as well as editor-in-chief, of the revered *Beacon*. Instead of wincing, or drawing back in revulsion, or tossing the contents of my wineglass (a California chardonnay Wally Szalla would have scorned) into the gentleman's face, I smiled gently, to allow my companion to know that of course I understood, his request was a gracious one, generously offered, in the service of doing me, the murder victim's daughter, a favor.

"Well! I know, it is a bit early. Maybe you are not quite ready to formulate your thoughts. Dale has been telling me that since, um, the tragedy, you have been living in Mt. Ephraim, in the family home you inherited, you've been turning in fewer features for us but those you have turned in have been first-rate, I've personally been impressed. Work is the great solace in time of personal tragedy, oh I know!" An inward brooding moment. Sipping of chardonnay. I had to wonder what Mr. Waldeman meant. What my relations with Dale Wilmer were at the moment.

We wavered from week to week. We were like a fever chart except not so predictable. It appeared that Mr. Waldeman didn't know, I failed to complete at least half the assignments Dale Wilmer gave me. "Failed to complete" a euphemism for "never got around to starting." I had to wonder if my relations with my editor Dale Wilmer were in inverse ratio to my relations with my married-man-lover Wally Szalla. If we were on good terms at the present time or not-so-good. If one of us, or both, were delighted/disgusted with the other right now.

". . . may discover kindred spirits. In the healing process. Those who have lost loved ones, too. Prematurely I mean. 'Violently.' We were thinking of a diary format. When the trial begins in December. With tastefully selected photographs. We feel that, given our readership, and a wish to extend circulation, the diary format is the most accessible to the most readers." A sigh. A lifting of the wineglass. A fleeting vision of *most readers* hovering in the air before us. "You would provide day-by-day copy. Very easy to e-mail. Dale could edit. No need for you to rein in your observations. Your feelings. 'Intimate.' 'Uncensored.' Perhaps I will have a hand in editing, too. A daily account of the trial, with the outcome not known. You, as well as your readers, Nikki, would be kept in suspense."

The nickel eyes glowed, for a moment almost lewdly.

Mr. Waldeman was admired/feared/disliked/avoided at the *Beacon*. Some staff persons claimed never to have seen him. Some, perhaps unseriously, doubted he existed except on the *Beacon* masthead. I knew that Waldeman existed because Wally Szalla knew him, in the way that Wally knew everyone worth knowing in the Chautauqua Valley.

Mr. Waldeman was assuring me that payment for the proposed feature would be "considerably higher" than usual. Whenever I wished, we could "negotiate." Perhaps a "formal contract." An "advance."

My heart was beating slower and slower. Strange! I wondered if it might cease to beat.

Mr. Waldeman spoke of my piece on the Christian punk band, that had been featured on the front page of the *Beacon* and had stirred some interest. In fact, it had been reprinted in its entirety in newspapers in Rochester, Buffalo, Syracuse and Albany. I smiled to think that Mom would have been proud of me. At the house I'd discovered a scrapbook devoted to NIKKI'S WRITINGS. Each article, each clipping, dating back to columns in our high school newspaper and features in college publications. The most recent was an interview with a local private school headmaster, dated May 8, 2004.

One of your best pieces, Nikki! Really, it is.

So Mom had assured me. Beaming with pride.

Like Dad's calendars, Mom's scrapbooks were scrupulously maintained as holy relics. You would not think they might come to an end so abruptly.

We must have ordered lunch. Food was brought. Our hefty silverware flashed. I pushed food around on my plate until, at an appropriate moment, a waiter murmured *Ma'am may I?* and whisked it away.

"Nikki. I hope I haven't offended you."

Alpha-male code for: you are not responding as I wish.

Alpha-male code for: you are not responding in a way to assure your own best interests.

The nickel eyes were guarded. Perpendicular lines bracketed the small smile. By this time my heart was beating so slowly, I had to wonder if I was awake. There was little likelihood of my tossing wine at my companion, muttering *Go to hell! I hate you! I quit!* and stalking out of the elegant dining room.

The check was paid. We were parting company. One of my hands was shaken. I heard myself say, in my bright Nikki-voice, "When I'm ready to 'share my grief,' Mr. Waldeman, it will be with the *Beacon*. I promise!"

time . . .

In the house at 43 Deer Creek Drive, time moved differently than it did elsewhere. Not in short frothy rapids that glittered in the sun but in large wide swaths you could not see the edges of and could not know where they began, how far they extended and where they might end.

If they might wash over you, and drown you.

Or bear you aloft, hopeful and unharmed.

"a good, safe thing"

It had become routine: Mt. Ephraim police now patrolled Deer Creek Acres.

At least twice a day, but not at predictable times, a metallic-blue Mt. Ephraim PD cruiser turned into the subdivision and passed with methodical slowness along the curving roads, drives, lanes. Gliding into and out of cul-de-sac "circles."

The cruisers were manned by youngish uniformed cops. Usually there was just the driver. I knew that Ross Strabane would never have ridden in the patrol car and yet each time I saw the car I thought of him and felt a stab of alarm, resentment. *I don't need you. I have a man who loves me.*

If I saw the cruiser I looked quickly away. My face beat with blood, I felt stricken, exposed. For of course the cruiser had to do with 43 Deer Creek Drive. With what had happened to my mother in that house.

Opinion in Deer Creek Acres was divided on the subject of the patrol. Most thought it was a good, safe thing, especially the parents of young children. Some older residents grumbled that it was annoying to see the patrol car, Deer Creek Acres wasn't a "crime ghetto."

If I'd been asked my opinion of the patrol I would have said yes certainly it was a good, safe thing.

In a time of emergency. When you need the police. Yes.

No one asked me. Except for a few of Mom's close friends, residents of Deer Creek Acres waved hello to me but otherwise kept their distance.

Her? The Eaton girl. The daughter.

That house where Gwen Eaton was murdered.

Through the summer, the police cruiser became an ever more familiar sight in Deer Creek Acres. Children waved at the uniformed driver, who waved back. Young mothers dawdled in the street with babies in strollers, toddlers, eager dogs. Often I heard laughter. I felt a pang of envy.

I didn't answer Strabane's letters. I didn't call him.

Yet it happened one afternoon, I was just parking my car in the driveway when the Mt. Ephraim cruiser appeared. And instead of looking away, somehow I was smiling at the cruiser, and waving.

"Hi! Hello!"

The youngish uniformed cop behind the wheel might have looked surprised but he smiled, too, and waved as he drove past.

And now I was suffused with a strange childlike happiness. For it had been so easy, what Mom would have been doing from the start: making the young police officer feel, not unwanted, but welcome in our neighborhood.

"where we all came from"

Every few weeks for as long as we could remember, Mom drove into the old, east side of Mt. Ephraim, to St. Joseph's Cemetery.

For a long time I went with her. Longer than Clare went.

As soon as Clare was in eighth grade she was too busy for such excursions. Jumping into the car because Mom called out in her cheery-adventure voice, "Who wants to go with me?" no longer appealed.

The east side of Mt. Ephraim was a hilly tumbling-down neighborhood near the river of row houses, potholed streets, derelict buildings and vacated mills with such faded names as Beame Ladies Hosiery and Carlyle Footware & Leather Goods. Here, South Main Street intersected with Spalding where Mom had once lived. The names of the streets were plain and utilitarian: Bridge, Front, Railway, Commodore.

Mom told us how as a child she'd been told that Commodore Street had been named for "Commodore" Cornelius Vanderbilt of the New York Central Railroad, a long time ago. It was said that Vanderbilt, the wealthiest man in the world at the time, had "disembarked" from his luxury car to visit with a Mt. Ephraim resident. Or, Vanderbilt had at least stood on the railway platform overlooking the street.

"Did you see him, Mom?"

"Did I see the 'Commodore'? That man died in 1877."

As a little girl I'd been concerned with dates, ages. Numbers were tricky, figuring them in your head. You had only ten fingers and ten toes to calculate with. The only birth-date that seemed to be permanently imprinted in my brain was October 8, 1973, when I'd been born.

Mt. Ephraim had once been an important stop on the New York Central Railroad. Trains had pulled into the station often, sometimes two or three a day; the east side had flourished. Now, trains thundered past hauling what seemed like miles of freight cars and the old depot was boarded up and covered in graffiti. Anyone who wanted to travel by train had to drive thirty miles to the station at Chautauqua Falls.

As a child I'd asked Mom why was this so? Why the trains didn't stop in Mt. Ephraim any longer?

Mom laughed. "Oh, ask *me*! As if I'd know."

Then, for Mom always pondered our questions to her, even those she couldn't answer: "I think it has to do with the economy, Nikki. 'Supply and demand.' You can ask Dad, he will know."

I was reluctant to ask Dad such questions. He'd squint at me suspiciously as if, at school, I'd already learned the answer and was testing him. Or, worse, he'd provide such a long and complicated answer I couldn't make sense of it. "Supply and demand" was what it all boiled down to.

"Will you look at these *weeds*! It's enough to break your heart."

Visiting her parents' graves in St. Joseph's Cemetery, in warm weather, Mom brought grass clippers, a hand hoe, potted flowers. If it was sunny she wore a crinkly straw hat to protect her face, which burned easily. If the grass was wet, she wore rubber boots. St. Joseph's Cemetery had become shabby and overgrown and Mom was fearful of snakes.

At her parents' graves Mom knelt in the grass. Always she was sad, subdued. This change in my mother disturbed me. I saw that my Kovach grandparents' graves were smaller than the graves of most of their neighbors and wondered if that was why Mom wiped surreptitiously at her eyes. Such plain dull-gray markers!

MARTA ANNA KOVACH	JACOB WILLIAM KOVACH
March 7, 1919	December 29, 1916
November 14, 1959	August 4, 1961

As soon as I was old enough to subtract numbers, I calculated the dates on the grave markers: Grandma Kovach had been forty when she'd died and Grandpa Kovach had been forty-four. You could see why they'd died, such old people!

In my bright schoolgirl voice I asked Mom how old you had to be, to die, and Mom smiled nervously saying any age that was old, much older than I was, so there was no need for me to worry—"You're just a little girl, darling." Impatiently I said, "No, Mom. How old do you have to be? *You*." For of course it was preposterous to think that Nikki would die, for "die" meant to go under the earth, and why'd I want to do such a silly thing?

Mom stared at me for a moment. Then laughed, and gave me a smacking wet kiss.

"Not for a long, long time, sweetie. Maybe never."

While Mom tended to the graves, clipped weeds and trimmed the English ivy she'd planted, wiped bird droppings from the markers, I prowled about, restless. It was hard to care about my Kovach grandparents who'd vanished so long ago. Dad never spoke of them and if Clare or I asked Mom about them her replies were vague and distracted and her smiles forced as if she was trying to keep from crying.

In St. Joseph's Cemetery there were some large, shiny grave markers. There were angels, and crosses. The small plain Kovach markers held no interest for me. I could not associate them with any actual people, not people who mattered. The cemetery was hilly and overgrown with shrubs, Mom couldn't see where I was poking around and if I climbed up onto gravestones. At the top of a steep hill there was a dumping-ground for old, rotted flowers and broken clay pots.

Sometimes from the top of the hill I'd lose sight of Mom. Then I'd see her, kneeling in the grass. Mom looked so little! I almost wouldn't have recognized her.

Distance makes people sad, I thought.

After a while Mom missed me and began to call anxiously: "Nikki? Nikki?"

It was the most delicious feeling to hide from Mom then to jump out from behind a gravestone, and run down the hill to her.

"Oh, Mom! I was here all along."

On the way home Mom sometimes swung around to Spalding Street to drive past her old house. The number on the front doorframe was 91. The house was weatherworn wood faded gray like the Kovach grave markers, with a sagging veranda. Mom had lived upstairs which seemed strange to me: other people lived *downstairs?* It seemed wrong, too, that the houses on Spalding Street were so close together, you could hardly squeeze through the narrow space between them. The front yards were small, grassless and ugly, nothing like the lawns in Deer Creek Acres.

Clare once snorted in disgust: "Some people! You'd think they'd be ashamed not to fix up their houses better."

Mom said reprovingly, "Clare. Not everyone has our advantages."

" 'Advantages'—what's that?"

"A father to work and take care of them and—love them. A mother who can stay home with her children. Enough money to—well, live."

Clare objected, "Mom, anybody can rake up trash! Anybody can shut their front door, and pull their curtains back inside the windows, for heaven's sake." At thirteen, Clare had a schoolteacher's indignation in the service of absolute fact.

Mom continued driving, biting her lower lip. Poor Mom! She never argued with us if she could avoid it. And more and more, Clare was seeing things that Mom seemed not to see, or didn't acknowledge seeing. It was Mom's *just-pretend* way, in Clare's words.

It was a relief when Clare was too busy to come with us to St. Joseph's. I suppose Mom missed her but I didn't, not one bit.

The last time we drove past 91 Spalding, I asked Mom if she'd liked living in that house? If she missed it, sometimes? and Mom said with a vague smile, "We're all happy where we came from."

So softly Mom spoke these words, she might have been alone in the car.

"comfy"

Come over to the cemetery, Clare? Around eleven this morning? I've got a rose tree to plant by Mom's and Dad's graves. Pause. *We haven't seen each other for a while. I've been missing you.* Double pause. *I ran into Lilja at the mall the other week, and* . . . Awkward pause shading off into silence and a brisk throat clearing. *Well. Drop by if you can make it. 'Bye.*

It was as likely that Clare would show up at the cemetery as it was she'd show up at the house. My call was primarily to make her aware of me, and to make her feel guilty.

The yellow Rose of Remembrance tree was a perfect fit between my parents' gravestones.

Now that Mom's marker was in place, an exact match for Dad's, this corner of Mt. Ephraim Cemetery with its predominance of Eaton names was starting to look comfy.

"Comfy."

Such a silly sad word, I had to say it aloud.

Made you think of worn old furniture, tattered old slipper-shoes like Dad's infamous moccasins. Dad's recliner chair, the leather seat shaped to ghost-buttocks. Those boxes I'd discovered in the attic containing baby clothes, little-girl clothes, hand-knitted blankets and hand-sewn quilts and long-ago school report cards for Clare Eaton and Nikki Eaton and such special projects as a watercolor booklet titled "Sparkle Bright the Kitty Who Came to Stay" I'd made for Mom in fourth grade, on the back of which Miss Jaime (I'd adored, I hadn't given a thought to in twenty years) had written *Nikki, this is BEAUTIFUL! Your mother will love this little gem.*

"Comfy."

In early June, when we'd been on speaking terms, Clare and I and a few close relatives had come to the cemetery to watch our mother's grave marker set into place. It was a larger, sleeker, more stately and much more expensive dark-granite stone than Mom would have chosen for herself. Now we had

Gwendolyn Ann Eaton	Jonathan Allan Eaton
April 22. 1948	February 16. 1941
May 11. 2004	January 8. 2000
Beloved Wife and Mother	*Beloved Husband and Father*

A "grave blanket"—a slab of turf unconvincing as a toupee on a bald head—had been laid on Mom's grave, not quite matching the lusher grass growing on Dad's. Numerous flowers still brightened Mom's grave including glassily plastic lilies, bluebells, and roses. The Kovach touch.

Delicately Mom had suggested to her relatives over the years that artificial flowers weren't a good idea, generally. Her bulldog cousin Lucille had stared at her in amazement: "The point is, they don't *die*."

For years we'd been repeating Lucille's sage remark. *The point is, stupid, they don't DIE.* Even Dad, whose usual response to the Kovach tribe was to sigh and roll his eyes, laughed heartily at such wit.

My hands ached pleasantly, spading up soil and struggling to remove the thorny rose tree from its pot. That morning I'd had a call from Wally Szalla asking when we could see each other again and I'd been evasive about naming a date: "But soon, Wally. I miss you."

This seemed to be a season when I told people I missed them while hoping I wouldn't have to see them. Somehow, avoiding the task of sorting through Mom's attic boxes took up most of my energy.

I was thinking that Mom would have been touched by Sonja and Sonny's gift. Yellow was her favorite color for roses, she'd have told them.

How Mom would feel about my living in the house, I wasn't sure. Of course, she'd be happy that Smoky was back in his old haunts and that he was gaining some of the weight he'd lost. She'd have been upset that Clare was angry with me; or, maybe, it was the other way around, I was angry with Clare.

You have your own life, Nikki. Save it.

"Go to hell. Save your own life."

It was a relief, Mt. Ephraim Cemetery wasn't cramped like St. Joseph's but spacious and attractive and far better maintained. Most of the graves were carefully tended and some were routinely festooned with flowers. There was invariably the roar of a lawn mower or a leaf blower to assure you that things were being kept up. You still felt sad and more than sad but not so guilty, walking away.

In June, Clare and I had been brooding and teary and hadn't much to say to each other. Mom's death had been so fresh, it was like trying to breathe through layers of gauze wrapped around our heads. But I'd managed to say, in a voice just loud enough for Clare to hear and no one else, "Mom preferred St. Joseph's, remember? That 'special atmosphere' " and Clare had flared up at once: "Oh, *Mom*. You know what she's like."

Actually, I wasn't so sure any longer that I did.

avoiding . . . (II)

Then there were the people I avoided.

Like "bugs" this was a large, loose category. Much of the time it included anyone who wanted to see me.

Ohhh Nikki! We miss Gwen so.

Just can't believe that Gwen is . . .

. . . want you to know you are in our prayers. If there's anything we can do . . .

One of these was Gilbert Wexley.

The exalted one, Mom had so admired.

Though I never called him back, Wexley left messages on my answering machine that were terse and cryptic: *Nicole. We must talk.* I knew that he wanted to plan Mom's memorial service and that his plans were becoming ever more grandiose and I could not bear it.

To my dismay I read in the local paper that Wexley had begun soliciting donations for the "Gwen Eaton Memorial" to be scheduled sometime in the fall, and for the "Gwen Eaton Citizenship Award" to be administered by the Mt. Ephraim Arts Council.

A stranger interfering in our lives! I could imagine what Dad would say, who'd distrusted "civic-minded" individuals from the secretary-general of the United Nations to the local, unpaid members of the Mt. Ephraim Township Board.

I called Rob Chisholm, to ask him to object. I didn't want to speak with Wexley personally.

Rob said doubtfully, "Are you sure, Nikki? People in Mt. Ephraim want to do something for Gwen. I mean, in Gwen's memory." Awkward pause. Audible breathing into the receiver. "What happened is still so . . . raw. It's like it happened to them." Pause. Then, quickly, before I could register my objection by breaking into hysterical laughter, "They loved Gwen, that's it. They don't want to let go."

"Well, they'd better 'let go'! I can't be involved in their emotions."

This came out sounding like a plea. I'd meant to sound merely unpleasant.

I'd meant to have a brief, reasoned conversation with my brother-in-law, in lieu of my mean-hearted sister who wouldn't speak with me, but here I was being emotional. Probably sounding, to Rob's startled ears, like Clare.

Rob said, "Gwen would have liked this, I think. The memorial service, at least."

"Oh, Rob. She'd have been embarrassed to death."

What a thing to say. I would wonder afterward if in some weird jokey way it had been deliberate. Poor Rob could think of no reply except a mumbled, "Well. I'll see what Clare thinks, she'll probably agree with you."

Pause. I would not ask after Clare. *I would not.*

"And how is Clare? I haven't heard from her in a while."

Rob didn't answer immediately. In the background were ambiguous noises. (I'd called Rob at his office, penetrating the barrier of his secretary with a steely *Family matter! Urgent.*) His voice sounded forced-bright: "Clare is, well—herself. More and more, it's getting that way."

On that note, Rob had to hang up.

All summer I managed to avoid Gilbert Wexley. I understood, I think, that a memorial service for my mother was inevitable, I could not interfere and maybe yes, Mom would have wished it. Some things, Mom would say, have to be done and so you do them, and try to be gracious about it. But I couldn't bear seeing Wexley, I didn't trust the man. I must have been offended by something bullying and condescending in his manner toward Mom, at that dinner she'd given. *Your mother. Dear Gwen. Such a wonderful person. So missed!* Like Dad, I had to wonder.

"Nicole? Nicole Eaton? Is that—"

"Mr. Wexley! Hello but sorry, I can't talk now. A friend is waiting outside in his car, he's come to pick me up, *'bye.*"

This encounter was in, of unlikely places, Voorhees Vacuum Cleaners: Sales & Service, in a strip mall on Route 31. (Where I was taking Mom's hefty vacuum cleaner for repair. I'd grown to like the drone of vacuuming, the routine of sucking-up-visible-dirt into a disposable bag and tossing it away. Recommended for all grieving "survivors.") Later I would figure out that Wexley had followed me inside, he'd been getting gas for his car close by.

Another time, I saw Wexley, or a tallish bulky middle-aged man who resembled Wexley, with identical toupee-looking hair and pompous manner, approaching me in the ghastly warehouse-sized/frigidly air-conditioned Wal-Mart at the mall, quickly looking away I sprinted up an aisle to escape. (Almost into the arms of a sexy black guy in his twenties who laughed, "Hey man! Must be on the team.") (Thinking afterward this might be a way to meet men: sprinting, colliding with them, stirring in strangers a wish to protect, advise.) (Thinking, too, that I hadn't had sex in about as long as my dyed-purple punk hair had been growing out.)

Another time I sighted a brooding bulky oldish man trudging up a graveled path in the Mt. Ephraim Cemetery, in the direction of Mom's grave, and I ducked out of sight. And yet another time, one dozen white roses were delivered to the house with the card *In Gwen's memory always. G.W.* I had to wonder if Gilbert Wexley who'd been Mt. Ephraim's perennial bachelor-about-town had been in love with my mother.

That would explain it, I thought.

I'd only begun sorting through Mom's massive accumulation of cards, letters, mementos, clippings and snapshots, scattered through the house in drawers and envelopes as well as in albums, but so far I hadn't discovered anything pertaining to Gilbert Wexley, which was a relief.

(Somehow, I was reluctant to examine Mom's things. I still had a sour taste in my mouth, recalling how pitiless Clare had been rummaging through Dad's desk drawers as if looking for evidence against him which she'd finally found in the calendars.)

When Wexley acquired my e-mail address he began to send me lengthy rambling messages about the memorial service and the citizenship award and what a "gaping hole" there was now in the world. I replied to the first of these messages in my staccato e-mail style—*Thanks for your interest in my mother, I can't be involved in your plans but I won't interfere*—but when the messages kept coming in a flood, I stopped reading them.

Messages Wexley left on my phone voice mail, I erased without listening to.

By late summer, things began to get strange.

Uninvited, Wexley began to show up at the house. Dared to ring the doorbell. I happened to know from something Mom had said to Wexley at the Mother's Day dinner that he'd never stepped into our house before that evening, and maybe I'm a hostile personality, maybe my sporadic efforts to be more like my mother are just spurts of optimistic zeal, but I would not open the door to Gilbert Wexley whom I distrusted, no matter how Mom might plead for me to behave graciously. As Wexley stood at the front door daring to ring the bell a second time and adjusting his hair/toupee I crept up to yell at him through a screened window to please go away, I had a visitor and could not be disturbed. I saw the abashed man retreat to his car parked in the street where he sat as if stunned, or waiting, now I was truly in a fury and contemplated dialing 911 to report a stalker except there appeared after a few minutes the familiar Mt. Ephraim Police cruiser, the sight of which must have frightened Wexley for he hurriedly drove away.

More e-mail. More phone messages. Another unannounced visit, this time in the early evening of a day when I'd been feeling more mellow, not so prickly and mean, and there came Gilbert Wexley bravely up the front walk to ring the doorbell another time, carrying a briefcase to signal this was business, so I invited him inside explaining that I had only a few minutes to talk, and Wexley clutched at my hands avid-eyed, smelling of whiskey, speaking in a rapid incoherent flood of words that had only intermittently to do with the memorial service but mostly to do with how much Wexley missed my mother, how he'd grown to depend upon her, he feared he'd sometimes taken her for granted, such a good kind gentle decent generous woman, he feared possibly he'd even hurt her feelings, not intentionally of course but possibly he had, he was eager to see me, maybe he could take me to dinner, the Fayetteville Inn was a favorite of his, so much for us to talk about, he was "very impressed" with me, what he knew of "Nicole Eaton" and the few times he'd seen me, my articles in the *Beacon*, how smart and talented I was, and how attractive: "You have Gwen's specialness, Nicole, especially when you smile. You should smile more often!"

This was a cue. I was on my feet almost literally pushing Wexley out the door. Though he had something in the briefcase to show me, I wasn't interested. Explaining that my man friend from Chautauqua Falls was due to arrive in ten minutes, he was the possessive type known to take down the license plate numbers of suspicious cars he saw parked in front of my house so that he could ask a state trooper friend to run them through the computer and find out where the owners of the cars live . . .

Wexley fled. Except for a few e-mails and phone messages he never bothered me again.

Clare: guess who's stalking Mom. I mean, me. Pause. *Only if you call me, Clare, will I reveal his name.*

The incident was too delicious to keep to myself. Like bait I tossed it out knowing that, this time, Clare would have to give in to curiosity and call me and so she did, with a pretense of only just casual, even grudging interest: "All right, Nikki, I give in. Who?"

"Guess."

A pause. Almost, I could hear Clare's forehead crinkle.

"Gilbert Wexley."

"Oh! How'd you know?"

I sounded like a balloon, rapidly deflating.

Clare laughed, in that thin-hissing-through-the-nose way of our father's, when Mom had said something naive. "He's been bothering me, too. But Rob dealt with him."

Hanging up, then. Quickly.

secret

Pulses are beating in my eyes. *Mom? Mom?* I am calling. At first I am not certain of my age: am I a little girl, or am I older? I am stumbling through the rooms of the house. I am pushing open the door to the garage. Oh! I am beginning to be impatient for what is this, hide-and-seek? Why is Mom hiding from me? A strange smell assails my nostrils. I am reluctant to switch on the light. I think that I can see in the darkness, I have no need of the light. I am annoyed, to have to switch on the light. For I can't find the damned switch, my fingers grope in the dark. Outside it was brightly sunny, inside the garage it's night. My mouth turns downward with the exasperated thought *I don't have time for games, for God's sake.*

Mom is hiding from me, Mom is lying on the concrete garage floor in her pretty blue clothes. This is ridiculous, I am thinking, this is going too far! I am angry with Mom, lying in a pool of something dark and oily, with a sickening odor. She is lying with her face turned to me. She is lying with her arm stretched toward me. She is lying with her eyes open and pleading. *Nikki help me! Nikki don't leave me!* At once I begin to cry. I am not angry now, I am very frightened. Clumsily I kneel beside Mom. Her skin is so cold! Just to touch her is to feel that cold go through me, into the marrow of my bones. I am trying to lift Mom but she has become heavy. My arms are too weak. If I could lift her! If I could help her to her feet. But I am not strong enough. I am not brave enough. I am helpless.

For it seems that I am a little girl after all. I am crying so hard, I am a little girl who has disappointed her mother. It will never be made right between us. I leave my mother in the garage on the dirty concrete floor, I abandon my mother to strangers.

This is my secret, I am revealing now to you.

the moth

Waking in the night. I'd heard a sound. As of something dropped, or falling. In another part of the house. The garage.

The garage! I had not entered the garage for a long time.

I knew: the overhead garage door was locked—"secured," as the police say. The door to the kitchen was locked. Each door of the house, each window (including basement windows) was locked. In several rooms low-voltage lightbulbs were on. In the kitchen, the bulb above the stove was on. Close beside my bed in my old girlhood room was a telephone, and my cell phone was nearby. I must have been sleeping twisted in damp bedclothes. I was relieved that I'd been sleeping alone, not beside Wally Szalla. For lately when Wally and I slept together, in Chautauqua Falls, we were not so comfortable as we'd been, it is more practical to sleep alone if you're prone to insomnia or nightmares.

In fact I'd been sleeping with Smoky cradled in the crook of my left arm but Smoky had jumped down from the bed, I must have frightened him away. I kicked off the damp sheets. I told myself it was nothing. It was a dream. I knew perfectly well that it was a dream yet still my heart beat like an angry fist. I fumbled to switch on the light: 3:10 A.M. I'd been awake and reading in bed, only an hour before. As soon as the light came on, moths began to throw themselves against the window screen a few inches away.

Moths! The largest was the size of a hummingbird, beautifully marked with powdery-gray wings throwing itself against the screen.

On the floor beside my bed, another excellent reason not to have a two-legged bed companion, I kept a claw hammer. For protection. This I picked up now, to take with me. My hand was badly trembling but the weight of the claw hammer helped. In the hall, there was Smoky with pricked-up ears staring at me. In the switched-on light, tawny cat-eyes regarded me warily. As I advanced, Smoky retreated. I spoke to him to placate him but he didn't trust me: disheveled, smelling of my body, gripping a claw hammer.

Joking, "What's not to trust? Come on."

Joking with a cat. Was Nikki her old crazy self, or what.

In the kitchen, though I wanted to laugh, I stood very still. I intended to approach the door to the garage and I intended to open it if only to assure myself that there was no one, there was nothing, inside, for the garage was fully "secured" and I knew this. Yet I did not approach the door, still less did I unlock and open the door. I stood without moving for several minutes listening to the silence in the garage. I told myself, "No one. Nothing." My hand gripping the claw hammer still trembled. My mouth was dry as old newspaper baked and yellowed by the sun. It was consoling, the lightbulb above the stove was burning. Though it was only thirty watts, yet my father would have disapproved. He'd been impatient with weakness, "acting silly." In a family of three females, he'd often been impatient.

I opened the drawer where Mom had kept cards. Plumbers, carpenters, lawn men, electricians. "Sonny" Danto the Scourge of the Bugs would be there. And the Mt. Ephraim detective whose name I kept forgetting. *Call me. Day or night. If you need me. Or just to talk.* I found Strabane's card, went to the phone and dialed the number and heard the phone ring once, twice, a third time before quickly hanging up. "Crazy! What are you doing!"

I was weak with relief, like one who has narrowly escaped a terrible danger.

By this time it was 3:15 A.M. The sun would rise at about 5:30 A.M. The new day would begin, that would have nothing to do with the old for no trace of the old would remain.

getting along

Three days later he appeared.

"Ms. Eaton?—Nicole? Need some help?"

I was clearing out the garage. For months I'd avoided the garage. But that morning I'd forced myself to enter the garage. The single place I hadn't been able to enter since moving into Mom's house: the garage.

Garage!—garage! beating in my head like deranged rock music.

I glanced up shading my eyes. A man? A man in dark glasses, swarthy-skinned, with weird bristly quill-hair at the crest of his head? A man approaching me in the driveway, with an urgent smile?

I was stunned to see Strabane.

But you can't know that I called you, the call didn't go through!

It was a balmy September day. I was dragging a clumsy lawn chair-recliner out of the garage, its canvas slats so rotted and cobweb-festooned they looked like cheap lace. Already at the curb awaiting Saturday morning pickup were boxes of household trash, rusted garden tools, a cracked birdbath, grimy lamp shades.

Strabane took the bulky chair-recliner from me and carried it to the curb with no more effort than if it had been made of plastic. He was a stocky-shouldered man, flushed with self-consciousness, edgy and excited. I wanted to run back into the house and shut the door against him, I wasn't ready for this.

"What else you got for me, ma'am? Those suitcases?"

272

Strabane grinned, flexing his fingers. In his unease he was trying to be funny. Playing the role of, what?—a handyman, trashman?

I tried to laugh. Well, it was funny!

Trying not to show the surprise and fury I felt. Tears of indignation welling in my eyes. But there was Mom's sensible advice: be gracious to all visitors.

I had dragged the "matched leather" suitcases out of a shadowy corner of the garage and into the sunlight. There were five of these including an overnight bag of my mother's she'd tried to press upon Clare first, then me, when we'd gone away to college. The suitcases were scuffed and covered in cobwebs but still handsome, impressive. What Dad called "high-quality." I had been staring at the tarnished brass initials *GAE, JAE.* Trying to imagine my parents as newlyweds, young and deeply in love and not yet parents, thrilled with such a luxury gift that must have seemed to promise travel, a romantic future.

Exactly when the matched luggage had been shifted from a closet to the musty garage, I don't know. It was too sad to contemplate.

I'd been thinking that maybe I shouldn't throw out my parents' luggage? Maybe not this morning.

But there was my unexpected visitor Ross Strabane, grimacing as he managed remarkably to grip the handles of all five suitcases simultaneously, even bending his knees in the way of a competitive weight lifter. For a man of moderate height he had big hands. The deftness of his movements, a swaggering sort of confidence in his strength, were fascinating to observe. I didn't know whether I admired such strength, or scorned it as show-offy. But I knew that I couldn't have lifted more than two of the large suitcases, in both hands.

Strabane hesitated, seeing something in my face. "No? These don't go?"

"I . . . I think so. Yes."

"This is real leather, I guess? Nice."

Strabane stooped to smell the leather. After years in the garage the russet-red leather still exuded a faint, luxuriant aroma.

"They were wedding presents to my parents, from my dad's parents.

See: 'GAE, JAE.' Their initials." Suddenly I heard myself telling Strabane about my parents, in a halting voice that sounded unused, scratchy. As if I'd been saving up such a family tale for the first person who came along, out of sheer loneliness. "Mom would have loved to travel more than they did, but Dad was, well . . . He always felt he needed to 'stay close to home' because he had a responsible 'executive' position at Beechum Paper Products and he didn't trust 'subordinates.' They'd gone to Key West on their honeymoon and every winter there was the vague idea of going back, Dad would sort of promise Mom but then something would come up, and they never got there. Actually it was sort of a joke in the family. Mom had wanted to go to Europe, too, in fact I'd been planning to take her this summer . . ." Was this true? I was stunned at what I was saying, so impulsively. And to a stranger, a police detective who'd led the investigation into my mother's death.

Strabane was listening sympathetically. He seemed interested in whatever I was saying. I felt uneasy, not able to see his eyes behind the dark hyper-reflective lenses of his glasses, in which my own miniature distorted face was reflected as in a cartoon. "Anyway, the farthest we went as a family was usually just Star Lake in the Adirondacks where my dad's family had a cottage and then sometimes we'd come back a day or two early, Dad got so restless."

"Star Lake! We used to go there too, some summers." Strabane had set the suitcases back down. Flexing his strong fingers. "Until my family moved away, I'd take them, too."

This was an ambiguous statement. Much of what Strabane said came out just slightly jumbled, not-coherent. The way he stared, and smiled, and twisted his face, and shrugged and shifted his shoulders as if they didn't quite fit him, was distracting. You couldn't know what he meant by *my family*: parents? or his own wife, children?

Strabane wasn't standing close to me yet it felt as if he was crowding me. I didn't like the feeling. I didn't know why he was here. It was true that I'd called him, I'd dialed his telephone number, but I hadn't wanted him, even then. And he couldn't know any of this. Could he!

No right to intrude. No right to remind me of something I want to forget.

At least, he'd shaved off the scruffy beard. His jaw was blunt and curiously dented, or scarred. His swarthy skin was fleshy as muscle. You had to be fascinated by the bristly quill-hair and the close-shaved sides of the man's head. No one else I'd seen in the small-town Mt. Ephraim Police Department looked anything like Ross Strabane.

Still he was speaking of Star Lake as if it had a special meaning to him, as it must have a special meaning to me. As if somehow the two of us had known each other from summers there.

"Except I'm older than you, Ms. Eaton. I graduated from Mt. Ephraim High in 1981."

I knew, I was expected to say when I'd graduated. But Detective Strabane already knew when I'd graduated. He knew "facts" about me and my family and he knew information acquired through interviews, of which I could have no idea and wished to have no idea.

Seeing how I wasn't responding to memories of Star Lake, Strabane hesitated.

"Well. These suitcases? D'you want them at the curb, or—"

"I . . . I'm not sure. If the trash men take them away, they'll be gone forever."

"Do you have any use for them? *You?*"

"I have my own suitcase. You know, the practical kind with wheels like everyone has now."

"So, these? You want them gone?"

"No, wait! I just don't know." I was becoming anxious, I had to think quickly. "They're 'high quality' leather, that's why they're so heavy. No one has luggage like this any longer. I mean, my suitcase is light as plywood! It came to me maybe these suitcases could be fitted out with wheels? That way, they'd be practical."

Strabane smiled, baffled. That just-perceptible edge of exasperation you'd see in my dad's face, when Mom was being "logical."

"These? That weigh a ton? Fitted out with *wheels?*"

"Is it a silly idea? On Animal Planet the other night I saw this program about dogs and cats whose rear legs had had to be amputated because they'd been injured, the animals were fitted out with ingenious little platforms on wheels. With their front legs they propelled themselves like kids on skateboards! They didn't seem to miss their original rear legs at all."

I didn't like sounding so naive. Animal Planet cable TV had been one of Mom's weaknesses we'd teased her about. But Strabane was listening respectfully. He had the air of a man practiced in considering seemingly naive remarks. "Maybe because the animals don't have the concept 'rear legs'—'original legs'—they get along pretty well with what they have. Like they don't have the concept 'crippled,' 'freaky.' "

It wasn't a rebuke but common sense. And maybe Strabane was teasing, just a little.

I said, "Animals don't have the concept 'animals.' We don't seem to have it, either, applied to ourselves though in fact that's what we are: 'animals.' We want to think better of ourselves."

"We sure do! I hope so."

I decided to give up the "matched luggage." I took the smallest suitcase from Strabane to carry to the curb while Strabane managed to carry the other four suitcases in two hands. He was showing off, was he? Thinking well of himself, impressing me. I tried not to wince as he dropped the suitcases on the lawn at the end of the driveway with a thud, like the most ordinary of trash.

"Thanks! I appreciate your help, Detective."

This was a signal for Strabane to leave. Another man would have picked it up immediately. But Strabane, flexing his fingers, wiping his cobwebby hands on his trousers, seemed oblivious. My mother would have invited him inside to wash his hands but damned if I would invite this intruder anywhere.

Offer him coffee, too. Banana nut bread.

You weren't brought up to be rude, Nikki!

Strabane asked if there was anything else I needed hauled to the curb and I told him with a bright quick smile no thank you, there was not.

You could see by glancing into the garage that there was plenty more that was bulky, cumbersome. But Strabane wasn't about to contradict me. When he removed his dark glasses, I looked quickly away.

A police detective's job was identifying lies. Liars. I didn't want this man looking too closely at me.

"Guess I'm intruding here, Ms. Eaton? I'm sorry."

"You can call me 'Nicole.' Please."

After the dark lenses, Strabane's eyes were unexpectedly warm, vulnerable. The eyes of a worried man. He'd been feeling the awkward strain between us. The fact that he'd written to me, and neither of us had acknowledged it.

"Well. 'Nicole.' Anyway I'm not the 'bearer of bad news' this morning. That's good, right?"

Strabane stepped closer to me. The gesture seemed unconscious, instinctive. He wanted to protect me but: from what? The worst had happened, all that was over. What had happened to my mother could never happen to me. I knew, it was only common sense.

I could smell Strabane's hair oil. Unless it was some high-octane male deodorant beyond even what Wally Szalla used. My heartbeat began to quicken as in the presence of danger.

Oh, I hated him! I hated the memory of him. I wanted him gone, so that I could lock myself inside the house, in my girlhood room, and bawl.

Specifically, I hated his clothes. Hadn't he anyone to supervise his clothes! Maybe small-town plainclothes cops have to wear the kind of neckties you only see heaped in bargain bins, in post-Christmas sales? Maybe they have to wear shirts of some thin synthetic fabric that's only nominally white, you can see their wiry-shadowy chest hair through the fabric?—shirts that, glimpsed from behind, show bats' wings of perspiration across the wearer's shoulders? I hated the flash of mismatched socks, one of them beige with small checks and the other a frayed-looking sand color. Only Strabane's shoes looked decent this morning, maybe because they were new and unnaturally shiny, like his belt buckle.

I hated the way he'd showed up at the house when I hadn't chosen to speak with him. I hadn't replied to his letters. I hated it that this was a sexually aggressive male utterly unaware of himself, clumsy and uncertain. Wally Szalla gave that initial impression, too: comfortable and harmless as an old shoe. But Wally's sexual intentions were never unconscious.

Strabane said, awkwardly, "Why I dropped by, Nicole: I'm wondering how you're getting along."

Getting along? Was I? I had no more idea how I was *getting along* than I knew what my white blood cell count was.

I resented the question. I resented the implication that there was a desired way in which I might be *getting along*, that I might not be living up to; that Detective Strabane might assist me. Innocently I asked, "How do I look?"

This was meant to be a joke for I didn't believe that I could be looking great in faded denim shorts, a grimy T-shirt worn without a bra, no makeup except a smear of purple lipstick where a mouth should be. My hair was now a stiff broom-sage mix of glinting sand, wiry silvery-gray that crimped and thickened in humid weather. For my most recent tryst with my married-man-lover Wally Szalla I'd painted my fingernails and toenails peacock blue spangled with gold. The fingernail polish had mostly endured but the sassy blue toenails were chipped. I'd been noticing my visitor's gaze drifting downward to my bare dirty feet, then lifting again quickly to my face.

"Beautiful." Strabane spoke quickly, as if embarrassed. He was tugging at his shirt collar, his fingers left a smudge of cobweb. "You look beautiful, Nicole."

I hadn't heard this preposterous remark. A nerve had begun to beat in my left eyelid. I wanted to shove Strabane away with the palms of both my hands: flat and hard against his stocky chest.

"That's why you've come here? To tell me—what?"

"To tell you that your life will begin again, Nicole, after the trial. You have to have faith that that's so."

The trial. It had been set for late October, then postponed to early

December. Just recently we'd heard that it might be postponed again until "after the New Year."

"I don't think about the trial. I try never to think of the trial."

"That's good, Nicole. Because the trial is not up to you."

"I think about my life in this house, day to day. Sometimes hour to hour. That's what I think about, and there's happiness in that, and I have a right to that."

My voice rose. Strabane nodded gravely. He was looking as if I'd shoved him in the chest. Surprising him, but he'd stood his ground. And now he was rueful, chagrined. But still he stood his ground.

I was saying, excited: "Clare promised to help me clear out the garage but you don't see her here, do you! She wants to sell the house but she can't force herself to come back. This matter of leaving garage doors open permanently, my dad thought it was a moral failing in homeowners. Garages filling up with junk and cars parked outside. 'People don't respect privacy any longer not even their own.' Dad would drive us around the subdivision pointing out lawns, houses, garages that were 'well kept' and those that were 'disgraceful.' He judged by appearances, the outsides of things, because after all that's what people see. 'A garage door open to the street is like a wall missing from someone's house so you can see inside where they're sitting around in pajamas or worse yet naked.' The way Dad said 'naked' was funny as a laugh line on *Saturday Night Live*."

The way I'd been speaking, rapidly and meant-to-amuse, was a definite signal, my visitor should leave. I was becoming overly excited, upset. My skin felt feverish and the nerve in my eyelid was hopping. Strabane edged closer to me, regarding me with worried eyes. He'd meant to console me, somehow. He hadn't meant to antagonize me.

He said: "I've got part of the day off. I'm here offering to help you. If you want help. I was hoping I'd hear from you."

"Well, you didn't hear from me. You won't hear from me. I don't need you."

Through much of this edgy exchange, Strabane had been glancing past me into the garage. It was a tic-like gesture, he couldn't help himself. Thinking how he'd been summoned to this garage, that evening in May. He'd been the chief detective at a "crime scene" in that garage. Not four months ago but it seemed like four years. The bright-lit interior of the utterly ordinary suburban garage where my mother had been struck down, fallen to the concrete floor. A woman's small broken body on that dirty floor, in torn and blood-soaked clothing. I'd wanted to ask if the professional cop had noticed how carefully sewn the blue linen jacket was, with its pale-blue silk lining. How beautiful the floral-print blouse.

Women's things, women's bodies. Women's lives of so little consequence, finally.

Strabane was watching me, curious. He was one who'd made a profession out of decoding secret thoughts.

I said, "I appreciate your help, Detective. But—"

" 'Detective' is my rank. 'Strabane' is my name."

"Yes, I know. Mr. Strabane—"

"People don't call me 'Ross,' my first name. Somehow, it's always been, even in middle school, 'Strabane.' Weird, eh?"

I had no reply to this. Something strange and tight was happening to the lower part of my face.

"—I don't need you, 'Strabane.' It's too much effort now."

"What is?"

Becoming involved. Inviting you inside the house. Inviting you inside my life. Or, just offering you coffee, banana nut bread baked from Mom's *Breadcraft* book.

Inviting you to wash your hands, soiled on my account.

"There's a man, we're planning to be married. He . . ."

Afterward I would realize, Strabane knew about Wally Szalla. For sure, Strabane knew about Wally Szalla.

He'd been "investigating" our Eaton lives. I knew this. Though exactly how much he knew I didn't care to imagine, except I resented this, I resented this stranger knowing anything about me.

"Right, Nicole. Got it!"

He'd replaced the dark glasses. Immediately he looked just slightly sinister, sexy. The lenses were flat and hyper-shiny and I couldn't see his eyes any longer and Jesus, what a relief. I hoped I would never see those eyes again.

Still, he didn't leave. You'd think *Good, fine, this is over, you've got it, goodbye.* He was saying, "Soooo. Well . . . If, y'know, you need me, Nicole, give me a call, O.K.? Any time it comes over you, like you want to talk?"

His hand moved toward a pocket, until he remembered he'd already given me one of his cards. At least twice.

I thanked him, I said yes. I wasn't even looking at him now.

Not wanting this man to take away the wrong impression of me. That I was attracted to him though I couldn't stand him. That I wanted him, not to go away but to come closer, so that I could shove him away with both my hands, shut into fists.

Squatting in the garage tugging at boxes of aged, warped records Mom had packed away after, sometime in the early 1990s, Dad had "given in" (his expression, uttered with philosophical disgust) and finally purchased a cassette-CD player like the majority of his fellow Americans. Oh, what to do with these records! I understood Mom's predicament.

How could I dispose of these warped classics in their grimy yet still colorful covers, *Highlights from Bizet's "Carmen," Boston Pops Orchestra at Tanglewood Summer 1981, West Side Story, The Sound of Music?* I brushed away cobwebs, and reboxed them. I worked until my knees throbbed with pain, from squatting. I had totally forgotten my visitor. I was not going to think about my visitor. Instead I was thinking *See, I am getting along. This is proof. If you require proof. I am not Nikki now exactly but I am coping in a way Nikkie could not cope. I have opened the garage at last. Proof that I am unafraid of the garage is, I have opened the garage at last. From now on, I will be parking my car in the garage. I will lower the garage door. None of you will know by driving past when I am home, and when not.*

breadcraft

It was so, I'd begun experimenting with recipes from Mom's much-thumbed flour-smeared *Breadcraft* book.

I wasn't a natural baker. Never much of a cook. Maybe I suffered from ADD like half the U.S. population. Lacking in patience, and patience is a kind of maturity.

In the kitchen, at the bread board, kneading dough in the way Mom had tried to teach me, I felt peaceful, and I was happy. For—almost!—I could see Mom in the corner of my eye. Almost!—I could hear Mom encouraging me.

Kneading is easy, Nikki!

Flour your hands. Add flour to the board until the dough stops sticking. Good!

Don't wrestle the dough! Just push pull roll the dough, push pull roll the dough, that's right, sweetie, find your rhythm, no need to hurry, use your instinct, take your time, kneading is happiness, when you knead bread you enter a zone of happiness, when you observe bread rising it's happiness, when you smell bread baking it's happiness, when you cool bread (always on a wire rack, honey) it's happiness, when you share bread with others it's happiness and it is happiness you deserve, Nikki, not sorrow.

Salt tears dripped from my eyes sometimes, into the sinewy bread dough. If I couldn't wipe them away fast enough leaving flour-smears on my face.

Miracle Bread. Whole Wheat. Cracked Wheat. Twelve Grain.

While the bread was baking I expected the worst to emerge from the oven and sometimes I was right and sometimes I was what people describe as pleasantly surprised. When I messed up, I tried not to despair but just avoided the kitchen for a day. And when I returned, there was Mom awaiting me in the oversized white apron we'd given her inscribed MASTER BAKER, that tied at the waist and around the neck.

Bread baking is fun, Nikki! Not like life that gets too serious sometimes.

Sourdough. Buttermilk. Oatmeal/bran. Raisin/yogurt/twelve grain. Banana nut.

These were Mom's recipes, I baked. The familiar smell of Mom's bread-baking filled the house. If I shut my eyes as in the sweetest dream I could see myself running up the driveway from having gotten off the school bus, pushing open the kitchen door to a smell of bread baking that meant that my mother was home and calling out *Hey Mom I'm home!*

I baked. I messed up but I baked. I became exasperated, I lost my temper and dumped rock-hard bread into the trash but I baked. I quarreled with my married-man-lover but I baked. I regretted not having invited the bristly-quill-haired detective into my kitchen, to give him a taste of Mom's banana nut bread that had turned out pretty damned good, but I didn't call him; I baked. Thinking *You don't need more excitement in your life right now, you need less.*

I baked.

Quarreling with Wally Szalla was a prologue to making-up with Wally Szalla which was always worth it. I think.

For Wally, I baked sourdough. Something simple, for a man who claimed to like things simple. "Nikki, this is *good*." A look of surprise. "You baked this, Nikki? *You?*" For my thirty-second birthday in early October, Wally took me for a romantic weekend at the Hotel Chateaugay on the St. Lawrence River, north of Massena at the Quebec border. He gave me a bracelet watch of white gold inscribed on the back *to N, love W* that was the most beautiful jewelry I'd ever been given, and made me cry.

In Wally's fleshy arms (the man was muscled, but you had to squeeze to find it) in an uncomfortable antique bed high as an operating table I cried. As Wally made love to me, I cried. Not asking why I cried as if, in Wally Szalla's experience, a naked woman crying in his arms was to be expected.

This was the romantic weekend away from Mt. Ephraim and Chautauqua Falls both, when Wally meant to speak seriously to me about our future. But somehow in the mist of champagne, wine, vodka and brandies, and Nikki's tears, the future was displaced.

This man wants me to adore him. Then he won't need to adore me.

I returned home to Mt. Ephraim, thirty-two years old.

I baked.

part four

have faith

Your life will begin again. After the trial.

In Mom's sewing room was her Chautauqua Valley Shelter Animals
calendar. When I took it over, I was surprised to discover that it was an
eighteen-month calendar, from January 2004 through to June 2005. So,
as the date of the trial kept being postponed, into the so-called New Year,
I could keep rescheduling: TRIAL.

calendar

Mom's calendar! Eighteen color photos of orphaned, abandoned, neglected and abused animals who'd been taken into the local ASPCA-affiliated shelter, prior to being adopted into "good homes." These were dogs, cats, horses, even a goat, a Vietnamese potbellied pig, and a glorious white cockatoo.

I'd taken over Mom's calendar when I moved into Mom's house, it seemed only logical.

Clare hadn't objected. When she'd seen the calendar, the days neatly annotated in different colors of ink that looked, from a short distance, like a combination crossword puzzle and spiderweb, she'd backed off.

Mom had never kept a diary, so far as we knew. (Oh, we were certain we'd have known!) But her calendar was so annotated, almost you could read it as a kind of diary.

As a kind of puzzle, in part. For while most of the initials and abbreviations were obvious, others were mysterious or indecipherable.

It was painful to see. To retrace Mom's days, weeks. She'd led what looked like a "busy" life. A glance at her crowded calendar suggested this. Each Sunday was church of course. Often on Sunday evenings were church-related activities. Mondays through Fridays were dense with initials: *chur com mtg* (church committee meeting), *SSC* (Senior Swim Club at the Y), *lib* (library, where Mom did volunteer work at the checkout desk), *hosp.* (hospital, where Mom did volunteer work in the gift shop), *HH*

(Hedwig House, an assisted living facility in Mt. Ephraim where one of Mom's elderly Kovach relatives lived whom she visited regularly), *art mtg* (arts council meeting). There were numerous initials that had to refer to friends and relatives, mostly women Mom's age, with whom she had lunch frequently. There were initials referring to medical appointments. Hair salon appointments. On May 9, the day of Mom's Mother's Day dinner, the last time I'd seen Mom alive, she'd marked the date with a column of red-inked initials headed by *Cl/Nik*—meaning *Clare* and *Nikki*.

The first of Mom's guests to have been invited.

May 11, the day of Mom's death, had been marked in blue ink: *class 10:30 A. M., HH 5 P.M.*

May 14, the day of Mom's funeral, had been marked in green: *SSC 11 A.M., hosp. 1–5.*

From January through to the end of May, the calendar was heavily marked. Most of the week of May 16 was marked, the last week in May had been less marked, turn the calendar to June and there were only a few scattered dates marked.

Beyond that, blank days. Stretching into eternity.

On a childish impulse, I checked October. And there, in red ink, on October 8, was marked NIKKI. My birthday.

Clare's birthday, on June 2, had also been marked in red.

I checked to see that both January 8, 2004, and January 8, 2005, anniversaries of the date of Dad's death, had been marked with a small black ✓ in the upper right-hand corner of the date.

I could hear again Mom's breezy remark, she couldn't live without her calendar: "If I don't write the least little thing down, I'll forget it. So I always write everything down, and I never forget."

missing clare

"I have news, Nikki. Prepare!"

Out of nowhere the call came. The husky elated voice was both familiar and not-familiar. Intimate and startling in my ear so that I was made to realize how much I'd been missing my bossy older sister.

How like Clare, to call with such a pronouncement. Assuming on this weekday morning in October that I'd be home, and awaiting her. That I wasn't immersed in my work ("Only just writing? That isn't *work*") and had time for her after so many weeks of silence.

Since she'd called me a squatter, and run out of the house, Clare had been avoiding me. Sometimes I was furious, and sometimes I was plain hurt, that Clare had so suddenly cut me out of her life. All the years she'd been criticizing me for not living closer to Mom, now I was living in Mom's very house and Clare had ceased inviting me to hers. I hadn't seen my niece and nephew in weeks. I hadn't seen Rob. If I needed to communicate with Clare on something urgent, I called Rob at his office. If, less frequently, Clare needed to communicate with me, it was through Rob.

My brother-in-law was embarrassed and apologetic: "Clare says you make her 'nervous' and 'sad,' Nikki. She's trying very hard not to be 'nervous' and 'sad.' "

This hurt. This made my blood boil. Damned if I would defend myself over the charge of making my sister *nervous* and *sad*.

Rob said, "Nikki? Don't take it too personally, you know how Clare is." After a pause, sighing: "You learn to make compromises in families, as in marriages. If you want to stay together."

The old Nikki would have brightly quipped: "Who? Not me."

The new Nikki murmured, "Don't I know!"

Since Detective Strabane had come by and upset me I'd been thinking a lot about Clare and her family: Rob, Lilja, Foster. They were my family, too. They were all that remained of my family. I'd been haunted by the fact I'd lost both my parents within the past several years. It seemed too soon. It was too soon! How I envied my friends who still had their parents. Even grandparents! I'd vaguely thought the "older generations" a not-very-exciting responsibility/burden but now I was wishing badly that I'd asked Mom more about my Kovach grandparents when I'd had the chance.

So many years I'd had the chance. Those visits to St. Joseph's Cemetery, I'd must have assumed would go on forever.

Mostly I was hurt by Clare's behavior. The more she ignored me, wouldn't return my calls, the more I wanted to contact her. I wanted to think that Rob must be exaggerating. Clare couldn't be afraid of seeing me! One day impulsively I drove to her house to leave a loaf of fresh-baked bread (raisin/yogurt/twelve grain) with my startled niece Lilja who stared at me as if seeing a ghost.

Stammering guiltily, "Aunt Nikki, I don't think Mom is h-home."

"Just say hello to her for me, Lilja. And love to all of you."

Obviously Aunt Nikki was in a hurry, couldn't have visited with Clare if Clare had been home.

Instead of calling to thank me for the bread, Clare wrote a cold little note on a Finger Lakes Wineries postcard.

Thanks for the bread. Quite a surprise you'd have time for baking. Rob & Foster have already devoured most of it. Nice to know you're settled in there & have time for bread baking.

Yrs,

CLARE

Yrs! Was that supposed to be short for *Yours?* Hadn't Mrs. Rob Chisholm had time in her busy suburban life to spell out *Yours?*

It was Rob who called to thank me for the bread: "It was delicious, Nikki. Did you really bake it? *You?*"

As soon as Clare swept into the house, before she even hugged me and left a smear of lipstick across my cheekbone, she announced her news: she and Rob had agreed upon a "trial separation."

I was utterly taken by surprise. I must have looked as if I'd been kicked in the belly.

Clare laughed at me. She was exhilarated, thrilled. A flush of sheer pleasure rose into her face, the pleasure of seeing how your news has surprised another. Clare was smartly dressed in a chic new pants suit in autumn-leaf colors, stylish black shoes with a lizard-skin look. Her face was carefully made up, glamorous and even youthful, and her hair was a startling coppery-red, lifting from her forehead in moussed wings. And she'd lost weight! The fleshy-moon face she'd been despairing of since high school was visibly thinner, the hips and belly were thinner. There was something fevered and crackling about Clare, like a live wire you wouldn't wish to touch.

"Oh, Nikki. Don't look so shocked. You remind me of Aunt Tabitha, that's exactly how she looked when I told her."

Aunt Tabitha! This was a cruel touch. This was not nice.

Cruel, too, to allow me to know that she'd sprung her bombshell news onto Aunt Tabitha, before telling me. Her sister!

I told Clare that I was sorry to hear her news and Clare said sharply,

" 'Sorry'? You? Why?" and I said, confused, "Well—where is Rob moving?" and Clare said, "Rob isn't. I am. Foster and I. Day after tomorrow we move to a new residence," and I said, staring, "You, Clare? And *Foster*? You can't be serious," and Clare said impatiently, "You sound like Rob. You sound like Dad, or Mom. I'm the only serious person I know, I have to save my own life."

Seeing that I was stunned, Clare took fleeting sisterly pity on me and gave me another hug: hard enough to make me wince. Here was a girls' coach hugging a temporarily demoralized team player, as much to chide as to comfort. Her hands on my bare arms were unexpectedly brisk and cold. Her perfume/hair mousse was overpowering. With a throaty little laugh she told me that Rob was "stubborn"—"in denial"—insisted upon keeping the separation secret from his family and at Coldwell: "As if you could keep anything secret in Mt. Ephraim! Dad used to say we were all a hive of bees, buzzing whether there's news or not." Yet Clare sounded grimly pleased, at the prospect of news being buzzed about.

I asked about Lilja, and Clare said, frowning, "Lilja is furious with me, won't speak with me. All this is interfering with her ninth grade social life. 'First Grandma, now Mom' is what she's stamping about the house saying, as if what happened to her grandmother was some sort of inconvenience for *her*. Lilja is welcome to visit her brother and me anytime she wants. It's out of the question living with us, there isn't room. And her temperament! If she chooses to side with her father, that will be her decision. This past year has been hell, let me tell you. That girl is tough as steel."

Tough as steel? *Lilja?*

"Yes! If you were that girl's mother and not her 'cool' aunt, you'd know."

All this while Clare was charging through the house. Too restless to stay in the kitchen, or the living room, or the dining room; charging into the back bedrooms, in and out of Mom's sewing room, Dad's study, even poking her head in the bathrooms. Whatever Clare was searching for she didn't seem to find.

I offered Clare coffee, something to eat (still I hoped to impress my sister with my bread baking), but Clare scarcely heard me. I wanted to clutch at her hands, and hold her; I'd been wanting to talk to her for months, and now she was moving away from Mt. Ephraim! I was made to recall how after Dad's funeral, Clare had pleaded with me to move back to Mt. Ephraim for a few months, to help her with Mom, but I'd been far too distracted by my own complicated life at that time—a new job and a new man who'd been exerting pressure on me to marry him.

Now, I'd have had to think to recall that man's name.

"I hope you don't intend to take Rob's side, Nikki. Like everyone else in the family. You of all people."

"Clare, I'm not taking anyone's side. I'm just—well, surprised."

"But you shouldn't be. I told you how I'd been feeling—stifled, suffocated. Oh, for a while I was happy, when Lilja was little, and Foster, I'd have liked them to stay that age forever, but it isn't like that, Nikki. If you have children, you'll learn for yourself. And there's Rob: you'd never know it from how easygoing Rob seems, but that man takes up all the oxygen in the house, he's what is known as a high-maintenance male. Just the way he smiles sometimes, it's a command and I'd better salute and obey. The way he'll say 'Never mind about *me.*' Oh! the way he doesn't want anyone in his family to know, or at Coldwell. He's so furious, so hurt in his *pride.* This man who has the most unbreakable habit of leaving any bathroom he uses a mess, wadding up and practically hoarding his soiled underwear and socks, kicked into a corner of his closet, and claims he 'forgets'!—how can you 'forget' when you can smell these things across the room! I'm so ashamed of my husband, I hurry around picking up after him before Maria arrives, and Foster is taking after his father, there must be a gene for hoarding dirty underwear, Foster's winds up under his *bed.* As for Lilja—if you saw her room at this very moment you'd think that a cyclone had rushed through it. If you even knock at the door she screams like she's being attacked: 'Go away! This is my private space! I have a right to my private space.' Poor Foster, his eyes never stop watering, it must be an allergy, some sort of sinus infection, he claims he can't *see*. So I'm taking him to an eye specialist this afternoon in Rochester. Rob doesn't think we should wait until we get settled in our new residence but of course it falls on me to make the drive to Rochester. Wouldn't you know, Foster starts his new school next *week*."

Now I did clutch at Clare's hands, to calm her.

"Clare, wait. Where are you going?"

"Now? To the bank, and the dry cleaner's, and—"

"No, Clare. Where are you moving?"

"Oh, didn't I tell you? Philadelphia."

Philadelphia! I'd been assuming Rochester, our closest large city.

"Nikki, I'm sure that I told you we were moving to Philadelphia, of course I did, you just weren't listening. As I've been telling Rob in so many words that I couldn't breathe in the marriage any longer, but he refused to hear. It's like Dad whistling, Rob sort of vibrates, a humming noise like static, these men refuse to *hear*. You know, Nikki, I am not going to be made to feel guilty about this. I am not. I married Rob because I'd been made to feel guilty about not being married, made to feel guilty that Mom was anxious about me, made to feel that Mom was sad about me, how 'exploited' I was by the school district which was true, certainly it was true, but the remedy needn't have been marriage, I should have gone back to school and gotten a master's degree or a Ph.D., I tried to explain to Mom but it was like speaking a foreign language, I mean—like trying to speak English, and the other person is answering you in a foreign language. 'Why, Clare, Rob Chisholm is the nicest man you've ever brought home to meet us'—'Rob Chisholm adores you'—'Your father respects Rob Chisholm, and you know how fussy Dad is.' " Clare laughed harshly, waving her hands about. "Well, Dad should have married Rob Chisholm. They could have whistled and hummed together, kicked their underwear together, pooled their dirty laundry. Mom could've done their laundry for them. Remember Mom running those huge loads of laundry, Daddy had a phobia about 'microorganisms' on bedclothes, we'd hear the washing machine down in the basement suddenly start to shake and shudder as if it was about to explode. The whole house was shaking, like an earthquake."

"Clare, I don't remember that."

"Nikki, you *do*."

"Well, maybe I do, but it happened only once or twice when the washing machine was overloaded. It was most unusual, when it happened."

"Everything in this house was 'most unusual' when it happened. Because no one wanted to remember it kept happening."

Clare spoke with such vehemence, you had to know that her words meant more than they seemed to indicate.

We'd blundered into the kitchen where Clare was staring at the sunburst clock as if she was having difficulty calculating the time. She had to get to the bank, she said. She had to stop by the dry cleaner's, Rob was running out of clean shirts. She had to get to Dr. Myer's to pick up a new prescription, and—something else that was crucial?—oh yes: she had to pick up Foster at his school no later than 2 P.M. She clutched at her curly-coppery head, laughing. "So much happening at once, no wonder I can't sleep without pills."

Carefully I asked Clare if maybe she was acting impulsively?

It had been only about five months since . . .

"It's been *years*. Since I've been able to *breathe*."

"But has something happened just recently? The last time I spoke with Rob on the phone . . ."

Clare said hotly, "Actually, Nikki, that's none of your business. If something has 'happened' between Rob and me. You can assume that plenty 'happens' between a wife and her husband and that it's private. My decisions are private. Stay here in Mt. Ephraim if you want to!—live here in this house the rest of your life! I won't interfere."

"I'm not 'living' here, Clare. It's only until things get sorted out and we can put the house on the market."

Clare laughed. Her cheeks were flushed with a ruddy color as they'd been years ago when Clare had played basketball at Mt. Ephraim High, one of the more aggressive players on the girls' team. Her expression shifted, meanly. "What about you and Mr. S.?"

Mr. S.! I stiffened at the question. I told Clare that Wally Szalla and I were fine.

"Are you!" Clare spoke in a way to suggest that she'd heard otherwise but would humor me in this.

"That's between Wally and me, Clare."

"No, Nikki. Between the Szallas and you."

I was furious with my smug sister. First, she disapproves of my love affair with Wally Szalla; now, she's sneering at me because the love affair isn't going well. I thought of showing her the bracelet wristwatch as evidence of—what? The gesture would have been childish and desperate but the sort of visual proof that would impress Clare.

I changed the topic: "But why Philadelphia, Clare? So far—"

"It isn't far! You know that I have a friend there."

This would be Clare's old college roommate Amy Orlander. How could I forget Amy Orlander, invariably spoken of as "a friend in Philadelphia" when Clare wanted to trump those of us lacking a friend who belonged to a rich Philadelphia department-store family, in whose lavish wedding Clare had been a bridesmaid and with whom Clare stayed on mysteriously intimate terms, though other female friendships had been allowed to wither away. How could I forget that the Orlanders had long ago issued an "open invitation" for Clare to visit them whenever she wished and to stay for as long as she wished.

"Also, there's an excellent private school in Philadelphia that specializes in challenged children, I've been able to enroll Foster in the middle of the term, with Amy's mother's help: she's on the board. I'm just so very, very grateful—"

Challenged? Since when was Foster, a sweet affable slow learner with a weakness for video games, *challenged?*

"—and Amy's husband has put in a word for me with the dean of admissions at the Philadelphia Language Institute, I'm going to enroll in a master's degree in 'language psychology.' So that I can teach, or go into private practice. The tragic thing was how I became burnt-out as a teacher, before I'd even begun a career. Stifled and exploited at that terrible school. The principal was a petty bureaucrat and he'd have never left, there was no hope for advancement for me. My creativity was stifled. My soul was stifled! You aren't the only one who felt that Mt. Ephraim was a straitjacket. —Nikki, what's this?"

In the midst of her excited speech Clare had wandered into the dining room where I'd set some of Mom's and Dad's things temporarily on the table. "These old records? Weren't they in the garage for years? You've brought them back *in*?" Clare lifted out of a box *Classical Guitar Favorites, New World Symphony, Mormon Tabernacle Choir Sings Yuletide Classics*. I said, "I haven't had a chance to sort through them completely. You know, some old records have become collectors' items." Clare snorted in derision, " 'Collectors' items'! Do they even manufacture needles for hi-fi's any longer? *Are* there hi-fi's?" But she soon became engrossed in the records, which were covered in dust and cobwebs and randomly boxed. "Oh. These are mine, I haven't heard these in *years*." Clare had taken out *Dirty Dancing: The Original Film Score* and *Tango!* whose cover was a sexy Latino leaning over a near-supine Latina in silhouette.

"And what's *this*?"

Also on the dining room table were photos and snapshots, mostly of Mom, I'd been arranging in chronological order. The earliest was sixteen-year-old Feather Kovach in her maroon cheerleader's jumper, taken with sister-cheerleaders on the Mt. Ephraim cheerleaders' "squad" (for, strangely, I had not been able to find any snapshots of my mother at a younger age): here was a girl with the most shining eyes and most hopeful smile you could imagine, dimples, wavy-curly darkish blond hair, pert little face round and luminous as a moon. There was Feather in pink-sherbert prom gown, and in a graduation gown that fitted her like a tent; there was Feather looking scarcely older than she'd looked as a cheerleader, in a dazzling white bridal gown beside her young, stiffly smiling groom (how thin Dad's face, how thick and weirdly styled his late-1960s hair) in a tux. There, basking in an unnatural sunshine, was the happy couple on their honeymoon in Key West, Gwen in tank top and miniskirt posed with a bright-feathered parrot on her shoulder, as Jon looked on somewhat doubtfully. There was Gwen with a baby (Clare), and there was Gwen with a baby (Nikki); there was Gwen with a plumpish little girl (Clare), and there was Gwen with a fidgety little girl (Nikki). And so through the years, the decades, a rich profusion of images that left me dazed and shaken when I contemplated them. Clare had taken up the most recent photos, claiming she'd never seen them before: Mom, Clare, Lilja and me posed with arms around each other's waist in front of a Christmas tree so overdecorated you could hardly see the tree. "This was taken at our house. It must've been Rob's Polaroid."

"Rob took these with Mom's Polaroid. I'm sure you have copies, Clare."

"No, I don't. I'll take this."

Clare continued to look through the photos. I knew she was pissed with me about the Post-its. I laughed.

"I'm glad that you're amused, Nikki. That's in character."

" 'Pissed over Post-its.' *That's* in character."

A quarrel was flaring up, but we decided to let it fade. Not just now.

" . . . I thought, if the memorial takes place, we could use some of these as mementos. I was thinking of putting together a little booklet of Mom's life, there's this printer in Chautauqua Falls who did a memoir of Jimmy Friday, remember him? It's not posthumous but it has pictures, it's very attractive . . ."

"Jimmy Friday? That old bluegrass singer? Why are we talking about him?"

"We're not. We're talking about a memorial booklet for Mom."

"Oh, that. The memorial."

Clare spoke flatly, as if annoyed.

"You don't want a memorial for Mom?"

"I don't know, Nikki. Do you?"

"Well. If it could be for Mom . . ."

"Exactly! But it can't be. It's for Mom's relatives, friends . . . for us."

"Not for us. I don't think that I could bear it."

"*I* won't be here. I'll be in my new home."

"Clare, you'd have to be here! For your own mother's memorial, you can't think of not coming."

"Yes, I can think of not coming. It's a thought I've already had." Clare laughed, daringly. For a moment she seemed almost elated. "In fact, Gilbert Wexley isn't well. So plans for the memorial are suspended."

"Wexley isn't well? What's wrong with him?"

I only now realized that the man had stopped bothering me, for weeks. I felt a small stab of hurt on Mom's account.

Clare said, not very concerned, "Rob says he's heard that Wexley has been drinking 'heavily.' He seems to have collapsed at the Arts Council last week. His female staff has been covering for him for months, people say. He and the 'reverend'—I won't say his name—but you know who I mean—have been disagreeing over some aspects of the memorial, what sort of music Gwen Eaton really liked, religious or 'secular,' I've stayed out of it, I refuse to become involved with these two male egos. Some of the Eatons—you know how suspicious Uncle Herman is—are grumbling that maybe Wexley has been misappropriating donations for the memorial and the award in her name, there's no evidence for this that I know of, but you know how Dad's family is. Not that any of the Eatons want to organize the memorial themselves."

"I hadn't heard about Wexley. That's very sad."

"I thought you couldn't stand the man, Nikki!"

"I can't. But I think he means well. I think he was in love with Mom and didn't realize it and now his heart is broken, he's confused and clumsy with grief . . ."

Clare shrugged. "It's hard to feel sorry for someone whose heart is 'broken'—it seems like a luxury, somehow." She gestured at the photos scattered on the table and I knew exactly her meaning: to be alive was all that mattered, the rest is extra. "Anyway, thank God Wexley never got around to asking Mom to marry him, she might've said yes. Now we'd be Gilbert Wexley's step-daughters."

" 'Dad' Wexley. Jesus!"

We laughed and shuddered together. For a moment we were girls again, in a sudden alliance against someone adult. Neither of us wished to think that, if Mom and Gilbert Wexley had married, Mom would surely be alive now.

We were standing close together, but not touching. Clare's skin looked as if it would be hot to the touch. Perspiration was oozing through her fastidiously applied makeup. I remembered how, after Mom died, I'd stayed at the Chisholms' house for several days and had had glimpses of my sister's splotchily pale, unmade-up face: the shadowed eye sockets, the lines bracketing her mouth, the way after she washed her face most of her eyebrows vanished. This was my sister's vulnerable face, I hadn't seen since we'd been girls.

Those days, I'd felt powerful surges of love for Clare. An anxious need to please her, placate her. She'd seemed so much stronger than I was. So much more capable, responsible.

At the time, it hadn't fully sunk in: what had happened to Mom had happened to Clare and me, too.

Clare was looking at more Christmas photos. There were several that had been taken in Mom's house, in front of Mom's Christmas tree that was smaller and less ostentatiously decorated than Clare's. We tried to determine when these had been taken, and by whom.

Clare sighed. "Oh, Mom always looked so happy! You can see why they called her 'Feather' as a girl." She paused, swiping at her eyes. "To think that that man killed this woman. *This woman.*"

"He didn't know her, Clare."

"But he did! He knew Mom."

"He was ignorant. Of what he did. Even of what he was doing to himself." My voice trailed off as if unconvinced. It was a man's voice echoing in mine, faintly.

"He *knew*! It was to get back at me, he hurt Mom. For the way I'd mocked him, insulted him. Ward Lynch stabbed a defenseless woman thirty-three times. He was stabbing *me*."

Quickly I said, "Clare, that isn't so. How can you think such a thing . . ."

For a moment I felt dazed, light-headed. What Clare had said was so terrible, yet so logical . . . I couldn't accept it.

"The police said it was a 'crime of opportunity,' Clare. It's ridiculous to blame yourself."

"You'd thought of it, though. Hadn't you."

"No!"

"Yes. You did."

"No, Clare. I never thought of it, and it isn't true."

Clare said bitterly, "Well, Rob thought of it. The night after the court hearing, when I was pretty upset. Right in the courtroom, that man *yawning*! I couldn't get over it. And Rob said, 'If you hadn't insulted him, Clare. Didn't you know that a man would want to take revenge?' Rob says these things that come into his head, it's like he has pulled back the bed-clothes and discovered a nest of spiders that have to be my fault some-how." Trying not to cry, Clare looked angry.

Now I did touch Clare, or tried to touch her. The way a cat eludes you without seeming to, sliding away from your hand, Clare eluded me.

"Clare, no. Rob didn't mean it. He was just . . ."

"Saying what came into his head. Exactly."

"I'm not going to let you blame yourself, Clare. This is like Mom's friend from church Mary Kinsler, 'confessing' and crying to me that if she'd picked Mom up for their crafts class that morning, as she sometimes did, unless Mom picked her up, none of what happened would have happened."

In a voice heavy with sarcasm Clare said, "Who do you want me to blame, then? Mom?"

. . .

It was nearly noon. Clare used the guest bathroom to freshen up her makeup. Clare then made three brief calls on her cell phone, took into her possession the *Dirty Dancing* and *Tango!* records and a clutch of photographs to take with her to Philadelphia. In mounting panic I followed her to the door. It seemed unbelievable that Clare was leaving Mt. Ephraim in a few days, as if it were the most natural thing to be doing. It wasn't just Rob from whom she was separating, obviously. It was all of us. It was Mom.

Seeing my face Clare said, exasperated, "I'm moving to Philadelphia, not to the moon." When I said, "But you'll return for the trial, Clare, won't you?" she seemed not to hear.

It was a humid October day. The sky looked like clotted cobwebs.

I walked Clare to her Land Rover, parked on the road and not in the driveway. Clare must have noted the closed garage door, my car not in the driveway, which meant I'd cleared out much of the cluttered garage, but she'd said nothing.

My selfish sister! I hated her.

At this moment, the Mt. Ephraim Police cruiser turned onto Deer Creek Drive. You'd almost think it was headed for us, Clare stiffened, staring, but of course it glided past at about fifteen miles an hour. The young uniformed officer behind the wheel lifted a hand to us, in greeting.

Clare said sharply, "That's new here. A patrol car."

"Not so new, any longer. Since May."

Clare climbed into the Land Rover. I could see that she was eager to be gone. I wanted to clutch at her, to pull her back. I wanted to hurt her. I said, "Clare, don't you love us?"

Clare said frankly, turning the key in the ignition, "Nikki. It's hard to love people now. Without Mom, I'm forgetting."

with regrets . . .

The invitation arrived. *Wedding nuptials, Szyszko and Danto, Mt. Ephraim Christian Life Fellowship Church, twenty-second of November at ten o'clock in the morning.*

Yes, I'd promised to attend. But damned if I would go.

Knowing that Mom would have been disappointed in me.

taboo

There came my brother-in-law Rob Chisholm to see me.

Less than eighteen hours after Clare and Foster had left Mt. Ephraim.

On the phone he'd pleaded: "Nikki! We need to talk."

Fifteen years we'd been in-laws. My sister had been the apex of the triangle. *Brother-in-law* is a taboo category meaning *no sex*. I knew, I had to see Rob now that Clare had left him; I could not push him away, not cruelly as Clare was doing. Yet I knew it was probably a mistake.

The way sometimes you see an accident looming ahead. You are driving into an intersection, you have the right of way. Except you see a vehicle approaching the intersection from the side and you see that the vehicle isn't slowing for the stop. And in protest you think *But I have the right of way!* And then you think *But I have the power to stop, I have the power to prevent the accident.*

It was dusk when Rob arrived. Immediately I saw he'd been drinking. His jaws were unshaven and his face appeared gaunt. His white shirt was rumpled. Though it had been blustery and rainy through the day, he wore no coat. He stumbled in the doorway, laughed and muttered something meant to be funny. His eyes, snatching at mine, were red-veined and glassy.

I wondered if he'd left Coldwell Electronics early. Or if he'd even showed up that day.

Rob surprised me, he'd brought a bottle of whiskey. Without asking me he rummaged in the kitchen for glasses. I knew the whiskey was expensive since Wally Szalla often drank this brand. Rob was hoping we might share it, he said. He'd also brought a rain-splattered copy of last week's *Rochester Sun-Times Sunday Magazine* for me to inscribe.

"For this old friend of mine, his father is a vet in the Adirondacks. He'll appreciate this."

A feature I'd done for the *Chautauqua Valley Beacon* had been reprinted in the larger Rochester newspaper under the title "The Lady Is a Vet." This was one in my series of interviews with Chautauqua Valley individuals of local distinction: in this case Dr. Eve Spicer, a seventy-eight-year-old veterinarian whose specialty was horses and the "larger farm animals." Dr. Spicer was a small fierce shock-white-haired woman who'd become something of a legend in the Chautauqua Valley, as much known for her eccentricities as her veterinary skill. Dr. Spicer had been married four times. Dr. Spicer "thrived" on emergencies and beat out her competition by making home visits at any hour of the day or night in her SPICER VET MOBILE minivan she'd painted all the colors of the rainbow because such colors signified "hope." Dr. Spicer boasted of "psychic rapport" with most animals and I saw no reason to doubt her, considering the way she'd peered at me through her bifocal glasses and with a look of astute sympathy pronounced me "wounded."

Rob was saying vehemently, "—this friend of mine from Colgate, lives in Potsdam, Clare knows him but you haven't met him I don't think, it's his father this is for, he's been a vet in the Keene Valley for thirty years, he'll get a kick out of 'Dr. Spicer.' " Rob was looming over me holding the magazine open to my article, so that I could sign above the byline *Nicole Eaton*. His breath smelled like gasoline fumes. He was being maudlin, sentimental as I'd seen him only a few times, at Christmas with his children. You'd think that Clare was somewhere within earshot, all this attention focused on her sister was for her benefit.

I was embarrassed, signing my name. As if "The Lady Is a Vet" was such an accomplishment! But I understood that some people who don't write and never see their names and words in print attribute a magical power to the printed word. Mom had always revered books, any kind of serious writing. My newspaper journalism was, in Mom's words, "parts of you that go out from you and into other people."

I'd never wanted Mom to know, and wouldn't want Rob Chisholm to know now, how quickly I began to forget these profiles. I spent hours interviewing subjects and conscientiously—sincerely!—"relating" to them; I spent more hours transcribing tapes, to the point of becoming mesmerized with the very tedium of the task; and then there came the hours of writing, and rewriting. (Most of "writing" is "rewriting." This is another fact non-writers don't know.) Since moving into this house I'd become obsessive about my work, staying with a piece until it was finished no matter how exhausted I'd become in the process. It was a way of missing Mom, or maybe a way of not-missing Mom, while I was working. But once I e-mailed a piece to my editor at the *Beacon*, a kind of misty-gray amnesia set in and I began to forget. By the time the profile appeared under the byline *Nicole Eaton* it would seem almost the work of another person, a stranger.

It was rare for me to see my interview subjects a second time. Sad to say, I forgot them, too.

Except in one case. Where maybe it would have been better if I'd never seen him a second time.

"Nikki, thanks! I appreciate this and I know that Hank will, too."

Hank? What were we talking about?

In an excess of drunken gratitude Rob squeezed my hand, hard. For an edgy moment I thought he might kiss me.

I'd been hoping that Rob would be content with remaining in the kitchen where I could offer him coffee to sober him up, and a slice or two of Royal Apple Bread (I'd baked the day before, from Mom's recipe), but Rob headed for the dimly lighted living room, whiskey bottle in hand. Before I could invite him, he collapsed with a wheeze on the sofa.

"Drink, Nikki? Join me."

I told him thanks, but—

"C'mon, Nikki! Party gal like you."

Party gal. If there was a term that didn't apply to me at the moment, *party gal* was it. In fifteen years of knowing him, I'd never heard Rob Chisholm call anyone *gal*.

Rob splashed whiskey into the glasses, and handed one to me.

" 'Auld lang sign,' Nikki! You and I go way back, about as far as Clare and me." Rob lifted his glass in a swishing festive gesture, and drank.

"I think it's 'auld lang syne,' Rob."

"Whatever. Fifteen years is *'auld.'* "

This was meant to be a joke, but came out sounding wistful.

I pretended to drink. Damned if I'd let myself get drunk babysitting my sister's distraught husband.

Rob said, with maudlin emphasis, "Fifteen years is *'auld lang whatever.'* " His laughter sounded like wet gravel being shoveled.

Before she'd left Mt. Ephraim, Clare had called to warn me—unless it was a kind of boast, the way she'd used to speak of guys in high school she'd broken up with—that Rob was taking their separation "pretty badly." I had to wonder how she'd expected him to take it after fifteen years and two children—"pretty nicely"?

With every day that passed I was becoming more furious with Clare. Everyone in the family seemed to be furious, too. It was fascinating how family members united in fury against one of their own who has behaved badly: relatives who hadn't spoken with me since the day of Mom's funeral had been calling all weekend, incensed. I was made to realize that in their zeal to condemn Clare, the formerly "good" sister, they were willing to ally themselves with "bad" Nikki, who'd long disgusted the Eatons by seeing (i.e., sleeping with) a married man.

"Hey Nikki! You're looking good."

Rob meant to sound genial but this came out like reproach. He hadn't seen me in weeks, we'd only just talked on the phone when sometimes I'd been emotional if not upset.

"Well. I'm trying."

" 'Trying'?"

"Not to let missing Mom make me a wreck."

Here was a surprise: I wasn't looking bad, considering. My hair (shades of darkish blond laced with silver) had grown out to fall in loose crimped waves around my face and in several strands I'd braided purple yarn to match a purple-and-heather mohair turtleneck sweater Mom had knitted for me at least ten years ago, I'd rarely worn. My jeans were faded, just snug enough to show my derriere to advantage. I was skinnier than Wally Szalla "preferred" me but I was making an effort to eat more regularly, fret less and not to forget: lipstick!

Without my rich-luscious-moist-grape mouth, my face seemed to bleach out like overdeveloped film.

"You're no wreck, Nikki. I got to hand it to you, you've got guts."

Guts! About as appropriate, applied to me, as *party gal*.

Seeing me wince, Rob said quickly, "I mean, living in this house. Dealing with what happened to your mother . . ."

To this remark, I had no reply. I stared smiling at the glass of amber liquid in my hand. I was noticing with a small stab of embarrassment that the rim of the glass was slightly dusty. Rob had found these glasses on a shelf of rarely used "good" glasses and china. I'd slipped into a chair across from Rob on the sofa, a hefty pedestal coffee table between us, feet drawn up beneath me, meaning to be polite, to keep smiling. Though I hadn't done more than wet my lips with the whiskey, I was feeling suddenly reckless. That old, lethal impulse to match a (male) companion drink for drink . . .

". . . d'you think? How soon?"

Rob was circling his true subject, Clare. I thought he must be asking when the house would be ready to list with a realtor. Vaguely I mumbled what might've been "soon" but which meant *None of your business. This house was left to Clare and me, not you.*

Rob stiffened as if he'd heard all of this. Saying, with an air of detachment, for this wasn't Rob speaking but Clare, ". . . upset! Oh, man! Saying you'd removed her Post-its from the furniture, and boxes she'd packed you'd unpacked, you were having some sort of 'selfish nervous breakdown' and 'reverting to childhood.' But I said to Clare, on the phone

Nikki sounds perfectly—I mean, almost perfectly—under the circumstances what you'd call"—Rob lapsed into a wheezing cough and wiped his mouth on the back of his hand—"normal."

I laughed. Damned if I'd be provoked into further fury against Clare. "Thanks, Rob! I think you're 'almost perfectly normal,' too."

"You do?" Rob peered at me doubtfully.

I'd told Rob, as soon as he'd arrived, that a friend was coming to the house in about an hour, so I couldn't speak with him very long, but I had the idea that Rob hadn't taken in this information, or hadn't wished to. The "friend"—in theory, at least—was my married-man-lover Wally Szalla, whom Rob knew, and knew of. From Clare, he'd certainly heard a good deal about Wally and me, none of it complimentary.

I made a mental note to remind Rob, after about thirty minutes, that he'd have to leave soon. I hoped, by that time, Rob was still in a condition to drive.

In the living room, Rob was glancing about with a look almost of dread. Though he'd been coming to this house, he'd been a guest in this living room, since 1988, he seemed spooked by the place now. *He has never been here, never sat on that sofa, without Mom close by. Probably in the kitchen, and in another moment she'll appear in the doorway . . .*

My breath was coming quickly. I could almost see the expression on my mother's face and I could hear what she was saying, her greeting to Rob Chisholm, except at a crucial moment static intervened.

Rob, too, shivered. He'd almost seen, almost heard, too.

Though you know better, you don't somehow "know." I'd become fairly adjusted to living in Mom's house without expecting Mom to walk into the room at any moment but now that I had a visitor, and the visitor was Rob Chisholm, who was family, it was very hard to shake the feeling that, at any moment, Mom would appear in the doorway.

"Oh! God."

Rob gave a start. Nearly spilled whiskey onto his wrinkled white shirt. For suddenly there had materialized in the living room doorway what appeared at first glance to be a steel-colored burly rat, but was in fact just Smoky: glaring at the intruder with hostile tawny eyes as if, though Smoky had surely seen and sniffed Rob Chisholm many times in the past, the damned cat had never seen him before.

Like Dad, Rob Chisholm wasn't crazy about household pets. Yet he held out his hand as if the stolid little tank of a tomcat might be coaxed into coming to him and leaping on his lap.

"Smoky? Hey c'mere, kitty. You know me . . ."

I assured Rob that Smoky knew him, of course. But Smoky remained wary of most visitors.

Still Rob called, as if to a small, stubborn child, "Smok-y! Kit-ty! Don't you know me? You *do*."

Absurdly, Rob sounded hurt. There was something in the big gray cat's pose, the way his stiff white whiskers bristled with indifference, withheld acknowledgment, that stung my brother-in-law in his weakened state.

My strategy was to ignore Smoky. Calling a cat with a twitching tail is an exercise in futility. It's a struggle of wills, you can't win. You make a fool of yourself begging a cat to come to you and the cat will simply walk away, when he's had enough of embarrassing you, as Smoky was doing now.

Rob was saying, ". . . the one who ran away? That night? Your mother's cat? After . . ."

I told Rob yes. Mom's cat. He shouldn't be offended, Smoky wasn't friendly with anyone much, any longer.

Rob fell silent, brooding. His unshaven jaws appeared longer and leaner than I recalled. His graying-brown hair, thin at the crown of his head, glistened with perspiration. His red-veined eyes, too, were glistening with moisture. From time to time, thinking I wasn't watching, Rob would swipe at his eyes with his fingers. *He has never been in this house without Clare. Rarely without his children. Never in this house with just his sister-in-law Nikki.*

I knew, I should ask Rob why he'd come to see me. Obviously the subject was Clare and the "separation." But out of stubbornness, or a kind of shyness, I could not bring myself to ask.

"Well, Nikki." Rob sighed. "I . . . guess . . . she's told you . . ."

I wasn't drinking but lifted the glass to my lips. Wanting to hide behind it.

". . . after all these years, more than sixteen years we'd 'been together,' Clare has discovered . . . we are . . . 'temperamentally incompatible.' "

Vaguely I found myself taking a small swallow of whiskey. Though the sweet-fiery taste going down was anything but vague.

". . . 'sexually incompatible' is what she means. Right?"

Rob's hurt mouth twisted in a grimace of lewd despair. I was shaking my head no, avoiding his eyes. All this was utterly new to me.

"Nikki! No bullshitting. No need to protect your sister, it's all out in the open like spilled guts."

Still I seemed not to know. Not me! I would play this scene inscrutable as Smoky the cat.

Rob plunged on, miserably, ". . . she must have confided in you, Nikki. She says it's been 'years.' But I thought she was happy! I mean, I never thought she wasn't. Now she's saying she 'can't breathe' in our marriage. 'Suffocating' she says and if I try to touch her she throws off my hand like a snake. I mean, like I was the snake. This woman that, how many times, she'd become emotional saying *I never touched her* which wasn't true, I swear. Or, if it's true it was only true sometimes . . ."

I didn't want to hear this! My teeth clicked against the glass, I hadn't quite realized I'd lifted to my mouth.

Thinking how expensive liquor is so smooth going down, like liquid fire. The very opposite of yet near-identical to ice cream which when swallowed immediately begins to melt. One is fiery and consoling, the other icy-sweet and consoling.

Party gal. Well, maybe. Back when my hair was sexy-punk-purple and my satiny-elastic micro-skirts so snugly fitted my crotch. And my naked feet in black platform glitter shoes!

Rob Chisholm hadn't ever glimpsed me in quite such a costume. In Mt. Ephraim and vicinity, in the suburban homes of the Eatons and the Kovachs, Nikki'd been pretty well behaved.

It wasn't exactly true that a friend was scheduled to drop by that evening. At 10 P.M. I'd turn on "Night Train" to listen to Wally Szalla's dreamy/sexy voice introducing dreamy/sexy jazz and at midnight when the program ended and the D.J. signed off over the melancholy notes of "Night Train" I would feel a pang of loss, I would wonder where Wally was headed now, to his upscale bachelor quarters in Chautauqua Falls or across town to his upscale family house or (but I didn't want to wonder this!) another place, unknown to me. I had to wonder though knowing it wouldn't be Mt. Ephraim, tonight.

Nikki I've been missing you. Give me a call darling.

Nikki are you angry with me? If it's about last Friday, having to cancel . . .

Lately when I didn't return Wally's calls, Wally didn't keep calling back as he'd once done. Didn't send flowers as he'd once done. Didn't show up unexpectedly with a bottle of Italian red wine. Didn't bring me miniature books of inspiration. By now, Wally had to know that Nikki Eaton had either been inspired or wouldn't ever be inspired, it was a project beyond his powers.

". . . every flaw in a man, like he's stripped naked, on one of these afternoon TV talk shows, so humiliated, every time the phone rings it's 'Aunt Maude'—'Aunt Tabitha'—'Aunt Lorraine' "—Rob's voice rose to a sudden mock-soprano—" 'Ohhh Rob! What have I been hearing! How can you and Clare be separating! What about the children, how can you do such a thing to your children, can't you talk sense into Clare, the woman is your *wife*.' " Rob paused, breathing hard. He'd clawed at his shirt collar, his face glowered with perspiration. His expression had become savage. "The worst is, God-damned 'Uncle Herman'—'Uncle Fred'—calling me at the office. 'Rob, what on earth is happening with you and Clare? A "separation"? For no reason? And your children so young? You must know that such behavior is unacceptable in our family.' And I'm, like, wanting to say, so shove the family up your ass, 'Uncle.' *I'm* not one of you."

Unacceptable. An Eaton expression we'd been hearing all our lives, and had joked about. Even Dad had made a joke of it, sometimes.

". . . funny, Nikki? Glad you think so."

I jammed my knuckles against my mouth to keep from breaking into hysterical laughter as Rob stared at me with aggrieved eyes. He was mis-understanding my reaction, that I should seem to be laughing at him when I was only just recalling how *unacceptable* began for me in ninth grade when suddenly I'd discovered *SEX* or, more accurately, *SEX* discovered me.

And how powerfully it was coming now, suffused through my body like liquid fire, the old, lethal impulse to drink with a companion.

Especially a male companion.

A not-bad-looking rumpled-sexy mistreated husband. A guy whose eyes had been moving on me, over me, in-between the crevices of me, for fifteen years.

"Nikki, can you? Tell me? I feel as if I'm drowning, I can't grab hold of anything solid to pull . . ."

I set down my glass, that was nearly empty. I hadn't been conscious of drinking. I was feeling like a Christmas tree warmly lighting up. Espe-cially the lower parts of me. The parts that were lonely for my married-man-lover.

Fuck you, Wally Szalla. Go back to your precious Isabel, I don't need you.

I shook my head to clear it. Shifted my legs out from beneath me, that had begun to ache. Damned if I would seduce my brother-in-law, at such a time. In Mom's living room!

I tried to assure Rob, who stared at me with glistening-hungry eyes, that Clare hadn't said a single word to me that was critical of him, still less a violation of his privacy. Whatever the relatives were telling him, they were exaggerating as usual. "It's just that, as far as I can understand her, Clare wants to have a career again. She wants to enroll in graduate school, get a master's degree and—"

Rob interrupted angrily, "But to leave me? Lilja and me? Our house she's spent a fortune on? To walk out? Take my son with her? Instead of enrolling at Rochester or Brockport where she could commute, enrolling somewhere in Philadelphia? 'I have a friend in Philadelphia'—that's some kind of riddle? All our married life, I've been hearing that. Are Clare and this college roommate of hers conspiring? Behind their husbands' backs? Like Philadelphia is some kind of safe house, Clare can escape to? How can Clare walk away from Mt. Ephraim with all that's going on here? After what happened to your mother, and what's happening with you, and the trial coming up in January—she says she isn't coming back, incidentally—and making up her mind practically overnight, and calling a lawyer before she'd even told me, and drawing up a 'legal separation,' and—abandoning me? Nikki, I thought she loved me! I thought she loved our family life! I thought she wanted all that we have!" Rob was speaking in short, choppy fragments as if he'd been running and was out of breath. My heart went out to him, I felt his distress but didn't want to be drawn in, I was fearful of such raw emotion as I'd have been fearful of a rapidly spreading fire. "*She* was the one wanting to get married so soon, not me. *She* was desperate to quit her teaching job, hated her job, the school was 'suffocating' her, she 'couldn't breathe,' she wanted to 'start a family,' wanted babies, wanted to stay in Mt. Ephraim where her parents lived, where she knew everyone and felt important, safe, when I could have worked in California, Texas, even Hawaii!—I had excellent offers from American branch offices in Tokyo, Sydney, Rome—I'd have liked to try the Peace Corps for a couple of years, the Ivory Coast, Kenya, but Clare squelched that fast— 'And come home with some disgusting parasite?— our heads shrunken?' " Rob so perfectly mimicked Clare's voice of indignation/outrage, I heard myself snort with laughter.

"And your parents didn't want us to, either. Especially Gwen, the idea of Clare going to Africa seemed to terrify her."

Rob splashed more whiskey into his glass. Swished it, sniffed it, glowered at me, and drank.

When in doubt, blame Mom.

The few mouthfuls of whiskey I'd had had gone to my head. Since not-seeing Wally Szalla as often as before, and not-daring to drink when I was alone, I'd become more susceptible to alcohol.

"Glad I'm so amusing, Nikki. I should be on TV."

"Rob, I'm not laughing at you! I'm not laughing—"

"Maybe it is funny. Women on afternoon TV talk shows, they'd find it hilarious."

I tried to speak somberly. Soberly. "I—I think it's temporary, Rob. The 'separation.' "

"You do?"

"Judging from what Clare has told me. About leaving Mt. Ephraim."

I wasn't sure if this was so. Vaguely I seemed to recall Clare having said—well, something vague.

Rob asked carefully, "She's told you—? What?"

"That she'll be back. When she gets her degree. I think. And when Foster begins improving in school . . ."

"Clare said that? She'd be *back*?"

"She has to come back, Rob. She can't abandon Lilja."

"Lilja! What about me?"

Quickly I said, "I didn't mean that, Rob. Of course, Clare loves you. She told me, just before she left, 'I love Rob but I need to be away, for just now. I love you all but . . . for just right now . . .' " This wasn't sounding like my sister, exactly. But Rob, gazing at me with hurt-hungry eyes, seemed to find it plausible.

I was distracted by Rob's hurt-hungry mouth. Thinking what a long time it had been since Wally Szalla had seriously kissed me.

Since any man had seriously kissed me.

Since any man had seriously made love to me.

Rob queried me further about what Clare had allegedly said. I had to wonder if I was inventing dialogue for my sister in the way that Dad used to accuse Mom of so badly wanting people to make up the differences between them, she invented their dialogue for them.

Mom always defended herself, passionately. In her mind, the dialogue was 100 percent authentic, she swore she'd heard it with her "own ears."

I could almost swear, yes I'd heard Clare with my "own ears." If she hadn't exactly said these sensible words, she'd meant to say them.

". . . she does love you, Rob. That's the main thing."

Rob was on his feet, swaying. I hoped he wouldn't stumble into the pedestal table, that weighed a ton: people were always banging their shins on it, especially men. I was on my feet also. Oh, my head was spinning! But it was a comforting sensation, I hadn't felt in a while.

One of those sensations you feel lonely for. Like a man's hands touching you, a man's mouth kissing you. Almost, the exact identity of this man isn't relevant.

I roused myself to say, staring at my wristwatch, "Well! It's getting late . . ."

Rob roused himself, too. He'd finished most of the whiskey himself and would leave the bottle behind. Though he pointedly ignored my hint he seemed to know that it was time to leave. Thanking me not once but several times and calling me *Nik-ki* in a voice tremulous with emotion. ". . . why I came here, I knew, if I saw you, things would make some sense. Of the two of you, Nikki, you and Clare, this goes back years, Nikki, it needs to be said, of the two of you, you are the one who . . ." Rob jammed his fist against his heart in a sudden forceful gesture, as if words were failing him. ". . . no matter what people say about you. See, people don't know *you*. They think they know Clare, Clare Eaton is the 'sensible' sister but oh man, I happen to know otherwise. You don't live with a woman like Clare for fifteen years and not know otherwise. Also you're nicer, Nikki . . . And smarter, and better-looking, and, well . . . sexier. Oh, man."

When words like this come lurching at you, maybe they're the fantasy words you've been wishing to hear, always they come too quickly, too suddenly, before you're prepared, and the man is coming too quickly at you, lurching also, in this case stumbling against the pedestal table. Rob must have banged his shin hard but in his emotional state seemed scarcely to notice. His fumey breath was in my face. His fingers took hold of my shoulders in the mohair sweater. Before I could react, he stooped to me, brushed his lips against my cheek and then, hot-mouthed, kissed my mouth. His lips were rubbery and wet and not so comforting as I'd anticipated yet a sensation like an electric shock ran swiftly through me, chest to groin.

"Nikki, hey. I'm crazy about you."

Rob was pleading. Yet it was a forceful pleading, and he wasn't relaxing his grip on my shoulders.

I was pushing Rob away, or trying to. Didn't want this to escalate into anything like a struggle. My brother-in-law was drunker than I'd guessed and a drunken man is very hard to budge.

"You're crazy about your family, Rob. Not me."

"No, Nikki. *You.*"

Suddenly, in the confusion of the moment, it seemed utterly plausible. My brother-in-law Rob Chisholm was crazy about me. Not Clare but me. *Me!*

The way he was looking at me, preparing to kiss me again if I didn't squirm out of his grasp, if I didn't decisively wriggle free of his fingers gripping my shoulders which I meant to do, or tried to do, except my knees were weak and my reactions slow as if underwater, or in a dream: one of those sweet/shameful taboo dreams you hope to forget as soon as you wake.

"Nikki, you like me, too, don't you? A little?"

"Rob, I . . ."

"Hey c'mon: you know you do."

This was so. This was true. Those years of flirting between us. In Clare's very house, and here in Mom's house. At family gatherings innocent and gregarious as outdoor barbecues, where Rob Chisholm himself was in charge of steaks, chicken, hot dogs sizzling on the grill. Always there were opportunities. Sly-secret opportunities. Moist-lipped smiles, unmistakable in meaning. Squeezing my brother-in-law's fingers even as, teasing-quick, I released them. When we spoke together—and always, at some point in the evening, we'd find ourselves speaking together earnestly and at length—lightly touching my brother-in-law's arm. Sometimes Rob Chisholm and I were so highly charged, except not always, especially at the end of a festive evening when we'd each had a few drinks. When I'd say goodnight to my brother-in-law in a luxuriant display of full-frontal teasing: "Goodnight, Rob! Love ya!" The full length of Nikki against the full length of Rob.

Once, at a noisy wedding, I'd given Rob a hot wet goodnight kiss at the edge of his mouth and Rob responded by grabbing my derriere with both hands, to press me against him a little harder.

I'd only just slapped at him lightly, and laughed.

Hoping that no one had seen.

(Or maybe I hadn't much cared if anyone had seen. Not Clare, not even Mom.)

I wondered if Rob had been remembering the last time we'd been together in this house. Mom's Mother's Day dinner. So close to the day of her death.

I'd been well aware of the way the men's eyes had moved onto me. Danto, and Wexley, and Rob Chisholm. Especially Rob Chisholm. No wonder Clare had been furious, in the kitchen. No wonder Mom had been disgusted with me.

How can you drift as you've been drifting. How can he respect you if you don't respect yourself.

I seemed to hear Mom. Somewhere in this room. I wondered if Rob had heard her, too.

I was saying, pleading, "Rob, you'd better leave. This isn't the right time, and it isn't the right place," and Rob was saying, "What's that mean, Nikki? This is where you are, and I'm here. You must know, I've been crazy about you for a long time," and I said, "Rob, no. It's your family you're crazy about, please believe me," and Rob said, "Don't send me away, I'm so lonely," and I said, "Lilja must be waiting for you . . ." and Rob said, half-sobbing, "Lilja! Lilja can't bear to look at me! She won't even discuss the separation, she's staying with her cousin Caroline, didn't Clare tell you? I'm so lonely, Nikki, I can't go back to that house . . ." and I said, trying to remain calm, "But you can't stay with me, Rob, someone is coming to see me, soon," and Rob said, "Szalla? Him? *He's* coming?" and I said, "Never mind who's coming, my private life is no concern of yours," and Rob said, "Szalla doesn't deserve you, Nikki," and I said, "You'd better leave now, Rob."

By this time I'd managed to back away from Rob who was looming over me, hot-faced and panting. My shoulders stung from the grip of his fingers. My mouth felt bruised, from the single hard kiss. I saw a glisten of resentment in my brother-in-law's face, a look of purely male anger. I hoped Rob wouldn't turn into a mean drunk. I had to realize I'd never been alone with him in such circumstances. I hoped I hadn't been leading him on though of course I'd been leading him on and we both knew it.

Rob staggered out of the living room, along the hall and into the kitchen, went to the sink and turned on a faucet. In a gesture meant to be clownish as well as pragmatic he turned the hand-spray onto his hot face, wetted his face, hair, shirt and splattered his trousers. Water streamed down his face like tears. "This is to cool me off. This will teach me a lesson."

Rob stumbled into Smoky's food bowls and spilled kibble onto the floor. He apologized, laughing. He would have stooped to clean up the mess except I told him please just leave, I'd take care of it myself. At the door he fumbled with the knob, I had to open it for him and urge him out and still he lingered, unsteady on his feet as an upright bear. ". . . just that, Nikki, you're too good for Szalla. Guy's too old and fat for you. Sweet girl like you. Sweet, sad girl like you. *I'm* the one understands you, not what's-his-name. Clare is out of it, see I don't want her back, it's Foster I want back, I want my son back, I want my sweet Nikki on my side, whyn't you come over to my house and make supper for *me*, this isn't good for you, living here isn't good for you, Nikki, your mother died in this house . . ."

Now I was upset. Now I shoved Rob Chisholm out the door.

"My mother didn't die in this house, my mother lived in this house for thirty years."

After Rob left I cleaned up the spilled cat food. I knelt on the linoleum floor, my tears fell onto the spread-out newspaper. Of course Smoky appeared, nudging against me and purring loudly. He had banished his rival, now he was famished.

In the morning, I would discover the *Rochester Sun-Times Sunday Magazine* on the kitchen counter, where Rob Chisholm had left it.

messages

Has he been to see you?

Has he been complaining of me, to you?

Has he been taking care of himself?

Has he been drinking?

Has he been missing work?

Has he, well—missed us?

Messages on my answering machine from Clare. Playing and replaying them I wasn't certain if I felt relieved to hear from my runaway sister, or resentful. Wanting to fire back *You're the one who has left us, do you miss us?*

church street

"You baked this? *You?*"

With a prim doubtful expression Aunt Tabitha lifted the slice of sprouted-wheat/almond bread to her mouth. Then, as she chewed, tasted, swallowed, a grudging-Grandma expression came over her face.

Where other elderly women turn frail, with rice-paper skin, my aunt seemed to be thickening and hardening. Her skin exuded a lardish lustre and her figure was pear-shaped, stolid. Her bluish-white hair, tightly permed, had a synthetic bounce. Her appetite appeared to be undiminished.

". . . a trifle airy for my taste. You know, like there are air bubbles in the bread. Of course, Gwen's bread was like this, too. There are people who prefer it this way."

Tabitha spoke so solemnly, I told her I was sorry.

"Oh no, dear! It is good. It is"—Tabitha hesitated, regarding me with unexpectedly moist eyes—"very good. Gwen would be proud of you at last."

After weeks, unless it had been months, of avoiding Aunt Tabitha, I'd finally gone to visit her in the drafty cobblestone house on Church Street. As Mom would have done, I'd brought a fresh-baked loaf of bread made from one of Mom's recipes. Unlike Mom, I wasn't going to be overly sensitive about Tabitha's enigmatic remarks. Truly I didn't know if she'd meant *at last* to be hurtful to me, or a heartfelt compliment. Even Dad had said of his older sister that she doled out compliments the way she doled out tips: "Grudgingly."

After Rob Chisholm, I'd been feeling guilty. Almost as if I'd slept with my brother-in-law.

Waking to feel myself sexually aroused. A taste of a man's soft-hard mouth on mine. Whose?

Maybe it was a guilty season, autumn. Not leafy/colorful autumn but leafless/dreary autumn with skies like eraser smudges when it wasn't raining which usually it was. I needed to feel good about myself which meant behaving in a not-Nikki way, not-selfish but good-hearted like Gwen Eaton, rushing about Mt. Ephraim visiting with elderly relatives and friends. It had been a revelation to me, how my mother's calendar was sprinkled with the initials of these females, how frequently she must have seen them. Tabitha was telling me now, even as she buttered a second slice of crusty bread, that she missed Gwen every day, how "sweet" Gwen had been to call on her several times a week to ask after her health, how "thoughtful"—"generous"—Gwen had been to drive her to appointments, since Tabitha was having trouble driving lately: "Not me, but other drivers! They are so young, and so *rude*."

Before I realized, I seemed to have agreed to drive my aunt to an upcoming doctor's appointment ("This terrible 'colonoscopy' it's called, you are given something to make you woozy, you are not allowed to drive a car afterward") and a Women's Garden Club luncheon ("All the way downtown, and then you can't find a parking space").

It was ironic that Aunt Tabitha so missed Mom, whom she'd taken for granted as her younger brother's "sweet" little wife. In the Eaton family mythology, Jonathan Eaton had married "for love"—meaning, beneath him. Mom had always been intimidated by the Eatons and above all by Tabitha who'd been the wife of a Mt. Ephraim businessman named Edmund Spancic III. (Which made Tabitha *Mrs. Edmund Spancic III*, a name she still signed with a flourish.) The Spancic house in the oldest and most prestigious neighborhood in Mt. Ephraim was twice the size of the ranch house in Deer Creek Acres and my childhood memory of this house was

one of brocaded fabrics and claw-footed furniture, "doilies" and "slipcov-
ers" and German-made "figurines" not to be touched. Unlike our floors
which were mostly covered in wall-to-wall carpeting, the Spancics' floors
were polished hardwood which meant you could run and slide on loose
rugs, or in your stocking-feet, if no adults were observing.

One of the deeply mortifying memories of my childhood was of a
stopped-up toilet in the downstairs "guest bathroom" of my aunt's house.
When I'd flushed the toilet, the urine-discolored water level rose terrify-
ingly and overflowed onto the tile floor and rose-pattern bathroom rug,
and though the mishap hadn't been my fault, the toilet had obviously
been malfunctioning before I'd used it, the commotion that ensued, my
aunt's fussing over the "ruined" rug and my uncle's fuming over my "care-
lessness," had been a nightmare. Twenty years later I was sure that
Tabitha regarded me with mistrust as her slovenly niece who stopped up
toilets. While visiting her, I took care never to use the guest bathroom,
to lessen anxiety on both sides.

Was this an amusing memory? Clare would think so: she'd teased me
mercilessly for years.

Dad had held his own with his bossy older sister but Mom had always
deferred to her sister-in-law. It was her nature to give in to stronger personalities: she assured Clare and me, she "didn't mind" the way Tabitha
treated her. For Tabitha Spancic had genuine silver, not silverplate; in her
living room and dining room, Tabitha had "real" Oriental rugs; Tabitha
had a "girl" to clean her house, and often a "cook" to prepare meals; there
was even a "yardman" for the property, which was smaller than our own.
The Spancics had two cars, one invariably a Lincoln, while the Eatons of
Deer Creek Acres had just one, which was Dad's. How many times we'd
returned home from Aunt Tabitha's with Mom silent in the car and Dad
trying to joke her out of being hurt: "Gwen, don't take it personally. You
know how Tabby is."

Tabby! My heart beat hard in resentment, decades later. Why hadn't
Dad intervened with Tabby, then? In his sister's house, to her face? In the
bulldog-presence of Edmund Spancic III?

Aunt Tabitha and I were sitting in Tabitha's high-ceilinged dining room, at an end of the massive mahogany table where two plastic place mats made to resemble white lace had been set. For an important social occasion, Tabitha would have whisked away the plastic and replaced it with genuine lace. My memories of this room were mixed: formal, interminable Thanksgiving dinners and occasional Christmas dinners, endured rather than enjoyed, until I was old enough (by the rebellious age of fifteen) to refuse to come. On the table were the same sturdy silver candlestick holders, with cream-colored candles whose wicks had never been sullied by any match, and between the holders was Tabitha's favorite German figurine, a buxom shepherdess with rosy cheeks. With my sprouted-wheat/almond bread we were having Earl Gray tea in dusty Wedgwood cups. Tabitha kept spooning sugar into her tea and sighing. She'd been grateful to see me when I arrived but, being Tabitha, couldn't keep an air of reproach out of her voice, complaining of how long it had been since I'd visited her, how long it had been since she'd seen her grandchildren, how windy and cold it was already in November, how heating bills were so high she'd been having to shut off rooms in the house: "And there you are, across town, in another lonely house. And yours is *so small*."

I swallowed a hot mouthful of Earl Gray tea, pretending not to have heard this.

". . . just last winter, your mother and I were saying, how sensible it would be, if Gwen moved in here. Except of course . . ."

Tabitha sighed fretfully. How like fate it was, to have thwarted her wishes.

I said nothing. I couldn't look at my aunt, who seemed to be staring intently at me. Tabitha's pewter-colored eyes were sharply defined as coins behind her glasses, not the old-woman misty eyes you might expect.

Oh, I would have to ask Clare about this! I was sure I'd never heard Mom speak of wanting to sell our house, let alone moving in with Tabitha Spancic of all people.

". . . and Clare? How is Clare, in Philadelphia?"

Philadelphia was enunciated as you'd enunciate the name of a loathsome disease. I had to disappoint Tabitha by telling her that Clare seemed fine, very busy with her new life, we didn't communicate often, if she wanted to speak with Clare she could call her, I'd given her the number, hadn't I? Tabitha ignored this, sniffing. "There isn't another man involved, I hope," and I murmured no, I didn't think so. Tabitha said, "And Rob, what about him?" with a little catch in her throat, as if this were a riskier question, and I murmured no, I didn't think so.

Though I'd been wondering lately. The hungry way Rob had looked at me, the way he'd grabbed and kissed me. The smell of his whiskey breath. Maybe, just maybe, he'd been unfaithful to Clare, and that was the reason for the separation. Rob was often at electronics conventions, in such places as Atlanta, Miami, Las Vegas . . .

I'd half-believed him, when he'd said he was crazy for me. I'd wanted to believe. But in the sober light of day, Rob had maybe just been a lonely man whose wife had rejected him and I was his wild/sexy sister-in-law looking lonely, too.

"*Do* you know anything about it?"—Tabitha's eyes were prying at mine.

" 'It'—?"

"Their marriage. Clare's and Rob's." Tabitha spoke impatiently as if to a retarded child.

"No, Aunt Tabitha. I do not."

"Clare doesn't confide in you? Did she confide in Gwen?"

I shook my head, not-knowing.

"That poor little boy. He has 'learning disabilities'—Clare told me? Since when?"

Again I shook my head, don't know.

"And Lilja! That girl. I've tried to speak with her on the phone but she's always in a hurry and lately she must have caller I.D. because she won't *pick up*."

Shook my head: baffled, too. Sad!

In fact, Lilja seemed to be avoiding me, too. I'd thought that with Clare gone Lilja might be wanting to talk to Auntie Nikki, might want to have dinner with me from time to time, even stay over at my house, but she'd declined with a little cry of alarm as if I'd suggested something obscene. Rob complained to me that Lilja spent as much time away from home as she could, usually at a girl cousin's house. So far as he could tell, she didn't miss her mother much: "The main change in the household is it's *quiet*." Once, Rob had thought he'd heard Lilja crying in her room but when he went to inquire he'd discovered that she was on her cell phone with a girlfriend, laughing.

Tabitha sighed. "Girls that age! Lilja will be growing up even faster than you did."

Meaning, *having sex* at an age too-young for one of Tabitha's pristine nature even to contemplate.

Before arriving at my aunt's house I'd calculated how soon I could slip away again, reasoning that anything less than an hour would be an insult, but now that I was here, I realized it would be much more difficult to escape. Almost wistfully it had been hinted by Tabitha that we might have dinner together and, taken by surprise, I'd murmured an ambiguous reply not quite yes, not quite no, feeling a faint stir of panic. *No! no!* It would be an ordeal to prepare a meal with my fussy aunt in her dreary kitchen, nothing like preparing meals with Mom in her cheerful kitchen where I'd fallen into the daughter/helper role, with Mom the boss. I couldn't imagine such intimacy with my aunt. I couldn't imagine what sorts of meals Tabitha might prepare for herself, alone in this house. The wild thought came to me, I should take Tabitha out to dinner. What fun! My old friend Sylvie LaPorte had recently called suggesting we meet for lunch or dinner, I'd ask Sylvie to invite her mother, or an elderly aunt, we could have a double date.

Tabitha said, sniffing, "I see you're smiling, Nikki! So good to know that someone is happy."

I chose to interpret this rebuke as a compliment. And a signal to depart.

Except as I stood Tabitha said suddenly, as if she'd just now thought of it, that a closet door in her bedroom had fallen "off its hinges," and could I help her repair it? The last time this had happened, Gwen had helped, and they'd fixed the door "good as new" in five minutes.

Of course, I offered to help. With Mom as my predecessor, it wasn't as if I had much choice.

So, leaning heavily on the banister, Tabitha led me up the stairs to the gloomy second floor of her house. So far as I could remember, I'd never been upstairs before. (As children, Clare and I had been forbidden to "explore" our aunt's house.) Immediately, a feeling of disorientation came over me. Not just I didn't want to be here but I shouldn't be here. Tabitha was breathing quickly, as if excited. Following her stolid pear-shaped body along a dim-lit hall with soft, plush carpeting that swallowed up our footsteps, I scared myself thinking that in one of the closed-off rooms we were passing, my long-deceased uncle Edmund Spancic III lay embalmed in a canoe-like coffin.

"Gwen was just so helpful after Edmund passed, you can't imagine. Why, I never needed to ask her a thing, she would ask me, 'Tabitha, is there anything in the house that needs seeing-to?' *She* would ask me."

I absorbed this in silence. Not asking meanly what Tabitha had offered to do for Mom, after Dad "passed."

Tabitha's bedroom was exactly what I'd have expected in such an old, stately house: over-large, yet with too much furniture; fussily decorated in the style of a bygone era, with faded floral-print wallpaper and heavy brocaded drapes and an ugly chandelier. The bed looked as if it had been hastily, even grudgingly made, lumpy beneath a brocade spread. The most striking piece of furniture, the only thing I might have coveted, was a faded velvet *chaise longue* on claw feet, piled with one of Mom's silk-square quilts and several of her needlepoint cushions which I recognized immediately as her handiwork. I told Tabitha that the *chaise longue* looked like something you'd see Joan Crawford lounging on in a black silk negligee, in some late-night TV movie from the 1940s. Being Tabitha, unresponsive to my attempts at wit as Smoky, my aunt simply stared blankly at me. "I mean," I amended, "it's glamorous."

Glamorous? With the disproportionately clumsy claw feet, the piece was purely camp. But I meant to be admiring.

Yet still Tabitha stood, staring at me. She was wearing, in her drafty house, a dark wool-looking dress whose hem fell to mid-calf, over this a hefty nickel-colored cardigan with wooden buttons; on her surprisingly small, though rather swollen-looking feet, sensible-grandma shoes, more stolid leathery versions of Mom's all-occasion crepe-soled shoes. Pressing her hand against her bosom, Tabitha said, breathless, "Oh! Gwen once said that exact same thing, about that sofa. One day when I was feeling poorly, and Gwen came with me upstairs and helped me into bed, she said, you know how Gwen was always sparkly, 'If you get tired of that spiffy *chaise longue*, Tabitha, don't give it to Good Will without consulting me. I could use some glamour over at Forty-three Deer Creek Drive.' "

It was stunning to me, to so suddenly hear Mom's words, Mom's voice, rendered through Tabitha Spancic. I wouldn't have thought that my self-absorbed aunt would have remembered such a remark, let alone recount it for me so vividly.

I couldn't think how to reply. I felt a terrible wave of loss sweep over me.

Tabitha said, "Oh, I wish I'd given it to Gwen! It isn't as if I ever use it."

We turned our attention to the "broken" closet door. In fact, it was one of four elegantly constructed louvre doors, on two good-sized closets facing each other in an alcove, that had been designed to open and shut on rollers. Not ordinary closet doors for the Spancics, but needlessly complicated white louvre doors whose slats were grim with dust. I could see how the door had slipped off its roller, but damned if I could see how it might be forced up into the mechanism again. Tabitha had left it tilted drunkenly against a wall. As she fretted and fussed, I tried to lift the heavy door, struggled with it for several long minutes, broke several fingernails and came close to crushing my fingers. Tabitha did absolutely nothing to help. As the door teetered, swerved, fell against my arms, tilted back against the wall, left a sizable scratch in the hardwood floor (which

Tabitha didn't seem to have noticed thank God) my aunt lamented, "Somehow, Gwen and I were able to force it back. 'It's nothing,' Gwen said. 'But it has a trick to it.' "

I said, "Well, it's broken now, Aunt Tabitha. Maybe it wasn't broken before."

"Gwen said . . ."

Were we arguing? About what?

"Can you call a handyman, Tabitha? You must have a man you call often, with this house."

"Oh, I do! But he passed away, this summer."

A sly thought came to me: "Maybe Rob Chisholm could help. Call *him*."

Tabitha said, in her way of coercive helplessness, "Oh, couldn't you call him, Nikki? I scarcely know Clare's husband."

I said, "*I* scarcely know Clare's husband. In fact, I scarcely know Clare."

I'd managed to tilt the damned louvre door back against the wall, as I'd found it.

All this while, I'd been distracted by a sweet, seductive scent of lavender emanating from my aunt's closet: Gwen's "potpourri cachet." Every fall, Tabitha said, Gwen had given her a fresh supply made of dried wildflowers and herbs. "Why don't you take some with you, Nikki? It isn't like there will be more."

In fact, there was an excess of my mother's potpourri at home. In every closet, in the guest bathroom and in Mom's sewing room. I'd become so habituated to it I rarely noticed it any longer, except when I entered the house out of the fresh, chill air. I didn't doubt that every female relative and friend of Gwen Eaton's in a ten-mile radius of Mt. Ephraim was well-stocked with the scent. Yet it was kind of my aunt to make the offer, and I thanked her.

Unexpectedly then, Tabitha began to pull items of clothing out of the closet to show me. These were "good" dresses, some of them made of silk, satin, cashmere wool, and all of them on cushioned hangers. There were tweed suits, there were blouses and vests and skirts, the sight of which caused Tabitha to laugh almost gaily. She hadn't fitted into some of these things since she'd been pregnant with Aaron more than forty years ago, and it broke her heart to see them go to waste. *Wouldn't I like to take something? Please?*

I admired Tabitha's expensive things but declined her offer. The panicky sensation returned, a sudden conviction *She will make me into her daughter, too.*

"It's you or Good Will, Nikki. Naturally, I'd prefer a blood relative to utter strangers."

"Well, naturally. Aunt Tabitha. Thank you."

Still, Tabitha wasn't to be discouraged. From out of a cherrywood bureau drawer she lifted a peach-colored angora sweater, wrapped in tissue paper like something precious. "Isn't this beautiful! You won't believe, your mother knitted this for *me.* Such a long time ago, I know I haven't worn it in thirty years."

Rapidly I calculated: thirty years? If Tabitha was remembering correctly, Mom had knitted the sweater for her when Mom had been in her mid-twenties, and Tabitha in her mid-thirties. Somehow I didn't want to think that my mother and her sister-in-law had been close at one time; or, worse, Mom had wished to think they were close.

"I never did wear it very much. It was always a bit snug in the bosom. Please do take it, Nikki! Gwen would want you to."

Reluctantly I took the sweater from her. Angora is so light, it seemed to float in my hands. Contemplating myself in one of my aunt's mirrors, I held the sweater against me. Peach wasn't one of my favorite colors. My eyes appeared oddly shiny, glassy. My cheeks were strangely flushed. Close beside me Tabitha hovered, stolid and nearly my height, smiling in the way Mom used to smile when I'd tried on things she'd made for me.

"Aunt Tabitha, thanks. But—"

"There, that's settled. Wear it for your 'man friend,' dear. I think you will find," Tabitha said gravely, "men are most impressed by 'feminine'— 'gracious'—items of apparel, in good taste."

The peach-colored angora sweater was certainly in good taste. It would have been suitable for a child, with slightly puffy sleeves and an eyelet neckline. Across the bodice was a small constellation of seed pearls.

If I wore this sweater braless, hard little nipples poking through the peachy angora, Wally Szalla would be impressed, indeed. Not to mention hot-eyed Rob Chisholm.

I laughed. I thanked Aunt Tabitha with a quick kiss on the cheek. Ordinarily we'd have both been shocked by my impulsive affection but there was something feverish/festive in the air in Tabitha's bedroom, intensified by the pervading smell of lavender.

Next, Tabitha insisted upon giving me a detachable white lace collar my mother had sewed for her years ago, that had gone just slightly yellow. ("You can wear it with the sweater, Nikki. It will be adorable.") And a red silk blouse with an enormous bow, Tabitha said was too small for her but "looked just right" for me. (It looked voluminous.) And a black jersey cloche hat, she claimed not to have worn in fifty years.

"Aunt Tabitha, you aren't that old. Come *on*."

"In their hearts, people age at different rates, Nikki. You will see."

A cryptic remark for Mrs. Edmund Spancic III to utter!

Mom hadn't sewed the cloche hat for Tabitha, I was sure. It fitted my head just loosely enough so that I could sweep up my hair inside it. I had to admit, I liked the look: if I'd discovered the hat in a thrift shop I'd have quickly snapped it up. It was difficult to envision my aunt wearing such a hat but I could envision a lover pulling it off my head and my hair tumbling—glimmering, rippling—down past my (bare) shoulders.

Naked Nikki, in just a cloche hat. And the hat stripped from her.

The thought came to me: Detective Strabane might like this hat.

And the peach-colored angora sweater with the puff sleeves and seed-pearl bodice, too.

Primly Aunt Tabitha murmured: "They were not a natural couple, I'm afraid."

"Oh. They . . . weren't?"

"Not what you'd call 'compatible.' That is the word, isn't it—'compatible.' "

I was reluctant to answer. The subject was my parents. My heart felt as if it had been gripped in a vise: Aunt Tabitha's sturdy hand.

Somehow—oh, don't ask how!—we were in my aunt's drafty high-ceilinged kitchen. Somehow, I seem to have agreed to stay for what Tabitha called "supper."

In fact, I seemed to be the one preparing the meal while Tabitha opened and shut drawers, peered into kitchen cupboards, with a vague, vexed look of being unable to find what she sought.

Aunt Tabitha's kitchen was a place where things weren't likely to be where you sought them. "Good, linen" napkins were discovered amid greasy cooking utensils in a lower cupboard, "good, crystal" water glasses turned up amid canned goods, mostly Campbell's soups, in another cupboard. The roll of paper towels had run out forcing us to use "good, cloth" hand towels in the interim. These vexations, and others, were attributed to the unreliability of a woman named Daniella who "helped out" Tabitha once a week, usually Thursdays.

Beyond Daniella, the fault lay more obscurely with Tabitha's grown children who never came to visit, even with the deceased Edmund, who'd left Tabitha a widow alone in such a big house. Daniella had not much to do, but, somehow, Daniella couldn't be depended upon to do this little as well as she might have, considering how "generously" Tabitha paid her.

I told Tabitha I could sympathize: I was so sure that hired help wouldn't work out for me, I never hired help.

Tabitha laughed at this, her grudging-Grandma laugh that sounded like the cracking of dried sticks. "Oh, Gwen used to say the exact same thing. With a little wink, so I'd know she was joking."

"Did she!"

"Of course, Jon didn't 'believe' in hiring help if he could avoid it." Tabitha smiled, even as she sighed pityingly.

As girls Clare and I had been told to stay out of our aunt's kitchen which had seemed strange to us: at home, and in the homes of our friends, the kitchen was the room you naturally hung out in. But not the Spancic kitchen which was twice the size of mine at home but far less efficiently designed. Everything seemed far away yet the space was crowded. There was even a "butler's pantry" with a swinging door. Instead of a cozy breakfast nook by a window there was a wooden table in the center of the floor, and this table was surrounded by six chairs of which all but one were stacked with flattened grocery bags, old newspapers and flyers and things meant to be discarded. Instead of being fitted into the counters, the un-gainly six-burner gas stove was free-standing. Overhead a lone forty-watt lightbulb shone dimly upon our efforts like the fading star of a distant galaxy.

As soon as she'd led me into this dispiriting room, Tabitha seemed dis-oriented. If we'd been rowing a canoe together, Tabitha was letting go her paddle. Her most decisive act was to extricate, out of a drawer of tangled things, an apron for me. "Gwen always wore this when she helped out in the kitchen. In fact, Gwen sewed the apron for me herself, originally." The apron was made of a coarse beige cloth with ties at both the neck and the waist. Its single large pocket was a sunflower patch. It was very attractive, unquestioning I put it on.

Next, Tabitha directed me to the refrigerator freezer which was stocked with TV dinners and quarts of "diet" ice cream. I was astonished to see how bare, and how not-very-clean, the refrigerator was inside: no fresh vegetables, no fresh greens for a salad. Commercial white bread, processed cheeses and opened jars of peanut butter, chocolate syrup, and pickles. At least we had the TV dinners and the bread I'd brought.

"I don't suppose you have any wine, Aunt Tabitha?"

"Wine? For just *us*?"

Tabitha's surprise was genuine. I dreaded to think of the newest fam-ily legend of Nikki Eaton as a drinker.

Unexpectedly, my aunt had a microwave oven in the kitchen. Though there was something amiss with its dials, I was able to rapidly thaw and heat two of the more promising TV dinners: "Stouffer's Tom Turkey 'n'

Giblet Gravy with Mushroom Bread Stuffing." This included small portions of mushy vegetables recognizable by shapes and colors as hashed-
brown potatoes, sliced carrots, and string beans. And we had my
sprouted-wheat/almond bread, which had never tasted better.

We ate in the dining room, at our appointed place mats. I could envision the two of us at these place mats, eating microwaved TV dinners
each evening stretching into eternity.

With the air of a finicky eater being polite out of consideration for the
cook, Aunt Tabitha finished every morsel of her Tom Turkey dinner, and
quite a bit of mine. "I hate to see good food go to waste. 'Just think of
the starving Africans' my mother used to scold us."

For dessert, Tabitha doled out large scoops of chocolate-chip "diet" ice
cream in bowls, and brought a bag of Pepperidge Farm chocolate-chip
cookies to the table. There was such a sugar rush in my mouth, it felt as
if virulent microorganisms were attacking me.

By the time I cleared the table, squirted liquid soap into the sink and
began to wash dishes which, in her vague fumbling way, Tabitha set onto
the counter to "dry in the air," it was nearly 8 P.M. and dark as midnight.
I had arrived at the dour cobblestone house on Church Street at about
4:30 P.M. with a naive hope of leaving within the hour and now my concern was avoiding spending the night. An unnatural lethargy had come
over me, a kind of numbed contentment. It was the way Smoky had slept
all but about ninety minutes a day through the summer as if exhausted
by his life.

Tabitha fretted: "I never eat so late, usually. Now I'll have trouble
sleeping through the night."

Damned if I was going to apologize for having made my aunt's supper
too late. I suggested Sleepytime tea, I'd noticed in one of the cupboards.

Tabitha sighed, as if the effort of preparing tea was beyond her. She'd
have had no idea where the box of tea was, I supposed.

"The thoughts that come into my head, when I can't sleep! Oh Nikki,
I miss them both."

Naively I asked who did she miss?

"Your mother, Nikki, and your father. Who else would I be talking about! All this while you've been here, Gwen has been with us, too—hasn't she? You must have felt her."

I could not believe what Aunt Tabitha was saying. Yet she was setting the last of the plates on the counter to "dry in the air," quite calmly.

"Really, Nikki. You've never been in this house by yourself, have you? I mean, without Gwen?"

This was so. I had not.

"Gwen will always be with us. In her way."

I glanced around, nervously. Was this so? Was Mom near? My aunt's kitchen was so dimly lighted, you could imagine a vague hovering shape in the farther corner, beyond the refrigerator.

Tabitha said, sighing: "It hurts so, Nikki, when people younger than you pass away. Why, Jon was only fifty-nine, and Gwen was . . ." Tabitha's voice quavered with reproach, as if my parents had betrayed her.

My impulse was to apologize. *I'm sure they didn't die intentionally, Aunt Tabitha!*

As if reading my thoughts, and disapproving, Tabitha said, in her grim-Grandma way: "They were not a natural couple, I'm afraid. Not what you'd call 'compatible.' "

My heart beat frightened and excited. It was as if, as she'd been absentmindedly opening and shutting drawers, Aunt Tabitha had suddenly opened a door to reveal my mother and my father inside, not the long-deceased Uncle Edmund. I wanted to protect them, yet had to know more.

"What do you mean, Aunt Tabitha? Mom and Dad loved each other very much . . ."

Tabitha fluttered her hands impatiently, as if brushing away flies. "Oh, of course! Of course they did. But 'love' doesn't mean 'compatible,' dear. Edmund Spancic III and I, we were 'compatible.' " She spoke with a kind of spirited pride, as if daring me to contradict her. "We hadn't fallen 'head-over-heels-in-love'—'in love at first sight'—as Jon seems to have done with Gwen—we'd known each other for years. It was a very different sort of relationship. Before Gwen, Jon hadn't ever cared for anyone, any girl I mean; he'd hardly seemed to notice them. Oh, your father was very picky! We never thought he would find a girl to take out, let alone marry, yet one day lo and behold he brought this little Gwen Kovach to meet my parents—'Feather' she was called. I guess Gwen was out of high school by then, but you'd never guess from seeing her: she looked sixteen! I never called her 'Feather' nor did Jon, such a silly name, but Jon liked it, I think, that other people did. Gwen was so pretty, and so sweet, so very friendly and bubbly, in the way that high school cheerleaders are, except Gwen seemed to mean it, she was always smiling. But she was never, you know, forward. In fact she was shy. She'd never disagree with anyone, she'd never dream of interrupting. She smiled so, and lit up the gloomiest rooms, but she wouldn't say much. Jon had never been one to carry on much himself, he kept his serious thoughts to himself, like our father, but with Gwen, he'd just stare at her, and you could see that he adored her. 'Gwen is nothing like me,' he'd say. 'She's nothing like any of *us*.' Because the Eatons have always been so serious, especially in those days, forty years ago. But Gwen could melt the iciest heart, I swear." Tabitha smiled, re-calling. "It wasn't until years later that Gwen confessed to me, right here in this kitchen, that it had been all nerves—'My mouth just smiles, like animals bare their teeth when they're afraid.' "

Tabitha's mimicry of my mother's voice was uncanny. I wasn't sure if I wanted to laugh, or cry.

I wasn't sure if I wanted to hug my big-bosomed aunt, or push past her and run out of the house.

". . . yes, Jon married 'for love.' And Gwen, too. I think. Of course, they had their difficult times. It can't have been easy, being married to a man like my brother. 'Was Jon always so quiet at home?' Gwen asked me once, so plaintive, not that she was complaining about her husband, Gwen never complained of Jon to a living soul, that I know of, and I laughed and told her, 'Quiet? Jon's nickname was "Clam." ' " Tabitha laughed now, recalling. "Another time, poor Jon came over here, so upset, I'd never seen my brother so upset—'Gwen is thinking of leaving me.

She won't explain why.' And that time I just laughed, too, hearing such a thing. As if 'Feather' could go anywhere on her own! And Jon said, with this anguished look, 'She isn't "Feather," Tabitha. She's never been "Feather." I married a girl named "Feather" and that girl never existed.' I said, 'Jon, you always thought that name was silly. Just go back home, and Gwen will come to her senses. Where can that woman go, with two little girls?' " Tabitha snorted in indignation, the notion was so absurd.

All this while I was staring at Tabitha, in dread of what I was hearing. Two little girls?

"Aunt Tabitha, what do you mean? Mom was thinking of leaving Dad—when?"

"Oh, I don't know. I hardly paid attention." Tabitha's hands fluttered impatiently. "You were a toddler, I think. Clare was in grade school. You'd been a colicky baby, crying through the night, and Clare was a husky little girl, very demanding. Maybe it was just too much for Gwen, with a husband like my brother. Still, running away was just plain silly, we all knew it."

"Did Mom ever say anything to you?"

"I told you, dear: never. She knew such notions wouldn't have been welcome, in this house."

All this while I'd been digging at a discolored sink sponge with my fingernails, crumbling it. For hours afterward I would feel the pressure of tiny particles of synthetic sponge beneath my broken nails.

"But Mom wouldn't have left Dad."

"That's what I told him. 'Close out your joint checking account, "Feather" won't go anywhere.' Exactly what I told him."

I didn't know what was more upsetting: my mother's alleged "notions," or my aunt's bemused disparaging of them.

"Mom wouldn't have left Clare and me . . ."

An evasive-Grandma look came over Tabitha's face. Her response was a noncommittal hum *Mmmmmm*.

It was a look, and a response, I didn't care to examine.

"Of course, Nikki, your father had certain ways about him. 'Slow to wrath'—whatever that saying is. If you offended him he could go for days without speaking to you, just kind of glare at you, then suddenly something would set him off and he'd be furious. Oh, Jon could be wounding! He tried not to show it in front of you and Clare, I think. As our father tried not to show the 'Eaton temper' in front of his children. Of course, Eaton men always control themselves at work, and in the presence of outsiders. Eaton men are thoroughly professional." Tabitha's voice dipped thrillingly, and her eyes shone behind the glittering bifocal lenses. "Clare mustn't know this, Nikki, it's bad enough I'm telling you because Gwen made me promise not to—but—well—your father didn't pass away quite as people think."

"He . . . didn't?"

"When Jon had his heart attack, it wasn't after watching *Law and Order* and feeling weak, lying down on the bed as Gwen told people, this peaceful look in his face, oh my no. He'd been furious as a hornet. The day before, Gwen called me sounding frightened, asking if I'd speak with Jon—and my brother comes on the phone like he's angry with me, for heaven's sake. Turns out the furnace in your house was having problems, breaking down and Jon would call the repairmen to come over, they'd 'fix' it and go away, and a few days later something else would break down, and not long before Jon had had your roof redone, which is very expensive, and yet the roof was leaking in a few places, and Jon was somehow blaming me, I mean he was blaming poor Edmund who had passed away eighteen months before for having recommended the roofers and the repairmen, I'm not even sure that Edmund did recommend them but Jon had it in his head he had, and you couldn't convince your father of anything once he'd made up his mind. Well! The terrible things Jon was shouting over the phone, I would never repeat, and have tried to forget. 'I can't stand this life'—'Owning a Goddamn house, taking care of a house, it's hell'—'I'm going to sue the bastards! I'll kill them.' " Tabitha pressed a hand against her chest, as if shaken. "Well. The next day, evidently, was even worse. Somehow, soot from the furnace got blown through the vents and there were smudged black patches all over the house, and when Jon came home from work and saw these he rushed through the rooms, red-faced and shouting, there was no reasoning with him, Gwen told me afterward she tried to calm him but he threw off her hand, he looked at her with a face 'so ugly and hateful, I almost didn't know him.' You can't wash soot off your walls in any ordinary way, you know. It has an oil base, and it smears. Gwen didn't know this, and had tried to clean away the soot before Jon saw it, but she'd made it worse, I think, and Jon was furious at her, 'My life, my life is breaking down, it's defective and there's nowhere to send it back,' things like that Jon was saying, then he went into the bedroom and slammed the door and next thing Gwen knew he was calling for her in this strangled voice, and she heard him fall to the floor, and . . ." Tabitha's voice trailed off. Her coin-eyes welled with sudden tears. ". . . the rest you know, dear."

By this time I'd shredded most of the sponge. My response to my aunt's revelation was a vague dazed smile of the kind a child might make, to indicate she's been listening.

"Of course, we had the funeral luncheon here. And it was a beautiful luncheon, I think. Your house, with soot on all the walls, was out of the question. And too small, anyway. Those 'ranch houses' are just too small. You step through the front door and you're right smack in the living room. You remember how calm your mother managed to be, she was in such a state of shock. Only I really knew. I don't think she'd even told that Proxmire woman, she was so close to. And I only knew, because Jon had been furious with me, that was how he was sometimes, so hotheaded! Anyway, I lent your mother Daniella, in fact I paid for Daniella to clean the soot off your walls." Tabitha laughed, recalling. " 'That oil soot is the worst, Mrs. Spancic!' Daniella told me. 'Like it has a life of its own, like the devil, you clean it off and it moves somewhere else. Nasty.' "

What an inspired mimic my elderly aunt was! I'd never known before, somehow.

I woke from my trance. Made my excuses and ran for my life, I mean I ran for my coat.

Tabitha followed me into the front hall. Wanting me to stay the night since it had begun to snow, large soft wet clumps like deranged blossoms blown out of the night sky. I thanked her and escaped to my car, stabbing the key in the ignition even as Tabitha called my name, appearing like a hooded apparition beside the car, a plastic raincoat flung over her head.

In the confusion of the moment I couldn't hear what my aunt was saying. Only just the accusation, "—forgot, Nikki!"

My aunt thrust a grocery bag at me. I thanked her, and drove away. Several blocks on Church Street before I realized I hadn't switched on my headlights.

The bag contained the peach-colored angora sweater with the seed-pearl bodice, the detachable white lace collar, the voluminous red silk blouse and the sexy black cloche hat, I would discover when I was safely home.

duet

My mouth just smiles. Like animals bare their teeth when they're afraid.
My life is defective. Nowhere to send it back.
Through that long night of soft-falling snow I would hear them.
A love-duet.
My mom, and my dad.

"feather"

" ' "Light as a feather"—that's what I want my soul to be.' This is
what Gwen told me, when we were first friends." Alyce Proxmire peered
at me with small moist sparrow-colored eyes. Her thin lips twisted into
a kind of smile. "This was in eighth grade, we were both thirteen. I was
new at Mt. Ephraim Junior High and very shy, with braces, and glasses,
and this pretty little doll-faced girl came over to me and said *Hi!* She was
the only one."

How like Mom's oldest girlfriend Alyce Proxmire, that a happy memory should be laced with something bitter.

We were in my house, which Alyce persisted in calling "your mother's
house," looking through photo albums at the dining room table. It was a
week after my Church Street visit. I was still shaken by what Aunt
Tabitha had told me. For months Alyce Proxmire had been leaving increasingly plaintive phone messages for me—*Nikki, may I come see you? I
miss Gwen so* . . . A long pause. A snuffling sound. *I even miss Smoky.*

From Clare and others, I knew that Alyce Proxmire had taken my
mother's death "very hard." Which was a good reason to avoid her: the
last thing I wanted was Mom's hypochondriac girlfriend breaking down
in my arms.

Oh God! One day last summer I'd seen a car creep into our driveway,
I'd seen an apparition in what looked like a nightgown (in fact, a raincoat) lurch up the front walk, recognized Alyce Proxmire and ran to hide

with Smoky at the top of the basement steps. As the doorbell rang, and Alyce's anxious voice lifted *Hello? Nikki? Is anyone home?* Smoky growled deep in his throat, tail twitching.

How long Alyce remained on the front stoop ringing the bell and calling for me in her plaintive nasal voice, I don't know. It seemed like a very long time. I hid my face in Smoky's coarse fur, overcome by a fit of laughter. *My life. This is my life now. In hiding.* I would learn afterward from the Pedersens next door that my visitor wandered around the outside of the house peering into windows. They'd debated whether to call the police except she'd looked harmless—"Like some old retired schoolteacher-ghost."

I would learn from Gladys Higham across the street that Alyce had rung her doorbell, too, to ask if she'd seen me, where was I, if I wasn't home, or wasn't answering the door, what if something had "happened" to me?

Since May, all of Deer Creek Acres had become a terrain where something unspeakable might "happen" to a woman with the bad luck to be alone.

I was furious with Alyce Proxmire, intruding in my life. I refused to answer her calls, I tossed away her meek little notes. The woman held no charm for me. Maybe I hated it, she'd outlived Mom.

This was a time when Wally Szalla and I had lapsed into one of our intense interludes. Possibly we'd quarreled, possibly it had been my fault. I was feeling raw and tragic and not in a mood to be patient with Alyce Proxmire.

Grief is like one of those roller towels in public lavatories. Shared with too many people, it gets soiled and worn-out.

These past few months, I'd come to feel differently. I mean, I was trying. I didn't seem to be so angry, at least not all the time. Since experimenting with Mom's bread recipes, and having some good results. Seeing people, mostly older women I'd been avoiding. One of these had to be Alyce Proxmire, Mom's "oldest girlfriend."

When I finally called Alyce, and identified myself on the phone, for a moment Alyce seemed to be too startled to respond.

"Ohhhh! Nikki! I . . . th-thought it was . . ."

(That it was Mom? Were our voices, that had never been confused while Mom was alive, so similar?)

As soon as Alyce arrived at the house, sniffing and clutching a wetted tissue, she fumbled to embrace me, and gripped me in her thin tremulous arms. Her emotions were damp, sputtering: "Ohhhh. Nik-*ki*. *Oh*."

It was a moment I had to endure. Except I seemed to recall that I'd already endured it on the day of Mom's funeral.

". . . since that evening, Mother's Day . . . haven't stepped a foot in this . . . Ohhhh."

Alyce Proxmire's grief was genuine but exasperating, like a leaky roof. I shut my eyes hoping she wouldn't lapse into a fit of sobbing. (I rarely cried any longer, at least during the day. At night, in my sleep, sometimes I bawled like a baby.)

There came Gwen Eaton's cheerleader buoyancy into my voice: "Now Alyce! Gwen would want you to be moving on with your life, you know."

"Ohhhh I know. I know, Nikki."

Alyce blew her nose, wetly. Since I'd seen her last, her faded-brown hair had gone almost entirely gray and was noticeably thinner. Alyce was one of those gaunt-girlish older women who "mature" from pre-pubescence to post-menopause with nothing between. Flat as an ironing board yet with a little potbelly, rounded shoulders and knobby elbows and knees. Her expression was sometimes meek, sometimes a smirk. From her days as a public school librarian she retained a peevish air of distrustful authority. Her clothes were wheat-colored, beige and brown, tarnish colors. Her scent was talcum-cobwebby. When Dad rolled his eyes over Alyce, Mom was quick to defend her: "Alyce is a good, loyal friend."

Certainly, Alyce Proxmire was loyal.

Saying now, clutching her tissue, ". . . every day, every hour I think of her. If only I'd been with her that morning except I had a dentist's appointment, root canal . . . Oh, it was awful!"

Alyce's medical problems were of two types: chronic ailments, and mysterious symptoms that hadn't yet been diagnosed as ailments. Out of politeness I had to ask Alyce how she was, and saw her brighten at the prospect of telling me. There was a tremor in her voice as she recited her chronic ailments (insomnia, asthma, migraine, "queasy" stomach and "fluttery" pulse) and the alarmingly new and novel (swollen neck glands, watery eyes, ingrown toenail, sudden fits of hiccuping, a ringing in her right ear like "a doorbell stuck at high-C"). Mom used to exasperate Clare and me by exclaiming over every symptom of Alyce's, we were sure this only encouraged Alyce's hypochondria, but I'd come to see that Alyce recited her litany of health problems because they were all she had to offer as "news."

Following Alyce's medical problems, the subject shifted abruptly to the trial. I was astonished to learn that Alyce regularly called the Chautauqua County district attorney's office, the Mt. Ephraim police, several local newspapers and TV stations, for any news—"They all know me by now. 'Miss Proxmire,' they say, barely managing to be civil, 'we will contact you if there is any new development in the Eaton case.' " Alyce laughed scornfully, to show she wasn't taken in by such lame assurances. "At least the trial seems to be set now: January twenty-second. That awful defense lawyer must have run out of 'motions.' Imagine, demanding that the trial be held somewhere else, as if jurors in Chautauqua County where Gwen was known and loved couldn't be 'impartial.' If I could be on the jury, I would be 'impartial'—oh, yes." Alyce was breathing hoarsely, through her mouth. Her sparrow-eyes were fixed fiercely on me. "To think that that man, that terrible man, the one who hurt Gwen I mean, all this while, Nikki, that monster has been living, breathing, eating and watching TV all day, while—"

"Alyce. We don't have to discuss the trial right now."

Here was a shaky moment. This woman in my house for less than ten minutes and it felt like ten hours. I had to fight an impulse to push past her and escape.

Alyce sniffed indignantly: "—well! It's just outrageous. I can't wait for the trial to be over and justice to be *done*."

I'd set the tea things onto a cleared section of the dining room table.

Mom's cheery orange glazed-pumpkin teapot and matching mugs, which she'd made in one of her crafts classes, and Mom's selection of herbal teas in shiny packets: Peppermint, Chamomile, Lemon Mist, Black Cherry Berry, Tangerine Orange, Country Peach Passion, Red Zinger, Raspberry Zinger, Cranberry Apple Zinger, Sleepytime. Alyce could be relied upon to choose the most boring of teas (Chamomile) but I found deeply consoling the array of samples from Mom's cupboard, their names like poetry.

That morning I'd baked bread especially for Alyce, with her dietary restrictions, from a recipe of Mom's invention titled "Alyce's Bread." Hardly my favorite of Mom's recipes, this was high-fibre but saltless and sugarless wheat germ carrot bread. Alyce blinked and smiled to see it murmuring, "Ohhhh Nikki! You shouldn't have," but was slow to eat until finally I asked, "Isn't this 'your' bread, Alyce? Maybe I didn't make it right . . ."

Oh yes! Quickly Alyce assured me, I'd made it right.

". . . so thoughtful, your dear mother. Always so considerate of her friends. When Gwen first baked this bread for me, nine years ago, I'd been put by my doctor on a salt-free diet, and I try to avoid sugar, you know, but then a few years ago I was allowed off the diet, and somehow I didn't have the heart to tell Gwen, by that time she seemed so, well— devoted to baking 'Alyce's Bread' for me. It was like your father giving Gwen the identical talcum powder for her birthday every year, that pretty blue box with the silver tassels—'Forget-Me-Not.' Why, Gwen passed along to me enough 'Forget-Me-Not' talcum to last the rest of my life! But she could never tell Jon, she had a dread of hurting anyone's feelings. When Gwen said, 'Alyce, here is "Alyce's Bread." Special order!' she seemed so happy, and in a way it made me happy, too. Because no one else likes this bread, really it hasn't much taste except a kind of sawdust-carrot taste, so *flat*. But 'Alyce's Bread' became, I guess you could say, a kind of . . . custom."

All this while Alyce was chewing and swallowing small chunks of bread with a look of stoic determination, smiling at me.

Oh, fine. Bread no one liked, not even Alyce Proxmire, I'd wasted a morning on!

Sometimes before going to bed, on those nights when Wally Szalla wasn't coming over, I'd have a few drinks and lapse into a fantasy of doing good deeds as Mom had done, not out of a sense of duty but out of the bubbly goodness of my heart, seeing more of Alyce Proxmire, and more of Aunt Tabitha and other relatives, lonely women from Mom's church, neighbors . . . I could trade in my Saab for a minivan to drive these women to luncheons, matinees, museums and flower shows, swim classes at the YM-YWCA . . .

"Alyce, do you like to swim?"

"Swim! Gwen was forever trying to talk me into joining her at the Y!" Alyce shook her head as if she'd narrowly escaped being seduced by some wild whim of my mother's. "I tried to tell Gwen, chlorine can't really kill all those microorganisms, absolutely not. As for swimming itself, you get wet, you start to shiver, you catch cold and next you know you have bronchitis, then pneumonia. You get wet, and then you need to shower to wash the wetness off, and then you need to get dry. And next thing you know . . ."

Well, I'd tried. Even Mom would have to acknowledge my good intentions.

We turned our attention to Mom's photo albums. This was really why Alyce had come over, not to visit with me. With childish eagerness she sought photos of Gwen in which she herself appeared, of which there were a surprising number. Though I was sure that Mom had made copies of these for Alyce, Mom was always making copies of photos for friends, Alyce reacted as if she'd never seen most of them before. "Oh, Nikki, may I borrow this? I will have a copy made and return it, I promise."

Alyce was most fascinated by the oldest photos, which were likely to be creased and wrinkled. How young Gwen was! How young Alyce was! These were Kodak snapshots of the 1960s, my mother and her best-friend-Alyce hardly more than girls, Gwen dimpled-smiling and Alyce shyly-smiling for the camera. Alyce was taller than Gwen, Gwen was prettier and more compact than Alyce, the two looked nothing alike and yet, arms around each other's waists, there was something sisterly about them.

I felt a stab of envy. Clare and I had never liked each other, really. I was sure we'd never posed like this, so naturally leaning into each other.

Alyce's hand trembled with excitement, passing me another snapshot of her and Gwen, taken outdoors. Here was Gwen in a summer dress captured in the midst of laughter, half-turned to her friend Alyce in something shapeless and dun-colored but sporty, and in Alyce's arms was what appeared to be a baby in pink polka dots, kicking her feet in little white booties. Gwen had fluffy blond hair and Alyce was looking startled and almost-pretty with reddened lips and hair trimmed short in a pixie-cut. The date on the back of the snapshot was June 1974.

Alyce whispered: "That's you, Nikki! I mean . . . us."

Strange: middle-aged Alyce Proxmire in November 2004 gazing wistfully at her younger self of June 1974, holding a baby in her arms; and that baby, now an adult, regarding both Alyces with what you'd have to describe as mixed emotions.

Somehow, I was touched. I hadn't ever known that "Auntie Alyce" had held either Clare or me.

". . . loved babies, you know. Oh, she wanted more than just two."

Seeing that I looked doubtful, Alyce said emphatically, "She did. Even before she was married, she'd talk that way. 'My parents had just me. It was like they were worried about running out of space, or money, or love. Like they worried there wouldn't be enough to go around.' " Alyce's laugh was a thin sad echo of my mother's more mirthful laugh. "When she was just a girl, in high school, Gwen was hoping to have four, five, even six children. All the Kovachs had big families except for hers, I think that was why. In St. Joseph's parish where they went to church, all the families were large. Only Gwen's family was just her and her mother and father, and then her mother died, and there was just Gwen and her father, but Mr. Kovach worked for the New York Central Railroad so he was gone a lot, and Gwen stayed with relatives, all the time I knew her. After she had Clare and you, and you were going to school, she was all dreamy-like talking of how she'd like more babies, but it wasn't realistic, the Eatons were not the Kovachs, it wasn't the Eaton way to have big families. Once Gwen confided in me, Jon had been reluctant about having children, actually. 'He'd thought he would be the baby of the family, and one of him was enough,' Gwen made a joke of it, that was Gwen's way, to joke about things that were serious to her. Why, Gwen once told me she'd had to pretend her pregnancies were 'accidental' and 'meant to be'—not anything she'd wanted. Later, when you and Clare were teenagers, she got it in her head that she and Jon could adopt a baby, but Jon wouldn't hear of it of course—as if Jon Eaton would want to bring up some strangers' crying baby!" Alyce spoke in a girlish rush of words, biting her lower lip. "Poor Gwen. I tried to explain to her, why Jon felt the way he did, it made sense to *me*. But Gwen was such a dreamer. Over and over she'd say, 'When the girls grow up and leave, what will I do, Alyce? They can't wait to get away.' Gwen was desperate to be needed, you see. She couldn't respect herself if she wasn't needed."

I was stunned hearing this. For a moment I couldn't speak.

Can't wait to get away. This was not true!

"Alyce, Mom never said anything like that to me. Never."

Alyce said primly, swiping at her nose, "Well, Nikki. Naturally Gwen didn't say such things to you, or to Clare. Or to Jon. These are things she only confided to *me*."

"It isn't true, Clare and I couldn't wait to get away . . ."

Alyce pursed her lips, not wishing to reply. I tried to remain calm.

"Mom was happy with just Clare and me. She was a very happy person. Of course she respected herself! Everyone knows this."

I think this was so. I wasn't sure.

(Those years, adolescence and beyond, when I'd been scornful of Mt. Ephraim and Deer Creek Acres: dinky look-alike ranch houses, silly suburban lawns and the Moms and Dads who came with them like matched doll sets.)

(. . . when I was negligent about calling home, frankly bored with Eaton family life, "disappeared" with boyfriends/men without always telling Mom where I was going . . .)

Alyce said, with a quick smile, "Oh! Here is 'Feather' in her cheerleader jumper. Isn't she sweet!" As if wishing to change the subject Alyce showed me several photos of Gwen taken at Mt. Ephraim High School in the mid-1960s, Gwen Kovach as the cutest American-girl cheerleader you could imagine: buoyant blond hair, dazzling smile, trim curvy little size-two body in a maroon jumper and long-sleeved white cotton blouse. In one of the photos, Gwen was leaping with arms widespread as a soaring bird's, head flung back and frozen in an ecstatic smile. We'd teased Mom plenty about these long-ago photos. I'd seen them many times of course but never looked at them, exactly, not wanting my scorn for high school jocks/cheerleaders/"popular" personalities to affect my feelings for my mother.

Alyce continued to look through the photos, which I'd sorted into decades. Exclaiming, smiling, wiping at her eyes. I was still upset and wary of the woman. *She is jealous of Gwen's daughters. She wants Gwen for herself.* Casually Alyce began to recount how she'd first met Gwen Kovach, in eighth grade: the "pretty little doll-faced girl" who'd been the only child in Mt. Ephraim Junior High to befriend her. (Was this true? I doubted it. But no one was likely to budge Alyce Proxmire from her sweetly bitter memories.)

" 'Light as a feather—that's what I want my soul to be. Blown in the wind, and no one could catch it.' " Alyce spoke with sudden lyricism, sparrow-eyes glistening at me. "Gwen had the strangest, most magical way of speaking, all dreamy-like, so you wanted to believe she must be right. In some way, somehow."

I was wondering suddenly if Alyce had ever stepped inside the house on Spalding Street. The run-down woodframe house where Gwen Kovach had lived as a child. Past which repeatedly she'd driven, as an adult.

Damned if I would ask her, though! I would not.

It was then that Alyce said, casually, as if her memory had been roused by one of the photos, "Before she met your father, when she was sixteen, Gwen was in love with a boy. It happened very suddenly with Gwen, like a sickness." Alyce paused, considering her words. "He'd graduated from the Catholic school De Sales. They met in the summer at Wolf's Head Lake where Gwen was a waitress. I never trusted him, the way he smirked. Why, he wouldn't even look at me, Gwen introduced us just once and he hardly saw me, so *rude*. Gwen insisted he didn't smirk, 'it's just Brendan's way of smiling,' but I knew better. He was eighteen, and seemed much older than we were. He'd be going to St. Bonaventure in the fall. There was some high-ranking priest in his family, a bishop in Albany. His mother wanted him to be a priest, she thought high school cheerleaders were 'immoral' and 'common' and she didn't approve of Gwen, not that she ever met Gwen. Ohhh, it was an emotional time! It was a very upsetting time, for Gwen but also for me, as Gwen's closest friend." Alyce had been speaking in a rush of words, all breathy innocence like a girl confiding in another girl behind the back of a mutual friend. I felt that faint panicky sensation I'd felt with Aunt Tabitha. *Don't ask! You don't want to hear more.*

Yet I heard myself say, encouragingly, "You were girls together, you and Mom. Like sisters."

"We were! Yet we weren't equals. Gwen was 'Feather' Kovach already in eighth grade, and all through high school boys looked at her as they'd never look at me. Though she behaved younger, sometimes very young, Gwen was actually older than me in her heart—because her mother had died, she 'boarded' with Kovach relatives and didn't have a room of her own exactly. Her father worked for the railroad and was away from Mt. Ephraim a lot, especially after her mother died. Gwen was only eleven then. I didn't know her then. We moved to Mt. Ephraim two years later. Gwen never talked much about her mother, you couldn't ask her certain things. She'd just change the subject, or hum! What I'd heard was that Mrs. Kovach had had some terrible wasting-away nerve disease, or cancer, she'd gotten weaker and weaker and died at home and when Gwen came home from school that day they wouldn't let her see her mother, she was never allowed to see her mother again. But she wouldn't talk much about it, and I wasn't one to ask."

Now I did ask about the house on Spalding Street: "You were never inside it, Alyce? I guess?"

"Ohhh, that house! Never." Alyce shuddered, as if I'd suggested something obscene. "That was where her mother died, Gwen would never go near it. Gwen would never walk on Spalding Street. She'd go way out of her way not even to cross Spalding on Van Buren, which was where one of her aunts lived. It was just something you didn't talk about and anyway, with 'Feather,' there was always so much to talk about, that was happy." Alyce paused to chew sawdust-carrot bread with a faint, sad smile. "That was why Gwen wanted to be light as a feather, I think. So she wouldn't take up space in her relatives' houses where she felt she didn't belong."

Was that it! I didn't want to think so.

". . . I always thought that people called Mom 'Feather' because she was so lighthearted, and happy. Because . . ."

"Don't be silly, Nikki. Most people called her 'Feather' because they'd heard other people call her 'Feather.' There was no more logic to it than that." Alyce paused, grimly breaking off another piece of bread. She'd discovered, as I had, that there was just perceptibly more flavor in the crust, and was concentrating on nibbling crusts in her hungry-rabbit way. "I never called Gwen 'Feather,' not for a moment. Between Gwen and me, it would not have been right."

I'd been waiting for the subject to revert to mysterious Brendan, the boy Mom had loved: what had happened to him?

Alyce said evasively, "Oh, nothing 'happened' to him. He just went away to college. I think he became a priest. His last name was Dorsey, the family lived out on the Ridge Road. They weren't rich—nobody in Mt. Ephraim is 'rich'—but Brendan's father had a car dealership, so the family could put on airs. And there was the uncle, or whoever it was, 'Bishop Dorsey' you'd hear of. Lots of other boys had asked Gwen out, she had more boyfriends than she could count, but none of them were serious, until Brendan. He was handsome, if you like that type. A momma's boy, is what I thought. That smirk of his, and the way he'd be always running his hands through his hair, that was wavy and silvery-blond. He was tall, too. Gwen was always attracted to tall boys. 'He has such good manners. He's so *nice*'—Gwen was always saying. But he wasn't so nice to Gwen, after a while."

Alyce paused, as if she'd said too much.

"How wasn't Brendan 'so nice' to Mom? You can tell me."

Alyce said, sighing, "Oh, at first he was. He took her to movies, and swimming, and summer concerts at Lake Ontario. He had some kind of fancy convertible, he loved to show off driving it. And Gwen loved that car, too. Brendan was a singer, almost good enough to be a professional, people said. He'd sung tenor in the De Sales choir. But, you know, boys can be 'nice' and then, when they get what they want . . ." Alyce's mouth was downturned as a fish's. You'd have thought from her profound expression that no one had ever uttered this insight, or these words, before. "Well. There was this Youth Retreat at Star Lake, that the church I belonged to had every year in the fall, a weekend at a campground, it was mostly a Bible study retreat and I'd been going through some phase of 'doubting' God, and being kind of emotional about it, and all this I'd shared with Gwen, I was truly afraid that Jesus had forsaken me, or didn't even exist, now it all seems exaggerated and silly but I'd cried a lot at the time, and Gwen was always so sympathetic. She'd never have tried to interrupt and argue like my parents. Gwen was the only person I knew who believed in God but didn't belong to any church and never argued about religion, in any way. Most of the Kovachs were Catholic except for Gwen and her father but Gwen never talked about that religion, ever. When I was a girl, I was very religious. I invited Gwen to come to church with me sometimes and she would, but that was all. She never converted like the minister was hoping she would. At the Youth Retreat at Star Lake, we were all at an evening prayer service except for Gwen. I didn't know where Gwen had gone to, I looked for her and couldn't find her and a panic came over me she'd run away with Brendan Dorsey somehow, but later that night I found her in the top bunk bed in our cabin shivering under a blanket, where she'd been kind of hiding, and she told me she'd been afraid for the past forty-three days, thinking she was pregnant, but that night 'It all came out in blood' she told me. I was so shocked! Poor Gwen was white as chalk. She couldn't stop shivering. I gave her my blanket, and tried to warm her by holding her hands, and I got her to pray with me, and that helped, some. 'God has spared you, Gwen. This is all for the good,' I told her. Because by this time Brendan Dorsey was gone away to St. Bonaventure, he'd just forgotten her it seemed. 'It all came out in blood, Alyce,' Gwen said. She'd had cramps, and went to use the bathroom, and if she'd been pregnant it ended in that way, and nobody had to know. Gwen took it hard and was broken up for a long time, she could hide it from other people, but I knew. She never told anybody but me, of course. She'd never have told *him*." Alyce spoke scornfully. "I vowed, right there at Star Lake that night, *I* would never fall in love with any boy. A 'nice' one especially. And so I never did." Alyce spoke with a spiteful sort of pride, loudly blowing her nose.

As Alyce spoke, I'd been arranging photos. Tidying the messiest of the albums. I had not been looking at Alyce, and could not look at her now. Thinking *You asked. You wanted to know. And now you know.*

". . . never knew, of course. Oh, Jon couldn't have accepted it! I think I was the only one who knew. And Gwen had a way of pretending it had never happened, even with me. Like she didn't know about sex. And almost it was like she didn't. *I* was the one who remembered, of the two of us." By this time I'd been quiet for so long, Alyce looked at me with worried eyes. "I shouldn't have told you, Nikki. I'm sorry."

Carefully I said, as if this were a prepared speech, "No, Alyce. Thank you for telling me. I feel that I love Mom more than ever."

I swallowed hard, close to choking on these words. I didn't want Alyce Proxmire to hug me.

We were on our feet. Alyce was leaving. She wasn't so tall as I remembered, and her middle-aged-girl's face was etched with tiny creases. Dad used to joke *Good old Alyce will outlive us all* but I wasn't so sure. In a wondering voice Alyce was saying, "Gwen is gone, and I'm still here, and I don't feel much older than when we were sixteen, and Gwen was so cold at Star Lake, and I hugged her to stop her shivering, and she said, 'Don't tell, Alyce! Promise,' and of course I promised and here I am, forty years later, breaking that promise."

Early next morning, a gregarious flock of chickadees would help dispose of the remains of "Alyce's Bread," in chunky pieces on the snowy rear terrace.

change

Next night my married-man-lover came to see me late, after "Night Train." We were ravenous devouring slices of cold turkey on sourdough bread, cheddar cheese and coleslaw and our favorite Chianti. For the first time, we made love in my girlhood bed. We were tender with each other as new lovers. I thought *I will never have a baby with this man, I am safe from him.*

"Nikki. There's some change in you."

"Is there! Good, or not-so-good?"

"Darling, don't know. Maybe it's a necessary change."

singapore sling

She'd been waiting an hour to run me down, she said!

Waiting months, years!

She was breathless and laughing. She was "medicated"—her eyes shone like gasoline. Braking the white BMW sedan beside me in the snowy parking lot behind the YM-YWCA with a sharp squeal like a pig in pain. So close, the car's left front fender grazed my thigh.

The driver was a pretty-petulant woman in her forties with a hard red rosebud mouth and flaring nostrils. She was wearing a massive mink coat that sprouted like her own fur. I must have gaped at her in astonishment, as she rapidly lowered her window to jeer: "You are 'Nicole Eaton.' Hel*lo*."

I knew without having to ask: it was Isabel, Wally Szalla's "estranged" wife.

That morning I'd gone to swim at the Y. On her calendar Mom had marked 10 A.M. to 11:30 A.M., usually three days a week. I went to swim at the same time.

At the pool, I'd met up with several of Mom's seniors, to whom she'd given swimming instructions. I would confuse their names and faces afterward but they were Beverly, Mimi, Katrina, Shirley. They were Annemarie and Lillian, two of the women who'd released white doves at

Mom's grave site. They were frail-elderly "Mr. M." who confided in me, he'd been in love with Gwen Eaton for years, and gregarious "Mr. E." who insisted upon shaking my hand repeatedly, and swimming in my wake like an amorous seal. There was beetle-browed Mr. Kempton who'd retired from thirty-six years of teaching chemistry at Mt. Ephraim High, whom I recognized at once. ("Do I remember you, Nikki Eaton? I sure do.") They were Miriam and Yardley Shafer, a matched-set pair who paddled about in the shallow end of the pool scolding and sniping at each other like peevish chows. There was sweetly vague Mrs. Cadwaller whose daughter-in-law brought her to the pool every morning, who'd once lived up the block from us on Deer Creek Drive and was eager, seeing me, to ask where my mother—"That nice woman who always smiled so"—was?

My hand was shaken. I was hugged. I smiled until the lower part of my face became unhinged. I heard myself say in my mother's buoyant voice *Oh yes Mom told me about you. And you, and you. How she'd loved the swim class, how special you were to her.*

Each of Mom's pupils had information about her to impart. From Katrina I learned something I hadn't known, or had forgotten: my mother's favorite way of swimming was the backstroke.

" 'Because your face is out of the water. Because you can get dreamy and into your own zone. Because you can see where you've been, if you remember to open your eyes.' "

From Lillian I learned that my mother had a curious sort of faith in water: it wouldn't drown you, if you trusted it.

" 'I love the water. It holds you up.' "

Strange and thrilling, to hear my mother's words in the mouths of others. If I shut my eyes, almost I could imagine I was hearing Mom.

Beneath the chlorine-aqua surface of the pool. Beneath the bright splotches of reflected light. Beneath the clamorous hum and chatter of voices. You resist opening your eyes underwater but it must be done, as

Mom tried to teach us. *You have to see where you're going, girls! You can't swim blind.*

It was tempting to hide underwater in the pool. Sinking slowly to the concrete floor that felt smooth against the soles of my bare feet. Beside me, near enough to touch, was a wavy tiled wall. The water glimmered aqua and was sinuous, caressing. At a short distance were the pudgy bodies, slow-paddling legs of sister swimmers. Ten seconds. Fifteen. Stubbornly I held my breath until my brain began to feel like something that could explode. And my lungs, my throat. Twenty seconds. Twenty-five. Twenty-six, twenty-seven . . .

I wondered how long Mom could hold her breath underwater. I wondered what she'd meant by "into your own zone." I wondered if she'd meant it truly, that water won't drown you if you trust it.

Like Feather, wishing to be blown by the wind, where others can't follow.

I surfaced, gasping for air. My heart was pounding. An animal exuberance came over me: a greedy delight in filling my lungs with air.

". . . gunning the motor and waiting. And this wicked thought came to me, *It could be an accident, there's snow and ice here, who would know?* Then I thought, *It's that bastard I should run down, not her.*"

Isabel Szalla laughed with surprising heartiness. Nudging me with her leather-gloved hand, to laugh with her.

We'd been seated at a window table in the cocktail lounge/restaurant at the Marriott. At this time of day, only the restaurant was much occupied. Isabel had suggested an "anonymous" place. As if expecting, here in Mt. Ephraim, that people might recognize her. For the walk through the lobby and the restaurant she'd fumbled to put on oversized dark glasses. She looked both glamorous and frazzled. She gave off a sharp, peppery smell. She was a smallish compact woman with rouged cheeks and a jowly chin, several inches shorter than me. As we were led to our table, my eyes were fixed on the stiletto heels of her expensive Italian leather boots. Isabel swayed as she walked, semi-lurched, righted herself, resumed her air of ruffled dignity, fending off my hesitant offer of support before I came anywhere near touching her. Once seated, and the massive mink shrugged off, Isabel was fine. Her first drink, something exotic called a Singapore sling, she put away in three practiced swallows.

"You haven't ever been married, eh? What I've heard."

I had to admire this woman's boldness. Here was a no-bullshit woman.

"Right. You've heard right."

"Me! Married twenty-four years, I'm a veteran. Like, from a war? A crippled veteran?"

This seemed to be a question. Isabel's penciled-arched eyebrows rose quizzically.

"I mean, a vet always supports the war he was in, in fact any war. Otherwise he'd have to acknowledge he'd made the worst damn mistake of his life, and he'd never unmake it."

Isabel laughed again, reaching over to poke me. I wasn't at the state where laughter is contagious but I tried.

For longer than I cared to remember, Wally had complained to me about this woman. She was "unstable"—"unpredictable"—"self-destructive." He'd complained that each time she seemed to agree to a divorce, in fact insisted upon a divorce, shortly afterward she had an "emotional meltdown." In the jargon of contemporary psychiatry, she was "bi-polar."

Yet there was something appealing about Isabel, even if she was crazy. A no-bullshit wife inviting the Other Woman to lunch after almost running her over.

If I'd had time to think, I would recall having noticed the white BMW occasionally in my vicinity. Cruising past my car as I parked in one or another familiar parking lot in Mt. Ephraim. Possibly, I'd seen the car in Deer Creek Acres, cruising past my house. I hadn't given it a second glance of course. Only if I'd been suspicious would I have linked it with a white vehicle I'd glimpsed parked outside Wally's condo in Chautauqua Falls, on one of my rare overnight visits there some time ago.

Poor Wally! In his underwear bulging at the waist, disheveled and unshaven before his morning shower, peering through the venetian blinds, cursing *Oh why couldn't that woman leave him alone why when she hated his guts why did she torment them both how could this end!*

". . . just as much a victim as I am. You should know."

"Well. I . . ."

"I said, *you should know.*" Isabel's voice rose warningly.

At the same time, taking advantage of our waitress's startled attention from across the room, Isabel smiled and signaled for a second Singapore sling.

"Won't you join me, Nicole? They're delicious, actually."

"Well. I . . ."

"You do drink, Nicole! I've heard."

Big-sister-bossy. I could relate to that. This woman and I would never be friends but we could relate.

So far as I knew, Wally Szalla's marital situation at the present time seemed to me fairly clear-cut. He and Isabel were legally separated. Their lawyers were "negotiating." There was the expectation that, sometime soon in the next year, the Szallas would be divorced and Wally would be at last "free" to marry me.

I believed this, maybe. It had become a comfortable belief.

Anyway, if marriage to Wally Szalla happened, it would happen on the far side of the trial in January. Nothing was very real on the far side of the trial as nothing was very real on the near side of the trial.

". . . the children. So ashamed! Distraught! They adore their father though knowing full well the man's hypocrisy, duplicity. Oh, they would blame *me*. Never forgive . . ."

Our lunches were brought. And two glasses of tart white wine. I didn't remember ordering. Numbly I began to eat, something crouton-crispy with large glops of a whitish dressing, black olives, tomatoes, grated

Parmesan cheese and raw purple-onion slices. Isabel stared at her plate with a look of peevish alarm. "... *raw onions?* Somebody take this away."

Through the plate-glass window beside our table, a snowy landscape glimmered white beyond the parking lot. And there was a wintry hard-blue sky. It was like holding my breath underwater to think how it had happened, time had swerved from that May evening at Mom's house to now. I would have liked to explain to Isabel Szalla that *now* was in continuous motion like high-scudding clouds overhead and that was why I'd recklessly accepted her invitation to lunch, because it could have no permanent meaning, and it would pass. While that May evening smelling of lilacs, when I'd last seen my mother alive, when she'd hugged me for the last time, was fixed and unshakeable as rock.

I would realize afterward, and be grateful for, the fact that Isabel made no reference to what had happened to my mother. Obviously, she'd known. But no personal tragedies engaged her except her own, probably she'd discounted what she had heard, and forgotten.

Saying now with zest, bloodshot eyes giving off sparks, "... his family, also. The Szallas. Oh, that clan! From them, Wally inherited his taste for the illicit. His confidence he'll always be forgiven. His father Otto, you know, 'distinguished' mayor of Chautauqua Falls for fifteen years, was close to impeached, for 'misappropriation of municipal funds.' His uncle Joe the U.S. congressman they're so proud of, had a reputation for messing with interns and got involved in some scandal, his Democrat cronies helped him wriggle out of, and retire. And Wally himself, all these interviews he gives about the 'environment'—'ecology'—'pride in the Chautauqua Valley'—'saving the local radio station'—why d'you think he's on the County Board of Supervisors for no salary, except to make a little untaxed money under the table? 'It is not bribery, Isabel, I forbid you to say such a thing ...' Did you hear, Nicole, your lover has been named 'Citizen of the Year' by the Chautauqua County Historical Society? There's a big holiday benefit dinner at the country club, one thousand dollars a ticket, Wally is begging me to attend as 'Mrs. Szalla.'" Isabel laughed, shaking her head at the prospect.

This was a surprise. I had known that Wally was to receive the award, we'd celebrated the other evening with champagne. But I had not known that he would be attending the dinner with Isabel, or with anyone.

Weakly I said, "I don't feel comfortable, Mrs. Szalla, talking about . . ."

Isabel laughed and poked me across the table.

"Call me 'Isabel'! 'Mrs. Szalla' was my mother-in-law."

". . . behind Wally's back, about such . . ."

"My late and not-lamented mother-in-law. *She* was the one who'd forgive her darling boy things he hadn't even thought of doing yet."

"Isabel, I think we can talk like sensible civilized adults without . . ."

" 'Sensible'—'civilized'—'adults'? *You* call yourself an 'adult'? Having an affair practically in public with a married man and father, lacking even the good grace to be ashamed? Why, you're ridiculous."

I was too shocked to react. Isabel's bloodshot eyes glared. She'd pushed aside her plate and was rummaging through a crammed leather handbag. For a panicky moment I thought *She has a gun.*

It wasn't a gun but a thick wad of glossy photos, slapped down before me like playing cards. ". . . that's 'Miriam' at the radio station, with the hair. This, she's moved away now, is 'Jolene Java' the girl jazz singer he'd been promoting a few years ago. This—"

I stopped the woman's hands, which were making threatening motions in my face.

"In his heart, Wally is in love with *me*. Because I am his wife, I was his *bride*. He is a sentimental man, Nicole. All the male Szallas are. They believe in 'family values'—you will see! Wally has his sordid little flings, his whores, then comes limping back to the family, and to *me*. I've been collecting evidence for years, I've hired private detectives. Wally says that you are 'unstable'—'unpredictable'—'self-destructive'—he's worried you might 'hurt yourself,' and it would cause a scandal. Of course, I've asked him to move out. He pleads to be forgiven but I refuse to allow him to defile my bed. And I will not give him a divorce because I will not be defeated and cast aside at my age—"

I wasn't hearing this. I was walking away from my loud-voiced accuser, not listening and not looking back. You'd have thought I was naked, the way every eye in the restaurant leapt onto me.

You deserve this humiliation, what the hell were you thinking!

Once through the Marriott lobby I gave up all pretense of dignity and ran for my life, I mean for my car.

the riddle

I wouldn't be seeing Wally Szalla for a while.

Telling him it's for the best, some distance between us, some space. Yes I know, but. Please.

Listening to "Night Train" that night. The gravelly-voiced D.J. played Ray Charles' classic "I Can't Stop Loving You"—"This song is for 'Nicole, with love from W.'"

I didn't respond. Damned if I would respond. In my heart I knew that Isabel Szalla was right about me, as I'd known that Mom had been right about me. Even if Isabel was crazy, and lying. Even if Mom had never really known Wally Szalla.

He called, though. Left messages. On the tape his voice was urgent, agitated. I could not believe that he was not sincere. . . . *love you so much Nikki. She wants to destroy that. She's frightened, this time the negotiations are serious. I will be a free man soon. Please believe me Nikki. Give me a call and tell me you believe me darling I need to see you tonight.*

Played and replayed this message. The words were a riddle I had to decipher yet could not.

no questions

Five weeks, three days before the trial of Ward Lynch on charges of first-degree murder, kidnapping, etc. was scheduled to begin, a call came from the Chautauqua County prosecutor's office with the news that it had been postponed to March 30.

I listened. I didn't reply when the voice at the other end of the line asked if I had any questions.

"Miss Eaton? Are you still on the line?"

I didn't slam the receiver down. Quietly I replaced it. I had no questions.

Noting the date on Mom's ASPCA calendar: March 30 *TRIAL*.

The March photo was "Sybil the black-faced goat with her two kids Easter and Lester" who'd been rescued from bad living conditions on a farm but are now "well and thriving" at the Mt. Ephraim Animal Shelter. For a long time I stared at Sybil, Easter, and Lester and thought how lucky they'd been, to be rescued. And how, before they'd been rescued, they could have had no idea what "rescue" was. If they could have thought, they would have thought that the "bad living conditions" were life, and not bad luck. Or, maybe, they'd have thought that they deserved it, their bad luck.

Jan. 6, 2005

Dear Ms. Eaton,

Just to say that I am sorry about the trial
delay. This is not uncommon in capital cases
and does not reflect a lack of interest or
respect in the case quite the opposite in
fact, I hope you and your family can
understand.

Also just to say that the case is in my mind
though I am working on others of course. You
also are in my mind. After your testimony at
the hearing your words were much in my mind
and this has not lessened over the months.

My interest in this is professional purely, I
need to make clear. There should be no
misunderstanding here.

Well—that is all.

Like before, Ms. Eaton please call if you have
questions or wish to talk on any aspect of
this case. As I have told you it will be ended
soon, the trial I mean and you will then get
on with your life as they say. In saying such

a thing people mean well and it is true, what
they say, mostly.

Sincerely

Det. Ross Strabane

Det. Ross Strabane, Mt. Ephraim Police

P. S. Here is my updated card.

DETECTIVE ROSS J. STRABANE
MT. EPRHRAIM POLICE DEPARTMENT
TEL: (716)722-4186 EXT. 31
HOME: (716)817-9934
CELL: (716) 999-6871
E-MAIL RSTRABANE@MTEPD.COM

On the reverse of the card, neatly hand-printed:

3817 North Fork Rd.
Mt. Ephraim

"it all came out in blood"

A few days later there came, to ring the doorbell at 43 Deer Creek Drive, a stocky man of late middle age who walked with a cane, in a black overcoat that fell past his knees like a robe. Behind him at the curb was parked a shiny black Lincoln Town Car that looked like a compact hearse.

The man was Father Brendan Dorsey.

Dropping by to "pay his respects" to me, though we'd never met. To express his "shock, grief"—"sorrow"—to ask me to accept his "heartfelt condolences." Since he was in Mt. Ephraim visiting his widowed mother.

"Naturally, I'd heard. Some months ago. The terrible news. My mother saves newspaper clippings for me . . ."

I invited Father Dorsey inside. I took his coat from him, that was softly heavy black cashmere. On his rotund near-bald head, a black fedora I took from him as well. Brendan Dorsey! I was stunned to see him: the man who, long ago when he'd been a boy, my mother had loved.

The man who'd impregnated my mother. Might have married her, if he'd wished to. Thereby supplanting my father, and Clare and me.

If you'd been nicer to Mom, I wouldn't exist. What do I owe you!

I wondered if Mom would recognize Brendan Dorsey, after so many years. This worldly man in his late fifties with a boiled-looking face, a slightly swollen flushed nose. Something boyish and spoiled about his mouth. His eyes were startlingly pale, a washed-out blue. Brendan Dorsey had been handsome, you could see, before he'd gained weight and authority. One of those men-in-power who, so long as you don't contradict them, are utterly charming, gracious. When I asked Brendan Dorsey what I should call him, he surprised me by saying, with an air of subtly offended dignity: " 'Father Dorsey.' "

Strange! If you aren't Catholic. Calling an utter stranger "Father." And this least fatherly of men, with pale staring eyes and steel-rimmed glasses, black clerical clothes and gleaming black cane. Brendan Dorsey was impeccably dressed, from his starched white priest's collar to his expensive-looking black leather shoes. Though clearly he was a man who ate and drank well, his face fleshy and a sizable belly protruding over his belt like a kangaroo's pouch. Almost, you'd expect to see a pert little face peeking out of that pouch.

To Mom, when she'd been Gwen Kovach, this man had been a boy named Brendan. Now he'd aged into Father Dorsey, a figure of importance who informed me that he was "assistant to the Bishop of Minneapolis-St. Paul." He was "co-chairing" a conference of Catholic theologians at Canisius College in Buffalo, and, as he'd explained, visiting his mother who lived, with his younger sister Ethel, in the family home on Ridge Road.

I'd asked him to call me "Nicole" and not "Miss Eaton" as he'd been doing. I told him that Mom had had two daughters, that she'd married a man named Jonathan Eaton and they'd lived in this house together for almost thirty years until he'd died in January 2000. Graciously Brendan Dorsey murmured, "I am sorry to hear that, Nicole. You must miss both your parents very much."

For a moment I couldn't speak. It was as if the priest had reached out to touch my raw, beating heart I'd imagined was safely hidden inside one of Mom's cable-knit pullovers.

I didn't doubt that Brendan Dorsey had plenty of practice comforting the bereaved but I had no intention to break down and cry so that he could comfort me more. I said, "We've never met, Father Dorsey. But I have heard of you."

"Have you! That's kind to say, Nicole."

He was thinking I meant his prominence in the Roman Catholic Church hierarchy. When I said, "I mean, in a personal way. In a Mt. Ephraim way," he blinked at me, startled. A slow flush lifted into his face.

"Ah! I see."

"Not from Mom but from Mom's friend Alyce Proxmire. Do you remember that name, Father Dorsey?"

Brendan Dorsey, seated in Dad's old, favorite leather chair in the living room, shifted his bulk awkwardly, fussing with the cane between his legs. He frowned, to give the impression of trying to remember the name of an individual who, forty years before, he hadn't given a second glance to. " 'Alyce Proxmire.' A friend, you say, of Gwen's?"

Gwen! The name seemed almost to have slipped from his mouth, inadvertently.

"Mom's 'oldest girlfriend,' she used to call her. They were in the same class at Mt. Ephraim High."

Brendan Dorsey smiled, as if he'd solved the riddle. "I didn't attend public school, Nicole."

The old Nikki would've said something bright and brash to make this fat old guy who'd broken Mom's heart squirm with discomfort in her house, but the newer Nikki, having taken Mom's place in the house, only just smiled and said, innocently, "Oh, I know, Father! 'De Sales High.' The best school in the Chautauqua Valley. Exclusively for Catholic boys whose parents can afford the tuition."

Even before Mom's long-lost first boyfriend arrived on my doorstep, it had been a complicated morning.

I'd driven to Chautauqua Falls, as I did from time to time, to meet with my employers at the *Beacon*. (Who was still hinting, in the most tactful of ways, that a "personal piece" on my loss would be welcome in the paper; better yet, a "personal piece" on the upcoming trial.) Afterward, I dropped by my apartment to check it out. (When it seemed that I wouldn't be returning immediately, I'd given away my potted plants to my downstairs neighbor. I was careful to keep the thermostat at a high enough temperature to prevent pipes freezing. Since I'd never exactly decided to move into Mom's house, I'd never gotten around to filling out a post office change of address form, so mail continued to accumulate for me, kindly deposited on a table in my apartment by the downstairs neighbor. Not much of this was first class mail, and all of it was disposable.)

My landlord waylaid me on the stairs: when was I coming back? *Was* I coming back? My lease would expire in June, and rent was being raised by fifteen percent.

Fifteen percent! I tried not to wince.

I told my landlord that I hadn't been thinking about the future, much. "When I do, you'll be the first to know."

The last time I'd visited Chautauqua Falls, I'd spent the night with Wally Szalla. This time, no.

I didn't make a sentimental journey driving past Riverview Luxury Apartments. Still less was I tempted to drive past the big red-brick colonial on Ashburn Avenue. But I did drive past the WCHF AM-FM radio tower outside town. There were a half-dozen vehicles parked there but Wally Szalla's trademark old tarnished-brass Buick was missing.

Oh, it was ridiculous! I felt a pang of loss. If the Buick had been there, I wasn't going to stop in.

Maybe Wally had sold the car, at last. Maybe one of the new, shiny vehicles was his.

Returning home, I drove a mile or two out of my way to take North Fork Road into Mt. Ephraim. I seemed to be taking this route unconsciously, for no reason. Since I hadn't made any attempt to remember the detective's address, I had no way of knowing which residence was his.

Any time. Day or night. Just to talk.

Have faith!

North Fork Road was two-lane blacktop, a road of no special distinction. Like most roads in the foothills of the Chautauqua Mountains it was steeply hilly. It ranged from beautiful rural stretches passing through rolling farmland with views of the Chautauqua River in the distance, to eyesore stretches of run-down houses in littered yards, trailer courts and boarded-up old farmhouses and barns waiting to be razed by developers. There were small ranch houses with asphalt siding, middle-income colonials and Cape Cods, subdivisions with names like Fox Hill Acres. Just outside Mt. Ephraim there was a scattering of pretentious brick Georgians on newly landscaped lots, like those in the Chisholms' neighborhood. And there was, ideal for singles, North Fork Villas (1- & 2-Bedroom Apt's Now Renting), a decidedly downscale version of the Riverview in Chautauqua Falls.

I felt a sudden happiness, driving my car past snow-heaped fields, on a brightly sunny winter morning. How like the opening credits of a movie. As the camera soars and sweeps along the roadside. The suspense of not knowing where the camera is headed. What the story will be, who it will involve. And what will happen.

"May I?"

Brendan Dorsey was asking if he might take, as a memento, one of the cheerleader photos of "Feather" Kovach. Sweetly smiling in her trim maroon jumper, blond hair flying and face blandly pretty as a doll's. I checked to see if there were other, similar photos, and told him yes of course. His eyes welled unexpectedly with tears as he thanked me.

"She was the very spirit of joy, wasn't she! Of course, you never knew her then."

"Only from others, who did."

Brendan Dorsey was peering at other photos on the table, blinking and staring. A look of hurt and yearning and a kind of greed came over his face, I knew he'd have liked to ask for more photos of my mother but damned if I would give them away to this stranger.

" 'Feather' they called her. Ah, she was so—young. We were both so young." Brendan Dorsey sighed heavily. "Different people, really."

Because I didn't like Father Brendan Dorsey, and didn't trust him, I was trying to be extra-nice to him. Thinking *Mom would wish this, Mom forgave him long ago*. I could imagine her in the doorway watching anxiously.

I had to wonder if he'd loved her. If an eighteen-year-old boy can love. I had to wonder if, through his life as a priest, and what looked like the success of his career as a priest, he'd remembered her sometimes, and regretted his behavior. But he'd never tried to contact her, evidently. He had certainly returned to visit his family from time to time but he'd never contacted my mother through forty years and now she was gone and he was blinking back tears, looming over the dining room table in her house.

I asked, a little sharply, "Were you very close friends with Mom?"

"Quite close. At one time."

"You . . . 'dated'?"

It was the speech of that era: "dated." A cruder sort of speech came to mind but I refrained from using it.

Brendan Dorsey sighed, pushing his steel-rimmed glasses against the bridge of his nose. The glasses had become too tight for his spreading face, pinching his flesh. "In a way, yes. For a brief while."

"When was the last time you saw my mother, Father Dorsey?"

"I . . . I'm not sure."

"Before you went away to college?"

"It would have been then, yes. And the seminary."

"You went to St. Bonaventure?"

Brendan Dorsey glanced at me in mild surprise, that I should know this fact. Yet, being a man of prominence, if not himself a bishop in the Church, it might make sense, that a complete stranger knew something of his background.

"Yes. And then to Holy Redeemer Seminary in St. Paul, Minnesota." Brendan Dorsey paused, as if hesitant to continue, for fear of seeming boastful. "Also, two years at the Vatican studying church law. An extraordinary experience."

"You didn't keep in touch with my mother, I guess."

"Well, no." Brendan Dorsey paused, as if he had more to say, but thought better of it.

How provincial Mt. Ephraim would seem, to one who'd studied at the Vatican! And sweet little Feather Kovach, utterly outgrown.

I said, "Of course, Mom wasn't Catholic. You wouldn't have had the church connection."

"Yes. I mean, no. There wouldn't have been that connection."

I'd offered Brendan Dorsey coffee, and a cinnamon roll. Gratefully Brendan Dorsey accepted the coffee, but demurred at the prospect of the roll. When I told him that I'd baked the rolls that morning, from a recipe of my mother's, he said, as if reluctantly, "Well, I could try one. Thank you."

Brendan Dorsey ate the roll slowly at first, then with more appetite. He was a hearty eater, who fears stimulating his appetite, for then he'll have a hard time curbing it. We were sitting at an end of the dining room table. I'd set out Mom's most exquisite embroidered napkins, which Brendan Dorsey used to wipe his mouth of sugar, and his sticky hands.

I said, "It always seemed strange to me, in a way mysterious, that my mother wasn't Catholic since most of the Kovachs are. They belong to St. Joseph's parish."

"St. Joseph's! Yes. There's a new man there, I don't believe I have met."

"At the time of her death, Mom belonged to the Mt. Ephraim Christian Life Fellowship Church. My father wasn't religious and never went with her. They're both buried in Mt. Ephraim Cemetery."

Only recently had I been able to speak like this, my voice not quavering. I was able to say such words as *death, died, buried, cemetery*. Like a small child just learning to speak, I was fascinated by the sounds of certain words.

As I spoke, Brendan Dorsey nodded gravely. He was eyeing a second cinnamon roll in the way of a cat calculating a leap that might result in an ignoble fall, yet might be worth the risk. I said again, more pointedly, "I always wondered why. Mom wasn't Catholic."

"My dear, did you ask her?"

"Oh, you couldn't ask Mom anything so serious! She'd float away like a feather, and turn it into a joke. I guess she said she 'believed' in God, and that was enough. The actual church didn't matter."

"And what is your church affiliation, Nicole?"

The pale blue eyes were fixed on me, behind the steel-rimmed glasses. For a moment I felt the powerful tug, the wish to please a man of such authority.

"Nothing, Father Dorsey. But I 'believe,' too."

"Well, good. That's good."

Brendan Dorsey had weakened, and was reaching for the second cinnamon roll. We watched his hand, stubby fingers yet neatly filed, impeccable nails. Eating, sighing, he said unexpectedly, "A heretic, my dear. Like your mother."

Heretic? No one had ever called Gwen Eaton a heretic before.

"What do you mean, Father? I don't understand."

But Brendan Dorsey wasn't in a mood to discuss theology. In this middle-income ranch house in Deer Creek Acres, Mt. Ephraim. With the hippie-looking daughter of a woman he hadn't seen in forty years and rarely gave a thought to, except at weak, sentimental moments. "Believing in human beings, and not God. Not Jesus Christ our savior without whom we are unredeemed." Though licking cinnamon from his lips, wiping his sticky hands on the embroidered napkins, Brendan Dorsey didn't look as if redemption was uppermost in his mind at the moment.

Impulsively I said, "Thank you, Father Dorsey."

"But—why?"

"For becoming a priest. For leaving Mt. Ephraim, and leaving my mother. It was the necessary thing."

Brendan Dorsey stared at me, uncertain. Possibly he'd detected a note of female mockery in my voice, not what you'd expect in Gwen Kovach's daughter. He said, frowning, "My dear, it was. The 'necessary' thing: God's will. The priesthood was obviously my vocation, not . . ." His voice trailed off. His sticky fingers gestured vaguely to indicate all that was not the priesthood: the dining room in which we sat, the tidy little suburban house, Deer Creek Acres, the world.

Afterward I would realize, with a stab of hurt, that Brendon Dorsey hadn't shown much interest in Mom beyond her cheerleader years. He'd done no more than glance through photos of her as a young wife and mother, he'd made no comment on our family photos, hadn't asked a question about Dad. His interest in "Feather" Kovach had ended abruptly in the mid-1960s. By the time Mom had spent the weekend at Star Lake with her friend Alyce, this interest was extinguished.

He said, "I pray for her soul, dear. I will continue."

Pray for your own soul, Father. Mom's soul is fine.

"Well, thank you, Father! I'm sure that's generous of you."

Brendan Dorsey thanked me again for the cheerleader photo, which he'd placed in an inside pocket of his black cleric's coat. He thanked me even more effusively for the coffee and cinnamon rolls. I said, "Let me wrap up a few to take with you, Father," and he said, quickly, "No, no! But thank you," and I said, "But Mom would be so pleased, Father. It's her recipe," and he gave in with a guilty sigh, "Well. If it isn't . . ."

"No trouble at all, Father. It was very kind of you to visit."

In the vestibule, we had a struggle with Brendan Dorsey's heavy cashmere coat, as I held the sleeves for him to shove his thick arms into, awkwardly. There was the matter of his "damned arthritic" knee, which had stiffened while he'd been sitting. And—where was his cane? (In my hand. I handed it to him.) Even as Brendan Dorsey was set to leave he hesitated, as if he'd only just thought of this: "In sorting through your mother's things, Nicole, I wonder if . . . You might have come upon some old letters of mine . . ." A hot flush rose in his face, his pale-blue eyes became evasive. "I was very young at the time. I was emotional, undisciplined. I can't imagine what I wrote, that Gwen would have wished to keep."

"I don't think so, Father. I don't think that I have."

I didn't want to admit that I'd avoided going through my mother's oldest things in the attic. I'd postponed the task for months. Each time I climbed the steps to the attic and stooped to enter that crowded, airless space, I'd been overcome by a sensation of dizziness and dread and had to run downstairs where I could breathe.

". . . asked her please to return them, as I was returning her letters to me. Oh, Gwen was so emotional! She thought nothing of writing down her quickest, airiest thoughts, like little flames of feeling they were, on scraps of paper she tied into tiny bundles with ribbons . . . and these I mailed back to her, every one of them, as I thought we'd agreed." Brendan Dorsey paused, settling the soft black fedora on his head. He frowned, but then he smiled. ". . . such silly things! Gwen made minia-ture valentines to leave in my pockets, and in my car, for me to discover, she made little birds and animals out of aluminum foil, there were birth-day cards, half-birthday cards, un-birthday cards, once she melted dozens of jelly beans to spell out *I LUV Y* . . ." He laughed, swiping at his eyes. "That was Gwen's way, to make a fuss over trifles."

"Maybe they weren't trifles, Father. To her."

I watched Brendan Dorsey navigate the icy front walk, leaning heav-ily on his cane. I was feeling sorry for him now, even a kind of sympathy. I did not blame or dislike him. I saw him as Mom had seen him, a boy-man, his soul unformed, like a bud that will wither without opening. Thinking *What do I owe him, I owe him everything.*

Hoping he wouldn't slip and fall and injure himself before he made it to his Lincoln Town Car, and somehow become my responsibility.

girlfriend

I could hear the sharp intake of breath.

"*Him!* I don't believe it, Nikki!"

"Yes. 'Father Brendan Dorsey.' He was here, in Mom's house."

"Did he . . . remember me?"

"Yes. He did."

"He *didn't*! He . . . *did?*"

"When I told him 'Alyce Proxmire' he described you perfectly, Alyce: 'Gwen's closest friend, a very nice girl with beautiful dark eyes.' "

At the other end of the line there was rapturous silence. Quickly I hung up the receiver to preserve it.

"time for you to know"

"Nikki. It's time for you to know."

There was Mom's cousin Lucille Kovach peering at me with small brightly glittering eyes. A square-built woman in her late fifties with a face blunt as a shovel, no taller than five feet two inches but weighing at least two hundred pounds. Yet Lucille wasn't fat so much as solid, compacted, in the durable way that scrap cars and garbage are compacted.

Lucille Kovach, my "second-cousin" whom I had not seen since the day of Mom's funeral. In XXX-sized jeans with a man's fly front, the steely zipper of which glinted between her hefty thighs. In a greenish lizard-skin jacket over a tight Metallica T-shirt. On Lucille's feet, wedge-shaped work boots with reinforced toes.

Half in dread and half eagerly I asked what Lucille meant?—what was "time" for me to know?

"About Gwen. When we were girls, on Spalding Street. When"— Lucille hesitated, gnawing her fleshy lower lip—"something happened."

I thought it must involve Brendan Dorsey. Certainly, Lucille would have known about my mother's involvement with Brendan Dorsey. They'd lived together in the same household, for a while. After Mom's mother died and her father, who worked for the New York Central Railroad, gave up a permanent home to board with relatives.

Unless what Lucille had to tell me predated Brendan Dorsey. Before Gwen had been taken in by relatives.

Mom had always been vague about those years. From Alyce, I now knew more. Yet there'd been a "shifting-around" time before Alyce knew my mother. "Shifting-around" was Mom's word for that time when she no longer had a permanent home but moved from one household to another, until she graduated from high school, met and married my father. *Light as a feather* she'd wished to be and so her memory of that time had become feathery, imprecise.

I'd never wanted to think that Mom just wasn't telling me the truth. It was better to think she'd long forgotten what truth there might have been to tell.

That afternoon in February, a week after Father Dorsey, I was visiting Hedwig House, an "assisted living facility" in an older section of Mt. Ephraim. Following Mom's example, I'd been visiting my elderly aunt Renate Kovach once a week. I hadn't known that, at Hedwig House, Mom had regularly visited several other residents as well. From the nursing staff I'd learned that Mom had brought everyone baked things, sweet pastries. She'd been the most popular visitor at Hedwig House and after several visits they were still telling me so.

Visiting one elderly relative was enough, for me. I hoped to emulate my mother but maybe not just yet.

"Aunt Renate! Hello."

When I entered my aunt's melancholy room crammed with remnants of her lost life, often the elderly woman would mistake me for Mom, smiling happily at me, clutching at my hands and pulling me down to kiss her papery-thin cheek. Aunt Renate Kovach had become a frail bent-back spidery-limbed old woman, who'd once been nearly as stout as her daughter Lucille.

"Ohhh! Is this for *me?*"

"Cherry-bran muffins, Aunt Renate. I hope you like them."

"Thank you, dear! Nobody ever comes to see me but *you*."

This couldn't be so. Often I'd seen Lucille just departing in her Dodge pickup when I pulled into the parking lot behind the bleak sandstone building, and if she saw me she'd wave vigorously through her windshield. Or, when I was leaving, I'd encounter Lucille lumbering up the front steps. ("Hey Nikki! How's my mom, still kickin'?")

I never contradicted Aunt Renate, though. Just smiled, and listened. And listened. It made me uneasy to be confused with Mom, but when I'd tried to correct my aunt her immediate question was *Then where is Gwen?* and words failed me, how to explain.

"Aunt Renate, I think Lucille explained to you? My Mom is . . . isn't here right now."

"Isn't here *where*? Then where is she?"

"I think Lucille must have . . ."

"Lucille never visits! Lucille has her own 'life'! Ask her, she'll tell you: 'I have my own life, Momma.' But where is Gwen?"

Aunt Renate was becoming anxious, suspicious. Clutching at me with talon fingers. Dad used to say of Renate Kovach that the woman had a "carp" mouth. There were family tales of her scolding and humiliating her grown daughters including Lucille. When I tried to reason with her, she began to speak angrily.

"Who are you, then?"

"Nikki."

"Who?"

"Nikki Eaton. Gwen's daughter."

" 'Nik-ki.' " In my aunt's pursy mouth, the name did sound improbable.

"Aunt Renate, I was here last Friday. Remember, I brought you some cinnamon rolls . . ."

The watery eyes fastened on me doubtfully. The first time I'd visited, Aunt Renate confused me with Clare; once, waking groggily from a nap, upright in an easy chair, she'd stared at me blinking rapidly and began to whimper: "Lu-*cille*. Where you *been*. Leaving me alone in this place like *garbage*. That's what you think I am, *garbage*. God damn your soul Lu-*cille*. Take me out of here Lu-*cille* don't go away again and leave me in this place like *garbage*."

It took several minutes to calm Aunt Renate. I knew, I'd been warned by the nursing staff and of course it was common sense, you don't want to upset an elderly resident, that's the last thing you want to do. Yet it required some coaxing, to convince my aunt that no, really I was not her daughter Lucille, I was her niece Nicole Eaton. "Lucille and I don't look much alike, Aunt Renate. At least, I've never heard that we do."

"Two-Ton Lucy" and "Tank" were code names for Lucille Kovach generated at 43 Deer Creek Drive. Dad made Clare and me laugh referring to his Kovach in-laws as "The Mt. Ephraim Hillbillies" and Lucille especially discomforted him. (None of the Kovachs dropped by the house when Jonathan Eaton was likely to be home.) Growing up, Clare was most critical of Lucille Kovach for Clare's standards of grooming, deportment, and respectability were very demanding. Oh! what a horror Lucille was! What an embarrassment! Not just that Lucille was a barrel-sized woman with a broad, blunt face who often wore men's clothes, but Lucille was lacking in modesty: you'd expect anyone who looked like her to skulk away in shame, but no. You'd expect that, lacking a recognizable female figure, she'd refrain from tank-tops and polyester stretch pants in the summer, but no. You'd expect that she would refrain from making a display of herself with a bugle voice and gut-ripping laughter loud as any man's, but no. What especially scandalized Clare was that Lucille made no secret of her craving for male companionship even into middle age, and continued to "hang out" in bars though she'd been married and divorced three times, most recently to an ex-Marine who'd served in the Gulf War but was now incarcerated at Follette Maximum Security Facility for Men, serving a lengthy sentence for aggravated assault, creating a public disturbance, and spousal abuse.

" 'Spousal abuse'!" Clare was mystified. "How could even a Marine abuse that woman!"

Clare's scorn was contagious, to a younger sister especially. I was inclined to share it out of a fear of provoking it against me. Yet I'd always liked my Kovach relatives, on those rare occasions when I'd spent a little time with them. Like most people I'd been intimidated by Lucille but her attachment to Mom, and Mom's to her, had to mean something.

Returning home from school, sometimes I'd see Lucille's rust-bucket Dodge backing out of the drive. Inside, Mom would be bustling about the kitchen trying to air it out: stove fan turned on high, windows open, folded newspaper fluttered to dissipate Lucille's pungent, unmistakable smell which Dad's sharp nostrils would detect: Camel cigarette smoke, fattish-female perspiration, axle grease. (Intermittently for years, Lucille had worked as an auto mechanic in a Kovach relative's garage where she was said to be "damned good.")

Mom would plead, "Oh, help me, Nikki! If your father knows that Lucy was here he'll tease so! And don't tell him, honey, please?"

This afternoon at Hedwig House, there was Lucille visiting with her mother, her bulk cozily propped against the windowsill as Aunt Renate fretted and fussed, upright in her chintz easy chair. The honey-colored afghan was wrapped about the elderly woman's frail body like a shroud. Lucille was looking stouter than ever, even her head appeared larger, capped by a springy mass of grizzled-gray curls. The XXX-sized jeans and funky lizard-skin jacket and a smear of lipstick on her fleshy lips made her quite a striking sight in that cramped space.

"Hey Nikki: great to see you. Thanks for coming to see Momma."

I was smiling bravely. Wishing I'd noticed Lucille's pickup in the parking lot, I might have waited until she left.

Lucille extended a hand to me, blunt stubby fingers and dirt-edged nails. Like all the Kovachs she was loudly friendly, liking to touch and to laugh. It was possible she'd been drinking, a few beers at lunch. Her eyes were moist and glittering and her mouth kept slip-sliding into a lopsided smile.

"Momma, see who's here? You got a visitor, see? Gwen's daughter Nikki, you remember her, eh? The skinny one, 'Nikki'? Not the other one, that's Clare the high school principal, this is Nik-ki the high school sex-pot." Lucille laughed, this was an old joke of hers. "See, Nikki's bringing you something, Momma? Mmmm smells good. For you."

Aunt Renate roused herself to wakefulness, blinking and smiling in my direction. She seemed to recognize me today. She smiled at me, and thanked me for the aluminum-wrapped muffins, which Lucille had taken from me to settle on her mother's lap.

"Well! This is nice. This is real nice. I heard you've been visiting Momma, Nikki. Like Gwen did."

Gwen. I wondered if it was a good idea to speak my mother's name in Aunt Renate's hearing. But Aunt Renate had begun to nibble at one of the cherry-bran muffins and was distracted.

Aunt Renate brushed crumbs from her lips. "This is delicious, dear. You were always such a good . . ."

Lucille said impatiently, "That's Gwen, Momma. This is Gwen's daughter Nikki. Get them straight, Momma. You can if you try." Lucille was ruthless in the way of a gym coach blowing her whistle. Damned if she was going to let her mother, eighty-seven years old, lapse into anything like premature senility. Telling me in a tone meant to tease Aunt Renate, "Momma's memory is still sharp when she makes the effort. Sharper than mine, lots of times. Oh man, Momma can remember the damndest things. Except she gets lazy in this place. See, they keep it too hot here. Like a hothouse and you can't breathe, unless, this happened last week, the damn furnace breaks down, and it's damn *cold*. Momma, look up here. What kind of mess are you making, those crumbs! You never used to be so messy with your food . . ."

This went on for a while. Lucille oversaw her mother's every move like a doting/exasperated mother. Amid her other smells, and the pervading odor of Hedwig House which I preferred not to analyze, Lucille did smell just slightly of beer.

She teased me about writing "some newspaper piece" about Hedwig House, was that why I'd been visiting?

Quickly I told her no. Of course not.

She teased me about this "married-man-friend of yours what's-his-name 'Zall-la' "?

Blushing like a girl I told her it wasn't like that, exactly.

"What's it like, then? 'Exactly'?"

I shook my head. I wasn't going to be interrogated. The rare times we spoke on the phone, when I called her, Clare always got around to quizzing me about Wally Szalla, too.

Finally I'd told her I wouldn't ask about her sex life, if she refrained from asking about mine. This shut up my bossy older sister, fast.

Lucille's eyes glittered with a kind of mirthful well-intentioned malice. She had the physical authority of a large dog that might lunge at you to bite or to lick your face out of sheer exuberance. She was eating cherry-bran muffins in three sizable bites.

I'd had the impression that Lucille had always liked me, much more than she'd liked Clare, and I wondered what Mom had told her about me; what they'd talked about in private, all those years. The secret lives our mothers live.

Suddenly Lucille asked what I'd been hearing about the trial? That "s.o.b. murderer Lynch?"

I was shocked, that Lucille would bring up such a subject. In her mother's presence, and in mine.

"This latest he's saying, he didn't do it? *He* didn't? Some other guy, some buddy of his from prison, the two of them, and the other guy, *he's* the one who . . ."

"Lucille, please. I can't talk about this now."

"Yeah, O.K. I s'pose not. But, Jesus! The things they let them say! 'Defense strategy.' I was reading in the damn paper."

My heart was pounding rapidly. I felt that I might faint. It was a solace to me, that my elderly aunt appeared oblivious to the subject Lucille had brought up, contented with a muffin.

Second childhood it used to be called. There might be solace in that!

Lucille said, incensed, "Lawyers should be arrested, they spread lies. You'd think there would be a law, wouldn't you! 'Perjury' is something you hear, it should be applied to lawyers. Like this lawyer who represented Harvey, when I brought charges against him, damn liars the things they concocted trying to blame *me*. Like, I 'threw the first punch' kind of thing, and Harvey threw the last. And this s.o.b. Lynch, if the cops'd been thinking straight they'd have shot him dead when they found him, where was it, down in Erie. I'd have, for sure. Give me a gun, any day. Everybody is saying, it's a damn shame there has to be a trial, not just living through all that again, poor Gwen, I was broke up at the time and it ain't much better now, but not just that, it's damn expensive, it comes out of our taxes. And that guy's lawyer, you can't say it isn't 'perjury.' *He* should be arrested."

"I think that, to commit perjury, you have to have sworn to tell the truth, in court. Lawyers aren't sworn in."

"Well, hell! They're the ones who should be."

I was managing to remain calm. Lucille was referring to a new "defense" fabricated by Ward Lynch. He had long ago recanted his original confession and was insisting upon a plea of "not guilty." Initially, one of his lawyers had entered a plea of "not guilty by reason of temporary insanity" but more recently, as the trial was approaching, he'd come up with a new idea, that another man, not Ward Lynch, had actually committed the crimes for which he'd been arrested. The assistant prosecutor who would be trying the case had explained some of this to me but I'd told him please, I didn't want to hear it. Rob Chisholm had called several times wanting to talk about this and other matters relating to the trial but I explained to him I could not talk about it, I could not think about it. *Please*.

Seeing the stricken look in my face, Lucille reached out impulsively to touch me. It was more of a rough poke of my shoulder than a touch, but I came close to clutching at Lucille's callused fingers, just to hold them.

Since Mom was gone, and Wally Szalla, no one touched me any longer. Somehow I had changed from being someone much-loved and not even quite realizing her good luck to being a sexless stick figure like Alyce Proxmire, luckless.

Lucille nudged me again, more gently. "Nikki. It's time for you to know."

Lucille glanced at Aunt Renate, absorbed in a cherry-bran muffin and oblivious to us. She had something to tell me in confidence, in a voice lowered and somber, for Lucille.

Oh, I wasn't sure if I wanted this! If I could bear any more news of my mother. From Aunt Tabitha, from Alyce Proxmire, from Brendan Dorsey I'd had surprises sprung on me. In Lucille Kovach's moist glittering eyes I saw there would be more to come.

"About Gwen. When we were girls . . ."

And so Lucille told me, what I had never known, and was certain that Dad hadn't known: when Mom had been eleven, and her mother Marta Kovach died, it hadn't happened that Mom had not been allowed to see her mother when she'd returned home from school that day. The eleven-year-old girl had been the one to discover her mother, already dead. And Marta Kovach had not died of some "wasting-away disease" but by her own hand, having slashed both her forearms with a butcher knife.

"See, it was kept secret. Only just a few people knew. It was such a terrible thing, that woman hurting herself so bad, in such a way, right in her bed, where Gwen was the one to find her. Gwen would never talk about it afterward only just around it, sort of, you know how she was, she'd 'talk' with me about it, sometimes. But nobody else. Her father brought her over to our house, that night. All he could do was drink, and disappear. Gwen stayed with us, she slept in my bed with me, it was O.K., we'd played together a lot and I always liked Gwen better than my own sisters, for sure. Momma here, she was partial to Gwen. 'My best girl' she called her. Nobody was all that surprised, what Marta did to herself, she'd always been heavy-hearted and kept to her bed a lot, and Gwen was the one to cook up supper for them when she was real little like nine or ten. When we lived together, we'd make meals together in the kitchen, Gwen and Momma and me, and that was fun. We did have fun! Later on it was sad, your father didn't care for us, I guess. So we weren't invited over to your house much, you were growing up. Gwen was kind of lonely there, she said. She missed a city neighborhood, sidewalks and more people. I mean, she had friends, and she had Jon's family. But she was lonely for us, she said. I told her, like I told Momma, that's how it is sometimes, it's no point in getting mad at anybody. In families, these things happen. The Eatons are a class of people in a 'whole different ballpark' as the saying goes. Gwen and I were girls together, though, and we never forgot. We helped each other lots of times. The things in my life, Jesus!—Gwen was the one I turned to, for sure. Your dad never knew, he'd have been madder'n hell, Gwen lent me money lots of times. It was money like twenty-five dollars, fifty dollars, not a whole lot but it saved my life more than once. Jon never knew because it was money Gwen made selling her knit things and crafts, like at those fairs at the mall. When I tried to pay her back, she wouldn't take it. 'You have a harder life than I do, Lucy,' Gwen always said, 'you have to work. I'm just a housewife.' When Gwen was still a girl, her dream was to be married and have her own house. And she'd be so safe in that house! Except, sometimes she'd be sad and say, 'Oh maybe it's wrong for me to have children, Lucy. Maybe there are bad genes in me, I shouldn't pass on.' Because it wasn't just her mother Marta who was so troubled in her mind, it was Gwen's father, too, but he never turned against himself in such a way, or anybody else, it was more like Jacob Kovach stayed so remote, and drank himself to death. But I said, "Hell, Gwen, I wouldn't let nothing stop *me*. And I wouldn't, neither. I had my own kids, and they turned out O.K. I told Gwen say God has some plan, it's a weird plan that wouldn't make any sense to us, but it makes sense to God, so if there's this guy comes along who wants to marry you, and wants to have children with you, just the fact he shows up, you don't even have to love him like in the movies, that's what God has planned for you. See?' And Gwen thought about that, and must've agreed because that was how it was, I think. Exactly."

Lucille smiled, pleased with herself. By this time Aunt Renate had dozed off in her chintz easy chair. Her head was lolling in a way painful to observe so Lucille adjusted a pillow behind it. With fussy tenderness she wiped muffin crumbs from her mother's collapsed mouth and brushed them from her knees. Saying, if her mother woke up suddenly not knowing where she was, and her glasses falling down her nose, she'd see the crumbs and panic thinking they were ants.

"Momma's got this thing about ants, scared to death of them and it's getting worse. Out home, trifles never fazed her."

We left Hedwig House together. We talked a while longer in the parking lot where Lucille immediately lit a Camel. I was feeling weak, dazed. I was feeling light-headed from the sudden fresh air, that made my eyes water. Lucille gave me a wadded tissue, to wipe my face.

"So, Nikki. This past year, it's been pretty shitty, eh."

Pretty shitty. I suppose, yes. You could say so. There was a succinct sort of eloquence in Lucille's phrase.

"Well. I don't know. I'm missing Mom, yes. But . . ."

"Living in Gwen's house. Wearing her things and baking what she used to bake. Her cat, and seeing her people. You think that's a good idea, eh."

This wasn't a question. Lucille wasn't challenging me. She was brash and pushy and yet, like all the Kovachs, most of whom had not graduated from high school, she would defer to Clare and me, because we'd "gone away" to college. She said, exhaling smoke in a massive cloud, "Well, it's your way, Nikki. There's others, worse."

I was wiping something sticky from my nose. Tactfully, Lucille seemed not to notice.

"It's nice of you to visit Momma. She's always complaining nobody visits her but she forgets, those who do. By the next day she forgets. She'll be eighty-eight next month. She's a tough old girl, for sure. Like I was saying, there's times she surprises us, the things she remembers. It's like her brain is some kind of sponge, you squeeze it and the damnest things come out. Like, things I did when I was a little girl. Things I said. The kind of cereal I liked—'Cream of Wheat.' Things like that, nobody else would know or care about. That, when Momma is gone, go with her."

"Aunt Renate seems happy . . ."

Lucille laughed harshly. "Bullshit. 'Happy' is a word people say around places like this, it makes them feel better. Being Momma's age is shit, and half the time it's actual shit. If you're not sitting in it, your roommate is."

I couldn't reply to this! Lucille was nudging me to laugh, she'd intended to shock me.

"See, when your mother died, it was so awful 'cause Gwen died before her time. Gwen died way too young. Nobody was ready for that, or could have been. Like"—Lucille snapped her fingers—"that. So you are spared what my sisters and I are going through, with Momma. There is that to consider. Where Gwen is, there isn't any pain. The pain is back here, like with you. See what I'm saying? Missing your mom can be a place to hide, see? Like that house. Like a cave. After a while, it's time you come back out."

Lucille had more to say but was distracted by a dark-skinned Hedwig House attendant in a green uniform, carrying trash to a Dumpster.

"Rigger! You tryin' to ignore me?"

Lucille called to the young man in her brash bugle voice, hands on her hips. The lizard-jacket was pushed open by her big, billowing T-shirt breasts. It seemed she and the young man knew each other, some way.

"Naw, Lu-*cille*. You know better."

"It looks that way. C'mon here, meet my girl cousin Nikki."

"Naw, Lu-*cille*. Can't waste no more time today, I'll get my ass kicked."

"Get your ass *here*, man. You need to meet this girl."

"I said, ma'am I *can't*."

Rigger laughed like one being tickled. Shook his head that was braided spikes. He carried himself with the swaggering aplomb of a black rap performer. He was thirty years younger than Lucille Kovach and good-looking and sexy in even the grungy green uniform and you could see that he liked it just fine that two white women were watching him perform though all he did was shoulder cumbersome trash bags into a foul-smelling Dumpster and trot back to the rear entrance of Hedwig

House where all the residents were elderly Caucasian females. Lucille brayed after him, "Snubbin' me, Rigs, next time I'm gonna snub *you*." Rigger waved a hand at us in farewell, possibly it was meant to signal genuine regret.

Lucille was revved-up, laughing. Walked me to my car where she gave me a hard, quick hug that might have cracked my ribs except I was wearing a down jacket. "Some night, girl! I'm gonna swing around to your house and pick you up. There's this great place out on Route Eighteen, halfway to Malvern, Zodiac? You never heard of Zodiac? There's male strippers, Thursday nights. Fridays, it's a wild singles scene. You come with whoever you want to and you dance with whoever you want to. Disco like the seventies. Even strobe lights. It's a free, fun scene. See what I'm saying? Good-lookin' girl like you, it's your scene. For sure, you won't run into any Eatons there."

secrets

That afternoon, I returned to the attic.

That afternoon, I resolved to "sort through" the attic.

It was the last region of Mom's house that I could bring myself to explore. Though I'd done a poor job of sorting-through other rooms at least I'd made the effort.

The attic was a dimly lighted chill place. When I'd accompanied Mom up here, stashing away things "not good enough to use but too good to throw away, just yet" it had seemed to be a warmer place, with better lighting.

I left the door to the stairs open, that warm air might rise and make the attic more hospitable. And so came Smoky in my wake, pussyfooting in places too cramped for me.

Baby buggy. Baby clothes. A shadeless brass floor lamp, I realized I had not seen in years. There were winter clothes in garment bags, there were boots in a sturdy cardboard box festooned with cobwebs. My breath steamed faintly. Smoky leapt atop a stack of boxes, to paw wildly at a mass of desiccated insect corpses in cobwebs hanging from the low-beamed ceiling like stalactites.

The attic had been Mom's region. Dad had rarely ventured into it. Clare and me, never. Yet so many of our outgrown/cast-off things were stored away here, clothes, school yearbooks, report cards, stuffed animals and dolls, it was as if we'd been here all along, without knowing.

Things not good enough to use but too good to throw away, just yet.

This had been Mom's principle of accumulation, not only in the attic but everywhere in our house.

In our lives.

"Oh, Smoky. You're driving me crazy, will you *stop*."

The burly gray cat was turning in circles, not very gracefully. A swath of cobwebbed insect husks had caught on his stubby tail and in a mild panic he was swatting vigorously at it.

I wished that Clare was with me. I hated my sister, that she had abandoned me in my grief.

Our grief, it was. It should have been!

No: my deepest wish was that Mom was with me. I'd rarely ventured into this attic except in her company. As a girl, as a child. I'd rarely ventured anywhere except in Mom's company.

It seemed wrong, now. To be alone.

It seemed unnatural, a mistake. Alone, at the age of thirteen. I mean, thirty-two. (Thirty-*two*? When had that happened?) Except for a cat that more resembled a comical-stuffed cat, a child's idea of a cat, than an actual, adult animal.

What had Lucille Kovach told me: *It's your way, Nikki. There's others, worse.*

Damn, I wished I'd hugged Lucille back, hard as she'd hugged me. Should've shared a cigarette with her. Should've acted more friendly, flirty, with Rigger. It had all happened so quickly, I'd been dazed and unwieldy.

Time to come back out.

But where?

Against one of the raw, unfinished attic walls were stacks of cardboard boxes. Some of these were marked in crayon with dates—1975–76, 1981–85—but most were unmarked, mysterious. Inside were not-very-mysterious things: postcards, birthday and Christmas cards, a few hand-written letters. Startling to see my own handwriting, on a postcard sent from Santa Fe, May 1993. *Dear Mom and Dad, Is it beautiful here! But windy & the altitude makes me breathless. Sorry I've been out of touch, I am pretty much O.K. & will call soon I promise. Nikki.*

Unbelievably, I hadn't even signed *Love.*

I felt a stab of dismay, disgust. Not even to have signed *Love* to my parents . . .

I'd been twenty at the time. In some long-forgotten phase of being hurt, angry. Complaining to the guy I'd been traveling with my parents were O.K. but mostly hadn't a clue who I was. I guess I must have thought Mom and Dad would live forever, there'd be plenty of time to make up.

My impulse was to tear the card into tiny pieces. Instead I replaced it in the box with the others, Mom had so carefully preserved.

I thought of elderly Aunt Renate, who'd once been a strong, stout woman and was now diminished so you'd never guess what her will had been, her soul. What Lucille had said of her, remembering the damndest things. It was the fate of mothers, to remember. What nobody else would know or care about. That, when they are gone, goes with them.

In the attic where the ceiling pressed low like a skull that has shrunk I searched for another hour and a half, before I found what I'd been looking for.

It was in a sewing box covered in a lavender Laura Ashley print. When I lifted the box to open it, a swath of sticky cobwebs came with it and an agitated spider ran over my wrist.

Beneath spools of thread, loose buttons, needles, safety pins there was a partition that slid open, and inside this, partly hidden by more sewing supplies, were packets of letters: Brendan Dorsey's letters to Gwen Kovach, she'd never returned as he'd requested; and Gwen Kovach's letters to Brendan Dorsey, he'd returned in a manila envelope with the initials *G.K.* in black ink on the front.

G.K.! As if Gwen would have needed to be informed whose letters these were, and for whom they were intended.

I tried not to hate him. He'd been only eighteen, maybe nineteen at the time. He had not meant to be cruel.

My heart was beating rapidly and lightly, like the wings of a small, fluttering bird. I knew that this was forbidden, I had sudden access to my mother's secret life. I would take the sewing box downstairs with me like a trophy.

I stumbled to leave. I switched off the attic light. As I was about to close the door, Smoky bounded past me, stubby tail switching.

I cleared a place at the dining room table. I was very excited by this time. My fingers were strangely cold. They were numb, spreading out Brendan Dorsey's handwritten letter, on a single sheet of plain white paper, of March 7, 1966.

It was Brendan's last letter to Gwen, apparently. There was no return address. His handwriting was craggy and slanting, as if he'd been writing quickly.

Dear Gwen—

I am sorry to be writing like this but there is no other way. I could not tell you the other night, you did not seem to hear me.

I am shocked and saddened by what you have revealed to me. I did not let on at the time, I did not know how to speak. ~~Since then, I have~~

Because of your mother you "have no faith in God." I spoke to Father Gorran at our church, he was upset to hear this. (I did not tell him the name of my friend who had said these words, of course!)

How many children have lost their mothers, and their fathers, throughout History. How many human beings have weathered such storms. Your mother, you told me, died "in her own bed" and "at peace" after 18 months of illness, but only just think of worse suffering, and a child losing her parents at an age younger than you were. Father Gorran says that despair is the most deadly of the sins against God because it is a sin "against creation" and is the sin not to be forgiven.

Just to have faith in "human love" is not enough. The human race is fallen. Only through our Savior Jesus Christ is the human race SAVED.

I am not saying these things, because it is time for me to leave Mt. Ephraim. In fact I am hurt, that you would think such a thing of me. I find it hard to forgive you, Gwen. To turn against me even as you say you love me. You will "never stop loving me" yet you doubt my sincerity in this.

It is not just your lack of faith but other differences between us. I was confused and mistaken in our friendship. I have confessed my part. I was very responsible being older than you, and so much in love with you, truly it was the case I was not "thinking straight." This matter of purity and celibacy is harder for men. I am grateful that no one in my family will know. I have been given penance for my mistakes and sins by my confessor and am grateful that this error in my life is behind me. I hope the same is true for you, too.

Please do not write to me again, Gwen. I am returning your letters and cards here. Please do not call me. I vow to always love you, as a sister. I will pray for your soul. But I will not see you, and ask you to honor this. It is all but certain, I will enter the seminary after college. My mother has long understood that I have a vocation and my life will be dedicated to serving God. I pray that my life from now on will be good, with no more secrets!

I am returning your letters. I would not destroy them for then you could not know their "fate"—but now, they are in your position to destroy as I truly hope you will.

I promise to destroy my letters, when they are returned. ~~I am ashamed~~

I hope that God will bless you as He has blessed me and helped me through this time of temptation and doubt.

Your friend,
Brendan Dorsey

There appeared to be only a few letters of Brendan's, tied together with a piece of green yarn. In the manila envelope marked *G.K.* there were many more, the envelope was crammed. After nearly forty years, still a sweet, flowery scent wafted from them. I had a glimpse of pink stationery, earnest schoolgirl handwriting that bore little resemblance to my mother's mature handwriting. One of the letters, dated Christmas Eve 1965, was twelve pages long.

"Forgive me, Mom! I have to know."

This girl I had never met nor even imagined. In 1965, young enough to be my daughter now. This girl who, when she'd been eleven, had lost her mother, too. Who had come home to find her mother in a way that would be a mystery to her, incomprehensible.

I wanted badly to know, I could scarcely breathe with the excitement of wanting so badly to know, yet, somehow, even as I held the letters, I was pushing them away.

That sweet flowery scent. My fingertips would smell of it, afterward.

And Brendan Dorsey's letters, I pushed more emphatically away. What did I care for Brendan Dorsey's letters, they had no value to me.

It would have been a (vaguely insulting?) gesture to return the man's letters to him without a word. But I wouldn't do this, either.

Instead, I returned all the letters—Brendan's, and Mom's—to the sewing box. Exactly as I'd found them, in the secret compartment beneath the sewing supplies. How like a child's hiding place it was! I had to laugh, I would have liked to tease Mom about the sewing box, to make her blush.

I wasn't sure what I should do with the sewing box, myself. I did not think that I could destroy it. But I would never tell Clare, certainly. I would never tell anyone. After the trial, I would be able to think more clearly. After the trial, my life would resume. I had faith, I knew that this was so. I loved the man who had promised me this. I think I loved him. Or maybe it was a wish, a childish dream. We would sell the house, Clare and me. Clare would have to return, we would prepare the house to be sold. I would move out, it was time. But I didn't think that I would return to the apartment in Chautauqua Falls, where unwanted mail was accumulating. Not there. No more. If Clare had moved away, even temporarily, I could move away. There was no reason, that I could not move away. There had been a reason, but what was it?

I was very happy suddenly. I could not think coherently, I felt as if I'd been awake for months, a terrible light shining into my brain. And now my soul was exhausted, extinguished. Yet I was very happy. I would stumble into my darkened bedroom, to fall on my bed. I would sleep for twelve hours waking to sunshine glaring like a beacon in my face. I would keep my mother's secrets, that had been entrusted to me.

Even those secrets of Mom's I would never know, I would keep.

part five

the trial

"bearer of good news"

I was ready. I was sick with apprehension and I couldn't sleep for rehearsing my testimony. *And then I entered the house. By the kitchen door. And I called Mom's name. And I knew that something was wrong but I could not turn back. And at the door to the garage I saw her. I saw her, where she had fallen, and I went to her. And I saw that she had been hurt, and she was not breathing. And I went for help. And I turned back, for it seemed to me that she was breathing, and I could not leave her. And I held her. And I talked to her. And I had to let her go, a second time.* I could not sleep feeling the scrape of these words in my throat. Hearing the inadequacy of these words in my mouth. I could not sleep seeing Ward Lynch at the defense table only a few yards away. He would be wearing a suit and a tie, he would be cleaned up, "groomed." Haircut, cleanshaven. Nothing like the scruffy WANTED: ARMED AND DANGEROUS Lynch who had murdered my mother.

Except for his eyes. His eyes would be unchanged. Sullen, impassive. Dead eyes of no repentance, no remorse. The last human eyes my mother had seen.

For Ward Lynch was beyond Mom's forgiveness. He'd never have wished it. Not from any of us, her survivors. He was beyond us, untouched by us. He was one whom "Feather" Kovach had not touched.

. . .

The trial! Looming before us like a guillotine.

After months of refusing to speak of it, insisting she wasn't returning, Clare had returned. "I couldn't let you go through this alone, sweetie."

Sweetie! This was my bossy older sister in her tender-Mommy mode.

I have to confess, I'm a sucker for Clare as tender-Mommy. I fall for it every time. I'm like my brother-in-law Rob. *Kick me, if you promise to kiss me.*

It wasn't just for the trial that Clare had returned to Mt. Ephraim, obviously. She'd brought Foster, they were living with Rob and Lilja in the Chisholms' upscale suburban house. For sure, Clare wasn't about to stay with Aunt Tabitha or other dreary/inquisitive relatives.

I said, "I'd think, Clare, if you and Rob are 'separated,' you wouldn't be sharing the same house."

"It's a large house, sweetie. There's a 'guest suite.' "

"Who's the guest, you or Rob?"

Clare laughed in a way you'd mistake as mirthful if you didn't know her. "Nikki, obviously you've never been married. You can share a bed, you can share a toothbrush, and you can still be 'separated.' And you can still be married."

Rob had told me that he'd been flying to Philadelphia to see his wife and son, on weekends. He'd brought Lilja with him and the visit had gone "pretty well, considering." He'd told me that he and Clare were "probably" going to get back together, but not to speak of it to Clare who hated being pressured and hadn't quite made up her mind. "Clare's biggest dread is people talking about her."

"Are we putting pressure on her? Are we talking about her?"

"Well, we want her back, don't we? We love her."

This was a phone conversation. Rob was sounding elated, effervescent. There was an almost inaudible clicking of ice cubes. For a weak moment I wished I was there with him, sprawled on a sofa in the Chisholms' cathedral-ceilinged family room, exchanging bemused complaints of Clare and sharing a bottle of Jack Daniel's. The upcoming trial scared me so, I hadn't dared drink in weeks. Once started, I might not have been able to stop.

I missed Rob, close up. I missed my flirty brother-in-law. Since observing Rigger in his soiled-green Hedwig House uniform, spike-braided hair and sexy swagger, I'd been thinking about men, and missing them. Not just sex (well, yes: sex) but men.

". . . a taboo subject, O.K., Nikki?"

Taboo? Was Rob reading my thoughts?

"With Clare so sensitive like she is. Thin-skinned, you might say. Any reference to her getting a D in that linguistics course, and this blow-up she allegedly had with her old roommate Amy Orlander, she'd be furious with me, and we'd be back at zero."

" 'I have a friend in Philadelphia.' "

"*You* do? Also?"

"No, Rob. It's Clare who has a 'friend in Philadelphia.' You must have heard."

We laughed together. We were feeling cozy together. After Clare returned to Mt. Ephraim, and to her marriage, I had a hope that she might return to me, too; that I could resume my old relationship with my brother-in-law, that had suited our needs just fine.

The trial. Postponed another time, to April 11.

"How can they do this! Keep doing this! When will this end!"

Angrily I crossed out *TRIAL* on the March date in Mom's calendar and wrote in *TRIAL* on April 11.

I felt a taste of horror, that Mom's animal shelter calendar would be running out soon. From January 2004 to June 2005. That was it.

(How I loved using Mom's calendar! Since the New Year, I'd been able to check each morning to see what Mom had been doing a full year before and even if I did not follow Mom's example, there was Mom's example to be followed.)

. . .

"The trial? No. I don't talk about it, thank you."

Quickly I moved on. In public places I was learning to move in a way that brought to my mind, for some wistful reason, Wally Szalla's son Troy as he'd been at sixteen, a brash beautiful kid not just fast on his feet but moving in an instinctive zigzag to elude pursuers.

Six days before the trial was scheduled to begin, Wally Szalla called.

In the house at 43 Deer Creek Drive in Mom's sewing room where I'd been experimenting with her sewing machine, for which I had as much aptitude as I'd have had repairing cars, I listened mesmerized to that voice so familiar to me.

"Nikki? Please pick up, if you're there. I have news."

A pause. Urgent breathing.

". . . if you're there, Nikki, please? Talk to me?"

In a panic I thought *He's divorced. He wants to marry me.*

"Darling, I have some good news, I think. I wish I could tell you in person. I wish we could be together. I know I've behaved badly and irresponsibly and so much precious time has gone by when we could have been together, but I have news now, darling, my divorce from Isabel will be final by noon on Monday. Darling, I'm on my cell phone just entering Mt. Ephraim on Route Thirty-nine, I'm five minutes from you please tell me you want to see me . . ."

Now I did panic. Rushed for my jacket, my car keys, fled for my life.

Wally, no.

I can't, Wally.

Understand, please Wally.

I loved you but that time in both our lives is past.

. . .

It was the Chautauqua County Courthouse. It was the brightly lighted first-floor courtroom in which the preliminary hearing had been held the previous June. I had been counseled by the prosecutor who would try the case to "dress conservatively" yet somehow it had happened, don't ask how, I had stepped into the courtroom naked. In a belated gesture of modesty, embarrassment, I tried to turn back but hands pushed me forward. And in the confusion of blinding lights I was also inside our garage at 43 Deer Creek Drive. Embarrassing to be naked in the eyes of strangers, yet more embarrassing that strangers were gaping at the messy interior of our garage, for all my housecleaning had been undone, everything I'd set out by the curb to be hauled away by trash men was back inside the garage, so crammed and cluttered I could hardly make my way to the witness stand, clumsily trying to shield myself with my hands. There were Mom's bloodstained clothes, the linen jacket, the floral-print blouse, I fumbled for these to cover my nakedness, still I was naked from the waist down in dream logic consoling myself *Well! If I am blinded by the lights I don't have to see who is watching.*

The trial of the *People of the State of New York vs. Ward W. Lynch.* This time, the judge had ruled, it would not be postponed.

I was the first prosecution witness. I was due to arrive at the prosecutor's office, close by the courthouse, by 9 A.M. of April 11. The trial would not begin until later in the morning, or in the afternoon, for a jury had to be selected and the voir dire, in a case involving murder, might take time. After I gave my testimony, I was "free to depart" the courtroom. But I would not depart the courtroom, I would see the trial through to the very end.

The prosecutor would bring into evidence, he would show to the jury, Mom's bloodstained clothes and shoes. He would remove from paper bags her bloodied and torn blue linen jacket, her blouse, her slacks and her underwear: brassiere, panties. He would remove from a paper bag her crepe-soled shoes, stained and stiffened with blood and of the size of a child's shoes. He would "enact" the murder. He would place a female-looking mannequin on the floor in front of the judge's raised platform and on this mannequin, in mimicry of the wounds in my mother's body, there would be bright red strips of tape to indicate where the knife had gone in. With a Swiss Army knife in his hand he would count out thirty-three blows to the mannequin. It would require some time, thirty-three separate blows.

Seeing the sick look in my face the prosecutor asked me frankly if I believed that I could bear to watch this. I said, "I don't know. Maybe not. But I will try. For my mother's sake."

The week before the trial. *What to wear.*

At night I lay awake not thinking of my testimony but of what I would wear. I had been warned that clothing, hairstyle, makeup and "deportment" weighed heavily with jurors. I was the daughter of the murder victim and would be expected to appear, and to behave, in an appropriate way. *Do you think I would wear a tank top, miniskirt, platform shoes? Did you think I would have my hair cut punk-style, and re-dye it purple?* (I didn't ask.) I had been warned that when I saw Ward Lynch, he would not much resemble the individual I'd seen at the preliminary hearing but would be wearing a suit, necktie, his hair would be trimmed, he'd be cleanshaven, unshackled. I had been warned that the defendant was "innocent until proven guilty" and that his clothes would signal innocence and not guilt.

Those nights before the trial was scheduled to begin I lay awake in my bed thinking of what I would wear and what Ward Lynch would wear. I did not think of my testimony. I did not think of seeing Ward Lynch another time, at so close a distance. I did not think of his sullen face and his unrepentant eyes. Instead I thought, in the way of an anxious schoolgirl: the darkish pinstriped jacket with the cloth-covered buttons and shoulder pads, a long-sleeved white silk blouse beneath, scarcely worn, that Mom sewed for me. Neatly pressed dark trousers. Better, yet: the flared black wool skirt, Mom sewed for me many years ago, I'd worn only once, at a family gathering, to please her.

I realize you don't wear skirts very often, Nikki. But this so suits you.

I love it, Mom! It's beautiful.

Are you sure the waist is right? I can adjust it.

It fits perfectly, Mom. Thank you!

Well. I hope it's something you will wear . . .

Absolutely, Mom. I will. With the boxy little pinstriped jacket, it will be perfect.

" 'Innocent until proven guilty.' I hate it!"

In her new, sisterly-tender mood, Clare did not accuse me of being a squatter. Her emotions were fierce and unpredictable but they were directed toward Ward Lynch and the protocol of the upcoming trial.

" 'Alleged' murderer, he's called. As if Mom is 'allegedly' dead."

In this mood, Clare allowed herself to utter the word *dead*.

Though usually we preferred *passed away*, or *gone*.

"My nightmare is, they find him not guilty."

Did I want to share my sister's nightmare, no thank you. I had my own.

Though she was right, of course. Lying awake at night choosing my clothes for the trial, I had time between breaths to think of this possibility.

"It's like Mom is on trial, too. Maybe they will try to blame *her*."

Clare spoke angrily but I knew that she was frightened. We were girls strangely alone together in our parents' house, uneasy because our parents weren't home, but might come home at any minute, unless maybe, and this was the really scary part, they were gone and were not coming home, it was only just us, Clare and me.

" 'Not guilty.' The jury handed that verdict to O. J. Simpson, remember. It can happen."

We were examining the darkish pinstriped jacket, the flared wool skirt. The long-sleeved white silk blouse with the eyelet bodice. These clothes were laid out on my bed girl-style. We were sisters contemplating an "outfit" one was going to wear for some special occasion. The older sister's opinion would count for more than the younger sister's though it was the younger sister who would be wearing the outfit.

Clare repeated, "It can happen, Nikki. For sure, they will try to blame Mom the way they blamed Simpson's wife."

I wasn't going to be drawn into Clare's madness. I wasn't going to discuss the Simpson decision! I would wait for Clare's emotions to run their course.

"He has concocted a story, we know this. He is claiming that another man, another hitchhiker, was with him in Mom's car, and came to the house, and Mom wanted to 'hire them as handymen' and Lynch was in another part of the house when—"

"Clare, stop. I don't want to hear this."

"In court, you'll hear it. We all will."

"All the evidence points to Lynch. There was never any second hitchhiker. The jury will know this. Please!"

Clare was following me through the house. She'd frightened Smoky with her vehemence, and now she was frightening me. "Rob says I'm being ridiculous, but what if, Nikki. What if. It would only take one juror, to poison everything. A woman, maybe. She looks at Lynch and falls in love with him, it could happen. Crazier things have happened. Ted Bundy's trial, a woman fell in love with him and proposed to him and they were married while he was in prison. These things happen, Nikki. Don't shut that door on me!"

I was trying to hide in the bathroom. Clare pushed the door open, glaring.

"Clare, that woman wasn't a juror. I'm sure she wasn't."

"But what if she had been?"

.   .   .

The trial. And after the trial, a second jury to deliberate the "penalty phase."

In the event that Ward Lynch was found guilty of the numerous charges against him, a second jury would decide if his sentence should be life in prison without the possibility of parole or death.

The second trial would take place immediately following the first trial. At this trial, members of Gwendolyn Eaton's family would be invited to testify. Clare would testify. Dad's brothers Herman and Fred would testify. Possibly, Aunt Tabitha would testify. And maybe Lucille Kovach.

I would be expected to testify. I did not see how I could refuse to testify. Though what could I say! *I want him dead* was the wish of my relatives and it was assumed that this was my wish as well but if I testified I would have to tell the court that my mother would not have wished for a death sentence, not Gwendolyn Eaton. She would have forgiven even her murderer, I believed. And yet, for me to testify *My mother would not want this man executed, speaking in her place I do not want this man executed* would anger my relatives, especially Clare.

In the night sleepless. When I wasn't thinking of what to wear at the trial, and the possibility of a jury finding Ward Lynch not guilty, I lay awake imagining my testimony at the penalty phase and the hurt and indignation of my relatives. Sweating and dry-mouthed I lay awake seeing myself trying to speak with Clare and being rebuffed. Trying to touch Clare's arm, and she throws off my hand like a snake.

In her fury crying, face distorted in grief, "Nikki, how could you! Betray us, and Mom! I never want to see you again."

I woke from the nightmare. For a brief moment I felt relief, it had only been a dream, then the realization swept over me like dirty water that the trial was still to come.

. . .

And then, finally, after so many weeks, months, days and hours of anticipation—"For once, Nicole, I'm the bearer of good news."

Three days before the trial was scheduled to begin, Ross Strabane called me. As soon as he identified himself, my heart began to beat rapidly. I knew, somehow. There was a barely concealed tremor of elation in the man's voice.

He wanted to see me in person, if possible. As soon as possible.

"I can be there in ten minutes. Prepare for some good news."

When Strabane arrived, he was breathless and he was carrying a bouquet of lilies. Waxy white calla lilies, dusky-pink day lilies with freckled petals. Beautiful flowers of a kind Mom had cultivated, that came to bloom in late June. As soon as I opened the door to him Strabane said, "The trial's off. The defendant has pleaded. You can relax, Nicole. You can call your family."

I wasn't hearing this. I was staring at the man's face. I had not seen Strabane in months and yet he was utterly familiar to me, as if I'd seen him the day before. He had to repeat what he'd told me, there would be no trial.

"In the morning you'll receive a call from the prosecutor's office, Nicole. I just heard now and I wanted to tell you as soon as possible."

"No trial? Has it been postponed?"

My fingers, that had gone numb with cold, were gripping the bouquet of long-stemmed lilies. Their fragrance was so sweet, I felt faint. I must have looked utterly shocked and bewildered, in the way of one who has just been informed that she hasn't after all a terminal disease.

Strabane explained that the trial had not been postponed. There was to be no trial. Lynch's lawyers had finally got him to agree to a plea of guilty in exchange for a sentence of life in prison without parole, instead of risking the possibility of a death sentence.

"But why? Why has he changed his mind?"

"For some good reasons."

Still I was fumbling with the flowers. My eyes were so filled with tears, I couldn't see. The lower part of my face was wanting to break into sobs.

I couldn't trust my voice to invite Strabane inside, so he came inside un-invited. He shut the door behind him. He was still breathless. He looked like a man who has completed a brilliant downhill ski run. Seeing that I needed to hide my face in my hands, he took the flowers back from me and said he'd look for a vase himself, in the kitchen.

I heard him opening cupboard doors. I wanted to follow him into the kitchen to direct him to a tall cut-glass vase of my mother's that would be ideal for long-stemmed lilies but my legs were too weak. I found my-self sitting heavily on the edge of the living room sofa. Like a child dazed by good fortune, distrustful of what she's been told, I murmured aloud, "No trial? *No trial?*" I meant to laugh but somehow my mouth twisted, and tears spilled from my eyes.

Strabane returned with the ideal vase. He'd filled water to overflowing and was leaving a wet trail in his wake. I remembered my father on some long-ago occasion carrying a vase of flowers to my mother, in his eager-ness dribbling water on the floor. Mom had laughed, and hadn't said a word except to thank Dad and kiss him in her bright pert way at the edge of his mouth.

I thanked Strabane, and took the vase from him. All our hands were trembling.

"They ratted on him. Even the grandma. I knew they would, if I could get the evidence."

Oh, it was a complicated story. I seemed to know that it was a story I would hear many times and each time it would become more compli-cated, embellished. It was a story of victory which was why I'd offered Strabane a victory supper.

First, coffee. Then, something to eat. Then, a bottle of red wine I'd been planning to serve Wally Szalla, months before.

I was in an emotional state. My mouth wanted to smile, and my mouth wanted to cry. My eyes spilled tears like a leaky but erratic faucet. Strabane pretended not to see. His face was flushed with pleasure, a kind of electric vigor in all his movements. I had not noticed in the past how strong his profile was. His jaws, his nose. The slope of his forehead. He'd shaved before coming here, quickly and not very carefully. He had a naturally thick dark beard and he'd scraped the underside of his chin in several places. I thought about offering him Band-Aids but couldn't summon the courage, the offer seemed so intimate.

Oh, the story! How and why Ward Lynch's relatives in Erie, Pennsylvania, had "ratted" on him! It might seem like a miracle, such an end to the case, but—"It's what I figured. If I could get the right people to talk, and the evidence."

For Strabane, it hadn't been enough that Ward Lynch was slated to be tried for my mother's murder. He hadn't been satisfied that the investigation was complete. So on his own time he'd looked into Lynch's criminal past since Lynch's discharge from Red Bank. He'd interviewed prisoners in the facility and guards who'd known Lynch. Eventually he pieced together "connections": he learned that Lynch had delivered stolen goods to certain of his relatives (including the elderly Ethel Makepeace), who'd either kept the goods for their own use or sold them and shared the revenue with Lynch. These were small-time burglaries from 7-Eleven stores and private houses, cases of liquor and beer, cartons of cigarettes, TVs and CD players, jewelry. Still, the crimes were felonies, and warrants were served to Lynch's relatives. "They were allowed to plea bargain a deal of only two years' probation, in exchange for testifying against Lynch. They're stupid but not crazy. They knew a good deal, even Grandma. I'm only sorry it took so damned long, Nikki."

Nikki. The sudden shift was marked by a rush of emotion in the man's voice.

By this time it was past 9 P.M. It was a wet, windy April evening. In my emotional state I did not want to be alone but had no wish to reveal the rawness of my need. Nor did Strabane seem to want to leave. Yet we were shy with each other, a man and a woman somehow in a canoe together in white-water rapids, rushing downstream sharing a single paddle. I was wearing a cable-knit pullover sweater with sleeves so long, I could draw my hands up inside them, to warm them. Strabane wore a sport coat that fitted his shoulders tightly, over a cheap nylon V-neck sweater that showed a patch of chest hair gray-grizzled and wiry as a Brillo pad. His corduroy trousers were of that hue of too-bright tan appropriate for grade-school boys. On his feet, which were big as hooves, a pair of rusted well-broken-in Nike running shoes. Strabane explained he'd been off-duty today, a friend had called from headquarters when the news came from the prosecutor's office. "Knowing of my interest in the Eaton case. Knowing I would want to call you."

He was awkward, edgy. He was a man not at ease with speech yet driven to talk, in head-on plunges. He made leaps in reasoning I could not follow. Yet I understood him, somehow. When he lapsed into silence, I felt that I understood him best.

I'd run to call Clare to tell her the good news and to ask her to tell others in the family, we'd been spared the ordeal of the trial. Clare, too, had been disbelieving at first. Then she began to scream. Then she began to cry.

She must have dropped the receiver. I heard her calling *Rob! Rob!* and in the background my brother-in-law's raised voice.

When I invited Strabane to stay for supper I saw him ponder the question. He seemed to be thinking with his face. He seemed to require running both hands through his bristly hair. I understood: he was committed elsewhere. He had a family, obviously. He'd dropped by my house on his own time, out of kindness. The sexual tension between us was—was not?—*was?*—palpable as the tension in the air before an electrical storm. He knew, he was a man of powerful sexual feelings, but also powerful emotions, so he knew, he was debating. Almost, I could hear *Thank you Nikki wish I could but I can't* except he said instead, in a cracked voice, "Yes. I'd like that. But I need to make a call."

In the kitchen where I had not prepared any meal for anyone except myself, this kitchen where, when Mom was alive, I'd helped her prepare meals for the family, I drifted about dazed and giddy and frightened and excited, at first wanly opening and shutting cupboard doors, staring into the refrigerator and seeing nothing, disoriented as Aunt Tabitha had been in her kitchen when I'd taken charge. I would prepare a gigantic omelette. Six eggs with yolks and one egg white. Stir-fried onions, green peppers, mushrooms. I whipped the eggs in a bowl until my wrist ached. Strabane was eager to help. He wasn't a guy, he told me, who liked to be waited on: he'd come from a big family, everybody helped out. I was embarrassed to direct him to search the refrigerator, see what he could find. Salad things? The remains of a loaf of oatmeal/dried buttermilk bread I'd baked a few days ago?

"Stale doesn't matter if you make toast. I'll make toast."

Strabane knew exactly where the toaster was. Afterward I would think *He knows this house. A crime-scene house.*

I wasn't sure that I liked this. That I could live with this. That, having resented the man's knowledge for so long, I could learn to be grateful for it.

Accompanying the omelette enormous as a hubcap was an enormous salad. Strabane opened the bottle of red wine. We ate at the breakfast nook, famished. Black rain splattered against the window overlooking the rear terrace and, invisible in the dark, the bird feeders my father had set up. Frequently Strabane peered past me into the pitch-black beyond the window as if he'd heard something out back. His forehead creased into knife-sharp furrows. I wondered what he was seeing there.

My victory meal was a success. Strabane finished every morsel on his plate. With a crust-stub he wiped up every glistening bit of omelette. He was drinking two or three glasses of wine to my one glass. He was becoming ever more elated, ebullient. A look in his face like he's about to stand up in the hurtling canoe.

Attracted by our voices, Smoky had appeared in the kitchen. Like an apparition of some bulk, weight and attitude. Male visitors offended him on principle yet he was approaching this one by slow degrees, tawny eyes alert. When Strabane saw the tomcat he leaned over to beckon to him. "Hey Big Turk! You're a big guy, ain't ya! C'mere, and be petted."

Strabane had a way with animals, you could see. Smoky was intrigued. He approached the man's outstretched fingers with exasperating slowness, yet he came; he was wary but flirty, half-shutting his eyes and sensuously arching his back in an invitation to be petted.

I asked Strabane who "Big Turk" was.

"Never heard of Big Turk? He's this funky cable TV wrestler covered in tattoos, must weigh three hundred pounds. He's got a shaved head and demon eyes. Turk is, like, the all-purpose villain. White guys, pure-blood Americans with blond hair, get to beat the crap out of him, but not right away." Strabane laughed. "Plus, Big Turk is a screamer."

I asked if he often watched TV wrestling?

"Jesus, no! There's enough bullshit in my line of work, I don't need more. It's my hundred-year-old grandpa is the fan."

All this while Strabane was rubbing Smoky's chunky head as if they were old friends. He scratched Smoky behind the ears vigorously, the way Smoky liked to be scratched. These were seasoned tomcat ears, scarred and part-shredded. Though Smoky had been neutered long ago, he was aggressive with other cats. Beneath Strabane's practiced fingers he erupted in a crackling purr and his big body shivered in feline ecstasy. Imagine our surprise when, a moment later, he turned, lifted his tail, and sprayed a thin stream of amber liquid onto Strabane's feet.

"Hey! Damn you."

Smoky retreated, flat-eared, to his food bowls on the far side of the refrigerator. His stumpy tail was switching.

Strabane was crestfallen, but tried to laugh. Quickly I gave him wetted paper towels to clean his Nikes that were already damp from the rain. "Smoky has never done anything like this before, I'm so sorry."

It wasn't a tactful remark. Probably it wasn't even a truthful remark. Flush-faced, Strabane was swiping at his feet. He tried to make a joke of it: "He has, sure, ma'am. You're covering for him."

I stifled nervous laughter. My hands were small fists drawn up inside the long sweater sleeves. Like a child in distress I'd drawn my feet up beneath me in the breakfast nook. Watching this man I scarcely knew swabbing at his shoes where a tomcat had sprayed him I felt so powerful a wave of tenderness, for a dazed moment I didn't know where I was.

"It's other cats he smells on me, maybe. Dogs! There's at least six dogs, mostly boxers, at our place. That big old shingle-board farmhouse on North Fork, probably you've seen it?—kind of an eyesore, used to be a farm property owned by some relatives of mine now it's going to be torn down next year and all that land made into a subdivision. It's about a mile north of that eyesore trailer court, where they never take the Christmas lights down."

I was astonished. "That's where you live?"

One of the doomed old farmhouses with stone foundations from the 1800s, in that beautiful hilly countryside. Not sleazy-chic North Fork Villas as I'd assumed.

Strabane explained that his life was "complicated" at the present time. Not his professional-cop life but his personal life. "I went to live with my grandfather last year, poor old guy couldn't handle all the family he'd acquired. We're talking about eighty years of acquisition. His oldest daughter, not living now, had this stepson from one of her hippie communes, this guy has been in the wind for twenty years but they keep waiting for him to return like the Messiah. It's Reuben's wife, this sweet sad woman who'd liked to think of herself as my mother, when I was in need of a mother which hasn't been lately, of course, and what keeps turning up of her family from West Virginia including some so-called cousins of hers that, looking at me, seeing who I am, they can smell the fact I'm a cop, start acting really nervous. Plus there's remnants from Grandpa's old bluegrass band, and old lovers of his must've been underage when he knew them, and 'fans' that show up and pitch tents in the pasture like the year is 1965 and we're into Flower Power. Jesus! My grandpa the celebrity, I think you met once—Jimmy Friday?"

Now I was truly astonished. "Jimmy *Friday*? Your *grandfather*?"

" 'Friday' was never his name. 'Harold Burkholtz'—my mother's name was 'Burkholtz'—was his name. The audience my grandfather was aiming for with his special brand of country-and-western music, he figured 'Jimmy Friday' had a hell of a better chance."

It seemed a lifetime ago, I'd interviewed the elderly bluegrass performer with the frothy white hair and slyly sexual manner, on the occasion of his memoir *Songs My Daddy Taught Me: The Mostly True Tales of Jimmy Friday*. After last May, I hadn't given Jimmy Friday another thought. To remember him now, the sweetly seductive old man eyeing me so wistfully, clasping my hand in his and lifting it to kiss in parting, was an effort like trying to haul a dream up into consciousness even as it's sinking downward to oblivion. Strabane was saying he hated to disillusion me but his Burkholtz grandfather hadn't any background remotely like the one "Jimmy Friday" had invented for himself, that seemed to have been modeled after the life of Johnny Cash, the man he'd most admired and envied.

I saw Strabane's mouth moving. I saw him smile. I saw that his nose was just slightly asymmetrical, must've been broken. I saw that his skin was olive-dark, there were fine, almost invisible scars at his hairline. And the hairline was corroding, at the temples. And the bristly-oily hair was threaded with gray, at the temples. The eyes, the kindly-moist eyes. The slightly red-veined eyes. The eyes of a man who has seen too much and who knows too much but maybe he won't tell you, for he is kind. I wasn't following much of what he was telling me about Jimmy Friday, the doomed farmhouse on the North Fork Road, six—six?—boxer dogs of whom one was the mother, the rest were pups. I was thinking how the Nikki who'd interviewed Jimmy Friday had been so *young*. Had been so *ignorant*. Fuming and cursing at her recorder. Playing the damned tape, trying to make sense of the interview, and Mom had still been alive.

That morning. "Jimmy Friday." My last chance to have saved my mother.

Strabane was saying he'd been married, too. For three years, in his early twenties. A girl he'd met on a blind date arranged by an army buddy. He'd been in the U.S. Army stationed in New Jersey and in Oklahoma and in South Korea—where the average American didn't know the U.S. has had soldiers for fifty years!—and in all these places "nothing was happening, and always the same way every day." His marriage hadn't lasted. Fell apart like wetted Kleenex. His wife who'd claimed to love him for all her life got herself pregnant at an embarrassing time when they'd been like 50,000 miles apart for months but they'd decided, for the sake of their families, to pretend the baby was his no matter the baby turned out to look nothing like him. But the consequence was, Ross Strabane was financially responsible for this dependent child, he was the legal husband and father and even when Robin divorced him, and was living with another guy, and later another guy acting as "legal counsel" for some questionable tribe of Indians hoping to be legitimized to operate a casino in the Catskills, still the state would not recognize any change in Ross Strabane's status. The state did not allow DNA testing after the fact, out of a legitimate fear that welfare rolls would be even worse than they are now. "I can see the logic of it. It's a social necessity. Half the guys paying child support might not be willing to pay if they learned who their kids' actual fathers are. As a police officer, I can see the point. But as a civilian, I wonder if it's fair. For sure, when it's you, it hurts like hell. Not that I would not have paid. Not that I would not have bailed out my ex-wife when she was desperate. I would have, and I did. Now the boy is almost eighteen, they're living in Yonkers and he's been twice in juvie hall, twice in drug rehab and dropped out of high school without graduating and his goal in life is to be the 'white Snoop Doggy Dog.' Anyway my ex-wife is remarried. She will make her way like a sleepwalker. Just that, by the time I was twenty-eight it was like that part of my life was finished. You know what a phantom limb is, you don't have the limb, you have just the pain. So I went into police work. This work has saved my life. I told you, Nikki, there was this older detective who'd investigated a case involving my family, he's retired now, but I keep in touch, he's been a model to me, it's like he is always with me, working on a case. Because what I do is mostly in my head, not on foot. I need to make connections. I need to work backward from what there is, which is somebody hurt, I work back to who did the hurting, and why. What I respect about police work, it has its own dimension. I never talk about my work with civilians. I have friends not on the force, I've had women friends, I don't talk about it. Women have objected, they say that I am 'secretive'—'in my own head'—'weird.' But I don't talk about it. With you, I needed to talk about certain things but no more, that case is closed. Another thing women object to, your time at work. Well, I'm a detective, I'm not a meter reader. I'm not a mailman. I don't have the same schedule every day. I can work ten-twelve hours on a new case and sometimes longer. I can't sleep, at the start of a case. Sometimes I sleep in my car, if it's an emergency. The way we located Lynch, it was an emergency. Because he would have hurt other people. He'd have hurt his relatives if he knew they'd rat on him. His old grandma, he'd have hurt. If there's like a kidnapping, an abduction. You have to act fast if there's any chance the victim is alive. Your own life, your 'private' life, is nothing." Strabane paused. He'd been speaking rapidly, passionately. I had never heard any man speak in such a way. "Any woman I loved, I would want to protect her from such knowledge. You can see that, Nikki, right?"

Yes. I could see that. But I couldn't reply, I'd drawn my legs up beneath me in the breakfast nook in a kind of paralysis.

Strabane said, "I know it's hard for you to be around me. I know, I remind you of certain things. But if you knew me better, I wouldn't." He paused. He ran both his hands through his bristly hair. "Each time you saw me, like around the house, the meaning of me would be lessened. The past would be lessened." Again Strabane paused. He was watching me closely. Like a man who'd backed himself into a corner, who had words to utter he could not fully comprehend, he said, finally, "The future becomes wider, see? As the past is lessened."

I untangled my legs. I went away. I went to my parents' bedroom where I'd left a selection of Dad's neckties, I had intended to give to Wally Szalla months ago. Except knowing that Wally wasn't the type. No Szalla was the type to wear a dead man's cast-off ties. I brought them to Strabane in the kitchen, and told him to take his pick, as many as he liked: "They belonged to my dad. Maybe his taste is like yours."

A shiny zigzag blue and silver tie. A Madras tie, a gift from me in maybe 1975. An oddly narrow tie with dizzying red checks that, when you looked more carefully, were tiny elephants. Another narrow tie, brass-colored, that looked as if it had been braided out of thistles.

Strabane said, "These are great, Nikki. I can use them all."

He'd been holding the neckties up, admiring. The ugliest of all, the braided-brass, he held against his chest. I reached for his hand, both his hands. I gripped them hard. They were nearly twice the size of my hands, but I gripped them hard. I embarrassed Strabane by pressing my warm, wet face against his hands.

"Don't leave, Strabane. Just yet."

There was a thin razor-scar across the knuckles of Strabane's left hand, but I took no notice at the time.

mostly true

In my apartment in Chautauqua Falls, I found my inscribed copy of *Songs My Daddy Taught Me: The Mostly True Tales of Jimmy Friday*. On its cover was a close-up photo of a sly-smiling elderly gentleman with a full head of very white hair, gripping and plucking at a guitar in a suggestive way. Elderly Jimmy Friday wore country-and-western attire, wide-brimmed straw hat, string tie, a belt with a large silver buckle *JF*. He was a remarkable handsome man, despite his creased and weatherworn skin. He was winking at the camera, and wetting his lips with the tip of his tongue.

I brought the book home to show to Strabane that evening.

" 'To Beautous Nicole From ' One & Only 'Jimmy Friday!' "

Strabane read the inscription aloud in a tone I could not determine. Later I would come to recognize this tone as guarded, wary. A tone that signaled the sensible query *What kind of bullshit is this?*

Strabane leafed through the pages of his grandfather's memoir, shaking his head. He'd read the book, various pieces which had been previously published as interviews, then refashioned by a series of ghost writers, as a kind of tall-tale chronicle, the biography of someone who might have existed as "Jimmy Friday" if there'd ever been a "Jimmy Friday." He said, "People are all the time asking, if there's somebody 'known' in your family, are you proud of him? You can't give the true answer."

"Which is?"

"Which is you never meet the person you're supposed to be 'proud of.' It's only out there, in people who don't know him."

"But your grandfather's music is real. I've listened to it, my mother and some of her friends loved it, lots of people I know." I was feeling emotional suddenly. Protective of the flirty old man who wasn't here to defend himself.

Strabane said, "If bluegrass doesn't drive you crazy it can be pretty impressive. Right." He looked back at the floridly handwritten inscription on the title page. "One thing Grandpa is right about, 'Beautous Nicole.' The old guy got that right, at least."

I foresaw that, in time, it would come to seem that Jimmy Friday had been the agent to bring Ross Strabane and me together, not a meth-head murderer named Ward Lynch.

windward

"Ohhh, yes! I remember all my honeymoon couples."

May was such a dismal rainy month in upstate New York, impulsively we decided to drive a thousand miles south to Key West, Florida, where the Windward Inn still existed! And here was the owner's elderly mother Carmen peering at the photos of my parents spread before her at the front desk. Assuring me, "Of course I remember your parents, dear. Not their names of course but their faces. They were so happy together, always holding hands. This, with Oscar the parrot, who's no longer with us I'm sorry to say, was taken in our courtyard where you can have breakfast tomorrow. Oh your mother, what a lovely woman! She made friends with Oscar right away. He had a way of pecking some people but not your mother. I can see that you take after her, dear. Doesn't she, Eduardo?"

The middle-aged son Eduardo, owner and manager of the Windward, was looking on with a faint, forced smile. It was off-season in Key West and both son and mother were eager to please their guests from the north who'd only just checked in. I would note Carmen's tact, not inquiring if Gwen and Jonathan Eaton were still living.

What Mom had fondly remembered as a quaintly small "historic" hotel was the most decrepit hotel on South Street, so overgrown with crimson bougainvillea your first impression was there wasn't any structure beneath, only just gorgeous flaming blossoms through which white-shuttered windows and white wrought-iron balconies too small to be anything more than ornamental protruded magically. When we drove up, Strabane leaned over to squint through the bug-splattered windshield of his car, doubtfully.

"This is it? 'Windward'?"

"I think it must be. Oh."

"Well. It's something we can afford."

We. As if *we* had had experience with myriad things affordable and non-, in the brief time we'd begun to have experiences together.

The Windward Inn was at the wrong end of South Street and on the wrong side of South Street with no access to the beach but if you could appreciate funny, funky places it had its charms. In the lobby were palm fronds and enormous seashell decorations, potted orange trees with dust-laden leaves, a pungent odor of gardenia air freshener and insecticide beneath. There was no longer the living Oscar but a stuffed brightly feathered replica in a bamboo cage near the stairs. In the off-season, rates had been enticingly lowered yet much of the hotel appeared to be deserted. Strabane and I had registered at the desk as two distinct entities yet Carmen insisted upon assigning us the "honeymoon" room, with a view of the shabbily romantic courtyard below.

Carmen, in her mid-seventies, had dyed-black hair drawn back into a sleek chignon in which a single red rose had been twined. She wore flamenco reds and oranges, spike-heeled open-toed shoes. When she moved, hoop earrings swung at her ears and a dozen glittery bracelets jingled on her arms. Each time she sighted me she called out gaily, "Such a pretty girl! Like your mother. And your father, too—such a gentleman. Ohhh yes, I remember all my honeymoon couples."

I asked Strabane if he believed Carmen.

"Mmmm."

I laughed, and kissed him. I liked it that my lover was a man who believed almost no one, almost nothing, almost never. My mother would have pretended in her childlike-Feather way to be shocked by such skepticism but in her heart she'd have agreed. She'd have whispered in my ear *Nikki, he's the one.*

As Mother's Day approached in Mt. Ephraim I could not sleep. I was terrified of the thoughts that assailed me and the phantom smells: the butcher shop on Mohigan Street. I was depressed by the cold wet spring but anxious on those occasional days when the sun appeared and the air warmed and lilacs began to bud. Strabane came to find me in the kitchen in the middle of the night, where I was curled in a corner of the breakfast nook like a child with my bare feet drawn up beneath me. He pushed in beside me, awkwardly he held me. He didn't speak for a while and then he said, "Maybe we'd better go away for a while. I have a week coming."

He wasn't an impulsive man. But he could behave as if he was, for my sake.

"But I want to help you drive. I love to drive."

"My car, I drive. Being a passenger doesn't work for me."

It was a dreamy trip. It was a trip into the future: cold rain and fishbelly skies gradually changing to sun, ceramic-blue skies, startlingly warm air. From time to time, Strabane did allow me to drive while he nodded off in the seat beside me. I smiled when, asking him if he'd slept, he said, "Not really. Just closed my eyes."

We listened to CDs: Eric Clapton, Joni Mitchell. We listened to *The Best of Jimmy Friday's Bluegrass*. In the interstices of the CDs, we talked. Through Pennsylvania, through Maryland and D.C. and Virginia and the Carolinas. Through the length of Florida to the very tip south of Miami, and at last Route 1, narrow, mesmerizing, through the succession of Florida keys floating in the pure-blue Gulf of Mexico, to the southernmost, Key West, we talked.

Often, it would seem that we talked aimlessly. Knowing that, if a subject was evoked, it might be dropped because it would be taken up at a later time.

On the morning of the second day of the drive Strabane mentioned, as if casually, that he'd been offered a job in Buffalo. A promotion to Detective First Class with the Buffalo PD. He did not tell me, but I could surmise, that the promotion had to do with the excellent work he'd done in the Eaton case.

The Eaton case. In the end, it had turned out well for the professionals. It had turned out very well. I understood that Detective Strabane couldn't help but feel pride in his work, in its well-publicized conclusions. I understood that my mother's death, and even the brutality of her death, had made this success sweeter, in some quarters.

I understood and I was not bitter, I think. In even the most secret recesses of my heart, that Strabane would never penetrate, I did not resent his success but was happy for him. I think.

I waited for Strabane to ask me if I might want to come with him.

I waited, and wondered what I would say.

At the Windward Inn we went to bed late, and we slept late. Often during the day we put the DO NOT DISTURB sign on the door. We ate in outdoor cafés, Cuban and Cajun food. Strabane drank Mexican beer, and I drank sparkling water. Once on a whim I ordered a Singapore sling but after the first swallow I pushed it from me. "Not good?" Strabane asked, and I said, "Too good."

On Mother's Day there was early-morning rain, then the sun came out bursting like an egg yolk. We had a late breakfast in the shabby courtyard. Oh, but it was a beautiful little courtyard, I thought. No matter the crumbling stucco, the cracked flagstones where weeds poked through. No matter the white wrought-iron tables and chairs needed repainting. The gorgeous crimson bougainvillea that, close up, had leaves riddled with tiny insects. Strabane was reading the Miami newspaper. I half-shut my eyes seeing in a corner of the courtyard my young mother, not yet my mother, a large upright gaily feathered bird with a hooked beak perched on her shoulder. I heard her laughter which would have a small cry of alarm in it, for surely the parrot's claws hurt her shoulder, the parrot is a sizable bird. I saw my young father, not yet my father, looking on vigilantly, to rescue her if the parrot should become belligerent.

A memorial service was planned for my mother, scheduled for mid-June. By that time, I would have moved out of the house at 43 Deer Creek Drive, I thought. The house would be listed with a realtor. Clare and I would have made our final choices, what to take with us from the house, what to put in storage, what to dispose of.

During the time we were away, Strabane made numerous telephone calls. Some of these were professional, others seemed to be personal. I made only a single call, to Clare.

"Nikki! Where the hell are you!"

"In Key West. At the Windward Inn."

"The Windward Inn? Where Mom and Dad went?"

"It's beautiful, Clare. It's changed from what Mom remembered but it's very attractive, romantic . . ."

"I thought you'd done something like that. Rob and I both thought. I'm pissed at you for not telling me but I don't blame you for getting out. I don't blame you at all, sweetie." Clare paused. It sounded as if she was in a bowling alley. "This weather! Hear that thunder?"

"Here, it's eighty degrees. The sky is clear. The air smells of bougainvillea and oranges."

"Are you with that man?"

" 'That man'—who?"

"The detective. You know perfectly well who."

"Clare, he isn't married."

"Isn't he! That's a change."

I couldn't determine if Clare was angry with me or in fact happy for me. I was reminded of her vehemence when she'd been captain of the girls' high school basketball team and felt the need to speak sharply to girls who'd made errors on the court even though the team had managed to win.

There was a need to scold, but also to celebrate.

I love the water, it holds you up.

Well, maybe. If you can swim.

On our drive south we'd stayed at motels and, in the morning, swam for a festive half-hour or so in the pools. Strabane was a fast, sloppy swimmer. He reminded me of a sea lion, over-large and graceless. I watched him in the corner of my eye. I stared at him openly when he wasn't watching me. For we were in that stage when the sight of the other still has the power to shock.

Covered in dark wiry hairs like a pelt. His chest, his forearms, his abdomen, his legs and even the backs of his toes. There was a swirl of spiky hairs hidden beneath his swim trunks, at his groin. It was curious how his face and forearms were olive-dark and the rest of his body pale. At a motel in Georgia he clambered from a pool streaming water, making a snuffling noise through his nose and rubbing his eyes, a man I'd never seen before, who excited and frightened me.

Outside Daytona Beach, we were leaving a restaurant to return to our car when we heard raised voices, saw several loutish guys bunched about two girls, and Strabane listened, and went over to them, and said something to them, and abruptly the guys backed off and got into their car and departed. And when I asked Strabane what he'd said to them, he said, "What I always say. 'Some problem here?'"

The Windward Inn! That it still existed, that I could climb the creaky stairs my parents had climbed, stand in the very place in the courtyard where my parents had stood thirty-five years ago, seemed to me wonderful. How badly I wished that I could tell Mom.

I'd have told her that Carmen remembered her and Dad. Even if it wasn't true, Mom would have wished to believe me.

Strabane bought an inexpensive disposable camera. We asked strangers to take pictures of us including one of us in the courtyard of the Windward Inn. I had to wonder what the fate of these snapshots would be after thirty-five years.

Such speculation is like staring into the hot white sun. You know the sun is there but you can't see a thing.

.   .   .

It was the day following Mother's Day.

In the man's arms I did not think of any other man. I did not think of any other place. I did not think of May in Mt. Ephraim: the sweet-sickly smell of lilac that had the power to make me physically ill. I did not think of the eleven-year-old girl pushing open the door to her mother's bedroom and the last, fleeting moment before she saw what lay inside. I did not think of pushing open the door to our garage and that last, fleeting moment before I saw what lay inside. Eagerly I kissed the man who was kissing me, the man in my arms, I held him tight like a drowning woman. I thought *This is now, I am here. This is now.*

Next morning I slept heavily as if my bones had turned to lead and my eyes were stuck shut. I was naked in an unfamiliar bed and there was a naked man beside me whose name, for a panicky moment, I could not have said. I felt the mattress ease and lift as he slipped from the bed. I understood that he was being thoughtful, or cautious. I heard the floorboards creak as he padded about barefoot. I heard the door to the room being opened and shut quietly and when some time later he returned, I was still in bed and probably I hadn't moved. Through shut eyelids I saw the man standing indecisively at the foot of the brass bed looking at me.

"Nikki?"

He waited, watching me. I was at the bottom of a pool of water, I was pushing myself up to the surface. My lungs ached, I'd been holding my breath for so long.

"Nikki. Hey."

Eventually, I came to the surface.

We were walking on the beach. The sand was crumbly, my feet sank into the sand and I was having trouble walking. Circling in the air above a pier were prehistoric-looking birds: pelicans. The sky above the Gulf of Mexico was purely blue, beautiful. I was very happy and yet a sudden sensation of weakness came over me, a terrible sensation of sickness, emptiness. I told the man I was with that I had to return to the hotel. I apologized, I had to leave him. Stumbling and staggering I returned to the Windward Inn. I returned to our room and lay on the bed. It was a bed with a slightly sunken mattress and a jiggly brass frame. It was a bed you would call quaint. I was very weak lying on this bed though it was a comfort to me. Through slats in the part-broken blind waning sunlight glowed. I wanted badly to be alone but the man followed me and came to ease himself onto the bed beside me. The weight of him in the bed! He was so heavy, he was so warm, he was breathing so audibly, almost for a moment I resented him. Intruding into my grief as if to steal it from me.

He gripped my hand. My fingers were icy and unresponsive. I thought *You can't warm me, I am ice.* I remembered how I had run from Mom where she had fallen in the garage and I had paused to look back at her and saw that she was alive, she was alive and breathing and her eyelids were fluttering open. She was looking at me—she saw me! She tried to speak my name. She was very weak from losing so much blood but she had strength enough to call my name. But when I returned to her, and tried to lift her, she had died, it was too late. And so I had failed her after all. And then I had abandoned her to strangers. I thought *I am on trial and the trial will never end.*

"You'll live with it, Nikki. I'll help you."

I waited for Strabane to say more. I knew him now: my lover.

I waited for him to reason with me, to argue with me. I waited for him to say those words we say to one another at such times. But he remained silent. He gripped my hand in such a way that his fingers pushed through my fingers, and held them tight. I understood that this was the reasoning, this was my lover's argument.

In this way ended my first full year of missing Mom.